ONE YELLOW EYE

ONE YELLOW EYE

LEIGH RADFORD

G

GALLERY BOOKS

New York   Amsterdam/Antwerp   London
Toronto   Sydney/Melbourne   New Delhi

G

Gallery Books
An Imprint of Simon & Schuster, LLC
1230 Avenue of the Americas
New York, NY 10020

This book is a work of fiction. Any references to historical events, real people, or real places are used fictitiously. Other names, characters, places, and events are products of the author's imagination, and any resemblance to actual events or places or persons, living or dead, is entirely coincidental.

First Gallery Books hardcover edition July 2025

GALLERY BOOKS and colophon are registered trademarks of Simon & Schuster, LLC

Simon & Schuster strongly believes in freedom of expression and stands against censorship in all its forms. For more information, visit BooksBelong.com.

For information about special discounts for bulk purchases, please contact Simon & Schuster Special Sales at 1-866-506-1949 or business@simonandschuster.com.

The Simon & Schuster Speakers Bureau can bring authors to your live event. For more information or to book an event, contact the Simon & Schuster Speakers Bureau at 1-866-248-3049 or visit our website at www.simonspeakers.com.

Interior design by Hope Herr-Cardillo

Manufactured in the United States of America

10 9 8 7 6 5 4 3 2 1

Library of Congress Control Number: 2024914573

ISBN 978-1-6680-8121-1
ISBN 978-1-6680-8123-5 (ebook)

Dad.
There is nothing we wouldn't have done to keep you with us.
x

Rage, rage, against the dying of the light.

—Dylan Thomas

CHAPTER ONE

Kesta blinked. Once. Twice. The third time deliberately enough for the lashes to press into the hollows of her eyes, enjoying that disconcerting internal crunch, the guiding vibrations, like the involuntary overture of a yawn.

Kesta thought a lot about blinking now because *they* did not blink. She hadn't noticed it at first. In the midst of chaos, important details can be overlooked. Witnesses are unreliable. When all around you people are bolting in terror and you happen to find yourself running away from one of them at full tilt, there is no time to turn heel, head back inside the laboratory, and jog up to the fourth floor for a slit lamp to take a proper look. It occurred to her only much later on—three or perhaps four weeks into it—when she had seen several of them die right in front of her—most of them shot by the army, although that one guy guillotined by the galvanized roller doors at the dry cleaners was pretty unforgettable—that they didn't blink.

It was when she had found one in the pathology lab, just wandering around as if he had worked there once as a porter. The missing arm had been a giveaway of course, not to mention the little it seemed to concern him, missing and bleeding profusely as it was, the humerus quite visible and not at all funny. It was when she had hit him, over and over again, at first with a chair that had been too awkward to wield successfully for a woman of her size, and then with the old microtome on Dudley's desk, which she still used for paraffin sections. Even as she beat it down on the top of his head until there wasn't one to speak of, he hadn't blinked once. She had made assiduous notes afterward.

Patient does not blink. Patient cannot blink. Lagophthalmos, proptosis, or tumor should be considered.

Kesta sighed. She did, to her credit, have a fair amount to sigh about. But then so did everybody else. Today was Wednesday, and Wednesday meant she was compelled to listen to the litany of misfortunes suffered by the eleven others at group therapy. Her job as a biomedical scientist mandated her attendance, because of what had happened to her. And so, she went.

The other people at therapy would often look at her with eyes searching eagerly for friendship. When this happened, Kesta turned her blinking up a notch so that she appeared either to be deep in thought or napping. This had worked successfully for four weeks, but she knew it would only be a matter of time before she'd have to articulate this rejection. When Tina, the resident gobshite, had suggested they form a breakout group, a few seemed pleased by the prospect of taking their talking elsewhere, to a pub maybe, or heaven forfend, into each other's homes. All Kesta could think of was that the group was metastasizing, and in her experience that was never a good thing. Spread meant death.

These meetings of the Zombie Apocalypse Recovery Group were always the same; slow, repetitive, clumsy. The irony wasn't lost on Kesta. She wondered what Tim would make of it all, him being bitten at the very end of the outbreak and her condemned to a life in therapy because of it. She wasn't always sure whose fate was worse.

Where she mourned Tim, others grieved for children, partners, parents, each one lanced from their lives with prodigious cruelty. And violence. Where her fellow ZARGs were desperate to purge the horrors they had witnessed, Kesta needed only to work through her grief and toward a cure. She had made a promise to Tim that she would do her utmost to find one.

And so, every Wednesday afternoon at four, Kesta joined the others in a forgotten room at the back of a steadily disintegrating London hospital, the one she worked at during the day, cluttered with the detritus thrown at people with problems—tissues, tea urns, plates of beige biscuits fingered by all and sundry. The room itself was a glazed annex, typical of the health service, in which you could expect only to feel much worse when you left than when you had arrived. Ossified green lino, a medley of chairs and side tables bought on the cheap but expected to last, utilitarian but somehow jazzy. It reeked of disinfectant, was scrubbed clean of hope, and was also used presumably for mother and toddler groups or to give the elderly advice on internet banking. Or bladder infections. It didn't matter; the room was suitably depressing to host a collection of the bereaved and the lost for an hour each week, with taxpayer-funded Dr. Walling. More than she resented the shrink, Kesta despaired at the inane posters that pockmarked the walls, instructing those in attendance to wash your hands and check your prostate. Even if Kesta had one, she doubted she'd supervise it.

As the ZARGs assembled, they began to leak with pleasantries. *How are you feeling? The nightmares have stopped, so that's something. That's nice, good for you.* Give it five minutes and their trickle of self-pity and bewilderment would explode into an unstoppable torrent of grief and fear. It had been three months since the last of the infected were rounded up and shot, but those in therapy were still stupefied by a cellular shock. All Kesta really felt was rage.

"Who wants to go first?" Dr. Walling asked the circle that had taken shape around her.

Talking helps, Dr. Walling had told the group repeatedly and in a soft baby voice. If there was one thing Kesta knew irrefutably, it was that talking absolutely did not help her. It changed nothing, did nothing, meant nothing. Talking was a pretense, an act of concealment, like gift wrapping a plastic turd. It was also the only thing they had.

"I'll go," blurted Carol, who seemed startled by her own urgency. Carol almost always went first. "Hi, everybody," she said, waving balled-up tissues toward the group.

"Hi, Carol," replied Dr. Walling and everyone else except Kesta.

"When Andy was bitten, I fell apart," she sobbed, as if addressing daytime television. "There was nothing I could do to save him. And now I have to live with that."

Dr. Walling removed her glasses and stuck one temple tip into her mouth—a sign she was on the cusp of a question—but Carol was in full flow.

"I'd seen the government warnings. They'd been on telly for weeks. The kind of symptoms an infected person would show. The groaning. The bleeding from the eyes. How to file the report with the ooo number, that bloody form you had to fill out online. It was just . . . surreal. Like a horror movie."

Others in the group nodded and muttered in sympathy with Carol's difficult experiences with the internet. They'd all heard this story before.

"But at the end? At the end, I led him outside into the garden and watched him get tasered into the back of a lorry. There were dozens of them in there, women, kids. And I never saw Andy again. Don't know what happened to him. I mean, I know what they *say* happened to him. That he was shot. In the head. But I don't know if he knew what was happening. If he was frightened. I was, I was fucking terrified. I only did it because of the children. He just wasn't their dad anymore. I still feel like it was all my fault."

Carol poked at her eyeballs with the remnants of her tissues, making little mewling sounds. Dr. Walling, her interest piqued by self-blame, returned her spectacles to their proper position.

"Why do you feel it was your fault, Carol?"

"Because he was my husband and I was meant to look after him," Carol replied, "and I didn't. I called the emergency hotline. I reported him as infected. I took Daisy and Joey and I closed the doors to our flat and locked us in. Locked him out, wobbling around in the road. On his own."

The story wasn't new to them, but the searing pain that came with it took everyone by surprise, even Kesta. The image of a loved one left to die alone, abandoned to their fate. A survival of the fittest, except that no one had survived. Each person in the circle retreated back into their own private grief. Kesta stared intently down at her own lap as if a gateway into another dimension might open up, and she could disappear into it forever.

"Carol, thank you for talking to us about Andy," said Dr. Walling, who shuffled her papers and looked at no one in particular. "What I'm hearing from Carol is that we need to come to terms with *the end*"—Dr. Walling made theatrical quotation marks with her fingers—"the end of our loved one. Death is rarely chosen. What's clear is that the manner in which the virus claimed the lives of those we held dear—and the fact that this was out of our control—continues to distress us."

The group looked at Dr. Walling as though her level of consciousness had transcended into a higher state, far beyond her second-class degree in clinical psychology. Kesta looked everywhere other than at Dr. Walling. She wasn't ready to talk yet. As the doctor conjured Michael's name out of thin air and not her own, Kesta felt a hot sweat of relief soak through her shirt.

"Michael, did you want to talk about Eddie today? The final moments of Eddie's life? What do you think?"

"Goodness, well." Michael was fanning his face with his hands and looking apologetically at the group. "I'll try. Please bear with me." Therapy made Michael overheat.

"I had come home early, because of an outbreak near Aldgate where I used to work. And Eddie was in the kitchen." Michael winced as he said *Eddie* and Kesta felt her heart sink for him.

"I thought he was trying to make a cup of tea until I realized he wasn't. He was holding the kettle over a cup, but nothing was coming out of it because it was empty. He shook it about like a baby's rattle. Then he threw it on the ground and seemed puzzled by the noise it made. He stood there, watching it rolling around on the floor." Kesta and the others held their breath, all wishing for a different ending for Michael's story. "I asked him what the matter was. I thought he'd had a stroke. When he turned to me, I saw the shirt I'd bought him for Christmas was covered in blood, and that something didn't look right with his mouth."

"Temporomandibular joint dislocation," Kesta blurted out loud. The others stared at her. She'd been thinking it, over and over, in her head, and somehow it had launched itself out of her mouth. "The majority of patients suffered from it. It made their faces look distended." She smiled awkwardly at Michael, who looked at her as if she'd just dropped her knickers at church. Dr. Walling shook her head, and Kesta realized too late that her bedside manner had betrayed her again.

"He still tried to speak through it," Michael continued, stoically. "He was conscious enough to know that he was changing. I think he recognized me. People have told me that would be impossible, that there wasn't anything I could have done to help him, and I have to pray that was true."

Shaking, he wiped the sweat from his hands down the legs of his jeans and took a deep breath.

"We'd had a stove fitted the winter before last. I used to love watching Eddie chopping logs out in our little garden. With an axe. Used to take the mick out of him about it, fulfilling all my lumberjack fantasies, you know." A fond memory coaxed a smile across Michael's lips before the usual resignation returned. "Six blows it took. I'll never forget it, the look on his face. But you don't let the ones you love suffer, do you? I have to live with what I did for the rest of my life. And I'd do it again. In a heartbeat."

"You put him out of his misery," said Tina, standing up and walking toward Michael with open arms.

"Had to keep his head in the sink until they came for him."

"I know, it's okay," said Tina, squeezing him tightly, muffling anything further Michael might have wanted to say about his husband's head circling the drain with her chest.

A gentle wave of applause rippled out across the group. Kesta did not clap. Dr. Walling rose from her seat and hugged Michael warmly, while

Tina stroked his back. Tina had killed her sister with a garden spade and their mother with a brick a week later. Kesta could hear whisperings of how brave Michael was, how much he must have loved his husband to do what he had done. Once Dr. Walling had restored order to the group and everyone had returned to their chairs, Kesta looked up to see that Tina's hand was in the air and that she was looking right at her.

"Oh, Tina." Dr. Walling seemed delighted to have a willing volunteer. "Do go ahead."

Tina raised an eyebrow deliberately. "I want to ask Kesta a question."

"Kesta, are you happy to take a question from the group, from Tina?"

Kesta wasn't happy about it at all. She nodded and Dr. Walling signaled to Tina that she had the floor.

"You work for the health service, don't you?"

Kesta sensed that whatever she said would be the wrong answer.

"You're a doctor or something, right?"

Kesta shrugged. It depended on who she was talking to. Sometimes she said doctor because it was easier for people to understand. When she said scientist, they tended to query whether the preface should be *mad.*

"Well, I want to know exactly what your lot are doing with our money," said Tina, leaning forward in her chair, confident she was speaking for everyone. "And why you haven't found a cure yet? It's been three months. What's taking so long?"

It had been one thing to live through a zombie apocalypse and another to be held responsible for ensuring it never happened again. Irrational though it was, Kesta did feel responsible. For everything, really. All the time. She worried she would stumble over her words if she spoke, say something that made her seem guilty or complicit in matters the group could never hope to understand. Tim had been the diplomat in their relationship, so much more proficient at managing other people than she ever was. He instinctively knew what people wanted to hear and so he said it, whether he meant it or not. He had always known what to say to make Kesta feel better about life, better about herself. She would have given anything to hear his voice at that moment, to see him wink at her the way he always did, to reassure her that things would be okay. But she could hear only her own condescending voice, creaking out of her dry mouth.

"I work in oncology," she said, as if it should matter to them, "cancer care. Also in pathology and histology, these disciplines are critical when you're looking at disease but then, this is, well . . . so . . ."

She heard herself tripping over the words, struggling to explain herself and what she knew, and they didn't. She should just have said she was a doctor.

"I have training in virology, obviously, but this is different. We don't have a baseline, the antigenic shift hasn't been established, if indeed there is one. We, well, they—"

"Who's they?" asked Tina.

"Um, well, the team working on the virus research. Project Dawn—"

"So, not you then?"

"Not me, no."

"What's the point of you, then?"

"Well, oncology as I said, but, well, the team assigned to isolating and treating the virus, the Project Dawn team, they're learning about it as quickly as they can—"

"Not quickly enough," Carol chimed in, irritably crossing her legs and folding her arms. Others grumbled in agreement. Kesta felt the circle closing in around her.

"What is the government going to do about it?" Tina demanded, jabbing a cattle prod finger toward her.

"We're stretched to breaking point," Kesta mumbled.

"Well, it's not bloody good enough! It's too late for my sister, too late for my mum!"

"Tina, I'm sensing a lot of misdirected blame here—" said Dr. Walling, trying to intervene.

"How can we trust that it won't happen again?" Tina raved. "Where is the cure? Is there a vaccine? How many more people will die, Kesta?"

"—and anger, Tina. And possibly also boundary issues. We might want to breathe and consider how triggering your tone could be for other people—"

"Guys, please," Kesta said, standing up. She was trembling. "I don't work at Project Dawn, okay? I work at a regular hospital. This hospital. We're all just doing the best we can. We were making great strides in extending life expectancy with many of the cancers affecting our blood cells—"

"What use is a cure for cancer if we're all fucking zombies?" said Tina.

CHAPTER TWO

By the time Kesta reached the bar, it was a little after six. She felt bruised by what had happened at group, more resolved than ever that therapy wasn't therapeutic in her case. She wanted to go straight home, but tonight was a special occasion. With any luck, they'd be the only ones in there. The bar was over in Farringdon, and before the outbreak, it had been artisanal, and gin-focused, and called Pour Decisions. Now, as one of the few bars to have gamely reopened since the curfew had been lifted—albeit with its neon signage disconnected and much of its curved glass bay windows still boarded up—it served anyone anything they wanted. Kesta had taken to drinking there because drinking there somehow seemed less ghoulish than drinking at home. She'd resolved to continue doing both in order to fully test her hypothesis.

A giant in a waxy raincoat stood before her, most of his face obscured by a mask covering his mouth and nose. A milky acrylic shield framed his face. He scanned Kesta's forehead with an electronic thermometer—not to check if her temperature was elevated but rather to discern if she was alive enough to register one—and asked her to raise both her arms high into the air, then to touch her toes, to prove she had full command of her motor skills. The doorman seemed almost disappointed when she passed, and he had to let her in.

Once inside, Kesta was relieved to see only a handful of isolated drinkers, festering around the edges of the room. Jess of course was sitting at the very center of the bar, her heeled feet extended out toward the neighboring stool she'd marked out for Kesta despite the obvious lack of competition for it. Jess spread herself about thickly. There was always so much of her to go around. She was the human embodiment of treacle.

Jess was in a black shift dress and stilettos, even though she must have come straight from the surgery. The smug expression she wore by default changed the moment she saw Kesta wavering by the entrance. It was one of those funny things about death. Some people cried because what had happened to you hadn't yet happened to them.

"God, I'm fucking useless!" Jess sniffed, wiping her nose with the back of her hand. She prized herself upward against the mirrored bar and was illuminated by dozens of little flames, votives across the countertop, refracting against the glass, and pillar candles on the shelves where the spirit bottles had yet to be replenished. Jess was glowing. She reminded Kesta of the Dia de los Muertos dolls she and Tim had seen in Mexico on their honeymoon. Arms outstretched, teeth gleaming in the candlelight, Jess lunged toward Kesta and began to squeeze the life out of her. In her arms, Jess felt about the same height as Tim had been. For a second, Kesta gave in to it and pretended she was holding her husband again.

"I started to worry you weren't coming again, and then I remembered you had group today," Jess said. At this, she beamed, her tears already dry. "So, I went ahead and ordered a bottle." She slithered back onto her seat to take a proper look at Kesta, who, feeling that she was under the microscope, smoothed out her denim shirt and fluffed her untrimmed fringe. She smiled politely at the barman, who ignored her completely.

"You do want wine?" Jess asked.

"Actually, I've given up drinking till Christmas," Kesta replied with faux cheer. Jess looked appalled. "Sorry, no, wrong grammar. I've given up. Drinking till Christmas." The joke fell flat. She must try harder to look the part in public, she thought. To be normal, sociable. Tim would have winked and told her to relax.

"You look slightly less shitty than last time I saw you," said Jess, narrowing her eyes at Kesta as she poured generously. "Have you put a bit of weight back on?"

"Yes, I think so," Kesta lied.

"Cheers, babe."

"Cheers, yes."

Kesta needed two hands to hold the glass, and her first sip made her cough. Jess summoned the barman with the flick of a wrist, and a glass of water materialized before her. She slid it over to Kesta. Jess drummed her inky nails against the countertop.

"Should I ask you about therapy or is that a taboo topic for tonight?"

"Same as every week," Kesta said, shrugging, "everybody's dead. Everybody's sad about that. Blunt knives make decapitation more challenging than it should be."

"Bloody government should just give them all free booze," Jess snorted. "I've actually thought about prescribing spirits at the surgery. Most of my patients just need to drink enough to forget about what happened."

"And what's the mortality rate of those registered at your surgery?"

"Fuck off. I'm an excellent doctor!" cackled Jess.

It remained a mystery to all who knew her why Jess had become a GP. She loathed children and old people, a doctor's bread and butter. She was squeamish and haughty and incapable of taking anything seriously. What had happened to Tim had been the exception. That had sobered her up.

She was complaining about staff at the surgery being off sick. About her own workload and about life not returning to normal quickly enough after the outbreak for her liking. The barman kept grinning at her, toweling off tumblers that were already dry. It was hard not to be spellbound by Jess. She was infectious. Kesta wasn't really listening. She was thinking about how nice it must be, easing through life wearing Jess's skin. All those easy qualities she herself didn't possess stitched together seamlessly. Jess radiated an innate confidence. Kesta radiated something, but her glow probably contained potassium and had a fallout zone. The barman's mobile buzzed inside the leg of his trousers, and he disappeared into a back room to answer it.

Now that the coast was clear, Jess leaned forward in her seat. "Any news," she whispered, "on you-know-what?"

Kesta shook her head.

"No, nothing," she said, deflated.

"You must be on the shortlist though? With your skill set?"

"Maybe there were a thousand other applicants. Maybe I'm not qualified enough. I don't know. Either way I'm just waiting for something to happen."

"You've always been shit at waiting," said Jess, "but you promise you'll let me know if you hear anything, won't you? I don't want you harboring a dirty little secret from me."

"I promise I'll let you know."

"I mean, I think you should give yourself a break, babe," Jess said, in between gulps of wine. "Because you've had enough to deal with as it is without feeling like you should be running Project Dawn," she whispered it elaborately again, the whites of her eyes sparkling in the low light, "single-handedly. And it's not your job to save the world. Right?"

Kesta didn't really have an answer for that.

She dreamed of working at Project Dawn. No, that wasn't entirely true. Kesta's dreams involved her running, falling, hunting, chasing, being chased, being hunted, and sometimes gouging out the eyes of strangers with her own fingers, that one time with a teaspoon. Kesta's dreams were bleak and bloodthirsty and horribly unsettling, and it wouldn't take a Dr. Walling figure long to unpick their hidden meaning because the meaning wasn't hidden. Project Dawn would find the cure. That's what they had all been promised. And then the nightmare would finally be over.

Kesta fantasized about working at Project Dawn when she was staring wide-eyed into the abyss at three in the morning, which was most nights. She thought about it as she trudged to work each day, the image of herself at the microscope, staring down the lens into revelation, to her eureka moment. She would cogitate over it in the middle of the day, and sometimes her excitable, wandering thoughts would stumble their way out into the open, somewhere between pathology and the vending machine down in reception. She would gabble on about her hypothesis to a woman who worked in hospital administration and who shared her craving for a midafternoon Twix to overcome the sugar slump. Kesta would share her own theories on the nature of the zombie virus—sometimes it was an abnormality in the spleen, sometimes it was a retrovirus possibly spread by rats—and the woman would nod politely and tell Kesta what she'd told her every time this had happened, which was that she worked in human resources, and she really didn't have a clinical opinion.

But I'm human and my resources aren't being put to good use, Kesta would think as the woman backed away from her with a glazed expression, hiding the Twix behind her back as though it would be the first thing Kesta would go for.

"I mean, what happened during the outbreak was horrific," Jess continued. "My niece's cat sitter got shot in the arse. Bullet was meant for the zombie behind her, but it rebounded off a car wing mirror, clipped her in the keister. Our postman died on my front lawn. Which was ghastly. Every day there were more infections, more deaths to contend with. How are we supposed to just get over it? But not everyone lost a husband!"

It was clear that Jess regretted the words as soon as they'd drunkenly left her mouth. She set her wine down on the countertop.

"You know, Kesta, I'm so proud of you," she said, starting to cry again. "You're the only person I know who lost the love of their life. And you're going gangbusters."

The barman placed a square of paper napkins on the counter between them. Jess took them all.

"I'm so sorry," she wept, delicately dabbing at her lash line, "I just miss him so much."

"I know. Me too."

"Thing is, Kesta," Jess sniffed, "he'd definitely want you to be happy. Can you ever be happy again?"

Kesta said nothing. She just nodded and smiled. People didn't have a clue what Tim had wanted, and yet these days, they seemed intent on telling her that he'd want her to move on.

"You had twenty great years together."

It was meant to be forever.

"You were so, so lucky to have found him in the first place."

Kesta didn't feel lucky. She felt the polar opposite of lucky.

"I hope you know that I'm here for you, always," said Jess earnestly, adding, "that I know what you're going through," with absolutely no idea what Kesta was going through.

"Thanks, Jess."

"Shall we do a toast then?" she asked, hoisting up her glass. Kesta felt her stomach churn. She didn't want to do a fucking toast. Such ceremony felt ostentatious. But she ought to go along with it.

"To Timothy Shelley," Jess said, her voice faltering. "Our beloved Tim. Our darling, bonkers, gorgeous, daft, witty, marvelous old Timbo. On what would have been your thirty-ninth birthday. We love you loads, we salute you, and we miss you like hell."

"I love you, Tim," said Kesta, and drank what remained in her glass.

The light was fading when Jess disappeared toward the verdant hills of Hampstead, via the Metropolitan line, and Kesta resumed her long walk to Wapping. Outside Pour Decisions, a handful of mourners had converged over a collection of photographs, candles, and flowers wilting behind the iron gates of Smithfield Market. Kesta stopped to watch their quiet vigil, for bodies that must have fallen there but would be denied the dignity of burial. The mourners were matted together, crying, throbbing like ganglion cells under her microscope. No one really seemed human anymore, least of all Kesta. Grief does that. It hacks great chunks out of you and what remains regenerates into a poor imitation of what existed before.

The air in London felt colder now, as though there weren't enough people left to keep the city warm. In the distance, Kesta could see two police vans parking up, blue lights pulsing without sound. Six officers leapt from the vehicles like urban foxes, hungry guns worn at the hip, patrolling the area, just in case. No one had been bitten in three months. All of the infected had been rounded up—by the army, the police, by their own loved ones—and exterminated. There had been no other option to contain the spread. It was kill or be killed. The officers surveilled the mourners from afar, muttering into radios that crackled in reply. Kesta stared blankly ahead as she walked past them. The front line was a brutal place to be. Everyone else had the luxury of obscurity.

London lay prone before her, a cadaver dredged from a riverbed, under a sheet of cloud, resigned and exposed. It was no longer the city Kesta had grown up in. This city was terminal, its life draining away through mile after mile of ancient sewers, out into the Thames Estuary and the North Sea. As she walked toward the Barbican, past its deserted tube station, heading east, she could slice through the lane dividers all the way down Aldersgate Street without a single car to bother her. The red Z signs spray-painted onto doors and windows of buildings where the virus had struck demarcated her journey. Government posters clung to their walls shredded and defaced. Huge billboards lit up the roundabout warning people to stay indoors. Leaflets and cards, printed and handwritten, clogged up the gutters along the pavements. Churches offering sanctuary. Instructions from the army on self-defense. Homemade posters for those who were missing, their expectant faces now dirtied by other people's footprints, staring up at Kesta from the ground, still hoping to be found. Evangelical flyers proclaiming the end of times and all the answers you needed at the end of a hotline for £6.99 a minute. The streets were littered with relics of the crisis that lay where they had fallen, in the doorways of shuttered shops and cafes where once the homeless might have slept. Kesta passed by an old pub, still boarded up, a single light on in the back somewhere, shining for no one. There were no homeless people living in London now. They had been amongst the first to die.

———

Coming home to no one was the hardest part of all. Before she turned the key in the lock, there was a split second of hope, that he'd still be there as she remembered him. The flat was so lonely without his endless chatter, always delivered in his outdoor, college bar baritone. Indoor voice, for God's sake, she used to say to him, the neighbors will hear you. Tim would give her that smile, her only weakness, and carry on as loudly as before. She had the indoor voice. And without him it was barely a whisper. What she wouldn't give to be embarrassed by the sheer volume of him now.

The blinds in the living room remained closed, had been for five months. Light would attract them, they were told at first, so everyone had drawn their curtains and waited obediently for it to be over. She had grown accustomed to shutting out the world because performing for it like a monkey—at work, at therapy, as people tried to engage her at the supermarket or the park—exhausted her.

She went to the fridge and removed a bottle of white wine from the night before, along with a cardboard box from the middle shelf. Aside from a pint of milk and a bag of ground coffee, the fridge was as deserted as the flat. Kesta did not cook; that had been Tim's pleasure. She struggled to eat at home now.

Anyway, the fridge was mostly occupied by blood bags. O+. Kesta's own. And a regiment of tiny glass vials where the eggs should have been. She poured herself a glass of wine, lifted a circular lemon sponge from the cardboard box and deposited it on a dinner plate, and rummaged in the kitchen's junk drawer for something she wasn't sure she still had. But there they were, the little pink candles, stuffed at the very back, in between a torch, a plug adaptor, and some crayons. Kesta slid the nicest tea tray she owned out from underneath the drinks trolley in the living room. She arranged her sorry celebration across it.

Kesta laid the tray to rest on the table in the hallway and began the arduous process of opening the four black dead bolts on the spare bedroom door.

The room was in total darkness save for the primary colors of the vitals monitor casting an eerie rainbow across the bed like a nursery light. Sporadic bleeps and whirs from the machine reassured Kesta that some life remained. She recorded these readings in the notebook she kept on the nightstand: heart rate, oxygen levels, body temperature. All abnormal but at least unchanged. Kesta returned to the hallway for the tray, sliding it across the nightstand.

One yellow eye watched her. It saw but didn't see, and it never, ever blinked. A graying arm upheaved into the restraints before falling with a defeated puff. Violence had fought its way out of that body, and now it was a scene of great suffering. It was unnaturally positioned, a marionette with its strings cut. A spider's web of ruptured vessels, scaly skin stretched taut and livid. Every inch of it was screaming. But there was no pain, no sound, no progress in the patient that Kesta could determine.

She lit the candles on the cake, and she showed the cake to Tim.

"Happy birthday, darling."

CHAPTER THREE

The cake was a mistake. Kesta had fantasized that by singing to Tim and striving to celebrate his clinging on long enough to have turned thirty-nine, something might stir inside him, a familiar tradition stimulating some response. Kesta the scientist knew that such spontaneous recoveries were incompatible with Tim's condition, but Kesta the wife still sang badly and ferried naked flames into her husband's room, only to be surprised to see him bare his teeth, convinced that she was going to set him on fire. Unsuprisingly, he hadn't been able to blow the candles out either. She had felt silly and guilty as she'd huffed out the candles and eaten half the cake, sitting on the floor. She'd gone to bed shortly afterward and cried into her pillow, praying that if he could hear her through the walls, he was incapable now of understanding that he was the very heart of her distress. Kesta did not sleep that night because she rarely slept. Instead, she listened out for Tim and played through moments from their once-happy marriage in her head.

Now that it was morning, Kesta watched her husband from the doorway. It was impossible to tell when he was asleep because his eyes were always open, always staring back at her. Never blinking. Eerily yellow. Their emotion and expressiveness all but faded away.

"Good morning, my darling."

She kissed his forehead and tried to remember what he used to smell like before the cocktail of drugs had altered his scent. The air in the room was thick and metallic because of it, as though burned sugar oozed from his every pore. Kesta opened a window to let a little air in, although she kept the blinds drawn. They rose and fell with a soft pat against the frame, caught by the breeze outside like a child's kite.

"Urgggggh," said Tim, which was presently the best she could hope for. For three months, their marriage had been reduced to the mechanical basics of human communication. She consoled herself that it wasn't then so different than everyone else's.

"You could do with some fresh air," she said, checking the skin on his arm underneath the restraints she had used to chain him to the radiator. It was ulcerated. She wondered if he could stand for her to debride it, and if she did it, could she stop it from becoming infected.

"Is it hurting you?" she asked him. Tim stared back at her blankly. He tried to lift the damaged arm, wincing when the flesh touched the metal. "It's okay, we'll figure something out." Kesta took her clipboard and pen from the nightstand and began to write the date and time.

Ulceration of the dermis due to friction contact with restraints. Consider debridement. Will need scalpel.

"Oh, and I must remember to ask Albert about borrowing that fan."

Every few hours Kesta would scour every inch of Tim's body looking for clues and transcribe her observations onto A4 paper. She had bought a ring binder. A highlighter pen. One of those upside-down watches nurses pin to their chests, though she'd used it only the once because Tim had tried to grope and then eat it. She assessed and recorded the signs of his alertness, pain, delirium, muscle strength, and mobility. She knew that evidence of change in these things was not necessarily evidence of improvement, but she tried not to let any decline in her patient cause her undue concern. Change meant that Tim was still alive, sort of, and that was all she really cared about. She knew she couldn't cure Tim on her own. She wasn't completely delusional. Her plan, if you could call it that, was to preserve her husband in the best kind of undead state possible, until Project Dawn called to accept her, until someone there found a cure. She'd obviously have to figure out how to break the news to her new colleagues about the zombie she had withheld from the authorities for months, itself a criminal act, but this was a problem for a future version of Kesta. She could worry about only so much at once.

Maintaining a drug regimen was an ongoing practical challenge. There were drugs to reduce pain, others to help Tim relax. Drugs to prevent his blood from becoming too thick, drugs to stop his blood from thinning, drugs to stop his body from rejecting her blood when she transfused him with it once a week. Drugs to stop him from becoming dehydrated, meal replacements that were essentially drugs pretending to be food. Three months of trial and error and fear and perseverance had played out inside this room, together with an abundance of watching and waiting and praying. The sum total of it was that Tim was still here, or at least, a form of him. For Kesta that was enough. His experience of it all might differ considerably.

"I'll try to get home at lunch if I can," she said, blowing him a kiss before locking up the dead bolts and heading off to the hospital.

London is an obstinate city. Pestilence and plague, pea soup fog, years of being bombed to smithereens and razed to the ground by great fires hadn't dimmed her shine. But even a city as indomitable as she had a limit to what she could put up with. London needed to be seen crawling with people again to foster the illusion she was in recovery. To prove that everything was normal.

It was much the same for Kesta. While she wanted to hide away at home under the 10-tog duvet of her grief, she didn't have that luxury. For her to keep Tim's existence a secret, and to successfully maintain his undeadness, she had to carry on giving the best impression of her old self that she could muster. And that meant going to work.

The hospital building Kesta worked in was a throwback from the sixties. Four floors of dark brickwork, a copper roof burnished green with age. Metal windows that were difficult to open and that fogged with condensation come rain or shine. Metal banisters painted black in hypnotic swirling shapes leading up to linear, sensible, regular corridors, off which the laboratories lay, the smell of latex, of formaldehyde, of butanol, all in competition with each other to burn the back of your eyeballs away. To Kesta, it smelled like home, albeit a little too literally these days.

By the time she arrived it was just after seven and the laboratory was as dead as a mortuary. The mortuary itself was in the basement. There was no one to keep her company other than the angry cells on the slide in front of her and the bodies on ice three floors below. Kesta preferred to work early, before there were colleagues to distract her, people filling up the space she needed to think and work in. She slipped on her starched white lab coat to examine the cellular profiles under her electron microscope.

The microscope always held the answers. It foretold the future. It sealed your fate. It bore hope and death together, clutching them in the same impartial hand. The microscope never lied at 350 times magnification. At a distance, Kesta had a fish-eye view over the ocular lens, globular and unfocused, but she could see a blossom of hematoxylin blues far too beautiful to be cancerous, throbbing and fluorescent, but there it was, nature at her most deadly.

Tell me what you see.

Carcinoma arising from the epithelial tissue of the kidney. Poorly defined. Stage four, yet to be graded.

Kesta sighed. This patient would not survive.

From the corner of her eye, she saw the light of her mobile glaring. A text message from Jess. How lovely it had been to see her. Was she getting enough sleep? When could they next have drinks? Kesta rubbed her eyes. She couldn't focus on Jess in between patients, she didn't have the bandwidth to conjure a reply, to write things she didn't mean, little white emoji lies to cover up the human-sized black one. Kesta positioned a second slide with the stage clip and squinted at it.

They were doodles in a supernatural hand, stained fluorescent by her own, and expertly. Interphase. Prophase. Metaphase. Duplication, thickening, and coil. The nuclear membrane in decline, beginning to fall apart. Suddenly it dawned on her. She was in the grip of mitosis, collapsing in on herself and splitting into two. A new version of Kesta had separated from the first, taking all the hallmarks of the original, but something other, something different. The two Kestas must exist as one: the grieving widow at work and the scientist nursing a zombie in her flat.

Kesta surveyed the remnants of her old life, which lay as tributes across her workstation. A diary Tim had bought her for her last birthday and in which she'd never had a chance to write. A stack of bleached paperwork, administration and its accompanying army of pens, pencils, elastic bands, and a stapler. A couple of scrunchies twisted together, strands of her hair stolen inside them. A fine silver-framed photograph of Tim in black tie, taken at their wedding, and all the better to look at because she wasn't in it.

Being separated from Tim during the day was agonizing. It had taken a while for her to relearn how to concentrate, to stop her brain from spiraling into negative speculation where clinical calm should exist. She had installed a webcam in the spare room and an app on her phone that allowed her to monitor him while she was at work. She opened it and waited for the swirling colored circle to resolve and the live feed to connect. But for the monitor and the handcuffs and the empty eyes, it looked like Tim was sleeping. She could expect the sedation to keep him quiet and still most of the day. It was a grim inevitability that he would develop a tolerance to the drugs she gave him. Each time she opened up the app, she felt her innards were on a spin cycle while it loaded.

Kesta spent an hour wading through the screening backlog. Just after eight, her colleague Claire bundled through the swing doors, mummified by her winter coat and scarf, even though it was July—Claire said it was always freezing in Hainault when she caught the train in the morning, and as Kesta had never been to Hainault, she didn't like to argue with her—the music from her headphones loud enough for Kesta to hear.

"Morning, love," Claire shouted. They were meant to be equally well qualified, two biomedical scientists at the top of their game, but Kesta had observed that most of Claire's workday appeared to involve making coffee, taking personal calls, and delegating much of her work to Kesta.

"You are so much better with fine needles than I am," Claire said as she slapped a mug of coffee she'd just brewed hard onto Kesta's station so that it splashed perilously close to her microscope. Coffee was Claire's go-to form of bribery. "You don't mind, do you? In the fridge by the sink."

Above the sink in the laboratory, a collection of curiosities sat along the windowsill. They ought to have been disposed of, but Dudley was rather protective of them. They were considered poor taste, the subject of lawsuits at other hospitals. This type of display had once shown off the skill of the scientist who staged it. No one knew who had laid them out, decades before, judging by their incremental decay. They had always been there, frozen in formaldehyde. An ovary, no bigger than an almond, caught in the teeth of a teratoma, a lock of blond hair encircling it, benignly. A cross-section of lung, breathlessly suspended, the bronchioles creeping out into the jellylike tentacles. Kesta's favorite was a perfectly developed embryo, a baby the size of her thumb, with its own thumbs and fingers, smooth and pallid and without flaw, suspended in time, ageless and unborn. It was all of creation imprisoned for eternity in a single glass womb. Noticing that the baby was getting too much sunlight, Kesta carefully moved the jar to one side, letting the other tissues take the hit. She found Claire's abandoned slides and took them back to her station.

The squeaking of linoleum preceded him. Then Dudley Caring, the pathologist, kicked open the swing doors with one brown loafer and staggered into the lab underneath a pile of manila folders.

"Morning, ladies," he said, then groaned as the files collapsed onto his desk. "Will you look at all this admin! I have to get through it before the multidisciplinary meeting at noon." He straightened the tie he always wore despite the fact it seemed to get in the way of everything he did. Dudley was, much like Kesta, a workaholic, and the most accomplished pathologist she had ever known. In the areas of his life he considered less important than cutting up dead bodies to discover what had killed them—which was all other areas of Dudley's life—he put in no discernable effort whatsoever. Once, when he had let his wayward tie drip into the chest cavity of a particularly messy cadaver, he had simply cut it off. Kesta had long suspected that the tie was still inside the man when Dudley had closed him up. *Dudley is the ghost of your future yet to come if you don't stay married to Tim,* Jess had prophesized cruelly when she'd met him at the lab's Christmas party years ago and he'd regaled her with a long story about a breast symposium he'd just been to in Derby.

"Kesta, I need to talk to you. It's important," he said without looking at her. Kesta often wondered what Dudley's point of view must be, given that he struggled to make eye contact with anyone, male or female, always searching around the body, never daring to look right at the face. Perhaps it was the reason he was so good at postmortems.

The telephone on Kesta's workstation interrupted them. She picked up the receiver and saw Dudley's face fall flat with disappointment. Their talk would have to wait.

"Pathology?"

"You said gangliocytoma. And you were right," said the voice at the end of the line.

"Good morning, Mr. Paphides."

"Everyone else thought anaplastic, diffuse, but you were adamant. You have a sixth sense for these things, don't you, Kesta?"

"How did the surgery go, Pap?"

"Very bloody well, thanks," he replied with that cavalier conviction possessed by men who land planes, send other men into battle, and equate rummaging around inside your brain looking for tumors with feeling for a pack of gum at the bottom of someone else's handbag. "Got it all out in one go. The lad's in recovery now."

"I'm pleased to hear it," said Kesta. "I needed a bit of good news today."

As she returned the receiver to the cradle, Dudley was up and over to her desk before she could say knife.

"I need to talk to you," he whispered, before casting a mistrustful look back at Claire. His face was an alarming shade of puce. He leaned against Kesta's workstation and began rubbing his fingers against the drawer fronts as if he might find the right words there, written in braille.

"Oh, Claire," Kesta called out, "I just remembered there's a leg downstairs that wants collecting from the morgue."

"Can't Phil do it?"

"Phil's dead, dear, remember? Something about a zombie apocalypse?"

"Shit, I'd forgotten about Phil. Poor Phil. I'll go down now." Claire strolled out of the laboratory bemoaning the demise of their former assistant, and Kesta watched as the swing doors swung to.

"I just wanted to tell you that I followed up with Project Dawn yet again and still no decision," Dudley whispered. "Sorry."

Kesta shrugged.

As soon as the government had announced that a specialist research team was being created to investigate the origin of the virus, Dudley had applied to join it. Kesta didn't know that he had applied on her behalf too until a month after Tim's supposed death. He'd told her at the time he hadn't wanted to bother her with the news while she was grieving, as though four weeks was entirely sufficient to properly process the grisly demise of one's life partner. Kesta had ultimately resigned herself to the fact that this was, in all probability, Dudley's awkward and inadequate way of trying to help her. He recognized her need to keep busy. He just couldn't have imagined how very busy she already was.

"So, how are you keeping," he asked her, "truthfully, I mean?"

"The same," she said.

"No better, no worse?"

"That's pretty much the size of it." Kesta tried to return to the microscope, but his hand was on her shoulder, squeezing it.

"Yes. Well, you know where I am," Dudley mumbled, "if you need anything."

"Right over there," she said, pointing toward his desk.

"Yes. Yes, exactly. I'm always right over there."

Dudley shuffled back to his paper mountain and started to dig through the files again. Kesta returned to her microscope, but there was something wrong. She hadn't seen it happen. Dudley was like a poltergeist. Tim's photograph was lying face down on her desk. This was the third time it had happened since she'd told everyone he had died. Kesta felt her face redden. She wiped the frame with her coat sleeve and put it back in pride of place, then brushed at her shoulder where Dudley's hand had lain.

———

The hours ticked by in celestial color, slide by slide. A soupçon of blood smears, a single serving of trachea, a sliver of small intestine, laid out, assessed, and understood. Kesta's eyes were beginning to strain from squinting down her microscope. As Dudley prepared for his multi-disciplinary meeting and Claire struggled to know where to begin with sectioning the dismembered leg, Kesta considered running down to the stockroom because she wanted to find a steroid cream for Tim's sores.

"It looks just like a frankfurter, doesn't it?" Claire exclaimed. "Without the foot, I mean. Oh, hello, can I help you?"

A woman in a black skirt suit was standing in the doorway, her voice like a flashlight, searching, blinding those it touched.

"Mrs. Shelley?"

Kesta didn't dare turn around. She felt a cold sweat flushing across her throat. Her fingers clawed into the chair beneath her. They know, she thought, this is what it feels like to be found out.

"I'm here for—Mrs. Shelley," the woman said again when no one answered, checking Kesta's name against a file she held in one hand. In the other was a briefcase. Kesta's thighs started to shudder. Tim would tell her she'd done her best, not to fight them, just to go quietly. But that wasn't in Kesta's nature.

"I can explain—" she started, but the woman didn't let her finish.

"Oh, and Dr. Caring. I'm after Dr. Caring and Mrs. Shelley. Is that the two of you, then?"

The air whistled out of Kesta's lungs and she managed to dig her fingernails out of her seat. They were white and bloodless.

"I'm Dr. Caring, hello," Dudley said, offering the stranger his hand, "and you are?"

"Come with me," she barked, leaving Dudley hanging as she clattered back out into the corridor. They followed, leaving Claire and her leg in the lab.

The woman marched more than she walked. She swung the briefcase triumphantly as though it was a head she'd cleaved from the shoulders of her enemy. Kesta had never seen her before. She seemed to be leading them toward the administrative department. She barreled her way into the office of the hospital's chief executive and sat down at another man's desk as if it was her own. She heaved the briefcase onto it, clicked the locks aside, opened its jaws wide, and withdrew an iPad. She creaked back in the leather chair and inspected the two people standing limply in front of her.

"I work for UK Defense and Security," she said at last. "I'm here to discuss your applications to Project Dawn."

Kesta felt the dizziness returning, pins and needles burning her extremities. She needed to sit down, to steady her breathing, but since the woman hadn't invited her to, she just stood there, stricken. This wasn't the end after all. It was only the beginning.

"You've cleared the threshold for acceptance." She continued, "Your qualifications and experience will be an asset to us, I'm sure. But the research you'll be undertaking is not without significant risk. It will be laborious. It will be dangerous. It's entirely possible you could trigger a second outbreak." The woman laughed like lye water burning as it hit them. "Then we'd be royally fucked. No." She swiped a manicured finger over the screen. "I shouldn't make light of this. I do not underestimate the work involved, and you shouldn't either. I'd advise you both to get your affairs in order. It's imperative that you're both honest with yourselves about this. Are you ready to join Project Dawn?"

"Yes!" Dudley blurted, then covered his mouth with both hands. He was shaking, gulping back delight and ambition, as though he'd just won a minivan on a game show. He reached instinctively for Kesta's hand, but Kesta could only brush it away.

She had waited for this moment since Tim had been bitten. Now it blindsided her, and she felt only terror! What if she couldn't do what she was asked? What if she failed? What if she let Tim down? There were so many variables, so much that could go wrong. Her ears began to ring. She teetered forward, grabbed the edge of the chief executive's desk. She couldn't think straight. She couldn't see. The woman's lips were moving, but Kesta couldn't hear her, couldn't focus on what she was saying. Something about biosecurity clearance. About taking a different route into work each day to avoid detection. About the need for absolute secrecy. All Kesta could think was, *I'm the GOAT at keeping secrets!*

Suddenly, the altitude shifted somewhere inside her brain. She swallowed and her ears popped clear, the uncomfortable heat of the near faint fading. Dudley was saying something.

"The Strand?"

And the woman replied: "Yes, technically it's underneath the Strand. Project Dawn was constructed around the platforms of the disused Strand tube station years ago, half a mile underground. It's really quite ingenious."

Kesta was dumbfounded. The location of the Project Dawn site was the subject of a media blackout. She had taken it for granted that all biological research was being undertaken at Porton Down, miles outside London in the empty Wiltshire countryside. Instead, a clandestine operation was in play right in the middle of the city. As Dudley scrawled his signature gleefully on the iPad, Kesta wondered whether she should open up a vein to write with.

"We were concerned, Mrs. Shelley," said the woman, dangling the iPad in front of her, "that this might be too much for you, so soon after the death of your husband. Are you quite sure you can cope with the rigors of Project Dawn?"

Kesta felt the fetus of her responsibility to Tim taking root inside her. She had been keeping him undead for three months. Now it was up to her to bring him back to life.

"Where do I sign?" she asked.

CHAPTER FOUR

They called it a catastrophic emergency. A major natural disaster. There were some militaristic references to levels of threat to life bandied around, which signified the degree of force with which this unprecedented virus would be met. To most people these levels just made it sound as though the virus had arrived already scarily proficient at *Call of Duty*. When they screamed on the news about readying for Level 3 emergency protocol—roadblocks, martial law, stay-at-home orders—Tim had asked innocently, what had happened to one and two? Most Londoners did as they were told because they could see with their own eyes exactly what happened if they didn't. You really had to be there to get it.

This virus was anything but subtle. It didn't employ stealth and deception in its contagion, like a good virus should. It didn't sneak into your system discreetly, like a burglar jimmying a window, stealing your immunity, leaving you blissfully unaware that anything was amiss until it was too late. This virus was physical. It was violent. It warned you it was coming because you saw it rampaging toward you, you knew you had it because it plunged its fangs deep into your arm, ripping out the flesh as it withdrew, mission accomplished. This virus claimed you rapaciously, a visceral manifestation of your imminent demise. And that's what people saw, looking on from the outside, too awed to look away.

It looked exactly like the end of the world.

It was spreading ferociously. It had no incubation period—Kesta saw that once infected, patients died and were resurrected and back to attacking and biting new victims again within minutes. It was a virus spreading in real time.

In many ways it was surprising that it took so long for them to do it. Three whole days. They had to kill the contagion. London had turned. She was metastatic. She was harmful tissue. They had to cut her off. To amputate her poison, to cauterize her disease, because there was no other option. London became an open grave; the rest of the world waiting in solemnity until it was safe to fill her in.

The outbreak lasted for six weeks, until every last infected person had been captured, when the quarantine was finally lifted. No one who'd been bitten had been left alive, every victim destroyed.

Except, of course, for Tim.

At the beginning of the outbreak, no one talked about a cure because everyone was too busy running away from the virus. The physical demands of looking and waiting and fleeing and hiding and thinking about all the ways in which your personal items could be used as weapons, or worse still, used as weapons against you, rather sucked up all the oxygen and left none for the brain to theorize. Being vigilant is a permanent, engrossing state of mind, and Kesta, not a natural athlete, found the first few weeks exhausting, trying to repress her rising horror. As with everything worth devoting yourself to, people became more adept at living under siege. They'd learned that no help was coming. Defending themselves became second nature. Everyone wore trainers.

Kesta compiled clinical notes drawn from her own observations as soon as the infection started to spread. She spent her dark days and even darker nights trying to make sense of the insensible. Without logic, without data, without proof, Kesta would spiral.

As with everything scientific, Kesta always knew too much, like if that spotting was a problem; whether you should see someone about that mole. But with this virus, Kesta knew nothing. It was the first time in her life that she had ever felt afraid. Real fear, not the showy, spidery kind, but deep inside her, as though a sarcophagus had formed itself around her heart. But she had to stay calm for Tim. She had to learn what she could, as quickly as she could, so that she could assuage his fears as well as her own.

Tim being Tim, he used humor as a means of distracting them both from the apocalypse outside. He didn't want his wife worrying about him being worried, so he pretended that he wasn't. He'd worked his way studiously through the canon of classic zombie cinema in order to develop the right language to describe what they were seeing.

"*Train to Busan* is a personal favorite and an excellent example of the zombie's ability to switch from dormant to active in the blink of an eye," he said, the two of them unaware at the time of the foreboding irony of this insight. "One minute they look kind of sleepy, like they've been lobotomized, the next minute they can run at high speed to hunt down their prey. Although I don't think ours are, like, *World War Z* fast. They're more *Shaun of the Dead*, able to jog in a pack," Tim said, pointing to his laptop where a scene was paused ready for her to review it, as soon as she'd finished reading *Clinical Infectious Diseases*.

"Their lack of motor skills and how we've watched them powering down do indicate a new kind of neurological abnormality," Kesta had said, breaking the book's spine and splaying it out across her legs on the sofa, "though there are cases of waterborne amoebas where patients experience a sort of flickering of their coordination, before they lose it completely." At the time, she wrote *consider brain-eating amoeba* in her notebook, determined to research it later.

Four weeks into the outbreak, and Project Dawn was just a rumor, spreading much the same way as the virus did, by word of mouth. It didn't have a name then. It was just an emblem of belief. Someone opening up their front door to let in a screaming stranger struggling to outrun a pack of marauding zombies, bringing that stranger downstairs into the underbelly of a pitch-dark house, handing them a cup of tea and a seat on the floor with the others hiding out together in the darkness—and their talk of a cure was like turning a light on in that room.

Now Project Dawn was the only realistic hope Kesta had of saving Tim.

As Kesta walked through the courtyard toward their apartment block, her anxiety began to distill into something closer to optimism. She felt excited to share her news with Tim, but first she had to get past Albert in the porter's lodge.

"You look tired," he said, peering at her over his peculiar glasses. They looked like he'd bought them at a garage sale or won them in a Christmas cracker. Kesta was sure they didn't have the proper prescription.

"Oh, thanks, but I'm all right, really," she said, trying to hide her various incriminating carrier bags behind her, in case Albert offered to help her with them. "You?"

"Can't complain, love, can't complain." He put down his newspaper to take a better look at her. He had been the manager of the building since it had been converted from a squat in the eighties, back when the whole of Wapping was a long-forgotten dump, much the way it looked again now after the virus had stripped it bare. Albert had served two tours in the Gulf, and he liked things tidy, in their proper place at all times, the residents included.

Nothing escaped Albert, except, so far, Tim.

"You need anyfin' up there?" Even his thoughtful gestures were delivered like a threat, all extra east end vowels and rough as sandpaper.

"No thanks."

"Cuppa tea?"

Albert believed that tea was the true Cockney cure-all. And he made a decent cup. He put love and time into it. Residents would arrive midway through the steep, inquiring about their post or moaning about a leak, and Albert would boom, "I'm brewing, mate, I'm brewing!" Kesta made sure to say yes to a cup often enough, but she only ever joined Albert in the porter's lodge. She'd contrived a convenient lie—for that was Kesta's so-called life, a patchwork of lies sewn together to make do—about how having guests upstairs to the flat would upset her too much. Albert couldn't handle women crying. Men getting their legs blown off in a war zone was one thing, that was natural, but a woman weeping for her dead husband? Nightmare.

"I should really get my dinner in the microwave," Kesta said, "but I was going to ask if you still have that spare fan in the storeroom. It's a bit stuffy in the flat."

"Old boy in flat forty took it last week," Albert tutted, "but I could get it back for ya? Bring it upstairs? It'd be no bovva."

Kesta muttered something about not wanting to contribute to heat-related deaths in the elderly and began lumbering toward the lift. Albert eyed her bags, trying to decipher their contents: wine, coffee, more wine, maybe a ready meal. He returned to his evening paper.

"You gotta take care a yerself, gel. Eat right. Cook from scratch. Get some sleep. You 'ear me?"

"I hear you. Night, Albert."

"G'night, darlin'."

Once inside the lift, Kesta slumped against the wall and felt her heart rate steady. She dreaded running the gauntlet of Albert. The closer to home she got, the more keenly she sensed the risk of discovery.

When the lift doors opened at the second floor, she paused. It was a constant worry that one of two things would betray them: noise or smell. She knew that Tim couldn't get out of the flat by himself, but there were other ways in which his presence might emanate to other parts of the building and trigger Albert to buzz her intercom.

There was no smell this evening. Kesta unlocked her front door and kicked the draft excluder out of the way. Removing her leather jacket and shoes, she slid in her socks to the kitchen, emptying out the wine, the extra wine, and the coffee she had bought. She opened the fridge door, removed a bottle of screw-top Chablis and a blood bag, and put one of the glass vials of sedative into the back pocket of her jeans. She knew that the alcohol was making everything worse—her anxiety, her insomnia, her overarching sense of impending doom—but Kesta was determined that, regardless of how things might appear, this was absolutely not quite rock bottom. Tonight she had good news. She shuffled back into the hallway.

"Hello, handsome. How are you this evening?" she asked as she pushed Tim's door shut behind her with a foot. It was a ridiculous question, but then didn't everyone ask it, particularly of people whose only legitimate response could be absolutely fucking awful, thanks. *Such a British thing, never to say what we really mean,* she decided as she unloaded her wine and the vial and the package onto the nightstand. "I'm sorry I didn't make it home earlier," she said, leaning against the side of Tim's bed, "but guess what?"

The yellow eye that wasn't scrunched into the pillow underneath him looked up at her as if she weren't really there. Sometimes he would grunt when she entered the room, an effort toward shaping the words. Sometimes she thought he seemed pleased to see her. But not tonight. Kesta cupped his shoulder with the palm of her hand.

"I've been accepted at Project Dawn!" she said. "I can't believe it. Dudley may have pulled some strings, I think. Anyway"—she leaned closer to his face, trying to hold his gaze—"it means we have reason to be hopeful, Tim. We'll finally be able to make some real progress to get you well again."

Tim didn't look very hopeful. The air hissed out of his lungs as he tried to shift around onto his back, stopped, surprised that he couldn't turn any farther, then looked quizzically at the handcuff holding him in place. He moaned, shook his wrist, tried to pull himself free. He looked up again at Kesta, the neurons firing up in fits and starts, the realization dawning somewhere inside him perhaps that she was responsible for this predicament. Watching him struggling to work it all out, to fit the pieces that had created this grim puzzle together, always upset her.

"It's okay," she soothed. "Let's see if we can make you feel a bit— I won't say better. But—let's aim for less awful."

He'd been alone in the flat for nearly twelve hours with nothing to do but stare up at the great expanse of white ceiling hanging above him, his tolerance for the sedatives growing by the week. Kesta didn't want Tim to be permanently stupefied. She'd simply learned from experience that it was better that way. On the one day she had decided not to sedate him at all, a red mist had descended over Tim, and it had been a bloody brawl between the two of them—Kesta reinforced by the wardrobe, and Tim with his one free hand slashing through the air toward her—to knock him out again. Without his medication, Tim looked every bit like the walking dead Kesta had seen for herself, belligerent and predatory. She flicked the air bubbles out of the syringe.

He was just a blank space where her husband had been. He seemed to be watching the syringe as it was emptied into him. His breathing slowed almost immediately, and he lay on one side, drawing his knees up into his chest. He had always slept that way, in as tight a ball as possible, like a shelled prawn. Kesta stroked back his pale blond hair and looked deeply into that unseeing eye as he began to drift away from her.

"Are you proud of me?" she asked him, gently massaging his chained arm in search for a viable vein in which to pinch in a new cannula. She hooked the blood bag up to its steel stand to let gravity do her worst. "What do you think it will be like there, at Project Dawn, I mean?" Tim did not respond, not even a flicker, but Kesta carried on as if he had, because after almost twenty years together, she knew exactly what he would say to her if he could still talk. "I promise I'll try to be as friendly as I'm ever capable of being and not piss people off straightaway." She winked as she set the timer for two hours and stood back to watch as the red cells trickled their way down through the plastic tubing and into his arm. "I mean, what if they're already on the brink of a cure?" She squeezed his hand to drive the blood into his system. "That would be incredible, right? We could fix you in a matter of weeks." Turning his arm over, she noticed a rash she hadn't seen before. Was he building up a resistance to the blood transfusions? She hoped not. She could do without something else to worry about.

"Do these hurt?" she asked, smoothing over the rashes with her fingers, knowing there would be no answer. She bent down so that she could kiss his fingers, breathing in a forgotten smell, abandoned somewhere behind the virus that consumed him. "Obviously, I can't tell them about you straightaway." She traced his fingers over her lips as she spoke. "But when the time is right, we have to let them help us. We're going to get you cured, Tim, I know we are. I promise."

It was such an intimate exchange, her blood replacing his, trying to wash the virus away. Keep him ticking along, clinging to life. For the three months she'd been nursing him, Kesta had employed a two-pronged approach to securing medical supplies; the discreet overordering of stock at the lab, and theft. So far no one had noticed. Tonight, a batch of injectable chemotherapy drugs had been left behind after the leukemia clinic trial.

Kesta had been loitering around the nurses' station for several weeks, trying to make small talk, hoping to strike it lucky, all the while eye-banging the contents of the fridge with the drugs in it. Tonight had been the first time she'd been able to trick her way through, past a consultant, two nurses, and a receptionist, and bring home the spoils. She'd never stolen anything quite so potent before, but she figured it was worth a shot, since the worst had already happened. She had been busy maintaining what little health Tim had left and trying to stave off further decline. She was taking a huge risk giving him this new drug at home, but she'd made peace with the odds. Kesta was relieved to see that the drug came with instructions.

"This one's going to be a bit cold," she warned as she emptied out her special package and rubbed the little glass bottle in between her palms like congealed nail polish to warm it up a bit. Every loving gesture had taken on a new complexion lately. "This might help to stop the virus from replicating inside your body," she explained to him. "Studies have shown that many viruses respond to chemotherapy, so it's worth a try. Isn't it?" Kesta withdrew the liquid from the vial and quickly, so as not to make a fuss, darted it into Tim's stomach.

Tim showed no response. Kesta pressed down onto the injection site with a circular plaster to mop up any blood. Nothing. She pressed again, a little harder this time, digging into the wound with her fingernail. The yellow eye glared up at her just the same, and somewhere far beneath the surface of it, Tim lay sleeping.

CHAPTER FIVE

A t five-thirty the following morning, Kesta brought a photograph into the spare bedroom and positioned it carefully on the nightstand so that Tim could see it. Perhaps it would trigger something in his memory, remind him of who he was. Maybe it would help keep him company while she was at work. If he turned around in bed, if the sedation wore off a little, he would be able to see her face looking back at him. She would be there, with him, even when she couldn't be. She straightened the frame, angled it away from the glare of the monitor lights. This photograph was her pride and joy, though she'd never admit that to Tim. It always made her smile. He was wearing a crisp white shirt and a navy jacket that would one day end up forgotten in a taxi on the way home from a friend's engagement party. Her hair, like black tea, was longer then, almost to the waist, her fringe swept to one side and tucked behind her ear. The dress she couldn't even remember buying. She looked at herself in the picture, and it was the unbridled optimism beaming back at her that upset her the most. They didn't know what was coming.

"Do you remember the night we met?" she asked Tim. He shifted his body around in the bed, little noises of effort, *ah, ah, ah*, as he twisted and turned against the sheets, only to end up beaten by the strain. He rested against the pillow and stared out into the room.

"I remember," she said, "like it was yesterday—"

He was using his body to block her path to the angry-looking man readjusting his gilet. He had taken her by the hand, both hands actually, encircling hers with his own, like a flame he didn't want to burn out yet. Hands he now held, having adamantly prized her fingers away from the gilet, a stubborn knot he just had to unravel.

"Let go of me!" Kesta shouted, angling herself away. She was indignant. The temerity of the man. Of both men. This was why she had a rule to avoid the college bar. Look what happened the one night she broke it, absolute carnage, the hands of strangers grabbing at her own, an almost fistfight, which would have been her first. She felt cheated. She wasn't a woman you could just touch because you felt the urge. She would show him.

With all the strength she could muster, she wriggled backward, wrenching herself away from the man, digging in her heels. The floor was slippery with spilt beer and unknown juices, and her shoes kept skidding. She was caught on his line, anchored only by his grip, which tightened each time she tried to pull away. She'd never seen him before. He'd come at her out of nowhere, hooking her out of an argument, reeling her in, and now here she was, flopping around on the dance floor, gasping for air.

"I can't do that," he said, his hair turning red, then blue in the garish disco light above them. His eyes were green, then yellow, his teeth like dentures in the neon glare.

"I can't do that," he teased, "because I have a strong feeling this chap, sorry, what's your name?"

"Mark."

"I have a feeling that Mark's mother won't recognize his face again if I let go of your hands." Mark in the gilet was peering over the blond's shoulder, looking at her as men usually did, at the weirdo who should be more grateful for their attention, solicited or not. The blond seemed to think differently. He couldn't stop smiling at her. He grinned down at her from his great height, and she felt like buried treasure; she felt dug up, found.

Kesta didn't really do other people. She certainly didn't do relation-ships. On a normal night, she would have shrugged this guy off like a cold. Said something sharp to give him pause, to force him into a retreat. Tonight, she couldn't even make a fist with her hands still held in his. His entitlement to her space—her fight—her fingers—would ordinarily have riled her. He smelled of oranges and bergamot and danger and freedom and all those things she'd told herself didn't impress her. She had always thought that the right side of her brain was entirely redundant. She was governed by her critical thinking, not her fleeting feelings. His silken, bronzed thumbs soothed over her knuckles, which were raw from hours spent dunked in paraffin and other curios.

"Who wears a gilet in a bar, for God's sake?" she said, hoping against all hope that the blond didn't own one. "We're not in Fulham."

"I know, right," he replied, "what a wanker."

"Total wanker." She struggled to suppress a giggle, and her voice squeaked out like the air from an old set of bagpipes. "Anyway, what does it matter to you?" she said, sea legs shaking, forced for the first time in their lives to resist the urge to kick her free. "I fight my own battles."

"I can see that," the blond said, winking, "but why is it your problem?" A hand brushed the hair away from her face and tucked it behind her ear with those fingers made of silk, his mouth still close enough for her to feel his breath against her cheek. She pushed the hair back to where she wanted it, covering half her face, and his smile broadened.

"Because action is more positive than inaction. Subjectively speaking, so—" She could feel her cheeks redden, her heart pounding, worrying that the hand he still held in his, the fingers having woven their way in between her own, might expose how awestruck she felt, this close to him, wavering in between one life and the next.

"Is it now?" he asked, looking her up and down, all five foot nothing of her.

"Anyway, I'm very good with knives," she said, not knowing why she said it, the histological dissection component of her course putting in an unhelpful appearance—*knives for heaven's sake, why had she said that?!*—and she felt immediately silly because she never, ever tried to be flirtatious. The blond's brows arched upward. His forehead crinkled into worry lines, but he was ecstatic. The air was dazzling with a supernatural tension, both of them blinded by the lights. His arm snaked around her shoulders.

"Jesus, I don't even know what to make of that," he laughed, squeezing her into his side as though she belonged there. "So, what did he do, this Mark guy?"

"He was rude to my—friend."

"Which friend?"

"That one, over there. Jess." Kesta turned them around as one to point Jess out across the other side of the bar—where she'd already moved on from the offense that Kesta had taken so personally on her behalf and was downing shots with two postgrads.

"Shall we say that he questioned her, um, morals?" Kesta stared up into graying eyes that seemed to know everything that would happen in the rest of her life.

"Bastard as well as a wanker." The blond gave Mark a disapproving look that caused Mark to draw his gilet a little closer.

"And it's not true," Kesta said. "Jess is lovely. Well, I mean she's—Jess."

The lights in the bar turned up to full beam. The sticky floor was revealed in all its horror, sweat-stained men and women with their makeup smeared shrinking away from its exposure.

"Not as lovely as you."

For Kesta and the blond, the light bathed them in a glory from which neither wished to hide. They stood silently revealed to each other, fate ignited in the sliver of space between them.

"Hey, Mark," the blond shouted, fishing about in his jacket pocket for something before thrusting it at him, never once letting go of Kesta.

"Take our picture."

Together they posed. It was the end, and it was the beginning. For both of them.

"So where have you been all my life?" he asked as Mark returned his camera.

"Waiting," she said.

———

Kesta pushed the fingers of her left hand through his and felt his lungs shuddering upward and down again.

"I have to go to work, darling. I'm sorry I have to leave you."

His hair had whitened ever since he'd been bitten, and it clung in vain to his scalp. She'd given him an extra dose of sedative, Midazolam, which was pretty hardcore, even for zombies, because she couldn't be sure what time she'd be home that evening.

Kesta sat on the very edge of the bed and lifted Tim's hand up toward her, resting his arm across her lap. With her index finger she traced his blackened veins as though they might lead her to an answer. She smoothed the mottled skin and caressed each finger and thumb, thinking all the while that she might have to remove his wedding ring soon if he lost any more weight. Tim would hate to lose it. She resolved to dig out an old necklace of hers or maybe a ribbon if she could find one, fashion it into something that would let him keep the ring close.

"Funny isn't it, how the thing I got right in my life is the one thing I had never expected to have," she said, tracing the slim golden band over and over with her thumb. "I used to think that work would be enough for someone like me. But what we had—have—it's the best part of who I am, Tim. And I'm not prepared to give up on it, do you understand me? I'm going to fix this."

She could sit for hours just listening to his breathing. He was still in there somewhere, and he remained her husband, for better or, in their case, the very worst you could possibly imagine.

But not right now. It wouldn't do to be late on her first morning at Project Dawn.

"Wish me luck," she said as she slid the dead bolts shut.

Kesta hadn't known what to wear to work on the front line of apocalyptic virology, some sort of armor perhaps, to reinforce herself and protect her vulnerabilities. When you lived in a white lab coat, your clothes became your underwear, and as long as they sort of matched each other, that was all the consideration she was willing to give over to fashion. She shrouded herself in a fail-safe black Henley, tucked into jeans, tucked into boots, and her battered leather jacket. This being England in July, to dress for England in November was pure prudence.

Wapping always felt to her as though it had been robbed blind during the night. Its crumbling warehouses sliding into the stinking sandbanks of the Thames reminded her of rummaged cupboards, doors broken open, shelves smashed through, their contents sunk forever in the water. If you closed your eyes and breathed in deeply along these arcane streets, you could still smell the spices—cinnamon, nutmeg, cardamom, vanilla, the exotic teas and intoxicating rums—of the shipping trades when this part of London had been vibrant with commerce and skullduggery. Old pubs christened centuries before, gin joints for pirates and hangmen, revolutionaries and drunks. They had survived wars but not the virus, some still cordoned off for deep cleaning with angry red tape, signs warning people to keep out. The clean-up was ongoing. No one could be sure that bleaching and power hosing off the remnants of flesh and filth would stop the virus from returning, but it still seemed like the sensible thing to do.

As Kesta passed by the Scandrett Street cemetery, a green parcel lined with trees that stood in solidarity with unknown headstones, their identities worn away by time, she had to stop. This was where Tim had been bitten. She had to walk past it every day, and every single time it brought her to a standstill, like walking into a wall made of grief. She had tried to rationalize it, tried breathing to get through it, but nothing had worked so far. She and Tim used to take drinks from the pub across the road out into the cemetery to commemorate the long-forgotten dead on summer afternoons. Now the sight filled her with regret. If only they hadn't gone out that day. If only they had pretended not to see the body lying in the road. Kesta bent down to touch the flowers she and Jess had last carried to that spot weeks ago and propped up against the metal railings that defended the graves. The flowers were brown and mummified inside their blue tissue shroud. Kesta must remember to replace them.

Climbing upward onto Lower Thames Street, Kesta saw a man approaching in the distance. A speck of black, a pencil outline, growing larger and larger until she could make out a hat, an awkward gait, a walking stick. The man, having seen her, began to shout at her.

"Hello, hello!" he cried as he approached her, crossing as far as possible to the other side of the pavement. "Are you . . . is there anything wrong with you?" He wobbled off the pavement and into the vacant cycle lane as he raised both arms as high as he could into the air, wielding the walking stick, fighting to keep his balance on his unsupported legs.

"You're all right. I'm not infected," Kesta replied, lifting her arms toward the sky, gracefully human.

"It's only my second day out, you see. Have to get to the doctor's."

"No one's been infected for three months. You'll be okay getting to your appointment."

"Never believe what they tell you," he said sharply. "Never trust them to tell you the truth." Kesta felt an urge to reassure him that he was completely safe from harm. But then she realized that when the old man said *they*, he could have been referring specifically to *her*. She was probably the closest thing to a palpable threat he'd come across since the outbreak. She stood back to allow him to pass.

"They lie. Be careful!" he said, stabbing at the air with the stick. He was right. People did lie. She was lying to everyone.

Three other people would enact a similar pantomime as she walked on toward Ludgate Circus and along Fleet Street. They each eyed her mistrustfully from afar, relaxing only when she was close enough to see, and to smell, to put their minds at ease. Strangely, an entirely deserted London, Kesta could make peace with. It was seeing it so pathetically populated, seeing the fear in the hollowed-out eyes of those stragglers left behind, that deepened her loneliness. Somehow that was worse.

As she neared the Strand, she saw Dudley waiting on the corner outside St Clement Danes church. His face was fluid with expression, rehearsing a conversation he would have later in the day. He was angling two takeaway cups like an old-fashioned pugilist. He was obviously as nervous as she was.

"Shitting bricks," he said, passing her one of the coffees.

Together they walked to the Strand tube station. Kesta realized she must have walked past this door a thousand times on her way to her university or to meet Tim in Covent Garden. Shabby and red, and with an ominous iron grill that looked rusted shut. The station had been abandoned in the early 1990s, its aging lifts deemed too expensive to be refurbished. Dudley began to wrestle with the iron grille, when a voice hidden behind the listed bars and brickwork blistered at them to wait.

Dudley dropped what remained of his coffee onto his loafers as the grille creaked open automatically. A woman with gray hair in a white coat appeared on the other side.

"Quickly," she spat, turning without introducing herself. The three of them entered into darkness as the grille closed behind them, before motion sensors triggered an illumination. An empty brown space. Paint that probably contained lead peeling from the walls. The woman looked back at them. She didn't smile. She opened another door using a lanyard strung around her neck. Another room, repainted but roughly, a security guard with a civil smile, a conveyor belt, and an X-ray machine. And a gun. A big one.

"Morning," said the guard, watching Kesta's bag slide innocuously through the scanner.

"Morning," she replied, wondering if a guilty conscience would show up on the X-ray.

The woman flashed her lanyard for a second time, and Kesta gasped as she followed her into another white void and was blinded by the light.

The underground station had been lost almost entirely to progress, embalmed behind a veneer of cutting-edge medical research. It was a nightmarish landscape devoid of humanity, automated, with the plasticity to regenerate and repair. Every surface that could be embalmed had been brought to a blinding sheen, icy whites cut through with antiseptic steel and strip lights following your every move. Color-coded lines smeared the walls at waist height and at the edges of the floor, leading the uninitiated through a maze of laboratories, storerooms, offices, freezers, and, somewhere presumably, a canteen, though Kesta would never find it, only the break room. Underneath the surface of central London, this laboratory had been cauterized from everyday life. Workers concealed behind layers of protective clothing lumbered like astronauts down the bleached-out corridors.

As they descended, following the woman in white farther toward the center of the earth, an inflated figure overwhelmed by a hazmat suit moved past them in slow motion pushing a screaming monkey in an aluminum cage. Ammonia spewed through the air all around them, getting under her skin, into her eyes and mouth, worming its way into whatever hermetic suit obstructed its passage. Kesta covered her mouth with the neck of her sweater. Whatever she had imagined about Project Dawn, it hadn't been this.

The woman led Kesta and Dudley to a communal changing room. She instructed them to put their belongings into yellow lockers already assigned to them and to dress in the white smock and voluminous white trousers they found inside. Nylon halos would smother their hair and ears. Their hands would be squeezed into blue rubber gloves. Their feet in ugly, matching synthetic clogs. A medical-grade mask to cover the mouth and nose, a plastic visor designed to protect them from acid sprays. As she removed her jacket and boots, stowing them in the lemon locker, Kesta noticed a bank of showers at the far end of the room, still steaming. The inevitable decontamination to unwind from a ten-hour shift.

"These are for standard clearance," barked the woman, referring to their protective gear. "Levels one to three. For level four, Dr. Caring, that's you, ask your supervisor for a hazmat. They're on level minus three. If your key card doesn't open the door, then you don't have clearance." The woman tossed a plastic rectangle the size of a bank card attached to a long yellow strap at each of them.

"Who is our supervisor?" Dudley asked, immediately dropping his pass on the floor.

"It should go without saying that you can't smoke in here, but someone did try once, and they ended up with tuberculosis," said the woman and left. Dudley looked at Kesta, his eyes as wide as petri dishes.

"Good tip," he said, "don't smoke around infectious bacteria. Who'd have thought?"

"With insight like that, you'd think they'd have a cure by now," said Kesta, sliding her feet into the clogs with the sound of a wet fart. "Oh good, we look like two evil clowns," she said, admiring their reflection in the mirror above a row of edgeless sinks. She secured her locker with Tim's six-digit birth date and strung the lanyard around her neck.

"Welcome to the party," a new voice bellowed from behind her.

Kesta turned to see a man prizing up his visor, pushing back the puckered hood of his protective smock. Wisps of ash-blond hair possessed by static wafted above his head.

"I'm Professor Lundeen. Team Leader, Pathogen Inactivation. You must be Shelley and Caring." He told them, he didn't ask.

He was diminutive, as short as Kesta, and it was eerie coming eyeball-to-eyeball with her superior like this. He grinned with an intensity she couldn't decipher and immediately distrusted. A blue-gloved hand thrust toward her and, with some hesitation, she took it. His grip was firm, the shaking relentless. Shaking his hand while wearing the rubber gloves felt like being the giblets inside a plastic bag inside the arse cavity of a turkey. Kesta could feel her bones collide.

"Quite, yes, hello, I'm Dudley and this is Kesta." Now it was Dudley's turn to have his arm wrenched from the socket by this competitive greeter. Kesta imagined Lundeen pumping out the energy from the people he met with his animated introduction, shaking out their life force, sucking it into himself. Perhaps he'd started out life as a parasitic twin? He had the look of a man who'd eaten his own brother in the womb, the little embryo who could.

"Just surnames. Thanks. Keeps things—clean," he said before

slapping Dudley on the arm so aggressively he wobbled backward and stood on Kesta's clog. "Come with me."

Lundeen schlepped out of the changing room, and Kesta and Dudley followed him, somewhat stunned. He waddled like a toddler, as if his hips had undiagnosed dysplasia, his tiny arms wrestling to re-dress himself in the visor and the hood. Kesta held her lanyard up in front of her visor to see the photograph from her old hospital work pass. Even upside down she could read only her surname and the initial K. Underneath there was a barcode and a cypher of numbers and symbols. Lundeen led them along a corridor marked with red, then another striped with green. The handful of people they passed were swollen up in pressurized suits, moving at crawl speed, everyone detached and confined by their clothing and the need for secrecy.

"We are in an information bubble here," said Lundeen, muffled by his mask and visor, pausing by a large double door. "It isn't just disease we can't have leaking out, it's speculation. You will tell no one that you're working at Project Dawn, do you understand me? No one. Medical research is a devilish business. If anyone's going to find a cure for those damned zombies, it's us."

He used his lanyard to bleep them through into a cavernous white room. There were researchers attending huge electron microscopes lined along glaring steel tables that seemed to stretch out into infinity, though most remained unmanned. There were no natural sounds, no conversation, just the steady hum and clunk of machinery and the man-made screech of latex. Faceless goggles glanced up at them as they arrived before immediately and obediently returning to what they were doing.

The laboratory was located on what had been the eastbound platform half a mile or so underneath the Strand. Lundeen showed Kesta and Dudley to their stations, where thick wads of paperwork lay in wait, demanding their signatures. He left them momentarily to confer with a colleague, and Kesta scanned through a list of long-dead diseases, rinderpest, smallpox, samples of which she might be required to handle on the job. She reviewed the onerous consequences of percutaneous injury, the dangers of ingesting hazardous materials, the threat of mucous membrane exposure to pathogens. She looked over at Dudley for reassurance but saw he had already printed and signed his name on the accompanying contract.

"Did you see they've got smallpox?" he whispered, hardly able to contain his excitement.

"Only the sexiest diseases here," she said under her breath, "though it would be nice to know what we're actually meant to be working on since we have to sign a nondisclosure agreement not to discuss it."

"You'll be reviewing the tissue slides we have in storage," said Lundeen, suddenly right behind her. Condensation was trickling down his visor as he spoke. "We have thousands of samples to review. You're here because we need fresh eyes and extra hands. It's proven incredibly difficult to . . ." He lost his train of thought, distracted by a man sneezing violently at the far end of the lab. Everyone stopped.

"Any blood?" shouted Lundeen, watching and waiting as the man removed his visor, then his face mask, inspecting it, replacing the face mask, then the visor, and finally shaking his head. "Good. Where was I? Oh yes, retain people. This work isn't for the fainthearted. People keep quitting. We're still blocking out tissue samples from the bodies that were brought in by the army. You'll be looking for patterns amongst them, shapes in the cellular structures, similarities between what's present in our zombie samples and the other viruses we have on-site."

"So, you don't yet know what it is?" Kesta asked.

"No."

"Or where it's come from?"

"No."

"Is it a hybridization of one or more naturally occurring viruses?"

"It might be, yes."

"Viruses that have mutated together to create a new pathogen?"

"Perhaps—"

"You don't think it's man-made, then?" Dudley interrupted.

"We haven't ruled that out."

"I'm sorry," said Kesta, "but what exactly have you been doing for three months?"

"Shelley, this is the most virulent virus in human history. Just processing the security clearances and the paperwork for any new screeners joining the Project is taking weeks." He clenched his tiny gloves together, his muscles strained like a ratting dog salivating over a fresh burrow. "I mean, we can't risk hiring any maniacs, can we?!" He laughed excessively, his laughter hybridizing with the clanking of machinery and the buzzing of the lights and the subterranean ventilation. Kesta felt the entire laboratory cringe with her. Then Lundeen stopped abruptly and leaned toward her.

"You're not a maniac, are you, Shelley?" he whispered, eyeball-to-eyeball. She noticed his were fluttering slightly as if he couldn't quite locate her, even when she was standing right in front of him.

"I'm as stable as iron," she said, but inside she thought, *Patient shows signs of benign essential blepharospasm.* She wondered if the stress of working at Project Dawn had literally made Lundeen twitchy.

"So far, we've focused on cataloguing the infected we have in the freezer," he continued, gesticulating, his suit squeaking as if someone were trying to make a toy dog out of little blue and white balloons. "There are thousands of them, so it's taking a very long time. We have to identify them all, access their medical history. Given the nature of the outbreak and the condition that many of them have reached us in—"

"The condition?" said Dudley.

"Yes, some of them are a bit soupy."

"It's a bit like looking around your kitchen after you've had a lot of people over for Christmas dinner and trying to make sense of all the leftovers," said an older woman at the microscope opposite Kesta's.

Lundeen nodded. "This is Cooke, by the way."

"Clinical trials of new drugs can take years, as you know," said Cooke. "I went to medical school with a man who specialized only in the workings of a single protein present in the lining of the heart. He retired last year having never worked on anything else for his entire career. He was seventy-five."

She stepped away from her microscope and stood with a hand on her hip, rattling jewelry hidden somewhere underneath her lab coat. "Research takes time, even decades. It's a long and backbreaking process, one of trial and error, heartbreak, and disappointment. We, on the other hand," she said, glaring at Lundeen, "are somehow expected to conjure up a cure for a brand-new, prolifically contagious, absolutely fatal virus that makes people bite each other in the time it would have taken my old colleague to put in his contact lenses in the morning."

"What Cooke is trying to say here," said Lundeen, "is that our research is at too premature a stage to rule anything out. None of the international labs that have the capability to manufacture a virus of this kind have reported a breach in safety protocol. No one has admitted to a . . . a *leak*. We're working blind, I'm afraid."

"You must have a working hypothesis, surely?" Kesta pressed him.

"We think it's an arenavirus but not one we've seen before."

"You haven't determined the antigenic shift?"

"Shelley," he shouted, running out of patience, "I can't give you information I don't have. We're playing catch-up here, working as fast as we can but from a standing start and with a limited staff. Miracles don't happen overnight, you know? Miracles take time and effort. And money. Now, if you'll excuse me, I have to go justify our budget to the Department of Health. Caring, come with me please. I have something of a more *specialist* nature I'd like to discuss with you."

"Ignore Lundeen," Cooke whispered as the two men walked off. She was rotating her shoulders, no doubt stiff from hours spent hunched over a microscope, with an audible crunch. "He has a huge God complex. And he's a massive . . ."

"Arsehole?" said Kesta.

"I was going to say bureaucrat, but that's close enough." She lumbered around to Kesta's side of the station, where she rested her bottom against the worktop. "Where've you come from?"

"University Hospital."

"I was there in the eighties," Cooke said. "I've been at the Marsden, the Royal Free. All over." She kicked her clog at nothing on the floor as she reminisced about her career. She was much older than Kesta, old enough to be her mother, but she had the figure and the mannerisms of a little bird. The bluest eyes Kesta had ever seen, ringed with blue powder and lashes like spider's legs.

"And before this?" Kesta asked, remembering the advice she'd imagined Tim giving her. Ask people questions about themselves; it puts them at ease. Cooke's eyes sparkled mischievously.

"Before this I'd retired," she said, rather proudly, knowing full well she didn't look old enough for the knacker's yard. "I'm nearly seventy. Took me out of mothballs they did. That's how desperate they are!"

Something in Kesta's expression must have offended Cooke, though it wasn't her intention to do so. Thin blond brows formed sharp eleven lines between them.

"Sorry," Cooke sniffed. "I didn't mean to imply that you were a desperate choice."

"It's usually me putting my foot in it," Kesta said, "or so my husband tells me. Told me. It's really admirable that you've come out of retirement to help. I always think the service retires us too early anyway."

"My thoughts exactly," Cooke said, nodding. "There's nothing worth putting on a slide I haven't reviewed in my time. And yet, they are missing material here that I really think should be considered."

"Such as?"

"Animal pathogens," Cooke explained, "things in animals that haven't yet made the jump to people. Those of us not scooping through the zombie porridge have spent weeks looking at every arenavirus you could imagine, but all of them with precedents in humans. Many of them eradicated, like smallpox. So, what's the point of that? This has to be a new virus, doesn't it?"

Kesta had to agree, although the idea was terrifying.

"I mean, I guess it could be a prehistoric virus that's escaped from a melting ice cap somewhere in the Arctic or something, but how did it end up in Hammersmith? And some people still think it was a bioweapon."

"Seriously?" said Kesta.

"I know, it's crackers, proper science-fiction stuff. That's why Lundeen's always at the Home Office and the Ministry of Defense. To tell them it remains our clinical position that this wasn't man-made. They thought the guy who got it first, Paul whatever his name was, Patient Zero—anyway, the theory was he'd been sent by the Russians to wipe out London and destabilize the UK."

Dressed head to toe as though she worked for Evil Incorporated, standing in that subterranean laboratory, Kesta didn't think that theory sounded so outlandish.

"Did you have any contact with the zombies yourself?"

"Only the once, actually," Cooke sniffed and Kesta couldn't quite tell if she was relieved or disappointed by this limited exposure to the virus in the field. "I was at the supermarket. Didn't see him come in. Did see him bite the security guard on the clavicle and then work his way through the customers in the frozen food aisle."

"What did you do?"

"I watched," she said, stepping closer to Kesta. "Sounds awful, doesn't it? But I really wanted to look at the mechanics of it. The bite strength was extraordinary. I heard the bone snap. Once the guy had his teeth in there, the guard—and he was a big bloke, mind—he couldn't even move. One bite and that was it. Then off he went, chasing down another. You?"

Kesta decided not to tell Cooke about how Tim had become infected, just yet. "A few times. Even once at the hospital."

"Did you have to kill any?"

"I mean, I think I did, yes. I didn't always hang around to find out."

"That's the problem with zombies, though, isn't it?" Cooke said as she retreated to the other side of the workstation to close up a box of translucent slides. "You can never bloody trust they're dead unless you . . ." She made a slashing motion across her throat. "Really, you have to kill them before they turn, which, if you think about it is, well . . ."

"Murder?"

"Murder, exactly, but it saves a lot of trouble in the end, doesn't it."

Kesta decided it was time to change the subject.

"So, what are you working on today?" she asked.

"These are transverse sections of lung," Cooke said. "A lot of my time has been spent looking at how the virus changes the organs in the body of the infected." She tapped on the box of slides. "I've spent the last two days asking myself how they managed to breathe at all given how much inflammation there is. The alveolar walls are just shot to bits."

"What can I do?"

"I've got a liver in a bucket with your name on it."

CHAPTER SIX

In all the years they'd been together, Tim had come into the hospital laboratory only a few times, to meet her after work. Usually, he would wait outside in the inadequately small staff car park, or out on the road by the entrance to A&E. He hated the chemical smell, and he couldn't bear to see the patients struggling, dragging drips along the wards, smoking crafty cigarettes, and slowly expiring. He said that hospitals made him feel queasy and vulnerable, as though the sliding doors would slide shut forever and that once admitted, he'd never be allowed to leave.

"You're confusing the health service with Hotel California," she'd said.

"I just don't know how you do it," he'd replied, cupping her face in his hands, smoothing loose hair behind her ear only for her to promptly push it back again. "How you manage to work surrounded by death and stay positive and normal."

"Because I don't see it that way," she'd said at the time, though part of her knew she couldn't convince him. It wasn't something people in general could be convinced of, it was just a truth about the job you had to experience for yourself. "I'm surrounded by the living. I'm keeping people alive, not watching them die. That's what my job is about. Life."

"Three floors above the mortuary?"

"Yes, I'm trying to stall the process of people ending up in there."

As most couples do, she had tried to share her work with Tim, at the beginning of their relationship at least. He'd wanted to know everything about her as she wanted to know every inch of him. But as time went by, invisible lines were drawn between them, delineating what ought to be kept secret. Deep down, Kesta thought his work in advertising was frivolous and that his clients were whimsical megalomaniacs. He liked to imagine that the slides she prepared at the lab were actually pieces of expressionist art, and that they weren't made of the flesh and blood of real human beings.

"It's like looking at one of those magic eye pictures," he'd said, trying out her electron microscope for the first time, dazzled by the vivid scrawl he saw. "I'd go blind before I could see anything meaningful."

"It's because you're looking too hard," she'd told him, holding his hand to relax him. "Stop looking, and it will appear right in front of you."

"Like you did, you mean?"

"You're such a sentimental fool," she'd said and kissed him.

—

The liver was dark brown. It looked ready to burst, thin yellow tendrils straining across its surface. With the whole organ to work with, Kesta could take a core biopsy, to ensure she'd have a generous amount of material to examine. She withdrew cylinders of tissue using a solid, spring-loaded needle to drill down into the mass before suctioning them out again.

"It's like a cookie cutter," she'd once said to Tim, "except the dough is a person."

She extracted several cylinders to give herself choice later on, secreting them away in specialist cassettes. She would need to fix these samples in a chemical solution to preserve and harden them, allowing her to revisit them indefinitely, cut into them again and again if she needed to. She worked with precision. A delicate touch now would be repaid down the microscope later on. Kesta loved histology, the microscopic study of biological tissue and its partner, histopathology, the detective on the lookout for diseased tissue. The identification of the suspect, in this case, abnormalities in the tissue caused by or resulting from infection by the virus. Kesta was searching for biological clues.

Next, she must soak the liver sample in a series of ethanol baths, each bath made more concentrated until the sample was devoid of water, entirely dehydrated. Then xylene, a clearing agent, was applied before she could embed the tissue in paraffin wax, which allowed her to cut it into thin slivers like sashimi, in a process called sectioning. What was left at the end of all this was a tiny speck of unbroken biological code, a gray blob begging to be deciphered. This was where the staining came in, the pure magic of histochemistry, and where Kesta could excel herself in employing all the colors of the chemical rainbow—hematoxylin blue, eosin pink, the cool brown of TP63—breaking the code into color points of interest, allowing her to differentiate between the normal and the abnormal, looking for bright shapes that didn't belong there, making sense of it all in Technicolor.

For the next two months, she cut and fixed and examined the tissue held in storage. But nothing made sense. She mostly worked independently, sometimes with Cooke, moving robotically around the laboratory, cleaning, wiping, slicing, dicing, staring into the bright pearlescent light, breathing in those crude preservatives, always working cautiously, diligently sifting through the remains in the underground, the world of Project Dawn existing in tandem with the real one above it. Looking down a microscope all day gave Kesta an otherworldly perspective. The laboratory around her, the people in it, the general throng of comings and goings, the screeching of trolleys and latex suits, the slow grinding thud of the automatic doors remained a blur, a thick custard in which she was suspended but not quite alive.

She would break briefly for lunch or a coffee with Cooke, and they would talk in hushed tones about what they had seen down the microscope but couldn't yet understand.

"It isn't what I expected at all," Kesta whispered as they huddled by the coffee machine one morning. Cooke was changing the filter with the same agility she used to suction bits of tissue from cadavers.

"The coffee or the research?"

"The research," Kesta said as she filled the clear cylinder at the back of the machine with water, right to the top. "How is it that we're still groping around in the dark?"

"Love, it's only been a couple of months. Don't lose heart," Cooke said, turning the machine on with a beep. The two of them leaned back against the worktop, exhausted by the daily grind, the smell of coffee wafting upwards and permeating the break room. "Do you have any idea how many of us were killed in the outbreak?"

"Us?"

"First responders, doctors, medical scientists of all shapes and sizes," Cooke said, dumping three brown sugars into a mug, stirring till her jewelry rattled. "Thousands died, trapped in hospitals, left to rot there when all they were guilty of was trying to help. Everyone here is doing their best. You're going to have to be patient."

"I just feel more like we're cataloguing rather than researching," said Kesta.

"So, let's talk about what we are seeing. How is it possible," Cooke slurped, before adding a fourth sugar, "that the virus has pulverized the cells in every organ I've examined, and yet it hasn't resulted in the victim's death?"

"Nothing looks the way it should do under the microscope," Kesta agreed. "The tissue samples are almost unrecognizable as human. It's as if this virus hijacks the host cells and puts them into some sort of stasis without actually destroying them. It's making it impossible to know which part of the tissue is human and which part is zombie virus—"

"And whether any of it is an immune response, a protein triggered by the human host that we could actually extract and make use of," Cooke added.

"Looking at the larger samples," said Kesta, "the limbs are completely atrophied, muscles pulled right back into acute angles. And do you remember, when they were walking around, the infected would look up at the sky, not in the direction they were traveling?"

"Of course I do." Cooke shuddered. "They move like babies who can't support their own heads properly."

"Look," said Kesta, "we call it a zombie virus because it's spread by biting and at terrific speed. But it is expressly different to what we've grown accustomed to in films and on television. Our infected have yellow eyes, which suggests an extreme abnormality in the liver."

"Or yellow fever," Cooke offered.

"Or yellow fever. And they bleed profusely without bleeding out."

"Like a mutated version of a hemorrhagic fever," Cooke added.

"Quite. But they do not have the full range of motor function. They can't lift their arms very high, presumably because of the wasting—"

"And that could relate back to a brain infection," said Cooke.

"I was thinking brain infection right at the start of the outbreak," Kesta said excitedly. "And they do not appear to need to eat each other. In most of the zombie oeuvre, cannibalism is a nascent symptom of infection. Once they've been bitten, they are called to transfer the virus to at least one other human host, but then they feed rather than repeat that infection sequence inexorably."

"If you look at measles," said Cooke, "around 90 percent of people who come into contact with an infected sufferer will also contract the disease, mainly because that virus can survive in the open air for hours on end. But with this virus, the transmission rate is essentially absolute. It's a hundred percent because transmission becomes the host's entire purpose. We have nothing to compare it to. It's why it has to be a hybrid of two or more existing or unknown virus strains, creating something brand bleeding new. I was thinking—"

Cooke never finished her train of thought because all thinking was obliterated by the sudden screaming of the laboratory alarm. An awesome shock, a sound so violent it made Kesta's muscles spasm so that she dropped her mug on the floor. She and Cooke stood rooted to the spot, watching as the room boomed an angry red, the warning lights firing, the wild siren wailing, Kesta's coffee shimmering across the floor. The noise of the alarm was physical enough to make ripples shudder out across the surface of the liquid. Kesta could feel it inside her, her heart and stomach buzzing with the frequency. Someone ran past the break room and shouted at them from the doorway, but they couldn't hear what he was saying. Kesta found herself grabbing Cooke by the wrist, and together they ran out into the corridor, following the green lines upward toward the entrance of the lab.

As they turned a corner, bodies appeared, filling up the space, more people than Kesta had ever seen at Project Dawn. A cacophony of unintelligible voices rattling, the alarm still wailing, feet and bodies thumping. People's features contorted in fear behind their protective masks. Kesta's ears were booming, her hand clawed on to Cooke. They waited, all of them afraid.

Why aren't they moving? Why aren't they heading for the entrance? Why can't they get out of the building?

Kesta stood on the tips of her clogs, trying to lift herself above the crowd, searching for Dudley. She couldn't see him. He wasn't there.

In any other workplace, the sound of the alarm warned the staff there was a fire. Half a mile underground at Project Dawn, the alarm could mean only one thing: there was a leak. Kesta began to spiral. How would anybody know they were down there? What could anybody hope to do to help them? If something happened to her, if she died down there, what would happen to Tim?

The alarm cut, and the flashing red light disappeared. Kesta tried to blink away the color that had burned itself into her field of vision. She heard the sounds of whimpering and desperate gasps for breath echoing down the corridor, and somewhere in that mass of bodies someone was crying. Then another voice, flinty and unfamiliar, addressed them from some hidden PA system.

"False alarm. Everyone back to work."

The bewildered workers turned and filed, one by one, down the corridor, to resume what they were doing before hell had broken loose. And it did feel like hell down there, after that alarm was triggered, so close to the center of the earth. No one knew what had happened, whether the alarm had been set off accidently or whether, as some speculated in corridor whispers, something had leaked and a technician had been injured or even infected. They would all be kept in the dark about it.

Kesta stopped minimizing the risks she was taking after the alarm. She had been in such a rush to join the Project, to get her hands on anything that might help Tim, that she hadn't stopped to consider just how dangerous the work itself was. At any hour of any day, due to fatigue or lack of concentration, hers or someone else's, she could become infected—any of them could—elbows deep as they were in the worst virus in human history.

After the alarm, Kesta understood she had been naïve about Project Dawn, unrealistic in her expectations for its progress. Yet asking Tim to be patient, to hold on a little while longer as she hauled up yet another saline drip or carefully shaved away his broken skin as he groaned, well, it felt terribly cruel. She had to keep it together, not just for him but for her colleagues. Project Dawn needed more time. They were a decent team, stretched and underfunded yes, but everyone was united by the same ambition, the same drive to discover the genesis of the virus—and with it that magical cure.

Each time she saw Lundeen, he would promise her somewhat glibly that soon she and Cooke would be allowed to review the postmortem of the first victim, Paul Mosi, the outbreak's Patient Zero. Kesta would then be able to see for herself what the virus had done to him. She would be able to prepare her own tissue samples and compare them with the ones she'd taken from Tim. But as the days came and went, the postmortem remained elusive. She wondered if Lundeen was making her wait on purpose.

Kesta hardly saw Dudley, and she certainly wasn't assigned to work with him. He was always with Lundeen, whispering and walking, his lanyard giving him access into an area of the building that hers did not. Sometimes she'd follow him down the paint-streaked corridors when he was too wrapped up in his own thoughts to notice. There were parts of Project Dawn that were off-limits to her but not to him. She understood that his biosecurity clearance was higher than hers, but Dudley had told her they would be working together. Now it seemed as though Dudley was working in another lab entirely.

There was little else to punctuate the monotony of Kesta's infinite investigations. Home and the lab. The lab and her home. Work and Tim. The light aboveground and the darkness beneath the surface, the two Kestas living in disharmony trying to make everything sing again.

Wednesdays came and went. ZARG meetings with Dr. Walling and company were missed. Something had to give. Now that she was fully operational inside the Project Dawn machine, how could she possibly sit there and face the Tinas and the Michaels and the Carols of the aboveground world knowing what they did not. That there was still no answer, no cure, no hope.

Jess phoned her most days. Sometimes she would pick up, hear Jess chatting merrily without really listening to what she was saying. Jess would ask her about her day and Kesta would shrug, evading her questions with bland anecdotes about things that had happened to her before, in order to create the impression she was still working at the hospital.

Jess would text her too, little words of encouragement to punctuate her day. She would send Kesta links to articles about grief she'd read online, snippets from her own life, the General Practitioner's Tale. Jess was trying to be supportive. Kesta knew that. She was trying to be a good friend. But to Kesta, such efforts felt forced and unwanted. These interruptions in her day when she was hard at work at Project Dawn were growing more and more irritating. The articles Jess sent her were inane at best and insensitive at worst, as if her loss could be tidied away with a few generic platitudes. A comment Jess found insightful provoked nothing but ire in her. Jess was inexperienced in the waters of bereavement. Kesta was drowning in it. The allegorical life rafts Jess tossed in Kesta's direction had the opposite effect of making her feel leaden, deflated, less able to stay afloat. Sometimes Jess's well-intentioned voicemails and text messages made her scream inside. And so, she picked up the phone less and less and didn't always text back. Jess kept on calling anyway because Jess would have told herself that's what good friends did.

After two months spent extracting, treating, blocking, and dyeing the flesh of the dead, raking over their graves, looking for new clues with her electron microscope, all Kesta could find were livid lumps that looked a bit like microscopic purple jellybeans. They were present in each and every slide, hiding out in plain sight.

CHAPTER SEVEN

A man had arrived at A&E in Hammersmith at a little after nine one morning. He was exhausted, dead on his feet, the duty registrar had said. He had a fever, a headache. Whenever he coughed, he coughed up blood. He was embarrassed by how awful he felt. He didn't want to be a nuisance.

So, he'd waited by the entrance to the hospital for a few hours, coughing as quietly as he could, trying not to inconvenience the staff. And they let him wait because they were very busy. It was only when he fainted with real flair, sliding off his chair and onto the floor, his arms and legs contorted, sparking in electric fits, his eyes rolling backward in their sockets, alarming the other patients waiting impatiently, that they remembered he was there.

A nurse sat with the man on the waiting room floor and took his blood pressure. It was frighteningly low, fifty over forty, and he felt icy to her touch. She examined his eyes and saw they gave no reaction to the light, no change in his pupils, which were shrunken into sullen dots.

"His eyes are a funny color," said a gentleman with an arm in a home-made sling.

"Could be cholesterol," said the woman sitting next to him. "My uncle Norman had that."

"Excuse me, nurse, but he has been coughing an awful lot. I could have sworn I saw a bit of lung come up."

"You ought to get him off the floor, dear, make him a strong cup of tea."

The nurse smiled politely as the patients volunteered their hypotheses. Perhaps he'd fainted at the sight of his own blood, she thought, but she was also worried about sepsis.

"I'm worried about sepsis," she shouted to a colleague, who ran away at speed, returning with a trolley. Together they coaxed the man off the floor and onto it and wheeled him to an empty bay. They wrapped a pale green curtain around themselves and paged the consultant on duty.

"He has a fever of 103, although he's cold to the touch, BP is still only 65/40, and he's been coughing up blood," said the first nurse, wiping a thin film of sweat from her forehead.

"How do you account for his jaw?" Dr. Daniels asked her without even looking at the man. The man's face was distended, the lower teeth exposed in a gallows grin, the left side of the mouth slipping off the chin in a landslide of flesh.

"Did he fall on his face? When he fainted, I mean?"

"I only saw him sitting. I didn't see him go down."

"Possible dislocation, but we should rule out stroke first. It's probably a stroke."

"What about the blood though, Dr. Daniels?"

"Embolism, then."

Nothing explained the discoloration of his dead, cold skin. Dr. Daniels had never seen anything like it before. He looked like someone who'd been in a mortuary fridge for a week, livid and lumpy. This wasn't a stroke. Then the man began to bleed, just a little weeping at first, the yellowed whites of his eyes blushing like blancmange, streaming down his cheeks into perfect circles blossoming against the pillow.

"He's crying blood," cried out the first nurse. "Oh Jesus!"

"Seal off the ward. It's Ebola," shouted Dr. Daniels almost proudly.

The sick man's body became the eye of a violent storm that tore through the hospital at great speed. Patients were evacuated. A&E was closed. An alert was sent up like a flare to all London hospitals warning them to be vigilant for any patients presenting with symptoms of Ebola. The man was fixed into a plastic sarcophagus, airtight, nothing getting in or out of it save for the probing hands of doctors wearing hazmat suits. Antibodies, fluids, and electrolytes were squeezed into his veins—antivirals, antifungals, every manner of *anti-bollocks* Dr. Daniels and his colleagues could access while they waited for a specialist team to arrive.

The first nurse had rifled through the patient's pockets and found traveler's checks and a passport. His name was Paul Mosi, and he came from Belgium. Dr. Daniels flicked through the pages looking at the stamps. Australia, China, the US, and finally the last destination before he'd flown into London, Madagascar.

Dr. Daniels had an epiphany: his patient could have Ebola and bubonic plague. You couldn't rule out a zoonotic bacterium in a visitor who'd traveled so extensively, especially through the Indian Ocean. He ordered further tests, as much blood taken as pathology could handle. In the afternoon, a biohazard team arrived from Porton Down. Frantic messages were left with the Belgian and Madagascan embassies. Who was Paul Mosi? When had he arrived in London, and why was he here to begin with? An official called the Home Office, who called the Border Agency with strict instructions. Any passengers on flights from the Indian Ocean presenting symptoms should be quarantined immediately. Or even better, sent back.

Everyone rallied round, united by decency and purpose. Doctors, nurses, trainees, scientists, all of them driven by the essential human need to stop a total stranger from dying. Where there was life, there was hope. Until there was less and less hope to cling to because there was less and less life to perceive.

At a little after four in the morning, a white flag of surrender was hoisted above the crippled body of Paul Mosi. The monotone of the vitals machine sounded the alarm. For fifteen minutes, doctors and nurses stampeded in and out of that makeshift room, crashing up and down upon the man's chest in flailing despair. Ribs were broken. The registrar wept. Then silence blanketed the room, muffling tears and mutual disappointment. Bit by bit, the ceremonial unplugging took place, the dewiring and careful extraction of tubes. The restoration of some quiet dignity to the patient they had failed. Though death may be inevitable, to those trained in the art of deferring it indefinitely, to lose a patient is to lose the battle.

Thirty hours after his shift had started, a defeated Dr. Daniels found himself recording his patient's time of death. The body would need to be moved with great care, and he was determined to do it himself, to accompany his patient on the long walk to the morgue. It was the right thing to do. Dr. Daniels summoned a hospital porter, and together the two of them began wheeling the body of the late Paul Mosi down underground, while up above them, dawn was breaking.

The young porter was the only witness to what happened next. He was sleep-deprived, working night shifts for the first time in his life. So, when he thought he saw the white sheet twitch underneath the blazing strip lights, he rubbed his eyes. *Must be my imagination*, he thought. *I'm dead tired.*

The elevator pinged. They were in the bowels of the hospital now, a short push from the mortuary. This floor still made him shiver. As they started heaving the trolley out of the lift, the sheet moved again, and the young porter thought, *I need an eye test.*

The hand was black and shrunken, the skin sucked right back to the bone. It slithered out from underneath the sheet like a cobra, striking Mr. Daniels at the wrist, using his weight as leverage to haul itself upward until all of Paul Mosi had risen again, still covered by that bright white sheet.

The porter did not scream. He let go of the trolley and watched as it sailed off down the corridor. It appeared to be careening farther and farther away, but it was he who was in retreat, staggering backward toward the lifts, his brain wiped clean, his heart hammering like a rotary drill. As he reached the lift doors, sweat-stained palms pressing frantically for the call button, the screams of Dr. Daniels being eaten alive thundered down the corridor. The porter couldn't take his eyes off them.

Mosi had Daniels by the throat, his head forced backward on a broken neck, sprays of blood flung up across the ceiling. The two men were drenched in it as Mosi pinned the doctor to the wall and feasted. When he was done, Mosi watched almost curiously as the body of Dr. Daniels slid down to the ground, leaving a bloodied shroud against the wall.

The elevator dinged, and Mosi turned his head toward the porter.

———

"So, I just don't know what they are," she said to Tim as she laced up her combat boots, a slice of toast in her mouth. "Can you hold this?" She took a bite and passed it to her husband so that she could finish getting dressed.

"Nnnfff," said Tim, frowning at it, turning it over to consider both sides.

"It's some kind of inclusion, I think, they look like kidney beans or jellybeans or some kind of bloody bean. I've asked Cooke, and she says they're present in all of her slides too," she said, retrieving the toast, taking another bite, chewing while she watched him watching her.

"Well done for not dropping it, darling." She'd been giving Tim things to hold, things he couldn't break—books, loo roll, even the TV remote, to see if anything provoked a reaction beyond him frowning at it and to see if he could hold it still. Which he could, and that seemed positive, to Kesta at least.

"Am I treating you like a Labrador?" She smiled, hoping he'd see the funny side.

"Nnnfff," replied Tim, reaching his free arm out toward her, feeling in the air for the toast, perhaps disappointed he couldn't quite reach it.

"Here you go, you have it," she said, putting it in between his thumb and index finger and gently pressing them together. "Sweetheart, I've got to go, I'm afraid. I know I've been telling you for weeks now that we're doing a postmortem on Patient Zero, but Lundeen swore on his mother that it would be today."

Tim wasn't listening because to him that half-eaten slice of toast appeared to contain the secrets of the universe.

"Anyway, they are so much further behind than I could ever have imagined, and I'm so bloody fed up with looking at bits of brain and kidney and intestinal lining, so I really hope we do the PM today, otherwise I shall be fighting this virus all by myself. Now stay!" Kesta said, trying again to make him laugh the way he'd always laughed at even her unfunniest jokes, because that's what you did with the person you loved the most. You laughed at their bad jokes, no matter how many times you'd heard them fluffing the punch line.

Tim stared back at her obediently before throwing the toast on the floor.

———

They huddled together in the mortuary at Project Dawn. It had become something of a theme over the past week, Lundeen keeping them in check by demanding they wait for him, usually somewhere perennially cold. Kesta was convinced he was doing it on purpose to exert his authority. This morning, Kesta, Dudley, Cooke, and a mortuary assistant Kesta didn't recognize but whom Dudley appeared to know, were all shivering by a bank of twenty icy tombs lining the wall, willing their supervisor to hurry the fuck up. Seeing Dudley's familiar face after weeks of lonely screening made Kesta feel a little nostalgic for the path lab back at the hospital. She tried to make small talk with him, but his chronic inability to make eye contact was even worse than usual.

"Are you all right?" she whispered behind her face mask.

"I can't talk to you here," he said cryptically as Lundeen breezed in, ten minutes late, and Kesta felt the temperature in the room drop a little further.

The body of Paul Mosi had been kept in deep freeze for six months. What was left of him was a crystallized patchwork of flesh and stitching, shriveled and flaccid, deep red, vivid green, black curdling into something like cold lava. The freezing process was usually reserved for unidentified corpses, helping them to cling on indefinitely as they waited to remember their name beyond the given paper tag around their toe. Most bodies were kept in a mortuary only ahead of postmortem, and some decay was to be expected as conditions were akin to the salad drawer of a fridge. Some small putrefaction didn't affect a pathologist's divination of death. Bodies didn't typically hang around. Paul Mosi was the exception, fresh-frozen as he was and utterly essential to them, no matter how threadbare his body became. They were compelled to return to it, time after time, like the necrophile who can't let the dead be and keeps digging them up for one last gross embrace.

The mortuary assistant unbolted one of the doors and pushed it aside. Then she heaved the steel gurney out into the room. She whisked away the ice-white sheet that protected Mosi's dignity like a flamboyant chef. All five of them stared down at what remained of Patient Zero.

The head was completely gone of course, as was Mosi's left arm. Kesta reviewed the notes she held against a clipboard. Lundeen had an iPad that he propped up crudely against what remained of Mosi's thigh. A chunk was missing from his chest where someone had smashed into him with a fire extinguisher. The rest of his torso protruded, the rib cage having been forced upward during the initial postmortem, pressed back down insufficiently when it was time to close him up again. People always forgot how intransigent bone was.

"Lost count of the number of postmortems where I ended up straddling the body, helping the pathologist sew them back up again," said Cooke, reading Kesta's mind.

"PM review of Paul Mosi, zombie virus Patient Zero, biobanking round three, pathologists in attendance . . ." Lundeen was prattling away into the tablet, recording himself, recording them. Dudley was busy trying to avoid being caught on camera. Cooke poked the body with a gloved finger to see how much resistance the skin gave up, her blue eyes gleeful behind their acrylic shield.

"Lumbar puncture, skin samples to be repeated. Organs removed at earlier PM. Genetic tests. Feasibility of mutational analysis from archival paraffin-embedded heart tissue . . ."

They would scrape new bits of Mr. Mosi's flesh away, keep them safe, look at them in detail later. That which had previously been harvested had been analyzed into dust, so they needed more skin and bone to work with.

"What was the official cause of death?" asked Dudley, needlessly, his nerves getting the better of him that morning. Lundeen waved his little hands dramatically toward the space where Mosi's head ought to have been.

"Well, usually this bit not being there is considered unsurvivable," he scoffed. "But officially, Caring, it's down as shotgun wound to the head," Lundeen replied away from the microphone. "Most of the head was lost at that point, but we were able to lay out some paraffin brain slides at the first autopsy."

"The brain stem needs to be cut completely to achieve death in all cases," Dudley muttered, peering over Lundeen's shoulder at his iPad.

"What did he do for a living?" Kesta asked. Out of the corner of her eye, she saw Lundeen pause recording and hold the tablet against his chest as if to protect it from her irksome questions.

"How exactly is that relevant?" he sighed.

"I want to know who he was," she said, "about his personal history. Do we have his medical records on file?"

Lundeen sighed and began to scroll down the screen, searching for something, huffing a little until—

"Actuary," he said without looking up at them, "What's that, that's like an accountant or something, isn't it?"

"That's the most boring kind of accountant," said Cooke.

"Okay, so he was one of those, Shelley. A boring accountant. Happy?"

"And he lived in Belgium?"

"Correct."

"And he'd traveled a lot, in the past year, I mean."

"Yes, I believe so."

"Including to Madagascar?"

"Yes. Including to Madagascar," Lundeen huffed.

"Well, it's just that, in the early days of the outbreak, I was making my own notes," Kesta said, trying to sound as unassuming and sane as possible, "and I had this idea, given the symptoms, that some kind of parasite could be involved. Like schistosomiasis."

"Schistosomiasis?" Lundeen parroted back to her.

"Freshwater worm, you get it from swimming in dodgy lakes. Nips in through the skin," said Cooke impatiently. "Keep up."

"Anyway, schistosomiasis is very prevalent in lots of countries including Madagascar. Which of course has high rates of yellow fever too."

"So, you think we should see if we can find any schistosomiasis parasites in Mr. Mosi here?" asked Dudley.

"As much as anything, it made me read up on Madagascar more generally. Do you know it's unlike almost anywhere else on earth? The biodiversity there is extraordinary. For instance, eighty percent of its plant species are unique to the island. They've also been persistently disrupted and threatened by humans, by agricultural slash and burn, by the introduction of alien species. My husband—"

Tim had always encouraged her to trust her instincts, but she felt embarrassed to mention him so carelessly over a postmortem examination.

"—sorry, what I'm trying to say is that surely we need to rule out the virus having originated in Madagascar because its biological makeup is so wildly unique."

Lundeen scratched his forehead. "Shelley, there were no reported cases of our zombie virus in Madagascar."

"Yes, I know that. But the truth is we don't know why Mosi caught this virus and we don't know where. The assumption has been that Mosi caught the virus here in the UK. But that's only based on his incubation period. We know that he was at the hospital for hours before he died and came back a zombie. We need to account for that. The likeliest scenario is that based on conditions we are presently unaware of, Mosi acted like some kind of human food processor for disease. Given the abundance of rare species and his apparent regular travel there, well, it's like a veritable petri dish of animal viruses that have yet to cross into the human population. Has a team been sent out to investigate the island?"

"Absolutely not!" said Lundeen. "Can you imagine the diplomatic nightmare that would unleash? For the British government to accuse the Madagascans of starting the most devastating outbreak since the Black Death? With no proof of genesis?"

"Isn't that exactly what we're looking for right now, Lundeen, proof?" she said, lowering her tone. "Do we know if there were any viral outbreaks in Madagascar in the weeks leading up to Paul Mosi getting on that plane and flying in to Heathrow? Yellow fever, dengue fever, anything?" Lundeen paused just long enough for Dudley to interject.

"Yes, there was actually, Kesta." He was staring at Lundeen. "Sorry, *Shelley*. But we can't seem to make it fit."

"What do you mean?"

"There was a cluster of yellow fever cases in the villages around Toamasina. That's a significant port, apparently. Fifty people were infected. All of them recovered. This was three weeks before Mosi flew to London."

Kesta considered the symptoms of yellow fever, a flavivirus spread by mosquito bites. Fever, chills, sickness, headache, muscle pain. In severe cases, kidney and liver function could be compromised, bleeding would be prolific. And the patient's skin and eyes could turn yellow with jaundice.

"So, we're saying that the incubation period is too long for Mosi to have had yellow fever when he traveled? But did the first postmortem reveal whether he'd had yellow fever before? And recovered from it?" She waited for an answer.

Cooke put her hands on her hips.

"Tell me you've checked?" she asked Lundeen, posing her most devastating questions like a disappointed grandmother. Lundeen shifted from one foot to the other, pretending to read whatever was on the iPad.

"It isn't yellow fever," he said defiantly.

"Because you've checked and ruled it out, right?" demanded Cooke.

"No, because it isn't yellow fever," he said flatly. "We didn't know about the outbreak in Madagascar until a month ago, and by that point it didn't seem relevant. People don't really die from yellow fever anymore, anyway. It certainly doesn't make people bite great chunks out of each other to pass it on. And as Caring said, the dates don't work. Mosi can't have been contagious with it when he traveled."

"Actually, up to fifty percent of infected patients still die from yellow fever," said Kesta. "What if this patient had contracted other viruses on top of the yellow fever? What if they hybridized to form a new virus in his system?"

"Where's the liver?" Dudley demanded. "Shelley, you and Cooke should biopsy Mosi's liver. We need to establish whether there's been an immune response to yellow fever there."

"We'll also rule out all other hemorrhagic fevers," suggested Cooke. "Ebola. Lassa fever. Marburg. Junin virus."

"All of which have already been discounted," said Lundeen.

"I'm sure Mr. Mosi won't mind us being extra-specially thorough. Will you, Paul?" said Kesta, standing at the top of the cold gray trolley in place of Mosi's missing head.

"You'll be wasting your time," said Lundeen, "but sure, be my guest."

"And I was wondering if we could review my clearance level?" she asked.

"Your clearance level?"

"Yes," Kesta said, looking to Dudley for support. Dudley appeared to have developed spontaneous selective mutism. "It's just that, I was expecting to be working with Dr. Caring, and I do have a background in virology. I just want to make sure that I am doing everything I can—"

"You're stuck at clearance level three I'm afraid, Shelley. Screening. Only experienced pathologists and virologists have biosecurity four."

"But it means I can't—"

"It means you'll review the liver as you've been asked to."

Lundeen left them to meet with more important people—as he charmingly put it to the three of them. Kesta, Dudley, and Cooke returned to the main laboratory having retrieved Paul Mosi's liver from deep freeze. Approximately half of the organ was left, and Kesta could see flat areas where whoever had biopsied it before had sliced it smooth and clean, ready for the next samples to be taken.

"You won't want liver and bacon for dinner now, will you?" Cooke laughed as she helped Kesta to prepare the ethanol bath while Dudley hung around them like a chemical smell. "What is it, Dr. Caring?"

"Just something I wanted to make you aware of re Lundeen," he said. "He's under an awful lot of pressure." He glanced over his shoulder at the other minions working diligently behind them. "And from what I understand, there are, shall we say, issues with the funding."

"How do you mean, 'issues'?"

"I mean that this place was built secretly years ago. It costs an arm and a leg to run, and we're on a very tight deadline," whispered Dudley. "If we don't make real progress, and soon, they've threatened to pull our budget and offer the research out for tender to private labs domestically."

"But we're a private lab domestically," said Kesta.

"They'd be happy to hand over Project Dawn to anyone prepared to deliver on the cure quickly and cheaply. It's a matter of optics. And they feel that the risk of information being leaked to foreign competitors—"

"This isn't a competition, though."

"Actually, that's exactly what it is," said Cooke. "There's gold in them hills for whoever can isolate the virus and find the cure or develop a vaccination for it first. Medical research is like the Wild West. There's money in information. Power too. If Project Dawn finds the cure first, then it can set the price for mass-producing it and selling it, were the virus to crop up somewhere else."

"All we can do is keep doing what we're doing," Dudley said, "and hope for the best outcome." He trudged toward the exit at the far end of the laboratory.

"Hang on," said Kesta, pulling him back by the arm. "Is there something you're not telling me?"

Still, he couldn't bear to look her in the eye, but she recognized the physical burden in his crumpled posture that comes from carrying around something heavy. Something secret. "Dudley, talk to me."

"The thing is, I really can't, Kesta," he replied, looking over her shoulder toward Cooke. "There are things we're working on here that I am not at liberty to tell you about. Can we just leave it at that?"

Kesta called out over the bright whir of their machinery, but Dudley either couldn't, or pretended not to, hear her as he trudged out of the lab.

CHAPTER EIGHT

"I'm only round the corner. I can be with you in, like, ten minutes."

Kesta felt a chill shambling all the way up her spine like a mallet on a xylophone. She'd meant to reply to Jess's messages. But somehow nearly three months had flown by since their tragic *it would have been your husband's birthday if he hadn't been killed in a zombie apocalypse* drinks at Pour Decisions, and now here Jess was, catching her off guard on a Saturday, threatening to turn up at the flat in person.

"Kesta, I know you don't really like talking on the phone, but you also don't particularly seem to reply to any of my messages anymore. So, what am I to do? I'm coming round."

"No! You can't. I can't have you here." Kesta was scrambling, easing the cannula from her arm and pressing down on the wound. "The place is a tip and—"

"You know I don't care about that sort of thing," Jess blustered on, although she did care about that sort of thing immensely. "We could get a pizza from that place round the corner, you know, the one where all those old Sicilians were shacked up together during the outbreak. I think I'm in Shad Thames."

Kesta felt a warmth unknotting the muscles in her shoulders. "Jess, that's much farther away from me than you think."

Jess never knew where anywhere was. She was the sort of person who took cabs everywhere so that her abysmal sense of direction was never tested. She deigned to walk only if Kesta was with her, acting as sherpa. For Jess, it was only her arrival at the destination that mattered, not the journey. Jess, triumphant at the top of the mountain, the frozen corpses of the guides who had succumbed to the perils of going anywhere with her strewn in her wake.

"I bet you're in heels?" said Kesta.

"Obviously. I was going to try to find a taxi but—"

"Do you realize how many cobbles lie in wait for you between Shad Thames and the end of Wapping Lane?"

"All the cobbles left in London?"

"Cobbles are your nemesis. Remember Bruges?" Kesta could hear Jess making huffing noises of frustration at the other end of the phone as she wondered what to do. Kesta pictured her standing precariously in her patent pumps, staring up at Tower Bridge, contemplating finding a man with a boat in that otherwise desolate part of town, and demanding he sail her across the river to Kesta's flat. This would seem like an entirely reasonable request to Jess, who had learned to expect life to open up and revolve around her, like tiny plates of sushi on a slenderized conveyor belt. Life had allowed Jess to wear exactly the wrong kind of shoes, shoes in which most people couldn't stand, walk, run, or really even sit in.

"It will take you an hour to walk to mine, and by the time you arrive I will have a double ankle fracture to try and set," Kesta said, tying up the laces of her trainers, her phone squashed between her ear and her shoulder. "Let's meet at the Tower of London. You'll only have to walk across the bridge. You can manage that."

Kesta pushed the door to Tim's room ajar. He was due another sedation, which she ought to give him before she left. But she intended to be quick with Jess. She would risk it. Do it when she got home. He was facing away from her, the chained arm fixed to one side so that his body was twisted, his legs tucked up toward his stomach. The machine was emitting comforting bleeps of life. She heard the bleeping become more frequent as she approached him. He could sense her presence. She placed a hand on his back, another on the chained arm.

Kesta kissed him on the temple, breathing in the vague tang of the fragrance-free moisturizer she had applied that morning to keep his skin from blistering. The bleeps quickened, and she smiled. She rested her chin against his shoulder, nuzzled him. Somewhere deep in Tim's throat a grumbling sound, a note of recognition.

"Darling, I'm just going out to see Jess for a bit, but I won't be long," she whispered.

"Urghpmf," said Tim.

"You're absolutely right, darling. I do look a fright. I should at least put some mascara on."

He grumbled again, turning on the bed, and she was grateful for it. It was the closest thing they'd had to a normal conversation in days.

———

Jess had claimed one of the benches in the grounds of the Tower and spread herself and an impromptu picnic across it. It was five o'clock in the evening, and Jess's one-woman happy hour was in full swing.

"It's screw-top, so it'll probably kill us," she cackled, slopping black-red Malbec into two paper cups she'd taken without asking at a coffee stand, "and I have crisps and sandwiches, which was all I could get round here. And look, ankles still intact." Jess kicked her feet while admiring her haul. She handed Kesta a cup of wine.

"This is perfect," Kesta said, helping open up a second packet of crisps. Her face was flushed from running. She pushed the sleeves of Tim's old sweater up, pulled at the neck to cool herself. She felt guilty for ignoring Jess. The longer she let the messages go unanswered, the harder it always was to reply.

"Cheers."

"Cheers, babe," said Jess, gulping, wincing at the wine's sharpness and then, "Bloody hell, Kesta, what in God's name is this?" She grabbed her by the wrist. "Have you been shooting up or what?"

Kesta looked down to see an angry purple bruise erupting from the crook of her arm, from the blood she'd been poised to take for Tim. She must have torn the cannula out too fast. This spongy hematoma had sprouted up on top of older yellow wounds. She pulled the sleeves down and fumbled for an excuse.

"There's a blood bank," she said, the obvious excuse being the safest, "on my way to work. I've been going there for a while. Giving . . . well, blood. Obviously. I've been giving blood."

"Why?" said Jess, bewildered by reciprocal altruism. "Anyway, aren't you a bit skinny for that? I mean, don't they have like a weight limit or something?" She was frowning as her eyes tried to bore through Kesta's shapeless clothing to take another look, vaguely disgusted. It did sound like something Kesta would do, give away her blood for nothing. "Okay, well, remember to keep some for yourself," she tutted. "You never know when you might need it."

"Duly noted. So, how come you're in my neck of the woods?"

"Oh, well, I'd agreed to have lunch with Eleanor Weston, remember her? Last year of uni, she was a fresher, sort of muscled into our crowd." Jess could see that Kesta was drawing a blank. "Brassy, had that irritating habit of manically winking at everyone all the time. She thought it was flirtatious. You thought she had astigmatism?"

"Oh, yes, her," Kesta said, vaguely remembering the supposed affliction if not the name or the description of the woman, adding Eleanor Weston to the long line of people she'd met and forgotten about. Jess had a habit of stockpiling her contacts, filing them away, and cultivating them sufficiently so that when she had an empty afternoon or evening in her social calendar, they were ready and waiting to fill it for her. Kesta ripped open a coronation chicken sandwich, flinching as the bruise pulsed at her elbow. She imagined everyone Jess had ever met standing in neat lines like those Chinese terra-cotta soldiers, row after row of friends and acquaintances hidden underground in the thick clay, patiently waiting for Jess to dig them up again.

"I saw her for lunch."

"Where?"

"Manon on Bermondsey Street. They've just reopened."

"Oh, good for them, I like Manon."

"I like Manon, but now I can't go there again because Eleanor Weston got drunk on, like, two tiny thimbles full of Crémant, and I had to get them to call her a taxi, which took an age."

Jess didn't touch the sandwiches. She sorted through the crisps strewn open on the silvery packet until she found the one she wanted. "She's got three babies at home now, all under five."

"Gosh, how—demanding."

"I know, ghastly. Anyway, simply can't drink anymore, lost her tolerance completely. I was so embarrassed for her."

"Does she have asthma? Low blood pressure? Hives?"

"It's not alcohol intolerance, babe. Her children have ruined her. It's not good for a woman to have dependents."

A few people scurried past them like rats crawling out of the sewers. Kesta sat back against the metal bench, paper cup of wine in one hand, sandwich in the other, and felt a moment of contentment. The evening was comfortable enough—the air along the river was quite still, and it was warm enough for them both to be sitting out in it without coats. She thought she could still smell Tim on the neck of the sweater.

"So, are we going to talk about it, or what?" asked Jess.

"Talk about what?"

"About *you know what.*" She mouthed the words. "Where you've been hiding for the past few months." Jess repositioned herself on the bench so that she was facing Kesta, a pale cheek cushioned against a closed fist as she propped her elbow against the back of the bench. She was smirking. "Did you think I wouldn't guess? You bloody well got in, didn't you?"

Kesta had taken it for granted that she'd be able to keep Project Dawn a secret from Jess, having gained so much confidence in her expertise as a professional liar, what with her undead husband handcuffed to a radiator. She should have known better.

"So, then? Did you? You can trust me not to tell anyone. Did you get in?"

Could she trust Jess not to tell anyone though? Given that Kesta wasn't a trusting sort of person, she shouldn't judge Jess specifically. Perhaps if she was honest with Jess about Project Dawn but swore her to secrecy, it would satisfy Jess's curiosity for the time being at least. It might earn her more leniency, get Jess to back off a little if she knew what Kesta was up against. She said nothing. Jess began to squeal.

"I knew it! The truth is always written all over your face," she said, toasting her wine in the air. "I've known you too long, you can't hide anything from me anymore." Kesta felt another twinge of guilt. The bruise on her arm was throbbing.

"Seriously, you can't tell anyone, Jess. They'd pitch a fit if word spread."

"Oh, screw them. I'm not going to say anything." She guffawed. "This is so exciting! I'm just pleased for you. No, I'm relieved for you to have something important going on in your life. Something necessary. It'll give you purpose."

Kesta had to smile.

"So, how is it going?" Jess asked.

"It's—it's intense. And the progress is slower than I'd hoped but—"

"What kind of stuff are you working on?" Jess asked as she fiddled with a bobble on the sleeve of her top, lifting it loose, letting it float off in the air. "Have you reanimated any corpses yet?"

"I'm reviewing slides, mostly. They think it's—look, Jess, I can't really talk to you about it. I can't risk getting fired."

"Okay, fine, well, you know where I am if you need to vent, though I will refuse to sign a nondisclosure agreement or any of that crap."

"I promise to let you know if I manage to bring anyone back to life."

Kesta nibbled at a sandwich. Jess splashed more wine into both their cups.

"Oh, by the way," she said, rooting in her handbag, "I got these for you as asked." She pulled out a slim paper packet and handed it to Kesta, who promptly squeezed it into the back pocket of her jeans. She felt her weight squash the box as she sat back down against the bench. "Babe, I know you can't talk about work, but you can talk to me if you're feeling depressed. Are you?"

Kesta didn't think she was depressed. Desperate, yes. Devastated, absolutely. A dipsomaniac, undoubtedly, and many other terrible D words to boot. But she wasn't depressed. The antidepressants she'd asked Jess to get for her, from a friendly GP who wouldn't ask too many questions, were actually for Tim. She had resolved to throw antidepressant medication into the mix to see if it changed anything for him, made life more bearable. She couldn't know how aware he was of his situation. She hated the thought that the virus was holding him hostage inside his own body, couldn't bear the thought of his unhappiness. He couldn't tell her how he felt. She was left to guess, to imagine, so of course she always imagined the worst. Kesta forced a smile and squeezed Jess's hand.

"Thank you for these. I'm okay. Just taking precautions."

"They're accumulative, you know, so make sure you take them religiously, don't give up after a week, okay?"

"In that case, you'd better get me some more."

Jess sighed. She slung her arm around the back of the bench. "You know what would do you the power of good? A holiday. Wouldn't it be nice to go away somewhere? Together?"

Kesta watched as a pigeon wobbled in imperfect circles. She tossed it a crust from her sandwich. It cooed as it bobbed down to eat. The picnic was beginning to spoil.

"No," she said, almost too quietly for Jess to hear. "No, actually, I have no desire to be anywhere other than here."

"In normal circumstances, I would have dragged you away by now," said Jess, wiping her hands against each other to brush away the crumbs. She placed a clean hand on Kesta's thigh. "I'd have swept you off to sunnier climes right after the funeral. I'd have moved in, packed your bags, and carted you off to the airport, whether you liked it or not." Jess looked forlorn, a little sullen, as though the outbreak had denied her an opportunity to co-mourn, which she would have relished.

"Well, I wouldn't have wanted to go," Kesta replied flatly, "because it wouldn't have made any difference."

"It would have made you feel better. Holidays make me feel better."

"Well, that's *you*, isn't it?" Kesta snapped. "Jess, grief isn't something you can leave behind in the long-stay car park at Gatwick Airport. It goes with you everywhere."

"I know that, but a change of scenery does everyone good."

"Not me. We are not the same!"

Jess looked stung. She crossed her legs away from Kesta and her face began to harden like putty.

"Kesta, we both know you have a tendency to wallow in self-pity," she said, "and that you consider yourself above the rules that apply to everybody else. But it stands to reason that having something to really look forward to is mentally and emotionally important when processing loss. Especially if you're depressed."

Kesta did have something to look forward to. Tim getting better. Although she tried not to tempt fate or to let her brain leap on ahead of her, it was the hope of his recovery, however faint, that was keeping her going. She wanted to cure him. She wanted their life to go back to normal. And if it took another month, a year, an eternity, well, then she'd wait. Kesta clung on to the pure promise of serendipity. She believed it could happen because it had happened before, the night she'd met Tim. He appeared before her to change the course of her life, and everything had been settled anew. Kesta had no faith to speak of, but she did believe in Tim. Tim would pull through.

She didn't want to fight with Jess. She had always been like this, a high days and holidays kind of person, not such a specialist in the prosaic in-between. Jess could be enormous fun. But when you weren't in the mood for fun, what was she then? Somewhat obsolete. Kesta remembered something wise that Tim had said. She couldn't remember why he'd said it. He was probably encouraging her to be more tolerant of Jess's exuberance.

After the music fades, Jess is still standing in the middle of the club, dancing all on her own. You and I get to go home together and unload the dishwasher.

"Sorry," Kesta said, softening. "You're probably right. I just can't think of anything worse right now. I can't imagine going away without him. But I do acknowledge it's not fair on you."

"I'm being selfish, aren't I?" said Jess. "Sorry. Maybe when all this is over, you'll think about it?"

"Yes, maybe then," Kesta said, pouring out the remnants of the Malbec to cheer Jess up. It wasn't Jess's fault that their priorities were so different, that the only thing she wanted to do to mark the end of the outbreak was to drink sangria on a sun lounger somewhere lovely and benign where the locals didn't introduce themselves with their mouths wide open and their intestines hanging out.

"How's Dudley?" Jess asked coyly, pulling a face as she said his name out loud, as though she had to regurgitate it.

"He's been great, actually," Kesta said. "Really supportive. He's got a higher security clearance than I have, which is annoying, but—"

"Oh, that must really stick in your craw!"

"It's frustrating. He does seem very distracted lately. Otherwise, he's been very helpful, and even though I'm not qualified for all the work he's doing, he's trying—"

Feeling a vibration, Kesta dug in her pocket for her phone. There was a notification from the monitor in Tim's room. Something had triggered the motion sensor.

"Honestly, I don't think I've ever met such an insufferable dullard as Dudley," said Jess. "I don't know how you stand him."

Kesta drew the phone close to her face and squinted at the camera app. She opened it and waited for the live feed to load.

"Do you remember that one time at Christmas, at that awful party you took me to, where he was dancing while wearing that fucking jumper?"

The picture was clear. Tim's stark reality in black and white.

"It said 'self-service' on the front. And then because you were wearing tinsel, and he wanted to copy you—"

Tim was pulling at the restraint with his free arm. The bed was rocking with his effort. He was alert and focused, feverish with industry. He was trying to break loose.

"—and I was saying to that woman you used to work with, what's her name?"

"Jess, I have to go."

"Claire! That's it. She was great. I liked Claire."

Kesta leapt up.

"Sorry, Jess, I've got to go." She forced a smile, pretending to be inconvenienced rather than royally panicked. "Albert's just messaged me. A pipe's burst in the flat, he needs to get up there."

"But—"

"I've got to get home to let him in."

"Doesn't he have a key?"

"There's water gushing everywhere. So sorry to eat and run. It was so good to see you."

"Can I—I mean, I won't be able to help, I don't do leaks, or plumbing, but—"

"I've got to go, sorry—" Kesta didn't finish because she had to run.

"—but I can handle irate porters. I could come with you?" Jess called after her, but Kesta was already gone.

She tore through the archway under Tower Bridge and over the walkway where the lock held back the Thames. She pounded over the crumbling cobbles, feeling the heat in her knees and her hips, flying past the cemetery with its ancient headstones like crooked teeth, felt their ghosts walking over her own grave at the place where Tim was bitten, down the road unchanged in a century, the thick brick warehouses stoic and unyielding, full of dust and memories of when the city was alive, toward the silver gates of the wharf, and finally home.

As she ran past the porter's lodge, an unfamiliar voice called after her.

"Miss, hey, are you in flat nine? Hey! Something's making a racket up there—"

Kesta's heart was banging in tandem with the banging in the flat.

She raced up the stairs, the ugly bruise on her arm pulsing frenetically. Drenched in sweat, hot and ice-cold at once, fingers fumbling for her keys, blinking back the stinging pain of her mascara streaming into her eyes. Her footsteps muffled by the carpet as she flew down the hallway, the thudding, the scraping of something fat and heavy being shoved and battered sounded in the hall, a grand piano being shunted through a doorway, a fridge tipping over backward onto a wooden floor. Her hands were trembling as she opened the front door, and the sound of the struggle was amplified as she did so. Tim was shouting, his wordless voice full of rage and indignation, banging something against the bed, the bed banging against the floor, the floor reverberating around the flat, the whole flat shaking just as she was.

Kesta unlocked the dead bolts as quickly as she could, and the commotion within the room seemed to suck the door away from her like a vacuum. Then she saw him, squatting on his haunches, his body contorted over the chained hand, covered in blood as he fought to break it through the restraints. He looked up at her, his eyes like amber, and she saw that his face was covered in blood. He had tried to bite through his own hand to free himself. Upon seeing Kesta he let out a scream, shrill and evil, the sound of the virus.

She stood on the threshold, her mouth wide open, unable to move or speak or think. Tim was jumping up and down, howling sharp, frustrated screeches. Those yellow eyes full of blame.

Kesta pushed herself toward the bedside cabinet, dropping and rolling to the floor as Tim swung at her with a clawed fist. She looked up at him, spitting and glaring, lurching from side to side, the bed at risk of collapse. She used the cabinet to lever herself up a little, pulled out the middle drawer where she kept a vial of phenobarbital at the very back. She had never intended to use it. It was much too strong. But Tim was scraping his arm through the air, trying to reach her, squealing like a shot boar. She groped across the glass top for a pack of sterile syringes, ripped one open, held it in between her teeth as she staggered to her feet. There was blood on the floor, and she smeared it with her trainers as she panicked and slid while trying to puncture the vial with the needle. She tapped the syringe, squirted out a little of the drug, and steadied herself for a fight. Tim was coiled on his haunches ready to spring at her, his eagerness foaming around the edges of his open mouth and against his pink tongue protruding.

She inched toward him on the bloodied floor, using her right hand to parry away falling jabs and swipes.

"I'm sorry, Tim, but this is for your own good," she said as she transferred the syringe into her left hand so that her right was free to defend herself. *Smack,* as she connected with his outstretched arm—*smack, smack*—smacking away her husband's bloodstained hands. He strained toward her, swiping like a feral cat, his tongue flicking lasciviously. She backed off a little. She waited.

Then she thrust her body forward and struck him cleanly on the bridge of his nose. He recoiled, holding his free arm up to his face in puzzlement. And then she struck again, only this time with the phenobarbital, jabbing it into his chained arm, pushing the plunger down, and tugging the needle out of his skin before he'd had time to realize what was happening.

Kesta watched him, panting, her hands covered in his blood, and now her face too as she wiped back her fringe to clear the sweat from her forehead. He was left stunned, hugging himself into a tight ball, feeling around his nose, the rage receding as his body began to loosen, his arms and legs slackening, the head rolling backward against the pillow, and a last look of failure before he sank into oblivion.

The sedation wasn't working anymore. She had been leaving him for too many hours languishing on a single dose while she was at work, and he was becoming ever more resistant to it.

"It's not your fault, darling. It's mine," she cried out to him. And she meant it too. She should never have left him to go and see Jess. She'd have to secure a different form of sedation from somewhere. She could sneak back to the hospital perhaps, use her old key card, and see what she could steal on her way home after work. Another bloody thing to worry about, something else to overcome. She bent over double, gripping her thighs, her lungs on fire, tried to suck in some air, holding back tears, disguising them in big gasps for breath. Much like talking, Kesta believed that crying didn't help her. It was just a temporary release, an emotional response to a situation requiring a practical solution.

I mustn't cry in front of Tim. Mustn't cry in front of Tim!

And yet the tears threatened to overwhelm her, clogging up her throat, filling her eyes so she couldn't see clearly. She clenched her teeth instead, kept her head down low so that Tim couldn't see her face.

The intercom buzzed and Kesta jolted upright. The porter downstairs, some new guy who worked only the occasional weekend shift, demanded to know what all the noise was about.

"Tumble dryer," she lied spontaneously, "pulled itself out of the wall and started drumming around the floor of the kitchen."

"Like it was possessed?" said the new guy.

"Yeah, something like that," she said and hung up.

CHAPTER NINE

When observed under an electron microscope, proteins were always thought to have held a certain shape, and this fixed form determined their specific function, like sending signals to other cells in the body. Then someone discovered a group of proteins that didn't look like the rest and that had previously been discounted as analogous or just plain weird, so no one had taken them seriously until said bright spark realized that the way they looked, the shape they took, in fact belied the purpose that they served. These proteins could do all kinds of things. These proteins were the wolves in sheep's clothing, the ones you underestimated at your peril because they did not fit the mold. And all the while, these super freaks of nature had been in charge of what was going on inside us. Regulating DNA, causing cells to separate. Intrinsic disorder proteins gave the order that made a red blood cell a red blood cell. They also told cells when they were cancer.

Intrinsic disorder. It described exactly how Kesta was feeling. It was also the thing she was examining that afternoon at Project Dawn, the strange fluidity of certain proteins.

For four hours, Kesta had been comparing slide after slide of ID proteins lifted from tissue samples Cooke had harvested from Paul Mosi's various remaining organs. It was coming up to three, and she had been at the lab since seven that morning. Something was certain now: Paul Mosi *had* been infected with yellow fever. Whether or not he had recovered from it before he flew to London, no one could be sure. When, where, and how he had become infected was a mystery and might always remain so. The role, if any, that the flavivirus played in her zombie virus was at the top of Kesta's list of *absolutely terrifying unknowns*, and she was resigned to working through it to the bitter end. The more you knew, the less you were meant to fear, but Kesta figured that whoever had come up with that gem definitely hadn't been a scientist. The zombie virus could be a super-charged yellow fever mutation. Or it could be an entirely novel virus, the stuff of her uniquely gruesome nightmares. Kesta had to focus through the frenzy until she could make sense of it all, clinging to her microscope like rosary beads worried through her fingers. Kesta must believe in the science until she saw and understood the truth, and what that truth would mean for Tim. But the more Kesta learned about the virus, the deeper the fear ran inside her. She was very worried about Tim. She would have to leave the lab as soon as she could if she was to head back to her old workplace to steal some supplies. Sedatives, pain relief, maybe a D-ring cuff if they had one, because after Saturday's debacle, she might need to replace the handcuffs.

Kesta had a headache from staring down a microscope into the white light, and as she stretched her arms high into the air to undo the knot at the base of her skull, Cooke lifted her visor and carefully wiped around her blue-shadowed eyes, looking as exhausted as Kesta felt.

"Cooke, have you seen Dr. Caring?" Kesta asked, trying to sound casual about it. "I haven't seen him in days, and whenever I pass him in the corridor, he looks really stressed."

"We're all stressed," Cooke said, mimicking her by stretching out her stiff joints against the workstation, "but no, I haven't seen him. He's always off with Lundeen."

"Are they working on something different from us?"

"Different how?" asked Cooke.

Kesta knew she ought to keep her thoughts to herself, especially in a place as clandestine as Project Dawn, but Dudley's comment about the site being dangerous and the little she had seen him in the week since the postmortem of Paul Mosi had played on her mind. "Different in that they seem to work in another part of the lab to which you and I don't have access?" She looked over at Cooke and saw that she had stiffened again, caught in the snare of her own indecision.

"Cooke?"

"I'm not so sure that we are the only laboratory on-site."

She walked around to Kesta's side of the table, carrying a box of slides. She held one up to the light as if to show it to Kesta in some grand pretense toward looking and acting natural.

"I don't know this for certain," she whispered. "It's just an educated guess. We're working down here underground in a secret but half-staffed laboratory, where our boss mostly has meetings with the Ministry of Defense and the Home Office." Kesta could only stare up at the fuchsia slides Cooke was holding in front of her, to allow her brain the chance to catch up with the new reality as it began to dawn. "I think there are two laboratories down here." Cooke's voice was just a sticky whisper behind her mask. "There's us. And then there's whatever they're doing on the floor below. Us officially working on a cure for the virus. Them downstairs . . ."

The moment before she said it was like sheet lightning, a cataclysmic flash before the rumble of thunder.

"Gain-of-Function. Has to be."

The words combusted into the air and then disappeared so rapidly it would be easy to imagine they had never been said at all, were it not for their jagged particles, which remained and which Kesta could feel herself inhaling, each breath drawing them inside her body like a nerve agent. Gain-of-Function research would mean working to supercharge the virus, not cure it. She felt Cooke's hand gripping her arm. Another slide held up for her to pretend to look at. Kesta breathed in deeply and felt the remnants of those words, Gain-of-Function, catching on her insides, scraping their way into her lungs.

"Shit. It can't be."

"What other answer is there? Our progress is so slow. We must be a proxy lab."

"So, we serve what purpose, exactly?"

"We present the face of the Project's operations," Cooke said, moving another pink slide up into the light above them. "We take our time looking for a cure for the virus. While they isolate and gamify it."

A terrible pressure began to build around Kesta, like stepping into a vacuum that at any moment could trigger her collapse. "Cooke, that kind of research is illegal."

"I know," she said, returning the last slide to its case, drawing their conversation to a close, "but any of the other biological sites in Britain could have been given the contract to research the virus. Why bring everyone down here? Why start from scratch? Because they don't want the oversight. Because it's not the cure we're really looking for here."

A man carrying a large steel tray began walking in their direction. When she saw him, Cooke stalked around the workstation to her own microscope. The man's visor was so steamed, his facial features were a gray void.

"You should come round to mine for dinner," said Cooke, nonchalantly and for the lingering man's benefit. "Can I help you with something, Royce?" she demanded, but the man ignored her and hurried on through the lab.

"Who was that?" asked Kesta.

"Colin Royce," said Cooke before holding a blue-gloved index finger up to her mask where her lips lay underneath it. "I know him from years ago. Worked in infectious diseases at Imperial. Nice enough chap. We used to call him Rolls."

Kesta pretended to change the magnification on her microscope as she tried to control her heavy breathing.

"Come for dinner. When you have an evening going spare," Cooke said again. "Be nice to talk. Outside work. And forget I said anything. I didn't mean to worry you."

Kesta nodded to her and decided to worry about it furiously.

———

Surely Cooke was wrong. Gain-of-Function research was outlawed by almost every international laboratory. There was more mystery surrounding it than any other scientific research. Opinion was split for and against. Some considered it to be a necessary risk to radically expand our scientific horizons; others felt it was explicitly dangerous, monstrous even. All Kesta knew was that such research served to take a virus and make it more powerful, exponentially so. To isolate a pathogen and make its kill rate absolute. Embracing its promise for discovery meant accepting its potential for destruction.

If Cooke was right, and there was another altogether more sinister intent at Project Dawn, then the search for a cure was little more than a hoax. *Does Lundeen want to isolate the virus and then make it worse, not eradicate it?* He'd be breaking international laws, although Kesta knew he must be doing it with government backing. Government funding even. There were stories about Western governments transferring funds through complicated webs of offshore accounts, payments made under the guise of charitable donations to institutions in murkier, less developed nations where they could take advantage of lax rules surrounding biosecurity and make other scientists take bigger risks on their behalf, all for the right price.

Gain-of-Function research did happen but never in plain sight, the awful truth of it nearly always obfuscated by an impenetrable maze of deniability. Kesta imagined a man in a suit in a shadowy building handing secret documents to Lundeen along with an open check, asking him to risk another zombie outbreak, even worse than before. Experimenting with the virus to increase its potency meant the risk of contamination to staff and a leak into the city was exponentially higher.

They'd never been told why the alarm had sounded almost three months ago. The ominous tumult that followed as they waited anxiously, captive inside the building, went unanswered. They had simply gone back to work. But what had happened? No one Kesta had spoken to knew what had occurred to trigger it, not even Cooke. Surely someone—in the break room, the changing room, even in the lab itself—would have presented a plausible account. Everything else in the lab that day had gone smoothly. And yet someone had been concerned enough, frightened enough, to have pulled the alarm, briefly bringing the Project to a standstill.

And they hadn't let them out, had they? The staff weren't evacuated from the building, away from the source of the threat. They were locked inside with it.

Could an alarm have been triggered somewhere else on the site? Had there been an accident in another part of Project Dawn she didn't even know existed? There was a chance that if Lundeen was gambling with Gain-of-Function research, it was in pursuit of developing a cure or a vaccine more quickly, to expedite their progress. But she couldn't know for sure.

She would have to talk to Dudley about it. She imagined a man like Lundeen would have no qualms about running two labs in tandem, about coloring outside the lines of accepted, moral scientific practice. When faced with such an unethical proposition, she imagined a man like Professor Lundeen wouldn't even blink.

———

Kesta got out of the lab as quickly as she could that evening and tried to walk off her suspicions. She went shopping for sundries for herself, things to lay on top of the bounty she was about to filch from her old hospital for Tim. Plasters, toothpaste, and cotton wool pads were especially good because they were bulky yet light, they could conceal anything she was going to steal but wouldn't add to the weight she must carry home. Each item she touched she imagined herself contaminating, spreading a manipulated version of the virus through the aisles and up toward the self-service checkout. She walked through the piazza in Covent Garden, along Long Acre, through Seven Dials, then along Shaftesbury Avenue once so full of people with no idea where they were headed, looking down at maps, idling in front of her, getting in her way. She missed them. Now it was a closed artery, with nothing flowing through it. Except for the Gain-of-Function virus threat, which she felt followed her every step.

It was late enough for the cleaning crew to be working through the hospital when she arrived, swirling in diligent circles with mops that looked like candida, the tail ends of mold specimens, one of science's little in-jokes. As she walked up the first flight of stairs and saw the bank of shining floor in front of her, shining as though it was yet to set, Kesta crept tightly along the wall so as to disturb only the areas the human eye was unlikely to notice. She reached the back stairs, climbed quickly, then another crawl toward the stockroom with its industrial coolers and cabinets full of so many pretty, necessary things.

Strips of solid white tubing crackled along the ceilings, lighting up the room, making it hum as she entered. Kesta put the cool box down onto a steel table, took her rucksack off, sat it down, removed a second bag from inside it, and opened that one up too. She moved about the room gracefully, taking only what she needed and disguising the theft as best she could. She removed blister packs of tablets from white paper boxes, leaving the empty boxes behind. She made her selections from the back of rows, from the far end of the line to delay detection for as long as possible. Her fingers worked energetically, precisely; she knew which drawers and cabinets to open and rifle through, and she knew exactly what she was looking for.

Topical anesthetic creams, analgesics, and, most importantly, a box of sedatives the size of a microwave. Anti-infective medicines, anti-bacterials; as much vancomycin, her favorite glycopeptide antibiotic, as she could carry. Tim's resistance to monoclonal antibiotics was a worry, because she was treating him the way one might treat a patient with Ebola, by mixing them all together. She stole another course of medication designed to treat leprosy for no other reason than it was there.

When she left the hospital, it was nearly eight o'clock, and she was so laden down with special cargo that she had no choice but to stop and wait for a taxi on the street. As she raised an arm to hail one, she dropped a pack of syringes into the gutter. As she bent down to pick it up, someone else's hand beat her to it. Claire's.

"I thought it was you," she said, moving out of the road to allow the taxi to pull up in front of them. "Jesus, Kesta, you look awful." She glanced down at the packet in her hand and frowned. The cabbie switched his hazard lights on, an orange countdown, tick, tock, warning, warning.

"Thanks for that," Kesta said, snatching the packet back.

"What are you doing here?" Claire asked. Gray storm clouds began to thicken the sky, and the air smelled like rain.

"I could ask you the same thing," Kesta said. "Bit late for you, isn't it? Don't tell me you're actually working?" She tugged open the cab door and started tossing her various bags onto the floor and across the seat. "Wapping, please," she shouted at the driver as she climbed inside. Rain began to fall suddenly and heavily.

"I know what's going on," said Claire, holding the door open so that Kesta couldn't close it.

Kesta stammered for the right words. "Going on? Claire, I'm not sure—"

"I know where you're working, I mean," she said. "I was just pleased to see you. That's all. And I miss you both, you and Dudley." She took a last look at Kesta's bags, then at her old colleague. "Good luck, Kesta. With what you're doing. It's so important." She slammed the cab door shut.

Claire waved as the taxi pulled out into the road. She seemed lonely. Kesta had been so consumed with her work that she hadn't stopped to think at all about Claire, left behind, just another relic from before. Over on the other side of the road, the doors to A&E glowed yellow and red, opening and closing automatically for patients who must be invisible because there was no one there. As Kesta drove past, she was so focused on trying to keep drugs and supplies from falling out of the bags and worrying about getting caught by Claire that she hadn't noticed that someone was smoking in the gloom of the hospital car park, watching her.

CHAPTER TEN

There was a heavy thud against the front door. Kesta dropped the spatula, sending a spray of red sauce streaking across the kitchen cabinets, dripping onto the tiles below. She picked up a tea towel, wiped her hands gently, and tiptoed into the hallway, listening. Tim was lying in bed, the door to the room wide open. It was Saturday. They should have been in Rome. Kesta had thought it would be a fitting tribute on their wedding anniversary that year for him to kiss her on the Spanish Steps. Tim had asked if that was a euphemism. They had never been to Rome. Tim had always wanted to go.

Instead, she was wrestling unsuccessfully with a scalding Bolognese sauce. After fifteen years of marriage, you were meant to be rewarded with crystal to treasure—not second-degree burns.

Three impatient knocks rattled against the door. She could hear beeping, muttering.

"Hello?"

Kesta slid as quietly as she could to pull the spare bedroom door to a close. She waited. She hoped that whoever was out there would go away. No one ever came up to her flat without her permission. That's what the service charge she paid was for. A toll for keeping outsiders at bay, held back by Albert and twenty-four-hour security.

"Anyone home?"

She didn't recognize the voice. She couldn't let him in. But what if this man went back downstairs and got the porter to ring up? What if he had already heard her in the kitchen, heard her before she knew she was meant to be listening out for him? What if he was from Project Dawn?

Since Cooke had shared her suspicions about the secret second lab, Kesta's thoughts were becoming undisciplined. *Am I paranoid? Did you know if you were paranoid?* Kesta didn't like this new feeling of being unsafe inside her own head, the inner torment, the sense of persecution.

He banged again, three times, louder, and Kesta jumped. Tim grunted. He didn't like noise. The man wasn't going away.

"Yes, what is it?" she said through two and a half inches of fireproof wood.

"I've got a package," he said, "for Mrs. Kesta Shelley?"

"Right," she replied. "Leave it on the doorstep."

"Excuse me?"

"Leave it there."

"I'm supposed to get a signature."

"Oh, for heaven's sake, I'm Kesta Shelley. Can you please just leave it outside? Thank you very much."

"You can sign up for signature-free delivery on our website—"

"Great, but can you just leave it there? I've got my hands full."

"Yeah, all right then."

She heard plastic wrapping squeaking against the door as the deliveryman slid the parcel to the floor. The sound of solid shoes padding away. The communal hallway doors by the lift patting shut. She gave it a minute, then pulled the front door open and bent down to retrieve the package.

"What's that smell?" He was standing at the end of the hallway, smirking. He seemed pleased to have succeeded in forcing her out of her flat. Kesta, startled, caught her shin against the package.

"Nothing. It's nothing," she said, rubbing her leg.

"Doesn't smell like nothing," he said, walking toward her.

"It's nothing," she said.

"Don't suppose I could use your toilet while I'm up here?"

"No!" she shouted.

The man looked shocked, then irritated. His mouth was turned down, though he could have been offended by the smell. She was cooking, after all.

"There's a loo by the porter's office, by the entrance."

"Whatever."

He muttered something else, but Kesta couldn't make it out.

She steered the parcel into the flat with her foot. Then she locked the front door. She went into the living room and peeked through the curtains, which were always closed, in time to see the deliveryman walking out into the courtyard. Either he could piss like lightning, or he hadn't used the toilet downstairs at all. Kesta pulled the curtains snugly together. The living room looked more and more like the stockroom at the hospital. Boxes everywhere; little pieces of folded paper, instruction leaflets scattered like confetti. Underneath them dust, fluff, dirt. She should clean. But today, she had decided to cook, and there wasn't time for both. She took a pair of kitchen scissors and went back to inspect the package.

"Darling," she said, walking into Tim's room proudly carrying the box, "I have a present for you." She stabbed her way through the top, slicing it open from end to end.

It was a new record player. Tim's original turntable had been bought at a vintage store on Charing Cross Road. It had been Tim's pride and joy. Music was the one area where Tim had been an unabashed nerd, taking his knowledge of musical history to an almost obsessive degree. The only time Jess ever tried to shut Tim up was when he was in midflow, lecturing—though he would say educating—his dinner guests on the finer points of Vyto B's seminal seventies album *Tricentennial 2076*.

"Oh Tim, not *Psychedelic Percussion* again!" she would cry, and Kesta would laugh until she felt sick, watching her otherwise debonair husband embarrassing himself in defense of his weird musical tastes.

"You'll like Hal Blaine eventually, Jess. Everybody does," he'd say, ignoring Jess's wails of protest, winking at Kesta, and putting the record on for the third time. "Just give in to it."

His music had died along with the turntable. Early one morning at the start of the outbreak, one of the infected had managed to get into the warehouse courtyard. She was wandering around vacantly until a man walked out of his flat and, not having seen her because he was busy reading his phone, walked right into her. The scream he let loose, which was earsplitting and terribly close to her face, rather set her off. She grabbed him with both hands and opened her mouth wider than seemed humanly possible, which only made the man scream louder. The turntable was the first thing Tim had grabbed, ripping it away from the side table, lobbing it out through the balcony doors, watching in amazement as it smashed into the woman's head, stunning her enough to set the man free. Tim had mourned the loss of that turntable as he would a close relative. Kesta had promised that when all this was over, she would buy him a new one.

Kesta missed Tim's music terribly. In the middle of the night, she'd woken to that cotton wool throb, the diegetic sound of low-level electricity humming in the walls, sound defined by the absence of human noise. She realized then that this was almost always how it was for Tim—muted and lifeless and ongoing. That she made Tim lie there, all day every day for months on end, with nothing but silence for company. That same night she'd ordered a replacement turntable online, and now finally it had arrived.

She set it up on the bedside table, shoveling boxes of drugs and other sundries into the drawer to make room. Yellow eyes focused, tracking her as she moved in and out of the bedroom carrying stacks of records, setting them on the edge of the bed. He watched as she brought in a candlestick, flinched at the flame she created out of thin air—she would take this as a positive sign that he was able to remember the birthday cake incident—sniffing as the smoke wafted over his bed.

He tried to lift himself up. He looked woozy, forgetting how things worked, things like arms and legs. When Kesta saw him struggling, she used the pillows behind him and padded them deep around his waist to prop him up in a sitting position. If Tim could have, he might have noticed that she was wearing a little black dress, her arms bare and her brown fringe brushed straight, less like a nest.

"I know that things are . . . different now, but we're going to celebrate our anniversary in spite of them," she said with a bright smile, her face glowing amber in the candlelight. "Got to keep the spark alive, if nothing else."

A nerve twitched under her eye. She'd already had a glass of wine while she'd been struggling to cook. She plastered the smile back on again. "We're going to have dinner together. And we're going to play your records."

Kesta positioned one of their dining chairs close to the bed. A bottle of red wine and two glasses, one of which was plastic and had been retrieved from their old picnic basket hidden at the back of the boiler room. She poured wine for the both of them, punctuating her actions with glances up at her husband, checking he was okay, hoping some part of him felt her affection. She always looked, even now, to Tim for reassurance. She wanted to ask him what he thought of her dress, if she looked nice in it, but since she'd had it for years and he'd seen her in it before in their old life and liked it then, that had to be enough for her.

Tim sat sedated against the pillows, staring at his wife. He looked down at the handcuffs holding his arm in place against the radiator. Every day they were a surprise to him. Every day he would lift the arm and wonder why it got stuck halfway up. Kesta had to dart into the kitchen, blinking frantically, because she didn't want to spoil this evening by getting upset.

Rome would definitely have been better. Rome was what Tim deserved. He did not deserve this. *Why couldn't only absolute bastards have been turned into zombies? Why hadn't nature designed a more discriminating virus?*

Kesta composed herself and returned with a tray she placed on the floor beside the chair. There were two deep dishes on it—one filled with spaghetti Bolognese dusted with Parmesan, the other with the sauce without spaghetti. She had slaved over it all day since she wasn't a natural cook and because she wanted it to be good and for him to enjoy it, if that was even possible. She lifted the tray onto her knees, which quivered under its weight, a table for two at the best worst restaurant in the world.

"I'm probably not supposed to give you this, but what the hell, you shouldn't have to lose everything in life, should you, just because you're—" She stopped herself and tapped the glasses together dully.

"Cheers, darling. Happy anniversary."

She helped Tim cup his plastic glass and watched as he breathed it in, over and over, refusing to commit to it, curious and unafraid, but guarded, wary, looking up at her, sniffing, not sure what it was that he was meant to do or what she expected from him.

"Like this, remember," she said, sipping her wine. "Mmm."

"Mmmph." Tim dove his tongue into the glass and began to swirl it around, a whisk made of flesh, lapping frantically.

"Steady on," she said, giggling. She set her own glass down on the stand and tugged at the plastic stem of Tim's, feeling him gripping it harder in return. Much of the wine ended up on the bedsheets, some was dripping slowly down his lopsided chin, but the glass itself was empty.

"Let me get that for you," said Kesta, dabbing around his lips with a paper napkin. He let her do it without complaint, and she liked that. It felt intimate and, for the first time in a long while, it felt normal. It wasn't medicalized. Even with his beautiful face so changed, even with his hair whitened through the roots, even though the stench of ammonia had burned through the oranges, jasmine, and bergamot that had always flourished underneath his skin, she knew she loved him more than anyone could ever love anyone for all time. Love is a wound from which you can never heal. She knew that he'd be the death of her eventually, but that it would be a happy death just the same.

Kesta ate quickly, as she always did, talking through her food.

Tim was upright in bed, covered in deep stains, watching her vacantly as they listened to Sam Cooke. She ate until she wanted to feed him too, taking her place on the edge of the bed, his hand in the handcuffs nestled inside her lap. She brought a spoonful of the Bolognese sauce up to his mouth, and this time he didn't sniff it. This time he trusted her completely, flicking out his tongue until it struck the underside of the spoon, making her lower it a little, so that the next time the tongue found the food and he drew the spoon into his mouth. He sucked at it, enamel crunching metal, gnawing at it like a baby with new teeth coming in. He couldn't chew, wasn't practiced at eating this way after months of meal replacements. But he took the spoon and ate the sauce his wife had spent ages cooking. Looking at Tim, even now, trying his best to eat for her, she felt the sense of belonging she had always known since the night they'd met. She cherished him.

"You used to love these old records," Kesta said, sifting through the old 45s at the end of the bed. They smelled musty, little puffs of dust ascending as she turned them over in her hands to read the sleeve notes, the edges of which were paper-thin, the colored covers fading to brown skin within. She wanted to help him remember what it felt like to be human. If she could trigger a response to the music, awaken something underneath the surface lying dormant in him, perhaps she could help him remember her. To remember them, together.

"How about Mable John? You used to love her."

Kesta slipped the vinyl out and held it up closer to the candle, looking for scratches on the surface in the light, faults that might make the music skip. The grooves were almost imperceptible, like ripples on a black lake. The record was flawless. She laid it down gently on the turntable, lifted the tone arm, and watched as the record came to life, spinning around and around without sound. Carefully, she placed the stylus on the vinyl and heard it crackle and the music begin.

"Let me go . . ."

She watched as Tim turned his face toward the record player. It seemed to her that each lyric and every note was stirring something in him, a memory, an image, the sense of who he was, of who they had been, flickering behind those yellow eyes.

"Do you remember us?" she asked him, sitting down to better see if he was moved by the music. She watched his free hand's fingers—expressive, uplifted, conducting something deep within, a physical remembrance.

"Uh-uh-uh," he said, as though he were singing.

Kesta's throat constricted. She blinked away the tears. She didn't want to ruin this moment. So she sat back and drank her wine and watched as her husband lived, just a little, from the confines of the bed, dancing with his fingertips. It was bliss.

"People are going to think you've been so brave, you know," she said, "because you have been, darling. Because you are. So much braver than me."

He seemed calm tonight, as though the vibrations of the music were working the virus out of his system, like tight knots in soothed muscles. There was something in his countenance, in how the sharp angles of his body had softened in the low light, that made her want to touch him, to be warmed by him, to feel him towering above her, sheltering her from the evils of the world. She wanted to know what love felt like again.

As Mabel John sang "Say You'll Never Let Me Go," Kesta unfastened the handcuff and laid it on the bed. Tim drew his hand sluggishly toward his face, seeing but not understanding why it was blistered and mottled with dark purple bruises. Kesta's hand was outstretched in front of her. Looking curiously at his own hand and then at hers, Tim mimicked her, reaching out into the space between them. What did he feel, Kesta wondered, as she pressed his hand lovingly against her cheek.

"We'll take it nice and easy," she said, taking both hands now and bending her knees so that he did the same. "And up," she said, watching him wobble, using her thighs to steady them both, him so tall and fragile, the limbs too long, the head heavy on an uncertain neck.

"I've got you; I've got us both," she said, moving one hand around his waist until they were standing upright on their own feet, anchored to each other, hand in hand, arm around the other's waist. She trusted

Tim not to bite her because she had to believe he still knew who she was. If he didn't, that would be an unimaginable horror. For both of them.

"Am I doing the right thing? With you?" she said, and she began to sway, barely, from side to side, shuffling just as he did, shuffling because it was all he could do.

"I'm worried about what they're doing at Project Dawn. I wish I had you to talk to about it. Tim, I don't know what I'm supposed to do. Something bad is going to happen. I just know it."

Kesta drew closer and laid her head against her husband's chest. She closed her eyes and tried to ignore the rattling in his lungs. His heart murmured. She tried not to think about that sound, the sound of struggle, of failure, as Tim's blood forced itself roughly through valves that, by rights, should have already collapsed.

"I'd do anything for you, Tim. You know that. Don't you? Anything." Kesta concentrated on the little life left inside him, on those vital signs. Her hands clasped in his, their bodies fused together, swaying to the music. So much like it had always been, just the two of them in love, and yet so very far away from what they'd ever meant by *until death*.

CHAPTER ELEVEN

Kesta watched as the security guard rifled through her bag, looking but not really looking, just wanting the day to be over so that he didn't have to touch other people's personal effects for a few hours. Outside on the Strand, Dudley was reaching into his old wax jacket for a packet of cigarettes. She'd told him she needed to speak to him urgently. She'd left voicemails and sent texts, and now it was Wednesday evening and he'd finally given in to her demands.

"I thought you gave up smoking?" she asked.

"I did," Dudley said, exhaling with pleasure, "and then there was a zombie apocalypse, so I took it back up again."

"I'm the same with wine," Kesta said, laughing. "Though I've just carried on drinking it continuously for the past twenty years."

"When was the last time you had a drink?"

Dudley walked with the cigarette between his teeth. Kesta thought that could be dangerous, knowing Dudley as she did.

"Last night," she replied.

"Oh, so nothing in the daytime?"

"Well, no, not when I'm at work."

"Well, you can't be an alcoholic then."

As they crossed over to Fleet Street, Kesta suddenly remembered her ZARG meeting.

Shit. How long had it been since she'd attended? Weeks? No, months? Definitely months. She'd lost track.

Since no one had mentioned it, she could only assume that no one had missed her. Dudley was talking about how and when he would try to stop smoking for the second time, when Kesta saw a man on his own outside the High Court building. He seemed to be waiting for someone. Kesta thought she recognized him. He had a beaten-up canvas messenger bag slung across his shoulder, like a deadweight. He locked eyes with her, and for a second she thought he was going to say something. She hugged in close to Dudley, who threaded an arm through hers, as if she might be chilly. Kesta glanced over her shoulder. The man with the bag was following them. A few steps farther, Dudley mulling over whether medication with cessation counseling was preferable to going cold turkey, and still the man was walking quickly behind them. Kesta didn't like it.

"Hang on," she said, before coming to a stop in the middle of the pavement. She turned and looked at the stranger behind them.

"What's the matter?" asked Dudley. Now he saw the man too because, like them, the man was standing stock-still on Fleet Street. They stared at each other. Dudley tightened his grip on Kesta's arm. But before she could say anything, the stranger darted into the road. A passing bus blasted its horn and the man had to sprint to avoid being hit, his messenger bag slamming over and over into his legs. He disappeared down an alley toward the Inns of Court. Kesta shuddered.

"I thought that guy was following us," she said. "He seemed familiar. Did you recognize him?"

"Nope," said Dudley, taking a final drag, "but it was weird. He did seem to want to say something. Come on. We both really need a drink now."

He flicked the cigarette butt off into the gutter, almost aloof. Gone were Dudley's persecution complex and the anal perfectionism he'd always carted around at work—or perhaps that was just the effects of the nicotine.

They had worked together for nine years, but this was the first time they'd done this, gone for a walk together, to a pub together, looking something like friends. Kesta had to find out more about what Dudley was working on at Project Dawn, to see if Cooke's suspicions about the Gain-of-Function research were right. She felt a little guilty, dragging him out like this under somewhat false pretenses.

"Do you remember that pathologist who used to work with us?" Dudley asked, interrupting her guilty thoughts. "Stevens? The one with the beard?"

He was trying, sweetly, to distract Kesta from thinking about the man with the messenger bag. She frowned.

"Well, there was a rumor he drank the embalming fluid in the mortuary. He was steaming most of the time, but he could do a great postmortem even fully loaded."

"That cannot be true, but if it is, it's just sad," she said.

"Sadder still, he kept his vodka in the freezers."

"With the bodies?"

"With the bodies."

"Perhaps he liked a Corpse Reviver," Kesta sniggered.

"A what?"

"Sorry, it's a cocktail."

"You would know, I suppose."

"More than you could imagine," she whispered.

The pub was down a side street near St. Paul's Cathedral. It was one of Dudley's favorites, or so he told her. It was much less spit and sawdust than she'd imagined. It had retained its Victorian leather booths, tucked away in discreet nooks and corners. There were original glass partitions to separate the drinkers, and the wooden floor looked stripped straight from the belly of a galleon. It was cozy and unassuming, and very Dudley. At the back of the pub, there was a pool table and a television above it playing silently. Two men standing on their own by the bar raised their glasses toward Dudley. They were the only other patrons in the place. The landlord beamed and stretched himself over the counter to pull Dudley in for a handshake, then a hug.

"Nice to have you back, mate."

"Good to see you, Ollie," said Dudley, blushing.

"You really are a regular here," Kesta said.

But Dudley was caught up in a whirlwind of backslapping and banter, so she wandered away toward the far side of the pub, to a table by the door. She watched them as they huddled together and wondered if they knew what Dudley did for a living. He was a brilliant pathologist, but he was shy and modest. He wouldn't brag about his accomplishments. He would keep Project Dawn's secrets. Kesta quickly checked the app on her phone and saw that Tim was lying motionless in the bed, though she could just make out the mellow rise and fall of his chest as he breathed.

"I did ask for their most enormous serving."

Dudley had returned with a drab brown pint and a serving of Merlot poured painfully up to the brim of an insufficiently sized glass for Kesta.

"Nebuchadnezzar with straw not optional, regrettably," Dudley chuckled.

"Looks like they had a good stab at it, though," she said. She had to laugh, wondering how Dudley, klutz that he was, had managed to breeze across the pub's buckled floorboards without spilling a drop.

"Good health," he said.

"Good health," she replied, and they drank.

Two more men arrived and waved toward Dudley as they walked through the pub to the pool table. The landlord fixed their drinks while they began racking up the triangle and dusting the ends of cream-colored cues with chalk. They kept looking over. Kesta wondered if this was the first time they'd seen Dudley with a woman.

"So, how are you?" he asked her, running a spare beer mat through his fingers.

"All right," she replied. "The work is interesting. But it all feels very slow. And I had expected to see you more around the lab."

Dudley didn't answer. Now that they were seated, he seemed wooden and vacant, like one of those dummies you practice CPR on. Kesta sensed that they were about to have a very difficult conversation.

"Are you all right, Dudley?" she asked him gently. "It's just that I've hardly seen you at the lab, and on the rare occasions I have, you seem . . . preoccupied."

He worked at the beer mat with his fingers, tracing its edges, rotating it, turning it over from side to side, searching for an answer. His nails were bitten to the quick.

"Will you humor me for a bit?" he asked, his mouth downturned. "I need a few drinks first." As he finally met and held her gaze, Kesta saw that he meant it. He was fearful. She nodded.

"Why have you never gone for a promotion?" he asked, trying to make idle conversation.

"To pathologist, you mean?"

"Yes," he said. "I mean, you're just as qualified as me, really. You could do my job standing on your head. You could be running multiple sites across London. Be the one in charge."

"What, like Lundeen?"

"Bloody hell, no, what an arse he is." Dudley shook his head.

"I don't want to be in charge," she said, shrugging. "I've never wanted to be in charge. I'm best looking down a microscope. I can control what happens between the slides and the living. I can see everything clearly that way. It's the most confident I ever get to feel."

"But your talents, they're wasted."

"How can I be wasted in screening? If I'm diagnosing people correctly, I'm helping to save lives. And what about you, Dr. Caring?" she teased, realizing that in all the years they had worked together, she had never pressed him on it before, never really taken an interest on a human level in how he'd lived his life before they'd met.

"How did you end up here? I've always thought you seemed more like a research scientist. You're made for Project Dawn."

She mock-whispered the last bit, and it made Dudley smile momentarily, before his smile was dislodged by a painful memory, judging by the way it tugged at the muscles around his mouth and between his eyebrows. He coughed and shuffled in his seat.

"You're right. I do love this kind of work," he said. "It's been extraordinary these past months. Everything feels so heightened, so vital. Even though it's not"—he stopped himself, the beer mat fraying at the edges—"what I expected." He drained his glass. "I'm a researcher by heart, a pathologist by circumstance."

"How do you mean?"

"It was all taken care of, you see," he said.

Dudley was telling the story to her, but he was talking to someone else, someone to whom he somehow felt the need to justify his choices. Someone on his mind, from his past.

"I actually worked at Porton Down for a bit, in my twenties. I felt invincible. The work we were doing there was so cutting-edge. Then I was asked to head up a team out in the Far East. I was going to be the lead scientist. I was only thirty. SARS was a big thing back then. We were all going crazy over mutations. The lab I worked for was—unorthodox."

Kesta felt her blood chill and the shiver of an entity cross her grave.

"Go on," she said, covering her mouth with her fingers to hide her mounting horror.

"Kesta. I've never told anyone this before. But"—his voice faltered, he sipped his beer, tried to pull himself together—"but I don't want to have any secrets from you."

Her chest tightened, a guilty pain inside the space between her ribs.

"I was—we were—I'm one of the few scientists working in London who can lay claim to having experience in—undertaking Gain-of-Function research. In playing God like that."

Kesta had no idea what to say. Dudley looked like a broken man. She leaned in across the table and listened.

"It was—dangerous, what we were doing. It's like putting your own hands over His, to create, to redesign. We had a few near misses. But it was everything I'd ever dreamed of, professionally. At the time, anyway."

He gazed across the pub, his eyes on the two men ambling around the pool table, innocently lining up their next shot.

"But then my mother got sick and I had to come home. You can't pause time, unfortunately, and my time passed me by. I lost my confidence after that and, well . . ."

"What happened to your mum?"

"She died in the end. But I was with her. That was what mattered most."

"Dudley, I'm so sorry," Kesta said. "Why didn't you go back out there afterward?"

He paused for a long time.

"Because with my mum, I understood that there came a point when I had to let her go," he said, sliding the beer mat away from him to the other side of the table. "Because it was the natural order of things. It made me understand that there are limits to what science can and should be doing. That it shouldn't interfere with that natural order. I knew I wanted to work with patients, not pathogens. I didn't want to hide out in a lab, waiting for a Nobel Prize. I wanted to help people, not hurt them. We work in a fatal industry, you and I. We go through the elaborate motions of holding people in a suspended reality for as long as we possibly can. But in the end—"

"In the end there is an end," she said, and the two of them sat quietly for a while and watched as the other patrons drank merrily and played pool poorly, without a care in the world.

"It's what they're really doing at Project Dawn, isn't it?"

There were tears in Dudley's eyes, his jaw set with sadness and resignation.

"It's why I was recruited," he said, "because I'd done it before."

"What was the work you were doing at the other laboratory?"

"We were gamifying respiratory diseases."

"To what end?"

"To make them more transmissible," he whispered, "and to give them a perfect kill rate. The strain we manufactured in the lab was fatal in all cases."

"But Gain-of-Function research is banned here?"

"That's why Project Dawn is cut off from the other biological sites.

Everything has been designed to allow them to manufacture the virus at will, without scrutiny or oversight getting in the way."

Kesta tried to swallow but she couldn't. The sensation of gagging, of drowning without water, of silently choking to death. Her throat was closing. She couldn't breathe, could feel her face straining and reddening, flashes of lightning, Dudley's doomsday prophecy playing in the background. *They want to make the virus* stronger *so that it spreads even faster, to weaponize it.* A terrible pressure was building in her ears, and the pixilation of abrupt unconsciousness broke across her eyes. She tried to blink it away. *They want to see what the virus is capable of.*

"Kesta, you need to keep breathing," she heard him say. "You've gone a really funny color."

She heaved the air inside her in long, deep breaths. She closed her eyes to stop the room from spinning. She didn't want to faint, not now. She needed to understand what was happening. She needed to know what to do. She felt Dudley's hand holding hers, and it felt like ice because Kesta was on fire.

"You should have told me." She wheezed, eyes streaming.

"I'm telling you now," he said, "because it was me who triggered the alarm. I was handling a sample of infected tissue, and I thought I could see a tear in my glove. I imagined it. My mind was playing tricks on me, but in the moment, I was convinced I'd broken the seal, that I'd touched the sample directly. So I pressed the alarm button in the lab. They kept me shut inside for three hours until they were satisfied that I'd made a mistake. Lundeen was furious."

Kesta was woozy with shock. Cooke was right. Project Dawn didn't care about a cure. Project Dawn didn't care about saving Tim's life. She withdrew her hand from his, wiped it down the leg of her jeans. Dudley brought her some water.

"Kesta," he said, "you have to believe me when I tell you that I would never, never have brought you into Project Dawn if I'd known the truth." It was only now that they were on their own, face-to-face, that Kesta saw the toll that the job was taking on her colleague. How much thinner

Dudley's hair appeared, how sunken his eyes and cheeks were, a little less alive, a livid rash beneath his chin from where he'd raced to shave each day. "I would never have put you through this, not after everything you've been through. Not after Tim."

To hear her husband's name evoked by another was eerie and surreal. It held a supernatural power over her. It brought her, quite suddenly, to tears.

"Oh Kesta . . ."

"No, no, I'm fine," she said, smearing under her eyes with the back of her hand, sniffing. "But Dudley, we need to have a plan. We have to find the cure."

"I know," he said, "and I do have something else to tell you."

Kesta held her breath.

"We've isolated the virus."

Kesta gasped. The virus was extracted from sample tissues and cultured to make it as pure as possible, allowing it to be reproduced and tested en masse.

"Oh Dudley, that's incredible. When can we start trialing it?"

"I have Lundeen's permission to inject a case group of primates as early as tomorrow. I've requested your assistance. I want you with me on this."

She could almost have kissed him.

"Dudley, the cure, it's more important now than ever, especially if what you're saying is true and they want to create a version of the virus that's even more potent."

"I know, I know," he said softly, trying to placate her. "And we will. We have to because it's the right thing to do. We have to give them what was promised. We have to give people hope."

"Do you really believe that?" she asked.

"I have to believe it, Kesta. And you should too. Look, we have to be able to trust each other. You do what you can at your end trying to find out what caused the virus in the first place. I will make sure to share my findings with you too. We'll work on this together."

The wine and the stress were exhausting. Kesta wanted desperately to go home and tell Tim about everything that had happened. But seeing Dudley so agonized by their work, she knew she couldn't bail on him, not now, not after he'd confided in her and shown her so much trust. So, she bought them another round, partly for him and partly for her, to help assuage the guilt inside. No matter what she told Dudley, it would never be the whole truth.

"I always liked Tim," he said as she put a fresh pint in front of him. "He was very lucky, you know."

"To get bitten by a zombie?"

"To have had your love all those years. He was a lucky, lucky man there." He accidentally kicked their table. He was tipsy. Kesta steadied their drinks. "How long were you together?"

"Nineteen years. Doesn't seem very long now."

"Nineteen years is a lot of love, Kesta. Especially if you think about those of us who never find it. I'm alone, and I'm fifteen years off retirement."

He looked crestfallen, half smiling at the table, regretting what he'd said, thinking himself foolish. Kesta didn't know how to help him; she had never felt alone because even now, she still had Tim. Just. She felt greedy for the way their love had always left her wanting more.

"Well," she sighed, "you were never going to find a suitable woman in the mortuary. Unless of course a pulse isn't a prerequisite?"

To her relief, Dudley laughed.

"I'm pleased we've cleared the air," he said. "I feel better already. I hope you feel you can talk to me too."

"Of course I do, Dudley."

"Really?" His smile disappeared. "Because I want you to. Tell me stuff. I don't want there to be any secrets between us."

Kesta put her wine down on the table.

"I don't have any secrets, Dudley," she lied, knees juddering under the table.

"Are you sure about that?"

He was setting a trap for her, wasn't he? What was it he thought he knew? Little ripples broke across the surface of her drink, as though a giant ogre was thundering toward her. And the softness had vanished in his face.

"Dudley?"

A pain in her chest, deep in the muscle, was gnawing at her ribs. Dudley opened his mouth to speak. Then he closed it. He frowned and shook his head.

"I saw you. At the hospital. Carrying a lot of bags. I saw you talking to Claire. What on earth were you doing?"

Kesta couldn't form the right lie quickly enough. She needed something that Dudley would find plausible. She needed something he'd respect, something to make him back off. *Unless he knows?*

Unless he'd seen what she was carrying. Or spoken to Claire. If Claire had told him about the syringes she had found. She was panicking, her mind racing. Then the right lie crystallized in her mind, and Kesta found her voice again.

"I have a microscope at home." She couldn't stand to look at him. It was a dreadful lie, intended to exploit his pity. Worst of all his admiration. One lie to cover up another.

Dudley looked contrite and then, worse still, guilty for having questioned her.

"I've been doing extra screening in the evenings," she lied some more. "I cleared it with Lundeen." Shit, that was a lie too far, one he could possibly check, so she added one that was worse. "I'm afraid I need the extra money," and then the worst one of all, she invoked her widow's privilege.

"I get lonely in the evenings."

"God, Kesta, I had no idea. You're sure you're not taking too much on?"

"No, not at all. It helps to keep me busy. Sorry, Dudley, I should have told you."

It mattered to Kesta that he believed her. She had to keep him on her side. So, she did a terrible thing because it seemed like the right thing to do at the time to get him over this uncomfortable bump in the road. She reached across the table and took his hand.

"Fancy another drink?" She smiled, though inside she felt a bit sick. Dudley put his hand on top of hers, so that she became the filling in the world's most awkward sandwich.

"Yes, I'd really like that," he said, squeezing back.

CHAPTER TWELVE

I t knew that something terrible was coming. Humans in hazmats always spelled terror. It shrank away from her in its cage, raising its little hands up to its face. If the monkey couldn't see her, then maybe she'd disappear altogether. Perhaps this was Tim's view of her now. That if he could only close his eyes she'd go away.

Kesta had cut up a lot of mice in her time. Guinea pigs too. But never while they were alive. Her specimens had always arrived gift wrapped by death, euthanized by someone whose job it was to exterminate rodents and other mammals for a living so that scientists like her could wade through their entrails looking for something like victory. Occasionally, she'd gassed the rodents herself, lifting fluffy corpses out of their chambers, her only real concern mathematical, mechanical, that the limp remains might reanimate once she was a scalpel blade inside them.

Kesta wasn't squeamish and she wasn't sentimental. Not until she saw this monkey, the scent of its fear palpable in the triple-filtered air in the laboratory, did she feel a pang of guilt snag at her guts. She had graduated from mice to guinea pigs, and now she was staring down at something 93 percent of herself. Something that had spent its entire life in captivity but that possessed the self-awareness to groom itself when handed a mirror.

She decided to call the monkey Liv.

"It's okay." Kesta tried to sound reassuring as she snapped the clamp shut around Liv's neck to hold her in position, feeling her straining, panicking, then slumping in resignation, the little hands smearing against the clamp, leaving behind the essence of futility. Even in thick gloves, there was a risk the monkey would scratch or bite, and the clamp helped to restrain her for as long as Kesta required. Without warning, her own throat closed up, obstructed by an overwhelming urge to cry. It was just as she'd restrained Tim by the wrist. There wasn't really any difference when she thought about it honestly.

Liv's limbs scraped at the cage, bracing and pushing against the metal, leaving imprints in her fur, the way that Tim thrashed about in the bed, arms scratching at thin air, skin tarnished by the struggle. Her teeth bared noiselessly, Liv submitted to Kesta with the same stoicism Tim showed, her eyes burning into the ceiling, lips stretched back. Liv tucked her tail in shame between her legs as Kesta injected her with the live virus Dudley had isolated from zombie flesh and cultured in the lab, the pure virus he'd lobbied Lundeen for permission for Kesta to use so that she could study it in a live host mammal. Liv didn't whimper, but her face grimaced in pain just the way a human's would, a human trying hard to be brave. Kesta disposed of the syringe, removed the clamp from the monkey's neck, and stood back to watch.

At first, nothing happened. Liv sat panting in her cage, wiping her pink face with her hands, tufted eyebrows cleaving accusingly at Kesta, her rib cage gasping in and out. Then her shoulders dropped, and she began to relax. Just an injection, nothing so bad about that. Nothing the monkey wasn't used to by now in her grim little life. As if to rid herself of any human contamination, though it may have been self-comforting, Liv began to groom, dabbing her armpits with wiry hands, fingers tugging at loose fur, as if she'd forgotten all about the neck clamp. She looked at Kesta only if she moved and startled her, so Kesta decided to pull up a chair. This could take a while. Liv tilted her head and yawned.

Then some ethereal surprise made Liv leap into the air. She turned around to see what it was that had made her jump, the febrile hairs around her nose feeling forward for a foreign smell and finding nothing, she tried to resume her washing. Then an impulse to run overtook her and she began to pulse about on all fours, smashing into the wire walls, racing round and round like a puppy. She was noisy now, screeching and gurning, panicked by the sensations charging through her body, of the other entity replicating on the inside. She scratched and scratched, furiously trying to dig it out, yelping, not through pain it seemed but bewilderment. Then she gripped onto the bars of the cage and wailed at her captor, her tongue curled back in her red mouth, the eye teeth dripping.

Liv's eyes darkened as blood started to pool around the rims. She panted for breath, smearing the blood around her face, blinking and wiping and yelping. It was the same expression Kesta had seen on Tim's face as he stood there in the lounge, dripping with blood, while she figured out what to do next. It was the powerlessness of the patient whose brain was shutting down without their permission. Liv's movements were labored, one arm hanging down beside her, the other hovering in the air, reaching out to nothing, having forgotten its intention. With another pant for breath her jaw slipped down, exposing a miniature row of tombstone teeth. Blood and saliva were oozing out of her eyes and mouth now, her breathing shallow and erratic as if she were slowly turning to stone.

Liv slumped to the floor of the cage, jaw broken, blood-soaked, her internal electricity emitting a final spark of life as a single fingernail scraped helplessly against the cage door.

Kesta was just able to squeeze her gloved hand inside the cage, to stroke along the soft down of Liv's chest and her arms, still warm and silken. She felt her take her last breath just as she had with Tim, holding his hand, feeling him disappearing into the ether, leaving behind a perfect shell.

One hundred and twenty seconds after the injection, Liv was dead. Kesta returned to her chair and waited.

One moment you were alive, a moment later not, the time in between imperceptible. Death never arrived; it only ever departed. The body was abandoned, the gift of life stolen forever. Kesta's eyes welled with tears. She couldn't take her mask off to wipe them away, so she closed her eyes tightly. When she did so, Tim was always there. As he had been. So very full of life. When she finally opened them, two yellow pinholes targeted her from across the room.

Liv was sitting upright in her cage, and even though she had expected it, Kesta jumped out of her seat. Liv let out a deep sigh that parted the fur across her chest like a strong wind flattening its way through a cornfield.

"Welcome back, Liv," Kesta said. She walked over to the cage. As she did so, Liv's mouth yawned wide, and her little fingers tried to slice their way through the bars. She was drooling, eager to bite.

They would need to monitor Liv for twenty-four hours before taking a blood sample to compare the virus microscopically against the zombie samples she and Cooke had been preparing. They would compare the virus in animal and human host, looking for similarities, antibodies, inflammation, anything that could influence their research positively and ultimately lead toward a cure.

The door to the lab puffed open and another hazmat entered the frame.

"How's she doing?" asked Dudley, squeaking as he squatted down next to the cage to look at the rhesus. Liv squealed, straining to reach him, so he and Kesta retreated to a corner of the room.

"She's infected," said Kesta. "She died for a bit and then came back to life again. Same as in the humans, although the process was accelerated." They watched as Liv swayed gently as though she was overcome by sleep, now that the opportunity to bite them had been removed.

"Are the physical symptoms manifesting in the same way?"

"Exactly the same—the temporomandibular joint dislocation, the head tilting backward, the hemorrhaging, the twisting in the limbs. The ocular jaundice."

"Poor little blighter," he said, stepping gingerly toward the cage. Liv curled her delicate fingers into tiny fists, and she began to pant.

"We've been given the green light to roll out the primate testing from Monday. I've made it clear to Lundeen that we have to push forward with at least finding treatment options for this virus, if not a complete cure."

"Is there anything else I can be doing?" she asked, watching Liv with a peculiar maternal pride.

"Don't get attached to that monkey," he said.

"Would I?" she cooed.

"Yes. You would. Anyway, she's your responsibility now, Kesta."

"She's called Liv," she said, and Dudley rolled his eyes. "Anything else, Dr. Caring?"

"Oh, I don't know, nothing much, maybe just find the origin of this sodding virus," he said flippantly. "We need to know where it's come from, what was mutated to create it, or, God forbid, whether it spontaneously developed out of thin air."

"I'm treating myself to a trip to the Royal Scientific Library tomorrow," she said, "and I'm not leaving there until I do."

CHAPTER THIRTEEN

Friday arrived. Kesta had worked late the night before, reluctant to leave her furry charge in someone else's care. If she hadn't had Tim to worry about, she'd have asked to sleep at the lab, to keep a closer eye on Liv. But she did have Tim to worry about. And Dudley, anticipating her tendency to overcommit to things, had encouraged her to go home.

She'd scraped together a few hours of sleep. She hadn't had any alcohol. For Kesta, that breezy Friday morning, she almost felt refreshed, but then her baseline was pretty awful to begin with. It was her first proper day off since she'd joined Project Dawn, and being away from it, away from Professor Lundeen, and outside during daylight hours inhaling deep breaths of air and not formaldehyde was invigorating.

Normal women would have spent their annual leave having brunch with an old friend. But not Kesta. She had work to do. She would spend her day researching animal pathogens at the library before having dinner with Cooke to discuss her findings.

The more that Jess begged to see her, even just to take her calls, the more Kesta felt inclined to freeze her out. It was easier to lie to Cooke, whereas Jess's familiarity made her feel scrutinized and hounded. She didn't have the energy to keep pretending all the time, and with Jess, she was required to fake it most of all. The more she ghosted Jess, the worse she felt about it. It was a cruel and vicious cycle, oddly masochistic, really.

But it was easier being with Cooke because they had more in common, things Jess couldn't relate to, like the unbearable physical pain of grief owing to two dead husbands, one more dead than the other. Kesta stopped to lean against the library wall to finish her coffee. She lifted her face up to the sun. A normal feeling. It was nice.

It was dark inside the library, and it smelled not of chemicals but of time passing. The shelves reeked of oily leather, dusty parchment, and glue made from horses. The air between the shelves was hazy, as though the fingertip skin shed by a thousand readers over a hundred years had been left behind. Tables stretched out like mortuary slabs, lit poorly by green lamps, around which lonely readers could browse through books that looked embalmed, not bound. *Pathology, Histology, Biology, Infectious Diseases* read the signs at the tail end of each aisle. Kesta ventured deeper inside the library, passing antiquarian tomes, precious items laid out like specimens in glass chambers, where you looked but could never touch. First editions, medieval texts on bloodletting, on pestilence.

The library was a tribute to the rigors of the human mind. It told the story of adventures in science. It was also a mournful reminder of all that mankind had endured since the first caveman caught a cold and died from it, whenever that was.

On the other side of history, Kesta walked through into a large room divided geographically, with books specific to the diseases of Europe, of the Americas, the Indian Ocean. Finally, there and smaller than she had expected, given its unique biological makeup, Madagascar. Kesta thought she might as well work alphabetically, so she began at the beginning.

African tick bite fever. Rickettsia africae. Dozens of imperfect violet circles, some singular, others overlapping. The histological slides were basic and sixty years old. She turned the page to images of coin-sized bites oozing on the legs of children, an adult's hands spreading the wounds wide for the photographer. There were other pictures of ticks nesting alongside the crevices of animal hooves. Bubonic plague, little bugs, stained pink and blue, some roughly circular, the others tight and ridged with legs poking out from either side, like fluorescent wood lice. Dengue fever, spread by biting.

It's always biting, she thought. *There's something horribly intimate about that, the kiss of death even if the thing kissing you has six eyes and wings.*

Later, hantavirus, spread by rodents running riot, biting everyone in sight. Hantavirus is airborne, so you risk getting it if you inhale their excrement or urine. *Seriously*, Kesta thought, *who is going around huffing mouse shit, and to check for what exactly?*

None of the human histological slides looked anything like her zombie cell samples. Hours spent poring through tome after tome, and she'd come up empty. She was about to head back to the front desk to ask the librarian for his advice when something in the distance caught her eye. A book on veterinary pathology. The study of disease and viruses in animals. It was worth a look.

Inside the darkest room in the library, only slips of light broke in through two narrow, horizontal windows high up by the ceiling. Two leather stools sat on either side of a circular mahogany table. Kesta felt around its edges for the light switch, clicking on a green lamp to illuminate an emerald pool across the surface. She saw that the dust hung even more gloomily in the air here, thick enough to make her cough. She wondered if the windows had ever been opened. The shelves inside the room were densely packed, like battery hens, standing shoulder to shoulder, without air or light or warmth. She picked up the first book she could find and perched on a stool, watching her hands turn green, then gray-pink again in the lamp light. She was sitting at a card table chasing the ace of spades, a dealer playing tricks without the full deck to hand.

She learned the names of viruses and infections she'd never heard of before. African horse sickness, camel pox, ovine pulmonary adenocarcinoma. Familiar ones too. Foot-and-mouth disease, retroviruses affecting sheep and goats. The West Nile virus. Lyme disease. A litany of mischiefs passing merrily between other mammals and human beings, as we came to live side by side.

In the ten thousand years since man began to breed animals in the Fertile Crescent, he brought them onto the land he farmed, into the garden he tilled, domesticated them. Until finally, he brought those pets into the home he shared with his children, even the bed in which he lay with his wife, the closeness between the species spawning disease.

Marcus Varro had called them "invisible animals," the bacteria and the viruses that passed imperceptibly to humans, all the way back in the first century when no one had an answer for anything. Later, by more than a millennium, when the microscope was invented, what you observed through the looking glass was named "the little animalcule."

It would take centuries until the world understood that this miasma didn't appear like magic, spontaneously manifesting in thin air. Kesta thought it took a long time and a lot of books, judging by the contents of this room, for us to really understand what we were looking at.

The dull tone of a PA system sounded to announce that the library was closing shortly. Kesta had been there for hours and wondered how many books she could check out in one go, wished she'd brought a trolley or a suitcase with her to ferry them all home. She was about to start making a list of them when a livid yellow eye stared back at her from across the far side of the room. The book had been positioned at the end of a shelf with its front cover facing outward like a portrait. The eye watched her intently. The pupil was a vertical slit cut through the yellow iris, signifying that the creature was nocturnal. The book's title was embossed on the page, and it shone like scales rippling even in the half light.

REPTILIAN DISEASE: A COMPLETE STUDY.

Kesta took the book from the shelf and pinned it down in front of her on the table like a butterfly on display, splaying the wings wide apart. She flicked through page after page of weird and near-supernatural ailments.

Chlamydia in crocodiles. Respiratory disease in turtles, accompanied by all manner of washed-out histological photographs of multicolored slides. Then she saw something she recognized.

The little purple jellybeans. An image of a cream-colored snake tied into an impossible knot. INCLUSION BODY DISEASE read the header. A disease unique to snakes, primarily the boa constrictor. Kesta turned the page backward and forward, looking at the cell structure, then the crooked, yellow-eyed snake. Then she read something that made her gasp.

Not yet found in humans.

———

"I wasn't sure you'd make it in the end," Cooke said, smirking as she stood with her arms outstretched in the hallway, waiting to take Kesta's fading leather jacket. Even though both women were small, they filled the entrance space to the flat. "I was worried you'd change your mind."

"I've been looking forward to it," Kesta said as she rotated her way out of her jacket with Cooke tugging at the sleeves. Cooke gasped in alarm.

"Christ on a bike, love, there's nothing to you, is there?" she said, jabbing a finger into Kesta's ribs, finding only bone, no cushioning flesh. She gasped again, out of pity, then she gently angled Kesta so that they could both inspect her shrunken frame in the narrow mirror by the door. Kesta felt ashamed, thought she must be blushing, but there was no color in her face. Next to Cooke sparkling in softness, bejeweled, a magpie's nest, Kesta saw just how sharp and sallow she had become, her face hollowed out like a carved pumpkin by the harsh overhead lighting in the hall, dark slices under the cheeks like dueling scars.

"This is what heartbreak looks like," Cooke said, rubbing Kesta's arms, resting her chin on Kesta's shoulder. Kesta forced a smile. She pulled the sleeves of her T-shirt down as far as they would go, to hide the bruising.

"How did you get on at the library?" Cooke asked before disappearing to hang up Kesta's jacket.

"It was very—interesting," she said. "I've got something I'd like to show you."

"As long as you eat something first," Cooke called back from another room. As she waited, Kesta saw she was surrounded by walls covered almost entirely with photographs, mostly black-and-white, of a much younger Cooke and a handsome man with a moustache that grew or shrank in size depending upon the decade.

"That's my Rodney," Cooke volunteered the way widows do, sensing apprehension but always so inclined to invoke the spirits of the dead by introducing them to strangers. Kesta felt herself flush with embarrassment. She scanned the wall. The photographs were arranged in silver-framed montages of varying sizes; some a single image from a Polaroid mounted alone, others grouped in neat inserts, some assembled like collages when the photographs were important, but their quality, their size was lacking, like memories bound together so that Cooke didn't forget that they had happened.

The two of them at their wedding leaving a bleached-out church, a mountain of sepia confetti dumped across their shoulders by a grooms-man with a cigarette in his mouth. Marriages of yesteryear were never anything other than a decidedly flammable affair. Another of them standing proudly on either side of a sports car that looked too low and too compact to fit them and may have belonged to someone else. Cooke in a bold-print swimsuit, slim, tanned skin a high sheen; Rodney in alarmingly brief shorts, hairy, laughing, looking at Cooke like she was gift wrapped, big hands reaching out to touch her. The homespun, sunbaked oranges and ambers of the seventies replacing the crisply tailored monochromes of their sixties provenance. A photograph of the two of them both holding tall glasses of champagne, Rodney dressed as some sort of curate, buttoned up, in horn-rimmed glasses, a dark brown pipe hanging dubiously from his lips; and Cooke, or rather June, in a short black plastic dress coat, her hair teased into something close to sculpture, her parted lips frosted pink, chandelier earrings caught in motion, patent knee-high boots like a lunar landing. The vicar and the tart. Rodney and June Cooke. Life interrupted, bashful, full of promise.

Kesta felt her own grief form a hard lump at the back of her throat. June and Rodney were her and Tim in another era, living the same life, loving the same way, enjoying and enduring iterations of the same human experience. The clothes, the staging, the weather were all different—but the love at the heart of each picture was the same. The same as the photograph she had of the night she met Tim. It was an eternal love that demanded a wall full of efforts to capture it.

"Roddie always loved a fancy-dress party."

Kesta turned to see that Cooke was no longer in the room with her. She was back at that party, in 1976, in the spring of her marriage, with her husband. Then, a wave of reality washed away the image and with it, Cooke's smile. Her face fell and she sighed, not a rueful sigh but the sigh employed by those skilled in pretending, the sigh that resets the emotions, staves off new tears because you've cried them all before. The sigh that pulls you back together again, breath by breath.

"Dr. Caring told me you like a drink, so I've got some of those cocktail cans in the fridge." Cooke wandered into the kitchen and Kesta followed her. "What was it you wanted to show me?"

Kesta heaved her bag full of books onto the dining table and withdrew the one with the picture of the snake's eye on the cover. She opened it to the page with the purple inclusions, cracking the spine and spreading it out flat for Cooke to look at, a cat coming home to mother with the gift of a freshly murdered mouse.

"I don't drink by myself anymore, hangovers for days if I do. I blame the menopause."

Cooke took a can of something livid and green, some kind of prepared mojito, and snapped back the ring pull. "You want ice in it, dear?" she asked Kesta, as if ice would somehow improve a drink made by a machine six months ago and that you were meant to drink fresh.

"Yes, please, that sounds lovely," said Kesta.

Cooke fought to contain the explosion of bubbles as the liquid shattered the ice. She brought the drink frothing and hissing over to Kesta.

"Is this what I think it is?" she asked, wiping her glasses clean with the hem of her sweater before leaning down to examine the histological imagery.

"Inclusion body disease," Kesta said, sipping cautiously. The cocktail wasn't as awful as she'd expected. Perhaps her standards were slipping.

"You know, this thing was everywhere in the seventies," said Cooke as she turned the pages, highlighting lines of text with a long pink fingernail. "People were obsessed with it. Mainly because of the ghoulish symptoms experienced by the infected snake. They wove themselves into corkscrew shapes because their muscles contracted in on themselves. And because it was so contagious. The scientific press was full of it for a few years. My Rodney always hated snakes."

"The inclusions are the same as in our zombie slides," Kesta said, circling the purple oblongs that signified the infection with an index fingernail that was bitten down to the quick.

"You know there's still no cure for it, right? And that it never made the jump outside of reptiles."

"June, I think it's made the jump now."

The two of them reviewed the book at the dining table in the kitchen. The table was too large for the space, having been brought from a house where June and Rodney had lived before. Cooke told Kesta about the hysteria she had witnessed in the scientific community, the snake fever over IBD when she was younger. She remembered outbreaks in Europe—she couldn't remember where exactly—when snakes had been imported as exotic pets. Pet collectors were forced to cull because they couldn't stop the spread. The money on offer at the time, the prestige of being the scientist to identify the virus and then cure it. The eventual conclusion toward the end of the decade that snakes didn't matter much to anyone, really; and so long as only their species was affected, no further resources should be wasted on exploring Inclusion Body Disease. Snakes should simply be quarantined if they'd been imported, and their cages kept cleaner in captivity. After that, the virus was largely forgotten.

Kesta and Cooke talked about the ways in which a virus can mutate. The antigenic drift, the natural method, in which viruses evolve slowly over time. The antigenic shift, the sudden change, a seismic one, where two viruses collide and make another, one that's usually much worse. Influenza was the archetypal example of different virus strains colliding and reforming into something deadlier than the original and therefore harder to treat. They worried about reassortment, the mixing of genetic material from one species to another, from one virus to another, and multiplicity reactivation, where a host's cells can be simultaneously infected by two very different viruses, enabling both to multiply at will. What if yellow fever and IBD infections had triggered a response—together and against each other—in the body of Paul Mosi? They read the pages on IBD in snakes over and over again, dwelling anxiously over the paragraph that told them how reptarenaviruses were the most unusual of all viruses known to man because their genetic diversity was unmatched.

"So, we could have a new virus that is a reassortment of snake viruses, human viruses, and other animal viruses, all blended together in a single host, with the reptarenavirus being the most complex and therefore almost impossible to treat?" asked Cooke as the timer on the oven pinged. "You know, you could just have brought me flowers."

———

Kesta took a seat where Cooke had marked out a place for her with cutlery and a sequined table mat. The chair was wooden and solid, and Kesta wondered how Cooke had managed to transport all this stuff made for marriage, made for men to carry around, into this polite little flat by herself. She thought about the things she lugged around too, the books she never read, the clothes she never wore, items so precious to her parents—best china, flea-bitten Christmas decorations—that were now her own to shepherd toward her own grave with no one to force them upon when the time came.

"I used to cook from scratch—loved it—every night when Roddie was alive. He did the weekends, cracking roast, quite experimental with a *jus* when the mood took him," Cooke said. She was battling with too many hot oven trays that she was tossing onto the hob above. "But now I'm a ready-meal woman. I hope you don't mind."

"I never cooked when Tim was—" Kesta stopped herself before she said it, because in a flat full of June Cooke's loss, her own felt like a fraud. "I barely stop to put things on a plate. Tim did all the cooking. Which was especially good if we hosted. I always got too nervous about timing in front of other people."

"You strike me as such a practical girl, not one for flapping about," Cooke said.

"Cool as ice looking down a microscope, but I turn to slush at everything else."

Cooke cackled. "Rodney used to say I was like Thatcher at work. Not one for turning. Now, as you can probably tell, I've got jumpers older than you and saucepans that don't heat up, but I can't stand to return them."

She slopped the lasagna out of a plastic tray and set about it with a carving knife, which she licked with the tip of her tongue to check that the lasagna was hot enough to serve.

"Moving here was the last and only nonclinical decision I made since Rod died, and I've regretted it ever since."

She was laughing, but there was no depth to it. Cooke was embarrassed to have a colleague over for a ready-meal dinner and a cocktail in a can, even though only she knew what she had been capable of delivering before.

"You came back to work, though, that took real steel."

"I had no choice there, dear. It was keep busy or die. Cheers."

"Cheers."

Kesta and Cooke clinked a premade cocktail and a glass of tap water together, and Cooke set about dishing up the salad to accompany the lasagna, tonging it, leaf by leaf, lamb's lettuce and butterhead, straight from the plastic bag.

"I did rinse it. I'm not an animal."

"You make me feel at home."

"Then we should both move somewhere else."

The food was more than adequate, and the company improved the flavor. Cooke chatted happily about her two boys who lived abroad and the grandchildren she saw only a few times a year.

"I get a lot of photos," she said with her mouth full, "and we do video calls, that sort of thing. But it's not the same." She asked Kesta about her parents, shook her head at the news they were both dead.

"Important to find someone you can lean on," said Cooke, "friendships, that sort of thing. You can't do loneliness by yourself." She paused with the fork an inch from her pink-frosted lips. "Working after Rod died helped me drain the hours."

These were the thoughts that Kesta fought to keep at bay. That without Tim, she was alone, condemned to live a life she hadn't planned for and didn't want. Even a widow pushing seventy, with children who'd left her behind, with grandchildren whose cuddles she was required to ration from one visit to the next, thought that Kesta was worse off.

Somewhere in between the physical ache of being alone and noticing that Cooke's ketchup had expired six months ago, she realized she wasn't doing all of this for Tim. She was doing it for herself, perhaps more so. She didn't want him to die because she didn't want to lose him, didn't want to accept that this irrevocable schism in her life was permanent. The tears came from nowhere. Cooke squeezed her hand before offering her two pieces of kitchen roll.

"I'm so sorry." Kesta sniffed, dabbing awkwardly around her lashes. "I never cry."

"Oh love, that's the problem." Cooke had opened another can, this time something masquerading as a martini, and forced it into Kesta's other hand. "We bottle it up, don't want to burden other people with our misery. You're like a Bunsen burner, dear, you've got to open the valve up properly, let the gas flow clean, light the flame fully, otherwise you get a nasty explosion, and no one can go within five miles of Cheshunt."

Kesta laughed. They laughed a lot that evening, sitting knee to knee in June Cooke's lounge on two sofas meant for somewhere else. They ate biscuits and drank endless cups of tea, neither of which followed lasagna well, but it didn't matter.

Cooke was the only person who really understood her. It was good to be understood. And as guilty and as fraudulent as Kesta felt about encroaching on another's grief, cannibalizing Cooke's loss as though it were her own when her husband still lived, albeit barely, she also felt soothed by it. With Cooke, she could feel the shape of her grief begin to transmute, its edges becoming malleable enough for her to push it to one side, even if just for a few hours.

It was nine o'clock when Kesta decided she ought to be getting home and Cooke sensed that time was running out. There was no wine to blame for it, as there would have been with Jess, so it could have been the Bunsen burner effect she had referred to, the consequence of dark secrets building up, destined to combust. It may have been that Cooke just wanted to keep her there a little while longer.

"I nearly did him in, you know."

Kesta stopped in the entrance hall. She walked back into the lounge and waited for Cooke to carry on.

"When it got too much for him. He wanted it to be over." Kesta sat down next to Cooke and held her hand tightly.

"He'd been ill for such a long time, and he was so bloody brave about it. But he had a bad night and—he was lucid," she sniffed, "enough to know what he was asking me to do."

"What—?"

"I didn't do it." Cooke let out a sob. "I had the pillow in my hands. I waited for him to get to sleep. I sat there with it for three hours. But I couldn't do it."

"What happened?"

"In the morning, he woke up. I was still in bits over it, and he said, 'Why am I waking up, June? I might have known you wouldn't go through with it.'"

"Was he relieved?" Kesta asked her, holding back tears of her own.

"He made it a joke, like he always did," Cooke said, "but I could tell that part of him—I don't know. I'd let him down."

"You'd have gone to prison for it though?"

"I know, I did tell him that. He said, 'Well, never mind, I'll be dead, so I won't miss you.'"

The two women held hands in silence. It lasted for only a moment, until they both began to shake with tears turning steadily to laughter. Their laughter filled the room, filled them both, reminding them that while it may be darkest before the dawn, the black and the white, the darkness and the light, both exist side by side, neither one precedes the other. You feel them both at the same time, such is the nature of life.

"I've never told anyone that before," said Cooke as Kesta was finally ready to head home.

"Did it feel good to share it?" Kesta asked her.

"I think it did," Cooke said, pleasantly surprised.

———

Kesta tore through the spare bedroom bolts like lightning. When she opened the door, Tim released a quiet moan, as if she'd just woken him from a deep sleep. She moved toward the bed, unlaced her boots, and slipped off her jacket and her jeans, leaving them in a pile on the floor. Kesta climbed into the bed beside him, resting as closely as the cannula and the restraints would allow.

I can never let you go. I don't want to ever let you go. I can make a life for us out of this. This is enough for me. I can accept you like this, forever.

He watched her. He smelled her. He said nothing, did nothing. Kesta understood the risk, and that Tim had always been worth it. Somewhere deep inside the body of her husband, where she had to believe he still existed, was the man she could trust not to hurt her that night. He was so thin beside her, so much thinner than before, and tonight his breathing sounded as though his lungs were filled with glass.

Kesta wrapped her arm around Tim, closed her eyes, and slept as though she were dead.

CHAPTER FOURTEEN

"Yes, I understand," she heard herself saying for the third time that Saturday morning as she paced across the living room. On hold yet again, to a song she imagined would drive even the most stoical to murder if they were forced to listen to it indefinitely, droning on from somewhere deep inside the receiver. She deliberated putting her phone onto speaker, but doing so always made her worry that the person on the other end wouldn't be able to hear her when she spoke and she'd have wasted her time, holding on for nothing, punished for having a little voice. Holding the middle-of-the-road music an inch away from her face, she smoothed her free hand across the back of the sofa.

She remembered sitting there, right up on the top, her feet planted firmly on the seat cushions below, Tim's arm supporting her ankles to stop her from tipping backward. It had been New Year's, and they were more than a bit tipsy, their parents having been forced to spend four whole days camping at their kids' new and mostly unfurnished flat, because Tim was determined that everyone should just muck in. Everyone should have stayed in the nice hotel round the corner, as Kesta would have preferred, but Tim had an idealized version of what festivity should entail and would inflict it on everyone, no matter how much it ended up putting him out. He'd bought sleeping bags from a camping supplies shop and extra pillows. He had not considered the musculoskeletal concerns of four sexagenarians.

"Let's go away next year instead," he would say each New Year's Eve, but they never did. She remembered a feeling of warmth and contentment, small but profound, of that night seven years ago, when she sat on the back of this sofa with her hardworking husband massaging her feet as their families blended into one. It was the last time they'd all been together, Tim and his parents, Kesta and her mum and dad. Seven years later, and Kesta was the only one left.

"Are you okay to keep holding, Mrs. Shelley?" the man's voice chimed back in before the music returned, before she'd had a chance to ask him not to put her back on hold. She sagged down into one of the arms of the sofa and saw a crimson stain the size of a five-pence piece on the edge of one of the cream scatter cushions. She knew it was red wine but had no recollection of when or why she had spilled it. As the man's voice returned to reel off the litany of reasons why he was unable to help her any further, the number of minutes she had already been kept on hold not translating into any obligation on his part, it seemed, Kesta turned the cushion around to hide the stain and lobbed her phone to the other end of the sofa.

It was becoming an issue, she realized. Keeping people away. Not asking useful people for help. She had allowed many friendships to fade over the years because she hadn't registered their significance at the time. Friendships seem to take such a lot from you, she'd thought—your time, your patience—filling up space in your brain with trivial bollocks that Kesta considered to be nonessential conversation. When there were over two hundred different types of cancer without a cure, how were you supposed to devote yourself to someone else's passive-aggressive office dilemma, the outcome of which, ultimately, hadn't proven fatal?

"Friendships are like plants; you need to water them often," Tim used to say, and although Kesta knew he was right, she'd still thought it was obsequious.

"Seems I don't own a watering can," she had replied, "but it doesn't account for how you manage to survive in these hostile conditions of mine."

"Ah, well, you could say that I'm like the hardiest cactus known to man, but really it's just that you make sure that I get all your water all the time. I'm almost drowning in it. Don't resent sharing any of it with other people because I promise you, I will not dry out and die without it."

Kesta had resolved to find someone she could call on. She needed to find someone who understood more about IBD than she did. She had to take the risk. She had spent the morning phoning various teaching hospitals and research centers, asking anyone who'd listen what they knew about diseases in reptiles.

Two decades of devoted scientific service, and she couldn't drum up a useful contact—a friend, an acquaintance even—who could shed light on her query, brainstorm with her, chip in with ideas.

Her attendance had been required at numerous symposia over the years, medical conferences up and down the country, and even one in Hong Kong, but those had essentially counted for nothing, it seemed, because she'd failed to make a connection with anyone she'd met.

Despite Tim's best efforts to spark an enthusiasm for networking, Kesta had remained intransigent. She had seen other, less intuitive colleagues shimmy their way up the career ladder just because they had favors they could call in or contacts in convenient places. Kesta was planted firmly in the shadiest part of the garden behind all the greedy sunflowers. She also failed to make any overtures whatsoever toward keeping in touch with anyone.

Kesta ventured out into the hallway looking for her address book hidden somewhere in the console table. Instead, she found a leather-bound photograph album, not of her wedding but from the days when people still bothered to have rolls of camera film printed. She paused, listening for Tim, the door to his room unlocked and propped open. Something like snoring emanated from inside, then the dragging of limbs across cotton sheets. She lived with the worry that one day she'd listen out for his breathing only to realize that it had stopped. She went into his room and unfurled herself into the chair beside him.

"Nffff," he said, the fingers of the chained hand signing a hello into the air.

"Look what I just found," she said. "I thought we could look at it together."

Tim had kept the photos, but it would have been Kesta who had laid them out in dead straight lines, pressed flat, in chronological order. The album contained images from the first five years of their relationship. She knew it immediately because her careful cursive had inscribed as much on the very first page.

Nights Out in London, 2003

There were images taken of the two of them huddled up in each other's arms at a bar in Covent Garden, and another one in Farringdon. Faded testaments to their courtship in its infancy, she looking coyly at the camera, black sweaters, scarves pulled up higher than intended to hide as much of her face as possible. Tim beaming like the sun in every image, big-collared shirts, polo necks, suited and booted, a singular source of radiant light.

"I'm turning into Cooke," she muttered to herself, realizing that her life had been reduced to an ancient collection of photographs of her doing things she'd almost forgotten about. "That's a lady I work with. You'd love her, she's kind of like your mum used to be."

"Umphhh."

As a couple they never dreamed of asking other people to take their picture—aside from the infamous image that captured their genesis—so most of the photos were of the two of them squished together, faces melting into a single organism, filling the entire frame. Some were of them kissing, the soft profile of lips locked, Tim's smile ephemeral, mercurial, becoming her own. A few pages on, and scenery began to smuggle its way into the pictures.

"Did we become less fascinated by each other here, do you think?" she asked, giggling. "We seem to have moved on to landscape photography?" Salmon beaches, churches, piazzas desolate and crowded, bridges at dusk and at dawn, secretive snaps in the bowels of galleries and museums.

"Do you remember this trip?" She held up the page in front of him and pointed at a photograph. "What about this guy?" The photo was of a man wearing only Day-Glo orange shorts, holding a fishing rod high in the air as though he'd just claimed the high seas. "He tried to sell us lobster, which we didn't really want, and then we realized that by lobster he meant weed. Do you remember that?"

Tim pointed with his free hand toward the fisherman. Kesta hoped he was remembering. He was likely just copying her actions through a daze of sedation.

The two of them off on airplanes, hands clasped, faces elated, then riding in the backs of rickshaws, drunk and apprehensive. Mountains with snow and without, the two of them in neon swimwear, sunscreen smeared in the new romantic style across cheeks and noses. So much laughter captured for eternity. One photo had Kesta brandishing an oversized tuna that someone else had caught but that Tim had wanted a picture of because the fish was more or less the same size she was. Kesta remembered the sights and sounds, not of the places they'd been to, but rather the sound of Tim's boundless joy for everywhere he went with her.

Toward the end of this particular album, Kesta realized that only she was in the photographs. There she was, in a navy-blue skirt suit with an orange lanyard around her neck like a Hawaiian tribute, motioning arbitrarily to whatever lay behind her, the thing itself out of focus. She looked like a surly air steward, pointing toward the exits.

In another photo, in the same blue suit but taken from farther away, Kesta the smallest in a queue of maybe thirty people, all wearing identikit badges, all giving the cameraman the thumbs-up. Behind them the dull parallelogram of an administrative building.

She couldn't remember it. *A hospital? A hotel?*

A conference center. A conference center in Florida. She had been there just the once on her own, to a symposium on bacterial infections.

Now the memory slipped into the slot like a coin into a jukebox, and a familiar tune began to play inside her head.

The next page of photographs gave Kesta the strange sensation of looking at someone else's life. She could barely recognize herself, though it was her, undeniably. She was the center of each picture, shrieking with laughter, sloshing a huge pint glass in her hand, her tiny body encased in a tight pin-striped dress, arms flushed pink and bare where ordinarily sensible sleeves would have covered them.

Then the flicker of something mentioned, a rumor shared amongst strangers, American ones, about her drinking only Guinness. She didn't remember drinking it before or since, and yet here she was, swilling it gleefully, thrusting the glass, so large in her hands, at the other people in the photographs, men in sweat-marked shirts, women with their hair ironed flat, pure white teeth, seemingly enchanted by her and none of whom she remembered at all.

She knew herself well enough to know that even back then it would have been utterly typical of her to make an offhand remark, a poor attempt at a joke, and be forced through sheer willpower to stick to it. She could see that happening and resulting in her drinking Guinness for four nights straight.

The last two pictures were of Kesta and another man. He was tall, taller even than Tim, vast and muscular, built like a barn door, and she a secondary hatch fitted into his side.

John the American.

How had she forgotten him? She had known him for a time, as a friend, not merely an acquaintance.

"Tim, what was John the American's surname? I can't for the life of me remember. It's been years."

"Dirrrrrr."

"I don't think it was that, but my memory's like a sieve." She blew an invisible kiss toward him, and he made the noise again: *dirrrr.*

"I need you for remembering all the things I've already forgotten. Was it Dillon? Do you think it was Dillon? I don't think it was."

Life had gotten in the way, filling in the space between the man's face and her reality—with negativity, unhappiness, tragedy, work, relentless minor grievances that obliterated someone she might have dared to call a friend. Still couldn't place the surname though. Just John the American. On and off for a handful of years in the earlier part of her relationship with Tim, a lifetime ago now. Then, over time, the contact became infrequent, petering out unintentionally like a shooting star that was there and then just wasn't.

He was Florida born and raised, she remembered that. That he was a vet, not a doctor. She opened her laptop and began scrolling through the endless lists of universities, veterinary hospitals, and private laboratories at which a John the American type might work. Nothing. She searched for a list of colleges and teaching hospitals and worked her way through the alphabet, looking at the staff photographs on the ABOUT US pages of each site.

Eventually, she came across the Technical Institute of Animal Medicine in Tampa. A face that seemed to fit the bill, though he was much thinner and had grown a stylish close-shaven beard. She showed his photograph on the website to Tim. John the American was John Diaz. She wrote what she hoped was a brief and dignified email.

Dear John,

I know it will be my fault that we lost touch. And I will completely understand it if you ignore this email.

You will have seen what's happened here.

Is it okay to ask for your help?

Kesta (Small, antisocial brunette you knew once who may have pretended she really liked Guinness.)

She sent the email.
She thought for a second that his reply was instantaneous. But it

was a message he'd sent her months ago in the middle of the outbreak, sitting there, unread. *Thinking of you both and sending you and Tim love. We're praying you both get through this. Please call if we can do anything to help.*

She hadn't replied. She hadn't checked her personal emails in months, what with everything that had happened. John had tried in vain to reach her. In another version of reality, she saw herself and Tim on the last flight out of London, landing in Miami to John's brotherly embrace, seeing out the outbreak safe from harm. She poured herself a glass of water and drank it quickly to calm herself down. It was difficult asking for help.

There was a phone number in his email. She called it.

"John? John, I'm so sorry to bother you. It's Kesta. Kesta Shelley."

"Well, hello there, Baby Tank."

Kesta blushed at John's tender voice and the sudden recollection of her nickname on that trip. Baby Tank. Because she was five feet nothing and could drink like an entire garrison on leave.

"John the American." So-called because there had been two Johns on that trip. The other was from Milton Keynes.

"Kesta, my God! To what do I owe this pleasure? How are you? It's been forever!" She heard a squeaking noise, heard John saying something with the receiver held away from his mouth.

"Sorry, John, am I interrupting? Oh, shit, it must be early for you."

John's voice was strained at the end of the line. "Not at all. My sweet Sofia is something of an early bird."

"Oh Christ, John!"

"Yeah," he said, his voice tightening from the effort of lifting an infant up onto his chest. "I'm a father of daughters, Tank."

"How many?"

"Sof's our third."

How lovely it was that someone else's life was normal, full of the ordinary extraordinary things.

Kesta heard the baby gurgling against the receiver.

"Kesta, I've been so worried. When I didn't hear from you—"

"Tim's . . . gone."

"Oh honey! I am so, so sorry."

In almost twenty years, John the American had never met Tim. All he knew of him was what Kesta had shared, in fits and starts, through emails that were scant and infrequent and sent forever ago. And yet John's condolences felt more sincere than anyone's. Perhaps because he had three baby girls he couldn't bear the thought of losing. Or because he had already imagined that Kesta and Tim were lost, had watched the zombie virus rip through London, a city he had never been to, on the other side of the world, where a woman he'd met in person only once was living a nightmare and he was powerless to do anything about it. He had already mourned her death, so the compassion in his voice was sincere.

For a while they talked about everything and nothing the way long forgotten friends do. They shared the universal inevitabilities that gave them kinship—the deaths of parents, urban living, the trajectories of their careers—skimming through the highlights and the lowlights of the ordinary human existence, knowing instinctively that the other would understand the disappointments and the joys and the pressures and anxieties brought about by age. Neither one of them had mastered life, it seemed. Neither one could claim to outwit it in its efforts to attack you by surprise. After a while, the conversation ebbed away, and the only sound to pepper the silence was the happy gurgling of John's baby.

"Kesta," he said at last, "there must be a reason for you to call me out of the blue like this."

How could she tell him in a way that he could understand? In a way that didn't make her seem callous or grasping or deranged? How could she tell him a version of the truth but not the whole horrible story? How had she learned so skillfully to edit Tim out of her life this way, pretending that he was dead to the world when he was chained up and stupefied just feet away from her? She did it because she had no other choice but to lie. As soon as a better alternative presented itself, she would stop.

She needed John's help and John would need something in return. A morsel of truth if he were to believe her, to take a risk on her behalf, to sacrifice something she needed. Just a little bite. She would be honest, not about Tim, but about her work. If she played up to John's altruism, he would find it easier to share in this secret.

"I'm working at Project Dawn."

She had to say it twice before the shock of it subsided. Sofie continued to gurgle.

"Shit, Kesta, seriously? Should you even be talking to me about it?"

"Of course I shouldn't, John, but I have no choice. I trust you. Things are complicated there, and I really need to accelerate the progress we're making. I have a theory and I need your help to prove it."

Over the sticky giggles of the baby, Kesta could hear John muttering his way toward a reply.

"You said you're still working as a vet?"

"Yes, I mean, I'm more into teaching now, less hands-on medicine but—"

"Do you know very much about reptiles, John?"

"We got a lot of boas down in Florida. It's not my specialty, but we have a huge department dedicated to reptilian health at the Institute. Kesta, why are you asking me this?"

"Because I need to know everything there is to know about snakes. About Inclusion Body Disease in particular."

The line went dead.

"John?"

"Kesta, please, please don't tell me what I think you're going to tell me. It's impossible to even consider. A contagion that's a hundred percent fatal in snakes, without a cure, without viable treatment of any kind."

"It's jumped from snakes to humans."

Kesta knew the implications of what she was sharing with him. "Look, we're in a blackout here. We all signed nondisclosure agreements. We're not allowed to ask for outside help. But—this is too big, too serious. I have a terrible feeling that they're going to suppress information about the virus. They're going to try to keep it quiet for as long as possible."

"I can see why they would," said John. "It would be a game changer. But the international community will need to know. To be forewarned and all. Kesta, you know I'll help you. But I'm not going to be able to keep a lid on it at my end for long. I'm going to have to tell someone that you're investigating IBD. The stakes are too damn high for us here, the US has a hell of a lot more snakes than you guys do in Britain. Do you know—"

"Don't ask me about antigenic shift species or anything like that yet."

She sat down at the dining table in front of her laptop.

"All I have is this hunch about IBD from the histology I've been working on and an old book I found on the subject. I could be wrong, of course."

She looked down the hallway to Tim's room and wondered if she should close the door.

"It could be a perfect storm of conditions within the patient. It could be an intermediate species that caused the jump to humans. We don't know yet. John, I want to email you something. Get an expert opinion on it," she whispered.

"For God's sake don't send me a thing," he said, "I don't want to get you in trouble. Clara knows how to send encrypted files. Give me a minute to wake her—"

"John, I don't want to put you out."

"It's no bother, hang on a second. Come on, Sofie, let's go get Mommy for Auntie Kesta."

Kesta waited patiently by the phone for John to return. She heard noises in the background, then a woman's voice—she had never met Clara, John's wife, but she heard the woman cry out. She heard John soothing her, and then the two of them talking, decisively, working everything out together. Then the muffled crackle of John picking up the receiver again.

"Kesta, Clara's logging on to a secure website. I'm gonna read out an address for you to type into your browser."

Kesta knew there was no turning back. She was breaking protocol because she felt she had no choice, piercing the secret veil that shrouded Project Dawn. It took half an hour, but by the end of it, Kesta had sent twenty JPEG files—photomicrographs of Tim's blood films, along with those from Mosi and another unnamed tissue donor, stained an alarming violet to enhance the differences between the details. Her hands scattering across the keys, hitting them like gibberish, shaking, questioning herself, accepting that if she wanted to help Tim, she'd have to accept some help for herself. She was desperate. John stayed with her on the line while she worked, stopping only to feed the baby, who had woken up again. Clara helped with the files, giving clear instructions in the background, which John then repeated carefully down the line to make sure that Kesta had understood them.

She heard muttering, the old-fashioned handset being passed between the two of them.

"I'm going to leave you with John now," Clara said. "I know he'll do whatever he can to help you. And Kesta?" she said tearfully, "I'm so very sorry for your loss. Tim will be in my prayers tonight."

"Thank you," said Kesta and put her hand over her mouth to keep from crying. She heard the regular tread of the woman walking away, a door clicking shut, then John cleared his throat.

"Kesta, you're sure these slides aren't from snakes, right?"

"No, these are human zombie epithelial tissue and blood samples," she replied, "half taken from early-stage patients, the rest from someone infected toward the end of the outbreak. Why?" She could hear John exclaiming to himself under his breath.

"Jesus Christ." He whistled sharply, a shrill crescendo soaring upward before falling violently, the sound of a bomb dropping.

"Am I right, John?"

"This is Inclusion Body Disease. For sure, Tank. The most contagious disease in snakes known to man has become zoonotic. It's made the leap to us."

CHAPTER FIFTEEN

She was out of breath, fogging up her face shield, standing with hands on her thighs as she came to a halt in the middle of the lab. The others stopped what they were doing and turned to look at her. Cooke was nodding at her and trying to give her a subtle thumbs-up, which was unsubtle in her fat blue gloves. Kesta said it again, more emphatically this time.

"It's Inclusion Body Disease."

"It's what?"

"Inclusion Body Disease," she repeated, steadying herself against the workstation. "It's a reptarenavirus. It's wildly virulent, and I believe that it has made the jump from snakes to humans. IBD is a contributing factor in our zombie virus."

Kesta had their full attention now. She could see Dudley's eyes crinkling with a smile behind his visor. As she began to position a slide for them to inspect, she felt his hand against her back, a double tap of pride.

"I have a blood film image from a boa constrictor here," she said, spreading a printout of a histological image John Diaz had sent her, "and this is a zombie tissue slide from Mosi." Kesta fired up her electron microscope, which illuminated the space around her. She took one of the unidentified tissue samples she'd shared with John and anchored it carefully with the stage clip underneath the lens. She'd used a Wright-Giemsa stain, and the light from the microscope turned a pale lavender. One by one, Lundeen, Dudley, and Cooke peered into the purple light, then back again at the printout on the workstation.

Suddenly the room was filled with silent tension.

"Where did you get this slide?" Lundeen demanded, pressing his glove onto the paper hard enough to leave a crumpled indentation. Kesta pretended not to have heard him.

"Reptarenaviruses are genetically one of the most diverse, so we should expect a high degree of—"

"Where did you get this fucking slide?" Lundeen raged. "Why do you have slides that are not in our database?"

Kesta had no choice but to brazen it out. There was no turning back now. She placed one hand on her hip defiantly and tried her hardest to tower over Lundeen.

"I've been undertaking my own private research because things here are moving too bloody slowly," she said calmly, quietly. "I made a call to a laboratory in Florida. I told them I was a biotechnology undergraduate at Cambridge. They were very keen to help me. I'm also expecting tissue samples to be airfreighted over. They should arrive by the end of the week. This is me notifying you to expect them, Lars—"

Lundeen bristled with indignation.

"—but please allow me to apologize for overreaching in my efforts to find the origin of potentially the deadliest contagion in history."

Kesta got as close to Lundeen's face as she dared. She could hear him panting.

"My contact is based in the swamps where they have a high number of snakes, both wild and bred as pets. IBD is a real concern there, and it's highly contagious. I have brought in an expert to assist; except he doesn't know what he's working on. Only I do."

"We don't have IBD in this country," said Lundeen, scowling. "We've never had it."

"She knows that. Let her speak," said Cooke. "Carry on, love."

"Mosi wasn't from here. He was from Belgium, and he'd spent time in

Madagascar. There's IBD in Madagascar! They've had terrible outbreaks of it in Belgium, too. I've been reading up on them all weekend. We need to ask the embassies to confirm if they've had any reported cases of IBD in Belgium and Madagascar in the past eight months. Possibly even in the States because Mosi had been there, too."

She'd have to hold off on admitting that information to John for as long as possible. She must remember to cross that bridge and only then to burn it down.

"Kesta, do you realize the implication here?"

Lundeen removed his mask. He was ashen and sweating. His eyeballs fizzed from side to side. "If the Americans find out about this thanks to your private research, if the WHO is alerted to the mere suggestion that IBD has made the leap to humans, they'll bloody well close us down. It will raise an international alarm. Our work will likely be iced."

"Listen to me," Kesta said briskly, "I know we're in uncharted waters here. My contact understands the pressure we're working under."

"And who is he, your contact?"

"Oh, some veterinary pathologist. He doesn't know what I'm looking into," she lied. "He thinks I'm writing an academic paper."

"He's willing to courier bits of infected snake across the Atlantic for a student?"

"Fuck's sake, Professor Lundeen, there's huge value to the Americans, to my contact, in us finding out more about IBD and how to treat it in snakes because there's presently no treatment plan or cure for it. Even for the bloody snakes! That's what he thinks I'm doing, researching viable strategies to treat reptarenaviruses."

"And you're expecting me to trust that?"

"You're going to have to trust me," she hissed. "Even now, all imported snakes brought into the UK must be quarantined because of the risk of IBD. If the virus transmits from one snake to another, both either die or they have to be euthanized. Look at this," she said, directing them toward the more vividly stained jellybeans lurking on the edges of larger ones. "Do you see how there are numerous lymphocytes in the white pulp from the zombie tissue samples? I've seen gross abnormalities in nearly all the histologic sections, including eosinophilic inclusions in the lymphocytes," she said.

She gestured to the darkest points, circles that had flattened in the middle into devious little oblongs looking for an escape from the larger entity to which they'd attached themselves.

"I've looked through thousands of slides since I've been here, so has Cooke, all manner of diseases and viruses, human and animal, and the only meaningful match I can find is in these inclusions. They appear in both the zombie samples and those from the boa constrictor. You have to take this seriously!"

"She's right, Lars, look," said Dudley. "You can't deny it."

Lundeen took another fleeting look down the microscope, tutting. "What are the main symptoms of IBD, in snakes?" he asked.

"They plunge into a kind of death spiral," she explained, "twisting in on themselves like a corkscrew through uncontrollable muscular contractions. And they do this thing with their heads." She had everyone's full attention now, even Lundeen's. "They call it stargazing."

The stargazing freaked her out the most, the snake's head wrenched backward at an unnatural angle, just like Tim's and every other infected person she'd seen, walking staring upward, not in front.

"The virus attacks the snake's central nervous system, their pupils are often different sizes, one larger than the other. The snake cannot balance. It cannot and does not eat. In fact, most snakes eventually, over a significant period of time, actually die of starvation."

Cooke, Dudley, and Lundeen were spellbound.

"The inclusion bodies can be seen in smooth muscle tissue, in peripheral blood cells, glial cells. We're seeing them present in the same way in the zombie samples, including in the brain paraffin we have. Including in Paul Mosi."

"The snakes get it from mice, don't they?" asked Cooke.

"Yes, they think so, through droppings infected with parasitic mites. As it happens, the shift from mouse to snake is also yet to be established." Kesta took a deep breath, releasing it sharply. "Look, we know that Mosi had been exposed to yellow fever. We can only assume that he caught it in Madagascar during the outbreak there earlier this year. We know that Madagascar's biodiversity is uniquely rich. We can almost guarantee there will be viruses in that country right at this very minute, animal and human, that are yet to be documented by the international scientific community. Completely *novel* viruses." Kesta could feel sweat trickling down her throat and over her chest, then pooling along the underwire of her bra. "We know that Madagascar has had outbreaks of IBD in its wild and captive snake population before. What if one had occurred at the same time as the yellow fever outbreak and wasn't made public? What if Mosi was on the island, caught yellow fever, and then as shit luck would have it, was bitten by an infected snake?"

"He wouldn't necessarily have needed to be bitten to become infected," said Cooke, shifting her weight from one hip to the other as she mulled over Kesta's theory. "They have wet markets on the island. Others elsewhere have been a significant factor in zoonotic virus transmission before, with bird flu and the like, so it's possible Mosi came into contact with the IBD by, say, eating bushmeat."

"Who on God's earth is eating snake ceviche?" Lundeen scoffed, flapping his little arms around incredulously.

With one hand barely touching Lundeen's shoulder, Dudley flicked his superior to one side, like a useless divider in a filing cabinet. "But no other cases of our zombie virus were reported there, and you would expect to have seen a localized zombie outbreak in Madagascar first, if local food sources were compromised."

"Not all wet markets trade in live animals," Lundeen interjected, trying to reassert his authority, "many only trade in meat that's already been slaughtered. Some don't sell animals at all. No, no, it doesn't add up."

"It does because it would present an opportunity for different species to come into contact with each other," said Dudley, moving in front of Lundeen like an eclipse, "potentially bringing different viruses into a densely populated area and allowing for them to jump, to mutate, from one animal host to another. But then, we know that Mosi was the *only* person to have come out of Madagascar carrying the infection."

Lundeen continued to mutter to himself about the irrelevance of this line of enquiry. Cooke shuffled from one foot to the other, clogs squeaking erratically, brain whirring frenetically. Kesta tried to dig out the underwire of her bra from her ribs, but it was impossible with gloves.

"If he was bitten by a snake or consumed infected snake meat, then there must be a specific reason why *he* developed symptoms and no one else there did," she mused. "I suppose it does rule out a wet market theory. So where did it come from?"

"Back in Tudor times, there was an outbreak of what they called sweating sickness in England," said Cooke, chunky bracelets clinking somewhere underneath her protective suit, "and it was aggressive. The patients shook violently, they turned cold, then feverish. They complained of a terrible thirst. Around half who caught it died within a day."

"What does this have to do with the price of fish?" asked Lundeen.

"Because sweating sickness just vanished," she replied, staring off into the middle distance. Kesta could tell that Cooke was consulting that Rolodex mind of hers. "After less than a century, sweating sickness had completely disappeared. The accepted theory is that it was a form of hantavirus. Some other fella whose paper I read on the subject was adamant it was an early example of anthrax poisoning. But the thing is, no one's ever going to know for *sure*, are they, because we don't have any DNA or RNA samples from five hundred years ago to investigate it fully."

"Cooke," snapped Lundeen, on the verge of a tantrum, "your point, please?"

"Her point, Lars," said Kesta bullishly, "is that if we must accept that viruses can just vanish into thin air we have to accept the chilling reality that they can occur spontaneously in the first place."

Dudley nodded, his eyes glazing over in deep thought. Lundeen let out a churlish groan and kicked at the workstation.

"Well, at least reptarenaviruses don't have any DNA to insert in their hosts," he said petulantly. He kicked the workstation again for good measure. "Because that would be really inconvenient."

Cold beads of sweat began to drip down Kesta's stomach. She heard

Cooke whisper *oh shit*, just as Dudley turned to look at her, his eyes and mouth wide with shock.

"Are we . . . are we looking at both here?" Kesta stammered, scanning their faces for insight but finding only stunned surprise. "Our zombie virus behaves like an arenavirus *and* a retrovirus." She puffed the air of out of her cheeks, then took a deep breath. "RNA viruses have a much higher mutation rate. They're harder to control. Harder to vaccinate against. DNA viruses, on the other hand—like herpesvirus, like small pox—insert themselves into the host's genetic makeup. They can lie dormant in the host . . . forever."

Lundeen laughed darkly. "But there is no precedent for such a mutation. Arenaviruses don't just become retroviruses, do they? It's a scientific impossibility."

Suddenly, Cooke doubled over and moaned. "It's happened before."

Kesta, Dudley, and Lundeen watched as Cooke slumped awkwardly onto the laboratory floor. She propped herself up with one hand and used the other to lift up her visor and pull her face mask down. "Jesus, I can't breathe in this," she said, gulping for air. Lundeen was about to chastise her for this gross breach of health and safety protocol, but Dudley held him back. "There was this random case involving LCMV—that's lymphocytic choriomeningitis—where the RNA was copied into DNA."

Lundeen lifted both blue gloves up to his face, almost cowering behind them. "But that's science fiction science," he said.

"*All* science starts out as science fiction science," Cooke replied, chewing the gloss off her lips. "It was under lab conditions, but it still happened. Just the once. But once means . . . that there's a precedent that LCMV can be made to shift between arenavirus and retrovirus, copying itself into the host's cells."

"You're like some sort of scientific oracle," Kesta said wryly as she helped Cooke stagger to her feet.

"Sometimes I really wish I wasn't," Cooke groaned.

"And let me guess," Kesta said, wrapping a supportive arm around her, "LCMV is spread by mice too, just like IBD."

Cooke nodded wearily. The two of them leaned against the work-station, Cooke taking jagged little breaths, Kesta glaring at Lundeen, who was still using his giant blue gloves as a shield. "So, if our zombie virus *isn't* man-made, then what we're looking at is the exception. The exception that proves the rule. Zoonotic IBD, a reptarenavirus that's mutated in such an astonishing and devious way that it's taken on DNA-altering capabilities. But how?"

Dudley perched next to the two women. "Cooke, what can you tell us about LCMV?" he said.

"I know it comes in two phases," she mumbled through her mask as she pressed it over her face again. "The first is a sore throat, a cough, glandular pain. The patient would then appear to recover."

"Enough to make them believe they were well enough to travel?" Dudley asked her.

"Yes, possibly. But then a more serious phase is triggered. Inflammation of the brain, the spinal cord. Acute neurological distress."

"The mouse—the rat, the fucking hamster, whatever—that's the reservoir host, right?" Dudley was struggling to process it all. "The creature that can carry both these viruses, IBD and LCMV, without becoming symptomatic itself. So, what's our intermediate host animal? In SARS it was a civet, if I'm not mistaken, and in MERS . . ."

"With MERS it was a camel!" Lundeen shouted excitably.

"Yes, dear, with MERS it was a camel," said Cooke, not entirely able to mask the condescension in her tone, "but that would take us back to the wet market theory and the need for another animal host to help the viruses mutate, which would have resulted in a localized outbreak in Madagascar first, and that didn't happen . . . ouch! Kesta?!"

Kesta was squeezing the life out of Cooke's left arm.

"It means that Patient Zero *was* the intermediate host. Sorry." She let go of Cooke, but the violent imprint of her hand remained. "One zoonotic virus, LMVC, has somehow facilitated the mutation of the other, the IBD. It's acted like an accelerant for the other, allowing it to infect its first human victim, in situ."

"And in doing so has created a new kind of reptarenavirus, with all the hallmarks of a retrovirus," said Cooke, rubbing her arm.

"We're going to need to move very carefully on this," said Dudley, eyeballing Lundeen to stop him from interjecting. "It goes without saying that we need to keep this information contained. We don't want to cause panic, not in countries where IBD is prevalent."

"Surely the priority here is to reach the proper diagnoses first?" said Kesta.

"Don't be naïve, Shelley," barked Lundeen. "We're all adults here. There's money in research, billions of dollars of it. If we crack the virus code first, then our careers, our funding, it's gold-plated for life. If there's a leak, then someone else may beat us to the punch."

"As long as we are taking this seriously," she snapped. "As long as we do employ all of our resources, and I do mean *all* of them." She saw Dudley looking nervously at Lundeen, worried he was about to twig that Kesta already knew about the Gain-of-Function research and the two labs being run in parallel at Project Dawn.

"This feels like an important break in our hunt for the origin of this virus, and I want to impress upon you, sir, that I will do everything in my power to establish a conclusive hypothesis. I want us to succeed in our mission here. This mission, not any other nefarious bollocks you might be beholden to."

"Kesta, that's enough."

Dudley held her firmly by the shoulders, his voice low and gentle the way Tim's would have been, trying to stop her from going too far. But Kesta didn't care, she just stood, panting angrily, wishing she had a vial of something nasty to stick into Lundeen's neck.

He came so close to her that their visors clashed. She edged backward, but Lundeen pressed himself more tightly into her personal space until she backed into the workstation and couldn't retreat any farther. She felt the cold metal worktable against her backside as Lundeen's eyes stared, blackened and unfeeling like a shark's in hunting waters she had unwittingly entered.

"I'll make sure you have what you need to see this through," he said, "and you must think yourself very fucking clever to have proven yourself so resourceful. But don't think I'll overlook any further breaches. You cannot go around discussing this project with anyone outside this lab, not even under the guise of some cock-and-bull story about academic papers. I'm watching you, Shelley. Don't think I don't know what you're up to."

"What do you mean by that? Lundeen?"

Dudley reached across and blocked her from reaching Lundeen, who stormed out of the lab. Her arms rose and fell at her sides, in a gesture of bewilderment, but Dudley ignored her too, trailing subserviently behind their boss. Kesta said nothing.

Lundeen left the lab and Dudley followed him, until he reached the automatic doors, at which point he stopped and looked back at Kesta. She took it as a cue, Dudley lingering on the periphery of one laboratory and the other, the search for a cure and the bid to make the virus even more deadly.

"Anything you want to talk to me about?" she asked.

"Only that you lied to me," he whispered, and his eyes were full of hurt behind the visor. "You lied. After we had promised each other that we'd work together and not keep anything secret."

"I didn't lie—about what?"

"About asking Lundeen's permission to review those oncology slides at home. He said he knew nothing about it."

"What gave you the right to ask him in the first place?" she rasped.

"Because I was worried about you," he said, and Kesta could see even in his thick suit that he was shaking. "I wanted Lundeen to lay off you a bit. You told me you were juggling two jobs. He said that was a lie."

"It's not a lie," she pleaded. "It's not a lie, Dudley, it's just that I didn't clear it with him. Because he would have said no."

"That's another lie. I checked at the hospital too. Had coffee with Lorraine Spiller at the weekend—"

Kesta blanched upon hearing the name of the human resources director.

"—and she said that no overtime had been signed off. In fact," he said, looking right at her, and she could tell that most of all he was crushed by her deception, "she wished someone had offered to review slides part-time. She would be grateful for the support."

"Dudley, please, look, I—"

"I can only assume that you've been working on this theory in your spare time?" His tone was dispassionate, as if they were strangers to each other.

"That you took old slides home from the hospital, even though you have a vault of material here. I can't make sense of it. But since you've made yourself the golden girl today with your IBD discovery—which is brilliant, by the way, and I do mean that, Kesta, you are completely brilliant—I'm in no position to challenge you, am I? But if you're selling stolen pharmaceuticals . . ."

"I'm not selling anything. I'm not doing that. I promise, Dudley."

"Jesus, Kesta, the hospital's strapped enough as it is. How could you steal from them?"

"Dudley, I didn't do that."

Kesta considered compounding the lies she had told him but decided against it. "I can't tell you," she said, "but I promise you I didn't sell anything to anyone. You have to believe me."

"I want to believe you, Kesta, but if I'm to trust you, you have to trust me enough to tell me anything, even if it's terrible. You and I want the same thing. An end to this. A cure. Never lie to me again, or I promise you, Lundeen isn't the only person with the power to have you removed from Project Dawn. You should count yourself lucky that I'm still just about on your side."

———

The light at Project Dawn was always stark and unforgiving, like the bulbs could all explode at any moment from the intensity of shining so brightly. They needed the white light to be practical, so that the scientists and technicians could always see what they were doing. The light was also essential to ensure that no one ever felt that what they did could go unseen. It was a naked light, a light designed to make you feel exposed. A scrutinizing light, or perhaps it would be the last light she would ever see, the one she would walk toward and never quite reach, the light that signaled the end.

When Kesta went home every evening, especially this evening, the dimmer switch was her best friend. There was comfort in the darkness of their flat. Sometimes Kesta would sit in the dark, clinging on to Tim's hand, wondering if she kept the light low enough that no one else could see her, she would simply stop existing.

CHAPTER SIXTEEN

I t was dark under the ground too, a mile or so from Kesta's flat, as dark as gestation. A darkness so profound we can never know or even remember it, an enveloping gloom right before we emerge into the world quite helplessly, blinking wildly as we see the light for the first time. Perhaps it is the light that banishes our memories of this black fog we know only at the very beginning. The ignorance of night before our own dawn. There was blackout and then there was a sudden, cataclysmic light. Either way, he couldn't tell the difference between the two, the darkness and the light, and he didn't blink once as he crept out of the crepuscule and onto Commercial Road.

A woman clipped past him on her way into the City. He followed her. The woman was berating herself. She should have worn flats and kept her heels in her handbag until the last moment, then clicked into their offices like a corporate femme fatale. It was only an interview after all, but she hadn't worked since before the outbreak; she needed to get her career back on track and make some money. She wanted them to want her, so she'd left the house in her very best heels, stood in them for an hour on the Central Line all the way from Loughton because the tube was still so infrequent—two paltry carriages and running once every hour—and now she found herself walking from Bethnal Green into the City because the driver had decided he was terminating there. The woman stopped for a moment, leaning against a wall daubed with faded letter Z's, and slipped her left shoe off so that she could rub the sole of her foot with a firm thumb. A passing van beeped its horn at her, and she returned the gesture with a one-finger salute.

He hadn't liked the noise the van had made either.

"Arse," she muttered, oblivious to the man standing behind her.

The woman's phone began to chirrup from the bottom of the briefcase.

"Oh my days, not now," she moaned. "Mum, if this is you . . ."

She cringed as she placed her bare foot on the damp pavement, her pelvis out of kilter, as she rummaged about for the phone under makeup, notebooks, pens, the printout of her CV. Her dancer's core allowed her to answer the phone, replace the shoe, and start up her walk again with a graceful plié.

He watched her, not understanding who she was or what she was doing, he was incapable of that. She was just there and that was enough for him.

"Mum, listen, I'm not even there yet, can I call you back when I'm finished?"

The man followed her. Given her heels, her pace was slow and, distracted by her waffling mother, she forgot to look and listen as she crossed the road and her mother droned on.

"It's up to you, but if you want them to deliver the sofa, you're going to have to let them both in the house," she said. Her mother never heard *I'm busy* or *can I call you later.* These words didn't feature in her daughter's vocabulary, as far as she was concerned.

"You could stay in the kitchen and watch them from there," the woman suggested, trying to be constructive when all she really wanted to do was focus on her interview, run through potential questions in her head. Holding the phone against her ear with her shoulder, she checked her watch. She was going to be late.

Behind her, the man stretched out an arm. He couldn't reach her. He groaned but she couldn't hear him.

"Mum. Mum, I have to go."

The woman picked up the pace, breaking into little jagged steps, swiveling at the hips in her skirt, a clickety shuffle, neither walk nor run, her heart starting to hum, and her ankles close to collapse—holding up the woman and the briefcase and her mother's growing anxiety about deliverymen on the other end of the phone. Still the wet left foot kept slipping and sliding, in and out of the high-heeled shoe. She landed awkwardly on a manhole cover and felt a twinge of pain in her kneecap. Beads of sweat began to form along her hairline, and she dabbed at them with the back of her free hand. Perhaps she should ring the office, tell them about the train's unscheduled stop, but not about the heels, obviously, because who would want to hire someone daft enough to jog for two miles to an interview in four-inch sandals?

"Mum, Mum, I've got a call coming in. It's one of the partners, sorry, love you, bye."

The imaginary work call was the professional woman's last resort. She needed to take a breath and make a plan. Taxis were scarce as hen's teeth, but she stopped where she was and turned to face the road, scouring the horizon for the golden beam of a vacant cab. There was only an empty bus headed in the wrong direction and a man who had come to a dead stop right behind her.

"You all right?" she asked him, instinctively raising her hands high above her head. The man kept creeping closer, one foot at an ugly angle. An angry mob of black flies darted around his head.

"Hands up, yeah, hands up." The woman was edging backward, hands flapping in the air, the sudden stench of rotting fish and burning flesh smacking at the backs of her eyes, which were fixed on the creature lumbering toward her, his limbs askew, clothes shredded and soiled.

She knew they'd all been exterminated, months ago. They'd been told they were safe.

Then she saw the yellow of his eyes, the mouth opening up to her, so much wider than intended, like the Kitum Caves, a tunnel toward death. The last thing you saw before the lights went out for good, the darkness that precedes the final bite.

———

Kesta and the other scientists stood around the television in the break room, transfixed. Flashing blue lights fading in and out of focus as the helicopter hovered on high to capture the scene. Armed police officers spread like black mold along the grout of Commercial Road. Armored vehicles clamping the road off from the City of London. A handful of brave locals were trimming the police cordon, supporting a young woman waving a pair of high-heeled shoes in the air, disbelieving. In the eye of the storm a man was wobbling from foot to foot, dazed by the lights and frightened by the noise of the helicopter, of the orders and threats being screamed in his direction.

Lundeen muted the sound.

"Initial reports suggest the victim is male, mid- to late fifties, Caucasian, and in surprisingly good nick for someone who's been living in a sewer for six months." He turned his back to the television to face the team, and Kesta was sickened by his elation. "They're bringing him back here now. Project Dawn, we have a live one."

Lundeen began clapping, deliberately, like an evangelist. The technicians felt obliged to do the same and spluttered into applause, one eye on the television, the other looking for the exit. Perhaps there was still time to escape before the *live one* was in the building.

The prospect of having to face another zombie in the flesh was daunting, frightening even. Kesta saw a woman heaving sobs into a tissue, hoping no one else would notice. Maybe she was contemplating the gruesome fate that would await this man upon arrival at the lab. Kesta looked over at Dudley and saw that he was mentally sharpening his scalpel, lips smacking at the prospect of a survivor to get his teeth into, the medical rendition of their dreams. At long last a live host in which to observe the virus at close quarters.

Kesta wavered somewhere in between. After all, she had skin in this game.

"This won't end well," said Cooke quietly as the clapping faded, "because they thought they got them all the first time. Prepare yourself for press intrusion, government oversight, and mass panic on the streets. Suddenly it'll be Project Dawn under the microscope. Everyone's going to want their pound of flesh, and that flesh is coming from us."

Up on the television screen, officers were tasering the man, his muscles crackling and jerking with electricity before he crumpled to the pavement, then descending on his body like a hunting pack, the woman with the shoes screaming, hurried away from the scene by a faceless guard twice her size. The television went black, and Kesta felt a hand on her shoulder.

"This is the moment we've all been waiting for," Lundeen said, standing much too close to her.

Don't let your face give you away, she remembered Tim saying because she could never hide how she really felt about someone she didn't much like.

She tried to force a smile, turned to Lundeen poker-faced.

"I'll scrub up," she said.

———

He was confused. That was the thing that struck her first. And he reminded her of Tim. He was bewildered by these people who were strangers, by the industrial soundscape, the whirring, clunking, humming noises emanating from big machinery, by the blinding lights, the surreal feel. It was as strange for him, in his own way, as it was for them watching him, watching them while sniffing the air curiously, like an animal smelling out new territory, so eager to mark it. When they came too close, he growled.

He was held in place by a clamp around his neck almost exactly the same as the one Kesta used to lift Liv in and out of her cage. Similarly, it kept the patient at a distance while neutralizing their ability to bite. At the end of the arm attached to the clamp were two men straining to keep him still. As he looked around the room, inhaling them all through his nose and his gaping mouth, the tongue hanging out to one side, almost white, dried up and desperate for another's blood to replenish its natural color, Kesta, Cooke, Dudley, and Lundeen also looked, incapable of speech.

A live specimen, the virus in situ. This was hope in the shape of a middle-aged man of five feet ten, astonishingly thin, dressed in the remnants of a dark blue suit, the trousers of which were covered in tears, one grinning kneecap exposed. The left sleeve of the jacket had come apart at the shoulder. In a drain somewhere, Kesta thought, there's a navy tie and a shirt that once was white, discarded in a puddle, making a nest for the rats.

Somehow Patient 2468 had decided to hold on to his jacket. His torso was naked, caved in, and caked in dirt, the hairs of his chest matted together, debris from the drains having fused itself to his skin.

"Is that—a sanitary napkin?" Cooke said under her breath.

Alongside feminine products, Patient 2468 had what appeared to be newsprint embedded on his upper arm. Perhaps he'd tried in vain to repair the damaged sleeve?

"Remarkable, absolutely fucking remarkable," said Lundeen, unable to contain his excitement. He moved away from their huddle, walking toward Patient 2468 with his iPad at the ready, keen to make notes. He leaned toward the zombie with all the wide-eyed curiosity of a child intent on pulling the tail of a stray cat.

Patient 2468 lunged at Lundeen, taking his two captors with him. He surged across the room, dragging the guards, their boots sliding along the floor, until he was right on top of Lundeen, who promptly fell over onto his back, holding the iPad up in front of his face, screaming like an infant. The guards pulled hard on the leash, yanking back the neck of Patient 2468 until he was almost cutting himself in two, he was so determined to reach Lundeen, his teeth dripping with hunger.

"Back away slowly, on your hands and knees," the taller of the two guards shouted at Lundeen, who scuttled away obediently, having abandoned the tablet to its fate by the feet of the patient.

"Jesus, he's a monster," Lundeen exclaimed, cowering against the wall as far away from Patient 2468 as he could get.

Kesta looked down at him and hoped he could see how much she loathed him. She wanted him to know her contempt.

"He's not a monster," she said. "He's a man suffering, a man in pain. It's not him you should fear; it's the virus."

She felt a hand grab her elbow. She turned to see Dudley yanking her away from Lundeen. He scowled at her. Since his superior was quivering in a puddle on the floor, Dudley decided to take charge.

"We need to work out a way of managing him, calmly and respect-fully. Kesta, what are your thoughts?"

"We're going to need to sedate him. Midazolam should do it," she said, knowing with earned confidence that it would work, at least for a while.

"How the hell do you plan on doing that?" squealed Lundeen from his corner.

"Not by rushing him like you did," said Kesta, "but rather nicely and slowly. He's responding to a basic need here, which is the impulse to bite us. We need to inject him with a sedative, so we must treat him like a child and distract him in order to do so, to avoid either frightening or antagonizing him."

"I'll prepare a syringe," said Cooke, disappearing to the end of the lab, returning with a steel tray containing a small box and a hypodermic. Dudley put his hands out to support the tray while Cooke removed the glass vial of sedative from the box.

"How much do we give him, do you think?" she asked as she drew the solution upward into the syringe.

"All of it."

Then began an ungainly interplay between science and human kinet-ics. For every doctor who has uttered the words *this is for your own good*, there has been a person on the other side of them and a sickeningly sharp needle disinclined to be struck by it. Magic and medicine are necessary bedfellows. Illusion makes the ominous appear benign. It's the *look at that lovely view over there outside the window* while someone with too-large hands is inserting a fetid tube inside your rectum. *Pretend this isn't happening while it's happening* comes just before the Hippocratic oath.

Dudley took the now-empty tray and walked closely past Patient 2468, like a matador. He moved quickly while keeping just enough distance, waving the tray in the air, letting the light catch it so the patient was intrigued.

Patient 2468 huffed. The foot that wasn't backward stamped on the spot. The patient prepared to charge, tracking Dudley's motions with his head rolling on his shoulders and his arms lifting slightly, but he couldn't raise them all the way up, so his arms hung loosely, waggling by his sides. He thrust forward from his pelvis, throwing one leg ahead, then the other, all the while grunting, enthralled by the light. Dudley stepped closer, then backed off again, allowing the patient to almost touch the tray before pulling it backward—hiding it, revealing it once more. He danced with it, to distract the patient, not to fool him, and especially not to hurt him.

Dudley courageously led the patient away from Kesta, leaving the newsprint-covered shoulder wide open, vulnerable to a woman as sudden as she. She could just about reach him, stretching up onto her toes, her hands like lightning even in those fat gloves, darting the needle into his skin. He swatted her away before she could remove the syringe, which dangled from his shoulder like a banderilla. Dudley stood firm with the tray and the zombie fixed his eyes on it, grasping at the lights he saw flashing off its surface. Together, Kesta and Dudley were able to take the virus by surprise.

The two of them retreated, then watched as the man began to power down, standing woozily, slouching forward at the waist, then folding at the knees down to the ground. His bare chest puffed gently in and out, his hands resting on his thighs.

He looked at Kesta, right at her. Somewhere inside, he was figuring it all out. The guards had to come a little closer to allow Patient 2468 to lie down. The metal chain around his neck made a clunking sound as it hit the laboratory floor. His body made no sound at all. The poor man was down for the count, though his eyes remained wide open. Kesta tugged the empty syringe out of the patient's shoulder.

The scientists approached Patient 2468 and stood in a tight circle above him. Lundeen had recovered enough to retrieve his tablet from the floor.

"Even after all these months underground, he's a feisty bugger, ain't he?" said Cooke, squatting down to touch the man, who remained perfectly still. She couldn't quite believe what they were doing. Kesta watched Cooke feeling along the man's leg, fascinated by the foreign-feeling femur, by his sunken muscles.

"You're a fighter, you are," she said, using Kesta's weight to lift herself back up to her feet again.

"Why did he attack me?" Lundeen asked Dudley, as though his newfound skills as a zombie matador had also come with a promotion. Lundeen was embarrassed, that was obvious. Embarrassed to have fallen on his arse in terror in front of inferior colleagues. But his shame ran deeper. Like so many managers before him, Lundeen had forgotten everything that had once made him a half-decent scientist.

Privately, Kesta had to believe that he might have always been one of those solidly average types whose mainstream failures act like buoyancy aides that, along with an unearned self-confidence, help them to rise to the top. Lundeen had fallen out of love with virology, with microbiology, with helping other people to live without disease, and he stopped being excited about it. Now he bowed and scraped to money and prestige. Kesta realized that, in a strange way, she had the upper hand. Where Lundeen had the grading, the pension, and the title, she had the skill, the insight, and the nerve.

Kesta bent down to take a closer look at the patient, now very much unconscious, his yellow eyes trained on the ceiling. He was in good condition, all considered. She wondered if this was what Tim would look like now, if she'd left him alone.

"He wants blood," she said. "We know it's how the virus spreads, and it's also how the virus sustains itself. I think that the virus actually becomes stronger the more it's able to transmit. Hence the constant drive to bite."

"So he's weaker now because he hasn't bitten anyone in a while? He hasn't eaten?" Cooke asked.

"What are you suggesting, Shelley? That we serve up one of the technicians as lunch?" scoffed Lundeen.

"Lundeen, listen," she said sternly, and for once in her life almost towering over another human being. "He hasn't tasted blood, which is what the virus wants, to transmit itself, voraciously, into the body of another. He gains in strength from the virus becoming more potent."

"Let me get this straight," said Dudley, "you're saying that the virus becomes stronger in one person by spreading to another."

"Yes. It's what we're seeing in the monkeys."

"So, if we wanted to increase the virulence of the virus in—"

"—Dave," Cooke interrupted. "We're calling him Dave. I can't keep calling him Patient 2468, it's ridiculous. It's dehumanizing."

"Dave, then." Dudley waved down at the sleeping man formerly known as Patient 2468. "So, if we wanted to increase the viral load in Dave here, we need to do what?"

"Allow him to bite someone," said Kesta.

"You're not serious?" Lundeen spat at her, which was silly enough, since the spray of his frustration splattered against his visor and he would be forced to leave it there, mocking him, until he was out of the biohazard zone.

"Yes and no," she replied. "Yes, giving him a virus-free human being to feed on will allow the virus to thrive. No, I'm not suggesting you sacrifice yourself, Lundeen. Though we would respect your decision to lay down your life at the altar of scientific progress."

"What do we feed him then, Shelley?"

"Meal replacements via a feeding tube if you want to control it. The snakes with IBD eventually succumb to starvation, so we have to try to fill him with nutrients somehow to stop that from happening. Liquids.

Electrolytes. Antifungals. Blood transfusion with packed cells, platelets separately because they seem to lose the ability to clot. Keep him in this state, this zombie state. Pain relief."

"What does he need pain relief for?"

"Well, his jaw is dislocated and his left foot's on back to front, which doesn't look especially comfortable."

Lundeen was shaking his head, either in disbelief or to dislodge the spittle still trickling down his visor.

"Shelley, how have you been able to reach this hypothesis?"

Kesta didn't balk. She stood up and folded her arms across her middle, not in hostility, but in quiet defiance.

"Because I've thought about nothing other than the practical transmission of this virus since my husband was infected with it."

She said it sharply. It had the effect she was after, which was to stem further scrutiny for fear of setting her off.

"I've been through the histology and the cytology, and I've spent weeks with you reviewing slides of every conceivable virus, modern and extinct. When I close my eyes at night, I see in microscopy, tiny bloody pathogens fizzing in Technicolor, driving me quietly mad. I was surprised, frankly, Lundeen, when I did start working at Project Dawn, by just how little thought your team had given it."

"Seconded," said Cooke.

The power of the angry widows squared put paid to any pushback from the higher-ups. Lundeen was in no mood to argue with her. He launched into conciliatory action instead, which was almost as annoying, cozying up to Kesta as closely as their suits would allow, tapping her visor with his own.

"Okay, okay," he said begrudgingly. "This is good insight. This is something we can work with."

"Hang on." Dudley rested his hand on her arm. "You said something just now. *They* lose the ability to clot. What do you mean *they*?"

Kesta swallowed hard and hoped that the look of dismay on her face could pass sufficiently for disdain.

"It's obvious, if you think about it," she said, perhaps too emphatically because Dudley flinched a little. "They all bleed, all the time. The ones from before, I mean, from during the outbreak. They break their bones. They are badly bitten and wounded. They bleed constantly, but they don't bleed out. Something is preventing their blood from clotting, and yet it isn't fatal to them."

"So, the virus somehow instructs changes in the infected so that their blood functions differently? Blood no longer serves the body in terms of delivering nutrients and oxygen?"

"Exactly, I think that the blood's purpose is purely to transport the virus. They can remain in this undead phase, if not indefinitely then certainly, as we're seeing here with Dave, for a significant period of time. We can't rule out the possibility of Dave having eaten vermin or waste materials while he was down in the sewers, but at the same time we cannot rule out the fact that he may not have eaten anything at all for many months. There's something in the blood, something in how it changes the person who is infected by the virus, allowing them to exist in this new state, almost like a kind of hibernation. The virus only really wakes them up when the opportunity to infect arises. The body is merely waiting in stasis. Waiting for the next host."

"Could it be worth us looking into the properties of animals who sleep for long periods of time?" asked Dudley. "Those who can function without eating or drinking?"

"Like sharks," suggested Cooke, "they can go for ten weeks without eating. I saw a program on it once. The more they starve themselves, the better they become at hunting."

"There are all kinds of species capable of living on the very edge of existence," said Dudley. "The olm is another, amphibious, lives its entire life in the darkest parts of the underground cave systems beneath the Dinaric Alps. It's entirely blind, but its other senses are acutely developed. It lives and feeds and breeds underwater, never needing air or sunlight. Studies have shown the olm can last up to ten years without food."

Cooke gasped. "Just like our Dave!"

"This is a virus capable of changing the host's DNA," Kesta said. "Look at Dave, he hasn't fed in months. He's completely emaciated. He only seems to wake up when we approach him, and with one purpose. To bite us. The virus is changing the basic mechanics of what it is to be human and alive, until . . ."

"What is it, Kesta?" Dudley asked her.

"The host becomes irrelevant. The virus doesn't need them to feed, or to stay strong, or to take care of themselves. The host can dwindle into almost nothing, and the virus can still survive. The host is needed only—to transmit the virus. What if only the virus is alive inside the host?"

"Which could mean that if we remove the virus—"

"The host would die."

An invisible force pushed upon her, a sickening weight, the sensation of spinning in a human centrifuge, moving her, crushing her, all at once.

What if by treating Tim, she killed him? What if it really was only his body that remained, chained to their spare bed, and that only the virus lay alive inside him? What if the two could never again be separated? What if the damage the virus did to the human body was so profound, that once infected, the changes the body was subjected to, right down to its primal coding, were irreversible?

At their feet, Dave began to twitch.

She had nursed Tim for five months now. But who had been looking after Dave? No one. And yet he was still undead if not alive, in more or less the same condition as Tim was. There was still so much she didn't understand about the virus. What remained unchanged was how much it terrified her. She had to focus.

"He's coming round," she said. "We should give him another shot and move him somewhere we can lose the neck clamp and make him more comfortable."

"The ward in the basement," said Lundeen as he stepped away from Dave.

He watched Kesta with suspicion. She seemed to know exactly what to do in this moment, she wasn't frightened of the zombie, she appeared almost at ease around him.

Turning to the two guards, Lundeen said, "Guys, we have D-ring limb holders fitted to the beds downstairs. Let's get Patient, er, Dave out of here as quickly as we can. Shelley, can you please—"

He was going to ask her to sedate the patient again, but he saw that she was already on her knees, the syringe was spent, and Dave's muscle spasms were beginning to recede.

"Some of them have a very high tolerance for . . ." she began but stopped herself, hoping that no one questioned what she meant by *them*.

Cooke groaned as she bent down next to her, muttering to herself.

"Don't mind me, I just thought . . ."

She didn't need to finish what she was saying. As Kesta tugged the needle out of Dave's shoulder, Cooke pulled her gloved hand out from Dave's inside jacket pocket.

"Look!" she said, gleefully waving it at Lundeen and Dudley. "A wallet!"

"How has he managed to hold on to it after all this time?" Kesta asked, tidying away the used syringe.

"Let's have a look, shall we?" Cooke already had the smooth leather unfolded, the two halves of it spread apart, her fingers sliding through the individual sleeves. She found a driving license and gasped.

"Our Dave is actually Jasper Armstrong," she said, showing the license to each of them in turn, "born in '68, so that makes him, what?"

"Fifty-five," said Dudley, taking the license from Cooke, holding it up into the light. "He lives in Eltham."

The four of them stood in silence. Cooke peered down at Dave, now Jasper, who had started to snore.

"We know who he is now."

"Yes, we know who he is." Lundeen approached the sleeping zombie and tapped him gingerly with the toe of his shoe.

"We'll be able to notify his next of kin, then," said Kesta. "Shall I start calling the relevant authorities?"

No one looked at her. They were all focused on Dave. Up and down his chest rose and fell, the eyes wide, the smell still pungent.

"We should inform his next of kin," she said again.

"You'll do nothing of the sort," said Lundeen.

"Excuse me?"

"He's ours now. No one knows where he is. No one is expecting your call."

He walked over to her. "No one is waiting for him to come home."

Kesta took a step backward. She looked to Cooke and to Dudley for support, but they avoided her gaze, both busying themselves with the sleeping creature.

"You're not seriously suggesting that we don't tell his wife or his husband or whoever the fuck is missing him that he's alive and—"

"He isn't though, is he?" Lundeen smiled as he said it, as though it was pleasing in its rationale. "He's been gone for who knows how many months. Whoever missed him will have given up ages ago and—"

"You never give up."

"Even if they haven't, they wouldn't want him back in this state. Think about it sensibly, Kesta. He can't go home and take his kids to the park, can he? He has to stay here. So what's the point of us having to deal with the bureaucracy, the red tape around some half-witted spouse, crying their eyes out begging us not to test anything on him even though the whole of humankind is dependent on it, because she's clinging to the daft notion we can actually send him home, with what? A bag of fucking adult nappies and a boot for his ankle?"

"But his family has to know he's been found."

"Kesta, dear, what good would that do?"

Cooke was squatting next to Dave, her hand resting on his stomach for balance.

"You of all people can't honestly agree with him?" Kesta shouted, jabbing her thumb toward Lundeen.

"Kesta, sweetheart—"

"Don't you patronize me, June. Christ, I can't believe this. The three of you, conspiring to keep the existence of this poor man a secret from his family?" Kesta glared at each of them accusingly in turn. "June, please, what if it was Rodney? Wouldn't you want to know he was alive?"

Cooke stood up.

"No," she said, "I don't think I would. Not like this. I wouldn't want to see him like this."

"But this is unethical! We have a moral obligation to tell his family he's been found!"

"I think that morally, we're in a gray area as it is," said Dudley. He was pulling every card out of the man's wallet, checking it, tossing it on the floor. Then an awful smile spread across his face. "But legally speaking, I might have just found our get out of jail free card."

The others crowded around him.

"He's an organ donor," said Dudley.

"Oh well, that settles it, then," said Lundeen, pinching the donor card from Dudley and shoving it into the pocket of his lab coat. "I think we can agree that he would want to do this. To make a personal sacrifice. For science."

"Lundeen, this is a real live person!" Kesta cried.

"Well, that's debatable," he sniffed, "and anyway, we shouldn't concern ourselves with something as trifling as consent in a state of national emergency."

"He isn't dead yet!" said Kesta.

"He's undead," said Lundeen. "That's good enough for me."

CHAPTER SEVENTEEN

"So, it is safe for me to go out then? Or should I lock myself in the bathroom like Shelley Duvall in *The Shining* and wait for you to text me the all-clear?"

Kesta had been on the phone to Jess for over an hour, trying to underplay the fact that a zombie had crawled out of a sewer five months after what they had assumed was the end of the outbreak. Striking the right balance between prudent resolve and spiraling into blind panic had never been more important. The city was in danger of free fall as the veracity of everything they had been told during the aftermath was relentlessly questioned.

All the infected have been terminated, they'd been assured. Conspiracy theories were running wild. Kesta remembered the old man she'd met on her first day at Project Dawn. Would he be hiding away at home brandishing his walking stick for protection now, vindicated that his suspicions had been right all along? That those in charge lie to us? Always. Instinctively. Necessarily.

"We're confident it's just this one *survivor*," Kesta said. And she *was* confident—more or less. She had just finished drawing a pint of her own blood and needed to refrigerate it.

"Can you give me a second?" she asked, putting the handset down on the kitchen worktop and tucking the red bag onto the top shelf next to a ready-meal curry she was defrosting. She removed a bottle of sparkling water that belched lightly as she opened it. She drank it straight down, returning to the dining room where she had scattered the contents of a box of plasters across the beech tabletop in an effort to find the small circular one she needed to cover the puncture wound on the inside of her arm. She went back into the kitchen, to her phone and Jess.

"So, you're freaking out, then?"

"I am freaking out, Kesta. I'm genuinely freaking out. Did your lot"—she was careful not even to whisper the name Project Dawn on the phone for fear Kesta's line had somehow been bugged by a hostile agency—"you know, are they checking? Online it says that the army is going to start searching key sites where the zombies might hide, like in the underground and the sewer system. They must be sure there aren't more of them? And how on earth has this one managed to survive this long?"

Kesta understood that nothing she said was likely to placate Jess. It was better to let her raving run out of steam.

"It's scary," she said, "and you're right to be afraid."

"What's he like, then?"

"The zombie? I'm not sure he's your type."

"Oh, shut up, Kesta. Don't take the piss. This is deadly serious. I mean what condition is he in? The press is eating itself for information."

"Well, they're not going to get any from me," she said, "and you know I can't tell you anything beyond confirming his existence."

"People at work are split between staying home and soldiering on, and you know as well as I do that I'm not the soldiering kind." Jess had to stop for a second to allow the sound of sirens wailing in the background to fade so that Kesta could hear what she was saying. "And I'm frightened. I mean, this was all meant to be over, and we were getting used to that being the truth. Now I don't know what to believe anymore. For example, they're still pushing ahead with the reopening of the cinema in Covent Garden. I had wanted to go to that. Do you think that's a good idea? Should I still do that? Do you think I'll get there and find myself sitting in row Z next to someone who's actually been there for five months eating rats instead of popcorn?"

Kesta wasn't inclined to include the relaunch strategy of a chain cinema into her burgeoning list of things to worry about. "I would imagine they need to reopen financially. But if going feels like an unnecessary risk to you, then it's not one you should take."

"Is your arse sore?" Jess asked.

"What?"

"Your arse, Kesta. Are those splinters from that fucking fence you're sitting on giving you any discomfort?"

"I'm not sitting on the fence, Jess. I'm just advising caution. Same as before. We need to remain vigilant and mindful for our personal safety. But the likelihood of there being another zombie," she said, glancing down the corridor to Tim's bedroom, where he was presently waving his free hand through the air like a paper airplane, "is almost zero."

"I would prefer absolute zero."

"Well, I'm afraid I can't give you that," Kesta said. "What are they screening, anyway?"

"A zombie classic triple bill," Jess sniggered, "Romero, Argento, and Edgar Wright."

"That's incredibly poor taste, don't you think?"

"Well, I think it's poor taste now, yes, but people will probably turn out for it facetiously."

Kesta heard a clunk coming from Tim's room and looked up to see that he had moved himself to the edge of the bed, his wrist still attached to the radiator. He was tugging at it absentmindedly.

"Oh, I don't suppose they'll cancel your ZARG meetings, will they?"

"I haven't heard anything to suggest they will."

She wondered why Jess would ask her this so unexpectedly, before realizing there was no reason why Jess would suspect that she wasn't going to her ZARG meetings because they were supposed to be mandatory. Kesta couldn't remember how many weeks she had missed, but no one had raised a complaint, and surely they were less likely to now.

"I'm sure they'll relish the opportunity to have something new to talk about."

Kesta looked down the hallway to see that Tim was gone. He wasn't in the bed and the handcuffs had disappeared from view.

"Call you back," she said and didn't wait for an answer. She dropped the phone on the table and ran down the narrow corridor into the entrance hall and through into the spare room. Tim had managed to yank the handcuffs up toward the far end of the radiator. He had pulled at it so hard that Kesta could see the brackets coming away from the wall. He had reached the bedside table and was standing there picking up the contents, sniffing boxes of drugs, licking plastic bottles.

She crept toward him.

"Darling."

"Eeergh," he grunted, waving a packet of oxycodone at her.

"Can you put that down, my love? And get back into bed, please?"

"Eeergh!"

"I know, darling, I know. Let me take that, will you?"

She took a step closer, reaching out toward the packet with both hands. Looking from his face, which was set in frustration, to his hands, which were squeezing tightly around the packet he did not want to give her. He started to shake the packet in his closed fist like a child's rattle.

It was amusing to him. Or was it ownership? He'd no wish to be parted from it. It didn't really matter, she could easily get more, but she didn't want him taking anything by accident, outside of her regimen. She reached a little closer, her hands outstretched. And that was when he struck her.

Kesta didn't make a sound because the shock clamped her windpipe shut. She fell to the ground, cracking her hip against the wooden floor. Her first reaction was to crawl away from him to the corner by the door where she knew he couldn't stretch to reach her. She cowered there as the vise in her throat released. She gasped for breath, sucking in oxygen and breathing out surprise. Her left cheekbone pounded as though his fist was still hitting it, and she could feel all the blood in her face surging to that area to repair it.

He didn't mean to do it. You tried to take his toy.

Shaking, she touched her cheek with her fingers and saw that he had cut her. She looked up at him from her nook near the floorboard, and she felt small and helpless. He was a giant. He was powerful. And he was staring down at her, staring at the blood on her face.

Tim screamed. Head thrown back on that crooked neck, every muscle and sinew in his body was raging. He began to beat his chest with his fist, inside which the oxy strips were crumbled into dust. He stamped at the floor with his feet, yanked again and again at the handcuffs, pulling the radiator farther and farther away from the wall. Kesta felt the whole room shifting, shaking, all its contents—including her—fixed into orbit around this monster who was the sun.

"Argh! Argh! Argh!"

"Tim."

"Argh! Argh! Argh!"

"Tim, it's okay, Tim."

"Urghhhh!"

"Tim, I love you. I forgive you. It's okay."

She used the wall to push herself back up again onto her feet. She wiped the blood from her face with the sleeve of her T-shirt. Tim stopped jumping and went quiet.

"See?" she said. "I'm okay. We're okay."

Kesta watched as the anger drained from his body, which hung limply like laundry. He was wobbling from foot to foot. Somewhere inside him, the old Tim was ashamed.

"It's all right," she said, to console him, when there was a knock at the door.

"Kesta." It was Albert, knocking little raps like gunfire against the wood. "You okay in there?"

Shit.

Nausea lurched inside her. Tim was still out of bed and Albert was

banging on her front door. She had no time to think, only to act. She had
to risk leaving Tim there without sedation while she dealt with Albert, who
she knew wouldn't go away without checking on her. She looked at Tim,
who was agitated by the knocking sound, and put her finger to her lips.
Ssshhh. Kesta drew the bolts across the door until Tim was safe inside.

"Coming," she said.

She sped into the kitchen, opened a bottle of gin, and splashed it
behind her ears and over her throat like cheap perfume. Then, back into
the hallway, she looked at herself in the mirror there. Her cheek was
livid. She bruised easily. The skin around her eyes was thin like tissue.
She already looked beaten up. She mussed her hair, digging both hands
in at the crown, so that her ponytail was disheveled and hanging on to
her head for dear life. Then she unlocked the front door, opened it, and
kept it barely ajar with her foot.

"Was I being loud?" she said, one eye peeking at Albert through
the gap.

"Ground-floor tenant rang to complain about shouting. Is everything
all right, love?"

"Yeah, I'm fine. Sorry about that." Kesta opened up the door a little
more, letting Albert see her shiner.

"Jesus, girl, what you done to yourself?" He tried to push his hand
through the gap to touch her, so Kesta closed it up again.

"Oh, it's nothing," she said, "just me not looking where I was going."
Albert waited for an explanation. "I was trying to clear out some of Tim's
stuff, and I stood up into a cupboard door that was already open," she
said, tucking her hair behind her ear so that he could get a better look
at the bruise. "Really bashed into it, didn't I? Such a wally."

Albert peered a little closer but was repelled by an imposing smell.
She saw it register on his face.

*She's been drinking again, in the middle of the day, and she's fallen
over, doing herself some damage.* It all made sense to him now.

"Woman downstairs said there was a lot of noise and—"

"I took my mortification out on the cupboard," she said, "really went to town on it." The silence between them was painful. Albert was so full of pity, so very kind. She remained a terrible if practiced liar. Then he touched her hand as it held open the door, only for a second, before jamming it sheepishly into the pocket of his jeans.

"You must be scared what with them finding another one," he said. "I am too. Brings back bad memories. But lay off the sauce, girl. It won't help. Take it from one who knows."

"Thanks, Albert," Kesta said, closing the door, signaling that the conversation was over. Back inside the spare bedroom, Tim was leaning against the bed, rocking back and forth, his shoulders hunched, whining.

"It's okay, darling," she said, edging toward him, showing him that her hands were empty, palms open to him. "Albert's gone now."

She kept her distance, her body angled away from his, to dig into the bedside table to find a sedative. "Be good to have a little sleep now, don't you think?"

Tim seemed resigned to it. She guided him back into a sitting position, and she injected him quickly because she needed to dig out his old toolbox from the boiler room to find something she could use to reinforce the brackets of the radiator. Images of raw plugs and crosshead screwdrivers flew through her mind, and she wished she'd paid more attention to those home renovation shows Tim loved.

She thought about Dave and about Liv and how they now most likely shared the same distorted DNA as her own husband's. The virus replicating inside the host, perhaps even replacing every single cell with something designed in its own image.

How much of Tim was left?

"There," she said, turning away from him just for a moment to tidy up the bedside table and close the drawer. Then she strained to slide it farther away, out of his reach in the bed. She stood upright, gasping a little from the effort. She froze as she felt his cold hand weave around her waist, and she trembled as it pulled her in tightly, snaking down toward her thighs. She felt Tim rest his chin on the top of her head. She felt him breathing her in, sniffing at her hair. But it wasn't her hair he could smell. It was the blood lying underneath the plaster in the crook of her arm, the blood pooling underneath her eye where the bruise was building. Her blood excited him as did the racing of her heart. She didn't dare move. She laid her hands over his and hoped the sedation would overwhelm him before he overwhelmed her.

Was this her husband holding her or was she in the arms of the virus?

Kesta held her breath. She had to believe it was still him inside. She had to trust that he still knew who she was, still loved her enough to resist the virus's urge. Knowing he could crush her, knowing he could turn at any moment. Knowing he might bite.

CHAPTER EIGHTEEN

Tim was becoming harder to keep sedated, and Kesta could sense his thirst for blood—the sinister impulse to allow the virus to spread—was making him hungry. He was losing weight and growing thinner, though his strength and his reflexes remained the same. When she looked at him now, she was beginning to see the outline of the bones inside him as though they too wanted to escape. When he slept, he made a rattling sound somewhere deep within, and Kesta imagined a miniature Tim dragging a tin cup along the insides of his own ribs, a prisoner striving to remind his guard he was still there, still serving out his time. Other than the fluids and the pain relief and the blood she gave him, there had been nothing new to try for weeks. If Tim was getting sicker, Kesta was fraying toward her last nerve.

She'd been working patiently and cautiously, overseeing Dave the zombie's bone marrow biopsy, staging it perfectly, then reviewing it over and over again, more or less on her own. Lost in that world of devious purple jellybeans.

Each time she visited Dave, locked up in his cage in a secure room, far away from her own laboratory, she thought of Tim. Sometimes she just stood outside with her forehead rested against the shockproof glass so that Dave had something to look at as he shuffled from foot to foot in his hospital gown, chained by the ankle to a bolt in the floor, not by the wrist to a radiator.

The second coming of Dave had caused considerable panic. Schools and some businesses had closed again. Police officers and army reserves had returned to the streets. Kesta felt relieved to see people she recognized on her commute were still heading into town, trying to carry on with their lives. She was stopped four times on one particular journey to work and was once asked to produce her ID by a baby-faced constable. Each time the officers told her to go home and stay indoors. Each time she continued on, regardless.

Until she saw the man with the messenger bag again, hanging around outside St. Clement's church. The man she had seen the night she and Dudley went to St. Paul's for a drink after work. The man who seemed to be waiting for someone. As she came into view, he began to walk diagonally across the street so that he'd cut her off before she could reach the junction. A bolt of adrenaline shivered over Kesta's shoulders. He had been waiting for her.

"Excuse me, miss, can I talk to you for a moment?" he asked, a fake smile plastered across his face. He slid into her personal space as though they were friends, and although Kesta ignored him as best she could, she instinctively clutched her bag into her stomach and picked up her pace.

His right hand held on to his messenger bag, his left hand grabbed her forearm, and Kesta could feel her bones inside it. "I'm just looking for a quick comment," he breathed into her ear.

A journalist.

"I just have a few questions about the zombie you captured last week. We should talk."

A journalist who somehow knows I work at Project Dawn.

"I don't know what you're talking about."

"Let me give you my details."

He frowned, looking at the cut on her temple from where Tim had hit her. "What happened to your face?"

"Leave me alone," she blustered, wriggling away while he was distracted by fishing inside the bag for his business card.

"You don't look very well, Mrs. Shelley. If you don't talk to me, others will come looking for you," he shouted after her as she raced off down the street toward Temple tube station.

She reached the entrance and yanked at the shutters, but the station was closed, so she sprinted around onto the Embankment, emptied out of cars and pedestrians. There was no one she could ask to help her. She glanced backward but couldn't see him, only the fossilized buildings of her old college, of the redundant station.

She could keep running, all the way into Westminster perhaps, or she could hide. She swerved into Somerset House, slipping underneath the chains designed to deter tourists and down the steps into its vast network of intricate brickwork arches. The arches were like old tunnels, like the insides of your blood vessels. And now Kesta was a single blood cell traveling through them.

How did he know she worked at Project Dawn? How long had he been watching her? How did he know her name?

She knew that she should report what had happened to her to Lundeen. She should warn her colleagues that their work might be compromised because certainly their location was. Kesta waited, huddled on the floor in the half-dark, absorbing the damp from the bricks into her spine. The man with the messenger bag didn't come for her. Nobody did. It took her twenty minutes to convince herself that he had gone and that she was safe to leave.

She decided not to say anything at work about the journalist. It would only be something else to draw unwanted attention to her. Better not to be stained by suspicion. There was a definite risk that if she called the guy's bluff and reported him to Lundeen, the matter would escalate out of her control. She would have to be more careful when arriving at and leaving for work.

———

She was still getting dressed in her lab gear and worrying about the journalist when Cooke burst into the changing room, panting.

"I put it straight in the freezer. I didn't want to open it without you."

Only her blue eyes were visible through the gap between her face mask and her hair mask, but they told Kesta everything. The special delivery from John Diaz had arrived.

Cooke took Kesta by the arm and marched her down the corridor as she struggled to fix her own face mask with one hand. They entered the cold store antechamber adjacent to the primary lab and walked over to the bank of refrigeration units at the back of it.

Kesta could see it then, staring out at them both, such a generic-looking thing, something you might pack full with sandwiches, or tiny quiches, or a good bottle of Chablis to be kept chilled for a picnic. The container was the color of bone with a solid black handle embedded in the surface like some kind of lesion, until you wanted to peel it back and pick it up.

"I just took off the exterior packaging when I saw it had come from Florida," said Cooke as she pulled the door handle upward, as high as her chin, and out again, yanking and groaning as she opened the freezer door. A cloud of ice blasted out, smothering them. Kesta could feel her skin shrinking back on itself. The warmth of her breath colliding with the frigid air turned her visor almost opaque in an instant. She could just make out the ghostly shapes of Cooke's blue gloves extended, reaching downward and plunging themselves into the icy chamber, where they disappeared in another *whoosh* of frozen particles, then, slowly, as though the time and space around them had frozen too, her hands emerged from the white clouds, claws wrapped around the container suspended in the air. All around them that supernatural dry ice hovered. They walked through it, disrupting the clouds with their legs and feet until it had vanished as quickly as it had appeared. That bleak feeling of a cold so deep it kills anything living remained on Kesta's skin and in her lungs. It was the kind of cold that tricks your brain into slowing down, giving up, and going to sleep forever, a nitrogen cold so vicious it might snap you in half.

"Do you want to do the honors?" Cooke asked her, still shivering as she gently placed the container down onto a steel counter safely away from the freezer. Kesta shook her head.

"No, you can," she said, instinctively closing her eyes as Cooke began to unlock the fat clips holding the lid in place. In the darkness of her closed eyes, Kesta saw Tim's face as it used to be, tanned and smiling and full of life. It gave her the resolve to continue. She opened her eyes to confront what was in the box. She heard Cooke gasp, and she did the same when she saw it for the first time.

The snake was colorless and twisted into a tight knot with its throat facing upward. Each and every scale glistened as just the slightest contact with the atmosphere appeared to moisten it. Though it was frozen, the undulating texture of its reptilian skin rendered it supple and fluid, as though at any moment it might slip itself out of that painful bind and slither freely out into the lab. Kesta and Cooke leaned in closer, their face masks wet with condensation.

"I've never seen anything like it," said Cooke, tracing the larger scales that covered the snake's belly with the tip of her gloved finger. She prized the snake away from the box.

"It's really quite heavy."

The creature was still so perfect, emitting little mists of frozen air, and so pure that its rigidity seemed perverse. As Cooke turned the snake around to inspect the other side, they both saw the dainty prongs of a forked tongue, peeking out from its seamless mouth.

"There is a protein unique to snakes with IBD," said Kesta as Cooke returned the snake to its container. "We need to find it and isolate it."

"Staining it is going to be hard going," said Cooke, straining to close the lid again. She folded her arms across the surface of the box with the snake inside, then rested her chin in the nest she'd made. Kesta had to admire her nonchalance. "We'll need samples from every major organ in the snake. Digestive tract will be our best bet. We're going to be up to our eyeballs in paraffin, you and I. And it's not going to be straightforward solubilizing the inclusion bodies."

"And we only have the one snake to work with. We have to be careful. But once we have the protein, we can look to stimulate antibodies in another host. Mice?"

"Mice should do the trick. They live among snakes with IBD but never catch it. And mice are carriers of LCMV. Then we'll be able to determine the antigenic specificity. We'll see how the rodent's immune system reacts to the IBD protein and creates antibodies that we can then, hopefully, hand over to Dudley."

Dudley. Where on earth was Dudley? Kesta was plagued by a sense of phantom limb syndrome, so strong was the sensation that her lab had been amputated from the other, from Dudley and the Gain-of-Function research team. She felt a permanent dull ache of there being something missing, and it throbbed each time she arrived at the proxy lab and saw that Dudley wasn't there.

Lundeen and Dudley and their private team stayed secure in their even darker recess of the Project Dawn site. She and Dudley had passed once or twice in the corridor. She had been pushing a trolley of yellow chicks buzzing in a tray ready to be gassed and dissected. He was talking to a woman in a black suit holding her lanyard fast against her chest so as to conceal her name. Kesta had stopped, turned to watch them disappearing from view, though not before Dudley had looked back at her. He said nothing, used his key card to access a room she couldn't, and disappeared.

They slowly thawed the boa for processing. They extracted tiny tissue samples from the kidney and the digestive tract. Then the spellcraft began. Homogenization. Centrifuging, mixing, and vortexing. Then incubation.

A witch's brew: insides of snake, plus the hearts and minds of two brilliant women. Science taking what it knows to be fact, disregarding it, remodeling it, redefining itself, never too proud or blind to say it was almost wrong before—how could it know what hadn't existed?—but open to continual renewal, to improvement, the radical evolutionary expansion of its understanding of the universe. Kesta and Cooke, pushing at the edges of the galaxy, to the point of discovery, to something inexorable and new. The cultivation of the preparation. The isolation of the IBD protein in the Florida constrictor and, finally, the culturing of the monoclonal antibodies in their test mice.

Their dogged determination, coupled with industrial vats of black, sugary coffee, early starts, and later nights, kept them running on close to empty, spurred on by even the slightest advancement on the previous day's work. Tim had always said that once Kesta set her mind to something, there could be no stopping her. She lived without his cheerleading these days, but watching him on the video monitor while she was at work, sitting with him in the evening when she collapsed, almost as half-dead as he was, at home, was all the motivation she needed to keep going.

Wednesday night—Kesta should have been at her ZARG meeting but had, of course forgotten all about it—neither could believe their eyes, eyes that zoomed in on that unmistakable Y-shaped molecule fixed inside the slide, the pretty polypeptides of success. The little Y antibody latching onto the evil inclusion, miraculously conceived to drive it out of the sample and protect the native cells. The mice didn't get sick because these antibodies protected them.

Kesta had isolated the protein causing the virus.

Cooke had cultured the antibodies produced by the mice in self-defense against it. Now it was up to Dudley to mass-produce the antibodies and use them to find a cure. A cure for Dave. A cure for Liv.

A cure for Tim. A cure for Kesta in a way.

———

She saw the journalist again a few days later, striding down the Strand as she was heading home for the evening, but he didn't seem to see her this time. She ducked into a pharmacy and hid behind the window display. MAKEUP FOR THE NEW NOW, proclaimed the ad, and Kesta feigned an interest in a postapocalyptic blush, the shade called RUN FOR IT. She watched the journalist hurry past, with another place to be, another headline to chase.

"You look like you could do with a bit of color in your cheeks," said the sales assistant, appearing out of nowhere. "And a good base can cover up a multitude of sins."

"You can be sure of that, can you?" Kesta asked, conscious that she'd run into the shop for sanctuary but now wanted to escape from it as quickly as she could.

"This brand is perfect for the woman of today on the go," the assistant said and grinned, holding up a bottle of yellowing foundation like the Olympic torch. "It stays put no matter what life throws at you."

Kesta was about to question the validity of the woman's claims, when her phone began to vibrate in the pocket of her jeans. She summoned a look of faux disappointment that was returned by the sales assistant. Kesta answered without checking to see who was calling her, the sales assistant similarly distracted by an imperfection in her own reflection.

"I need to know what's going on, Kesta," said John Diaz, half a world away in Florida. Kesta felt like she was being watched on all sides, at home and abroad it seemed. "Is it what we feared? Has IBD spread to humans?"

"John, I can't talk to you right now."

"You have to talk to me. You owe me something. I need to plan for how to manage the fallout at this end. When it comes out."

"We need more time, John."

"I don't know how much I have to give."

CHAPTER NINETEEN

After her run-in with the journalist, Kesta could feel her own suspicions spawning inside her like a fungus. Her brain whirred endlessly, imagining what awful progress the Gain-of-Function lab must be making toward heightening the capabilities of the virus she was trying her damnedest to cure. She held imaginary arguments with Lundeen in her head, she thought about reporting him to the authorities, having his research condemned, but the only guarantee that would bring was that she would be shut out from any findings herself. She'd have to beg her way into whichever new biological site was granted the contract to investigate the virus, and she didn't know how much longer Tim could be expected to hold on as he was. If she was honest with herself, she didn't know how much longer she could hold on either.

We have to find a cure first. Only then can I risk reporting the Project. Got to hold it together. Don't lose your nerve, Shelley.

She hissed at the mirror in an unconventional affirmation.

"Who are you talking to?" Dudley said, standing in between the swing doors of the changing room. Kesta saw his reflection in the mirror above the sinks and pretended to tease out her thick brown fringe. She couldn't remember when she'd last washed her hair.

"Myself, obviously," she said. "There's no better conversationalist. Good morning."

"Morning." He was smiling genuinely enough through his visor. "You're going to want to see this." He pulled up his face mask, stretched out a glove for her to take.

"See what?"

"Come with me."

Kesta secured her face mask and her visor, and the two of them squelched down miles of corridor toward the areas of Project Dawn where her key card didn't work. He was leading her into the Gain-of-Function quarters of the site, toward the room that Kesta had seen him entering with the woman in the black suit.

Inside, the space was divided into two and separated by a thick glass wall. A viewing room with chairs, dimly lit, a dashboard befitting a rocket launch, and then a stark lab with one steel gurney in it. Two men whom Kesta didn't recognize were already seated in the viewing room, leaning against the dashboard as though they were about to cut an album, waiting for a performance to begin in the next room.

"I knew you'd want to see this," Dudley whispered. He wasn't friendly, it was more of a neutral tone.

"What's going on?"

"Just wait. Wait here."

A door she hadn't seen opened up on the other side of the glass. Two more hazmat suits wheeled in a trolley, inside which sat an infected monkey in a cage. It was Liv. She looked dopey, as though they'd just woken her from an incomplete sleep, yellow eyes subdued by a medical glaze. She swayed gently on her haunches. Kesta felt a maternal twinge. She wanted to touch her, to reassure her. She didn't know what was going to happen any more than Liv did.

Then Dudley appeared through the same hidden doorway—she had been so focused on Liv she hadn't noticed him leave the viewing room—and he held in his blue gloved hands a large syringe. He was carrying it like the holy grail, and he moved across the room with a serene purpose. He looked up at the glass, to Kesta, and even through the plastic and the industrial glass, even through that distorted prism, she could see him smiling. As she watched him, little Liv tilted her head upward and silently bared her teeth.

The neck clamp was on her and she flinched. Tense fingernails tapping against the metal. Out of the cage she came, down on the gurney she went, the metallic pats of her nails audible through the live feed echoing into the viewing room. Liv made panicked sounds, *aah, aah, aah,* but Dudley was stroking her back, knowing she couldn't free herself to bite him. He looked once more at Kesta before sliding the needle into Liv's abdomen, against which she stiffened herself in noiseless terror.

Dudley stepped backward, nodded at the two hazmats, who raised the monkey by the head again and back into her cage. The three humans left the room. Liv was all alone in there, and Kesta wanted to comfort her. In that moment, she hated Dudley for things he was and wasn't responsible for, hated him for doing this, whatever it was, to Liv, and for being privy to a part of Project Dawn that was determined to exclude her, that mocked her efforts to find a cure for the virus it was treating with venal abandon. She hated him for staring at her almost lovingly all the while it was going on, as though she'd wanted it to happen. But most of all, she hated him for making her hate herself. Because she did want to be in an illegal lab half a mile underground, watching a primate get tortured with man-made poisons, content to look the other way and leave her ethics at the door because she was so very fucking desperate.

A door swooshed open, air came in. There was a heavy hand on her shoulder.

"I wanted you to see this for yourself."

Before she could turn to speak to him, Dudley had taken up a chair in the middle of the viewing room. The others remained quiet. It was obvious they deferred to him, obvious it mattered little to them who she was. Kesta sat with her hands in her lap waiting for him to explain.

"I've just given Liv something we've been working on," he said. Kesta noted the *we*, designed to privatize the endeavor. "It's based on our preliminary cultures on the IBD protein sample you and Cooke isolated in the snake from Florida. I haven't tried it out yet."

"So, you thought you'd stick it in my monkey, did you?"

"I wanted you to see what happened. I've tried it on four rats so far. The sooner we can get it ready to trial—"

Dudley didn't get to finish what he was saying because Liv had started jumping up and down in her cage. She inspected her belly where the needle had pierced, soothing it with eager hands. Up and down her head rose and fell as she peered at it, then sniffed the air, then down again, then around and around in tight spirals she flew, her body energized, more alive than before. She began to shriek, not a fearful cry, but a flat sound as though she was talking.

Then she went still. But after a moment, she began to groom.

"She hasn't done that since we infected her," Kesta said, mouth wide in surprise, leaning into the dashboard to get closer to the glass that separated her and the monkey. "Dudley, she's grooming!"

The hidden door opened with a *pfft* sound. Another hazmat entered, big gloves cupped around a small bowl. The bowl was placed just outside Liv's cage. The hazmat left the room. Kesta watched in awe as Liv showed interest in the contents of the bowl, lively mealworms wriggling, tapping at them with an outstretched finger, her nose sniffing. Kesta was enthralled, and on the verge of tears.

Liv was eating for the first time in weeks, and she was grooming. But Kesta's tears didn't come to fruition. Out of the corner of her eye she could make out Dudley grinning at her intensely, almost salivating over her reaction.

"We're making progress, Kes, real progress."

"I thought you were only working to gamify the zombie virus?" she said.

"We are," he replied sheepishly, and she could see that he was as exhausted as she was, "but I've been trying a few things myself. This is being developed using the yellow fever vaccine as a foundation, as well as other hemorrhagic arenavirus strategies. We're trying to block the virus's entry point and inhibit its ability to fuse with the cells in the host."

Dudley led Kesta down toward a floor of the Project Dawn site she'd never been to. They walked through a long room set up as a hospital ward, with rows of empty beds, open cabinets, monitors unplugged, curtains pulled back. For now, at least, unoccupied.

"This is where we'll hold the human trials." Strip lights crackled, illuminating their passage through the ward toward heavyset doors, a room within a room, another room for viewing, like the room she had been in, only this viewing room would observe real people. As they left, Kesta noticed the doors to the ward were alarmed. There were security cameras in every corner, just in case whoever was stationed in the viewing room wasn't paying close enough attention.

Dudley swiped his key card, the green light flashed, and the door clunked open. They walked through it, into another corridor, over to another laboratory. Kesta felt the air cool, and she wondered how far below the surface of the city they were. It was an oceanic chill, the feeling of descent. She paused before following Dudley into the last lab. It felt like a point of no return.

The cold was coming from this lab, which was kept close to freezing. Kesta could see her breath inside her visor, little droplets forming. She could hear her heart rate slowing as she moved across the lab to a bank of refrigerators lined with little bottles, backlit, awful. She tried to listen to Dudley as he told her about the cure in progress, but all she could think about was Tim, lying in that ward, being pumped full of hope until he exploded.

"This is it, Kesta," said Dudley as he placed the vial onto her gloved palm. "It's what we've been waiting for."

As she looked down at the vial, she saw the label on it, REANIMATOR-A. Dudley's name was underneath, along with a jumble of letters and numbers and the laboratory stamp. Another label, farther up toward the bottle's neck: TOXIC! NOT TO BE REMOVED. One of a dozen bottles waiting patiently inside the fridge.

"This is our discovery, Kesta."

Dudley was so busy evangelizing the miracles of scientific research, about testing and making and clinical trials, about mass production, and something about a knighthood, in the long run, if they felt he deserved it, obviously, that he didn't see that her face was blank to conceal the dark whirlpool churning inside her head. He had placed the cure or something like it right in the palm of her hand. And she, with the expert sleight of hand of one of those close-up magicians she used to run away from at parties because there is no magic, only trickery, and Kesta didn't like being tricked herself, nodded and cooed and smiled and helpfully closed the chiller cabinet, distracting him with her resting interest face, nodding about the Nobel Prize, agreeing that a knighthood would be reasonable compensation for finding a cure for the worst disease in history, Lord Caring of Cheam or similar, it seemed appropriate, he could sit in the House of Lords and lobby on medical matters until he died at ninety-three in the bar at Westminster and people would say there goes the greatest man who ever lived. As Kesta reflected Dudley's dream scenario back at him, he was duly oblivious—as she needed him to be—to her ignoring the special label on the bottle that read NOT TO BE REMOVED.

She took it.

CHAPTER TWENTY

What doesn't kill you makes you stronger, someone fond of platitudes had once said. Kesta wasn't sure what idiot had come up with that, but she doubted they'd ever been a nurse. Just because it hadn't killed her yet didn't mean it wouldn't eventually. She didn't feel strong but she also wasn't dead, so perhaps there was some truth in it. Perhaps that platitudinal preacher was right.

"I'm not sure if I should give you this now," she said as she sat on the side of Tim's bed with his chained hand resting in her lap. His fingers were tapping against her thighs, though his eyes looked right through her as though she were transparent like tracing paper. She hoped there was a song playing somewhere inside his head.

"We trust each other, don't we? We have to trust each other to do the right thing because we have nobody else, just us two." She stroked the less mangled side of his face, and her hand felt moist. Tears had formed and fallen somehow, weeping from those eyes that couldn't blink.

"Tim, I don't know what to do. I don't know what you want me to do."

"Nnnnfffff," he moaned.

Kesta felt her lips and her chin begin to quiver with indecision, with the weight of responsibility she had taken on.

What doesn't kill you makes you stronger.

She had to be strong. She had to be strong for them both. Looking down at her husband, withering away before her eyes, knowing everything he had endured over the past few months, she knew in her heart that he was the strong one, not her. It hadn't killed him yet.

"What do I do next?" she asked him. "What do you want, Tim?"

Tim lifted his unchained hand up to her face.

"Llll . . . mmm."

The self-awareness of human beings allows us to endure levels of pain unknown to other mammals because we understand its purpose. Our consciousness enables us to weigh up a situation, evaluate its risk, measure out the possibility of a successful outcome. This allows us to tolerate pain more readily. We alone know what is coming for us. And we know it's going to hurt. Babies are born in agony, delivered through industrial feats of teeth-gritting and ripped skin, as women tear themselves apart to bring forth new life. There is no end to the suffering for which we will not volunteer ourselves if we can hold on to hope, if we believe that the light at the end of that long dark tunnel is just that. Light.

"Tim, I think we have to try, don't you?"

Kesta closed the bedroom door. She couldn't know what would happen next, and there was no textbook to consult, no case study to reference, no guiding light. Just her, the patient, and the drug. Life was all experiment. It was a gamble she was choosing to take because she alone was happy with the odds. Not happy, exactly. She had accepted them. On Tim's behalf. No, on their behalf, because you made decisions for the whole, not the half.

As she slid the needle into his skin, as his yellow eyes stared blankly out to nothing, she wondered if she had robbed him of his humanity through the drugs she had given him, through the restraints she'd used to bind him to her, through her inability to bring him back to life. Had she conjured the illusion of hope where there was none to be found? Had she unwittingly created a monster?

Am I that monster?

———

"There, it's done," she said, returning to her chair by the bed with her notebook.

Patient administered 100 mL of Reanimator-A. 9:05 pm, Thursday October 14th. Intravenous injection, left arm. Blood pressure 55/30. No immediate change noted.

As she sat there in the afterglow, she knew she had been deluding herself. She'd thought they were in this together, she and him, as they had been since the night they met, when they gave up their own lives to share a single life between them. But Tim was in this alone, wasn't he? He was soldiering his way down to the abyss without her. We're all of us dying from the day we are born, but she had been made acutely aware of it, losing him in slow motion, day by day since he'd been bitten. She had tried to take on the inevitable, she'd been fighting Death. Was she destined to fail? Could anything you did in the name of love ever be considered to be wrong? Love was hope and hope was love, wasn't it?

In the electric monitor light, the air over Tim's body began to pixelate, microorganisms sparkling in a hawkish duel. It appeared then to hook him at the middle, wrenching him upward, folding him in at the center. His head and feet stayed fixed as the core was raised in increments into the air, a tug-of-war between this life and the next.

Kesta stood up, shaking, dropping the pen, which skittered across the floor. The noise that bellowed from him wasn't human. It was gut deep, raw, and blood-soaked. Still, Tim's stomach was dragged higher, his arms and legs distorted, splayed at either side as though he were splintering apart from the inside out. The primal wails of life being lost, of war being waged, of the whole world coming to a desperate end and not with a whimper but a thunderstruck howl.

Wide-eyed, Kesta walked toward the bed and braced herself against it to watch what was happening to Tim—what *she had done* to Tim. His skin was bubbling, melting across his arms, the surface layers erupting and sliding in a lava flow, shoulder to elbow, magma boiling beneath the dermis.

Kesta was transfixed. She grabbed at Tim's hand, to let him know she was still there with him, to reassure herself, but her fingers slid across the back of his hand, which was hot and slimy, and as she prized her fingers away, she saw his flesh follow, dripping from her like cooking fat onto the floor.

Is this an allergic reaction to the drug? Is this it working to drive out the virus? Is this how it's going to end? What the fuck do I do now?

She could think of only two things. Adrenaline and steroids. She had both inside the bedside table but couldn't remember where they were. She ripped out the drawers and threw them onto the floorboards, smearing their contents frantically out in front of her, reading the labels, ripping open boxes, panting, frantic, and all the while Tim was howling. She found the epinephrine, jammed it into his leg, then followed one shot with another, forcing a corticosteroid into his system. When he stabilized, she could give him fluids, she thought. She could transfuse him again, anything to get the Reanimator-A out of his system.

She was beginning to hyperventilate as she stood there clinging to the bedside, gasping not breathing, her ears ringing with alarm. Before her eyes, his skin began to crackle and peel, piling away from Tim's body, the snake shedding its skin.

It isn't working, why isn't it working?

And still that moaning, rumbling in the darkness as his body convulsed against itself and the bed, until Kesta couldn't stand it any longer and she did what she had to.

She pressed her hands over his mouth.

The yellow eyes looked up at her. Lips bitten together, her face twisted with brute force, she closed her eyes and pushed down against his face, pinching his nose together, leaning into him with all her remaining strength. Holding her breath until his stopped. She felt him kick beneath her. She heard the jangling of the cuff against the radiator. She opened her eyes and saw his tears, tears he could not blink away, that she'd brought to bear in him. And then his free hand grazed against her cheek, resting there in quiet submission, in absolute love. Kesta heard his voice inside her head: *You always know what to do, Mrs. Shelley, I trust you. I love you. You always know what's best.*

But Kesta couldn't do it. Her tears came like oxygen and hydrogen in a glass balloon. He'd lit a fire underneath her and she exploded into violent gas, turning to water in his arms. She'd never let him see her cry, not in all these months, but she couldn't hold it in any longer. Her grief was alive inside her and she had to let it out. She held Tim's hand against her face and wept, wiping away the tears beneath his widened eyes. She only wished she had the strength to finish him, to take away that sorry look, to undo everything, to have let him die when there was still life inside him. But she couldn't. She just couldn't lose him.

———

The neon strip light in the bathroom blinked into action. She turned on the hot water tap and thrust her hands into the sink. As the water ran and the steam began to rise, she saw the mess she had made. It was splattered across the porcelain, a bloody sprawl of tissue and fluid congealing around the toothbrush holder. She looked in the mirror but couldn't see herself in there any longer.

The second Kesta had succeeded in cannibalizing the first. The hair was the same, dark but now dank, clinging limply to the monstrous shape of her skull. The eyes still blue but milky and sunken. The peaches and cream skin had soured, rotted by new veins and bloated from crying, from struggling, from self-neglect. No, her appearance was altered because she had sheltered this terrible secret for so long. It was eating her alive.

Kesta was a stranger in her own face and in her own life. This stranger in the mirror had no answer. The two women looked at one another. She dried her livid hands on the towel underneath the sink before scraping her hair away from her face and leaning closer to the glass, crushing her pubic bone against the sink, feeling the urge to break it, to smash herself in two. Dying is waiting. For a moment she had wavered, she had wanted him to die more than she had wanted him to suffer and live.

The groaning started up again in the bedroom. Kesta switched the light off but lingered for a moment, her shadow trapped by the light from the hallway like a ghost. Her arms hung helplessly about her sides, and her head jutted to the side as if she could no longer bear her own weight. Without her, Tim might die. With her, Tim might die.

He has to survive, no matter what. Prizing one foot from the floor, Kesta lumbered forward, shuffling toe by toe to the door, then using her hands to pull herself around the bathroom door and into the hallway.

The sheer force of love propelled her back into the fire.

———

Liv was screaming. Everyone in the lab, Cooke included, kept staring at the zombie monkey willing her to be quiet. Everyone except for Kesta, who was oblivious to Liv's noise because the screams oscillating in her own head were at much the same decibel. Nothing more had happened to Tim that night. She had waited up until daybreak, making notes on the hour, checking his vitals, praying for change. She had staggered in to work. Whatever had happened to him had stopped, and he had seemed more stable when she had left him.

"You're over the worst of it," she'd reassured him on her way out, though really this was for her own benefit, not his.

Kesta reached a glove through the bars of Liv's cage to risk stroking the fur on her legs. Each time she touched her, the monkey would groom the area where a human hand had been.

"At this rate, you'll be taking her home when this is all over," Cooke said without looking up from her microscope. "I thought about getting a cat when Rodney died. But I'd probably end up killing it."

"Not on purpose?" Kesta said, not really listening.

"Can't promise you that. Not if it looked at me funny." She peered up at Kesta and the monkey. "Like the way that monkey is looking at me right now."

"Liv doesn't like other people, that's all."

"No, dear, that's you. You don't like other people."

Kesta wanted to check her phone, but she couldn't risk doing so until she had a break and could sneak off to the changing room and get out of these ruddy gloves. She wanted to watch through the video camera in Tim's bedroom to see what was happening to him now. She felt lightheaded, queasy with lack of sleep. She drew another vial of Liv's blood. It was still black in color like bitumen and sat solidly inside the vial. She slid it across the worktop to Cooke, Liv's eyes following its journey past her cage.

"Do you want to do the blood film for this, or shall I?" she asked.

Before Cooke had time to answer, the laboratory doors were flung open and two soldiers in fatigues walked in. They were carrying guns and were flanking Lundeen and a woman in a dark gray suit. It was the woman from UK Defense and Security, the one who'd co-opted her and Dudley into Project Dawn. They were marching right toward her. Liv shrieked again and covered her eyes with her hands.

"Is that you under there, Kesta Shelley?" asked the woman in the suit.

Fuck, she thought. *This is it.*

A billion cells inside her brilliant brain, and all she could think was *fuck*. At best, Dudley could have told them she'd been stealing from the hospital and they'd come to arrest her. At worst, Tim had escaped the confines of their spare room and ravaged half of Wapping, and they'd probably take her straight to the Tower for execution. Kesta didn't have a cunning plan, and there was nowhere to hide in the lab.

"Yes?" she gulped. The woman in the dark gray suit consulted a letter she was holding, then whispered something at Lundeen, who nodded in reply. "Kesta, do you know the whereabouts of a Mr. Colin Royce?"

Kesta looked at Cooke and Cooke looked at Kesta. The two of them turned slowly to point in the direction of a man who was holding a petri dish up to an ultraviolet light at the far end of the laboratory. Without reply, the soldiers and the woman approached him. One soldier snatched the dish from his hand and gestured at him with his gun to step away from the workstation. Instinctively, the man raised his hands into the air, walking backward without looking until he bumped into a colleague who'd been too frightened to get out of the way. Still Liv's screams punctuated the air.

"Someone shut that monkey up!"

"What on earth is Rolls meant to have done?" Cooke muttered under her breath.

"He'd been in touch with a lab in Germany," said Lundeen, who waited next to them while his heavies dealt with Colin. He spoke quietly. The three of them watched as one of the soldiers twisted Colin's arms behind his back, securing them at the wrist with a plastic tie.

"I had a tip-off about it. He broke protocol. There are consequences for that."

"I didn't do anything. Honestly. This is madness! It wasn't me!" He was shouting at Lundeen as the soldiers escorted him out of the laboratory. The woman in the dark gray suit came over.

"Thanks for reporting this, Professor Lundeen. We'll handle things from here."

Lundeen and the woman shook hands. With that, the soldiers stalked out of the laboratory. Everyone left behind stood still, shell-shocked but above all relieved in that moment of dreadful calm not to be Colin Royce. Lundeen leaned against the workstation and sighed. Liv stretched her hand out toward him through the bars of the cage, but he was too far away for her to reach him.

"We've lost a few bottles of the Reanimator," he said. "DO NOT let this information leave the room." He went to wipe the stress from his brow, having forgotten he was wearing his visor. "Royce has a sister in Berlin. He'd been emailing her about us, quite openly. Seems he was willing to sell our findings to the highest bidder. A German weapons manufacturer apparently."

"Not Rolls, surely?" Cooke shook her head, disbelieving.

"He had a flight booked for next weekend, and two substantial payments had been made into his account."

"Never did like him," sneered Cooke, sticking her finger into Liv's cage, letting the monkey hold on to it with all her tiny might.

———

She let the water run hot against her skin. Steam thickened the air around her so that she could no longer see out into the empty changing room. She forced herself under the roaring jet, shielding her eyes from the worst of it the way Liv did, the humidity making her dizzy.

She held her breath. How long could she stand such intense heat without injury? She felt her shoulders burning. She jammed the tap shut and walked through the steam cloud. Her shoulders were red, but not scalded. *Decontaminated but still unclean*, she thought. She should soak a towel in ice water and bathe her shoulders to take the heat out. Instead, she dried quickly, easing her arms into the sleeves of her denim shirt, fastening its buttons with her fingers still shaking.

She left the laboratory still dripping, thinking only of getting as far away from Lundeen and the others as possible. And Cooke had been right; she did want to take Liv home with her, keep her hidden away with Tim as some strange comforter for them both.

Out in the city, she felt a stiff breeze, her wet hair forming a cold cap against her scalp. October and the arrival of autumn churned up the air. Leaves were falling too early, torn away from trees not yet prepared to give them up. As she walked down Fleet Street, she heard a siren's wail, a noise distorted by the rush of the wind along the empty road. She turned to look around her, but there was nothing there. Only when she tried to carry on did she see him walk out from the entrance to the station, to stand in the middle of the road, knowing full well that she had to pass him.

A suede bomber jacket that had seen better days zipped right up to his chin, that messenger bag slung across his body. He had a swagger, that was clear—not from being attractive. He certainly wasn't that—if anything, his face was the very definition of forgettable. Even staring right at him Kesta thought, *If he does anything to me, I'll never be able to pick him out in a lineup.* He had a swagger because he thought he was smarter than everyone else.

"I don't know if you remember me?"

"I remember you."

"You're not Kesta Shelley, by any chance?"

She said nothing.

"You live in Wapping, don't you? Used to work at University Hospital?"

Kesta stood still, kept her mouth shut as she prayed for an exceptionally fast but silent bus to drive into the forgettable-looking man and pummel him into the tarmac.

"And now you work at Project Dawn. Don't you?"

"If you have all the answers already, we have nothing to talk about."

She tried to pass him, but he blocked her, making himself seem bigger than he was, a goalkeeper ready to jump off his line.

"Look, if you don't talk to me, you're going to have to talk to someone else," he said, smirking at her as though it was all just a very funny game to him. "We just have a few questions. Can I—"

"We?" Kesta said.

"I work for the *Standard*," he said.

Shit.

"And we're concerned about transparency. Can you confirm that a man has been arrested?"

How does he already know? Colin Royce had been taken away from Project Dawn only that morning. Her face gave her away.

"So, it's true?" he said. "Someone was arrested? Can you tell me what for?"

"I have to get home."

"Was the arrest to do with the illegal research being conducted at the lab?"

Kesta felt the marrow in her bones freeze.

"I don't know what you're talking about."

"They're doing something they shouldn't be down there, aren't they?" he said. "Something that's outlawed in this country." He began to rummage in his bag for his mobile phone. He was setting it up to record their conversation.

"Where are you getting all this nonsense?"

"Obviously, if we were to run a story about the illegal research being undertaken here, right in the middle of London, especially since the city has suffered so much tragedy—"

"You don't know what you're talking about."

"Then explain it to me. Tell me what's really going on at Project Dawn," he said, trying to smile, but it was a true journalist's smile. It didn't reach his eyes. It was just his lips telling you to believe his version of the truth.

"You already have a source?"

That fake smile again. "We need someone we can trust on the inside. To help us hold the Project to account. It's in the public interest."

"I think what's in the public interest is us finding a cure, don't you?"

"So, you do work for Project Dawn?"

At last, a bus pulled up toward them as the traffic lights turned red, and they had to move off the road and onto the pavement. Kesta wanted to get as far away from the journalist as possible, and she thought about banging on the doors and forcing the driver to let her board. But she had to get home to Tim, not go on a joyride in the opposite direction. The lights turned green, and she watched him drive away from her as the man put a hand on her shoulder.

"Don't you fucking touch me!"

"Look, we just want to hear your side of the story," he said, and they both moved toward the tube station entrance, he thinking about finding a safe place out of the wind to talk, she considering routes of escape.

"Can you tell me what they're working on? Can you give me something?"

"You have no idea, do you," she said, "what it's like to save a life? What it's like to really help people?"

"Information helps people," he said. "The truth saves lives, Mrs. Shelley. Can I call you Kesta? My job is to defend the truth so that people have power, the power of knowledge."

"Well, mine is to stop them from dying," she said, "not to fuck around with words, speculating and making people's lives a misery in the name of public interest. Trust me, the public doesn't want to know what we're working on. You couldn't begin to imagine—"

"So, tell me," he said excitedly, the messenger bag pressing against his groin. "Tell me your story. Tell me what they're working on. Tell me how thanks to you, there's a cure on the horizon. If you give me something, in exchange I'll hold off on investigating the claims of Gain-of-Function research. For a while. Just give me something on the zombie they brought in."

Kesta kept backing away, thought about running down the stairs and into the station, but she was just so very tired.

"I just want to go home," she said. "I have nothing to say to you. Please, just leave me alone."

"Kesta, this won't stop, you know?" he shouted right in her face. "People will come for you. Other newspapers. Less reputable ones. I'm someone you can trust. It's best to tell your story now, control the narrative before the narrative controls you . . ."

"It's not a story; it's my *life*," she screamed.

——

She bumped into Albert in the courtyard outside the warehouse. It was just beginning to rain. Albert's glasses were covered with little drops of water, which he wiped clean with the driest part of his sweater.

"You're soaking," he said. Kesta hadn't noticed she was wet from the shower, wet from the rain, and wet from the icy-cold sweat of her encounter with the *Standard*.

"I went to the gym," she lied.

"Pull the other one," he said, laughing. She thought she'd gotten away with it when he said, "But it's good if you are, Kesta. Exercise helped me when I quit drinking." They blinked at each other through the drizzle.

"You're going to?" he said firmly. "Like I told you to. Drinking never helps." She wiped the rain away from her face, though it may have been a tear.

"I'm trying, Albert. I'm really trying."

"At the end of the day, gel, that's all anyone can ask."

As Kesta opened the door to her flat, it dawned on her that this was no longer home. Home was where you felt safe. Closing the door behind her and locking herself inside, she knew she couldn't be home because she didn't feel safe here anymore. The men and women in gray suits were literally closing in. Today they'd come for Colin Royce, but tomorrow it could be her. Her relationship with Dudley had devolved into a fractious truce, but she knew she had disappointed him by lying, and she couldn't trust him not to share his concerns with Lundeen about her vulnerabilities, whatever he imagined them to be. Perhaps that's why the woman from Defense and Security had asked *her* to identify Colin Royce rather than anyone else in the room. Perhaps it had been a test. To let her know that they were on to her, and that betrayal would not be tolerated at Project Dawn.

She was just so very tired. Her eyes were twitching, the nerves upset; she had a ringing in her ears like when the television programming would stop at midnight when she was little, that final fuzzy tone carrying you off to bed.

"Stop it! Stop it. You're panicking," she berated herself out loud as she tossed her keys into the bowl of coins on the table in the hall. She shivered and she shook, but it could have been a chill, it could have been the shock. That journalist was following her, waiting for her to trip up. She was worried he knew where she lived.

What if he finds his way inside the building and tries to trick his way into my flat?

A sudden sound jolted her out of it.

"Keeerrr—"

"K . . . K . . . K . . . keeeesss—"

He was sitting upright at the edge of the bed, his feet planted firmly on the floorboards. As she came into view, he raised his free hand. It was almost a wave.

"K-k-k-k-kees," he tried again, and this time she could watch his lips and the muscles in his hopeless jaw working together, determined to get the word out.

"Kesta," she said for him, throwing herself at his feet, resting her hands on his knees, looking up at him, his head wobbling, trying so hard to hold it level. "Kesta."

"Ke-k-k-k-keesss," he hissed, and she saw the masseter muscles tighten and an emotion that wasn't pain or rage or distress opening up across his face, enlivening his eyes. She saw a new frustration twitching in his cheeks, cheeks that seemed pinker than before. A sense of self-awareness possessed him now. A sense of who she was, not his carer but his wife. The woman he had loved.

He held out his unchained hand toward her. Yesterday he was shrinking away into nothingness, his skin deflated and his limbs crippled by the virus—as though all the life was slowly draining out of him, sucked up into the room where it hung above them in the stale air. Now, nearly twenty-fours after she had given him the Reanimator-A, Kesta saw that some human essence had returned to him. His arms were no longer twisted. His legs, which had been nothing but bone, now draped over the bed, some musculature restored. His chest broadened as he took deeper, longer breaths, and his posture straightened, each vertebra unlocking itself from the next. Tim's eyes no longer gazed upward to the stars. They looked right at her.

Kesta took his outstretched hand and pulled it toward her, kissing it feverishly and looking at her husband in wonderment. It was close to miraculous. Tim was no longer undead. He was almost alive.

CHAPTER TWENTY-ONE

There are moments in our lives too good to be true. That doesn't mean to say they're perfect, because perfection is subjective and entirely dependent upon where your baseline was to begin with. Bliss is rarely diamond hard and champagne infused. Bliss is often just quiet days and unbroken nights.

In Kesta's case, her husband was a better kind of deathly ill than he had been before. For a little while at least, that felt perfect. It was enough. It was more than they'd had recently, if much less than before. When Kesta woke each morning, she thought about what they might do together in the future, not whether the things they had already done had been for the last time. There was a stay in the inevitability of his looming execution.

She should have known it was too good to be true.

On these perfect days, Kesta did laundry. For the first time in months, she washed her clothes, her underwear, her towels. When the airer was full, she laid them all out to dry on every surface in the flat she could make use of. She put her knickers over the doorknobs and slung pairs of black jeans across the top edges of the doors. She cleaned every surface with a fragrant spray so that the rooms smelled like jasmine, not bleach. She Hoovered the floors. She washed them with a furry mop. She reordered the cupboards in the kitchen, having wiped them clean. She went shopping for candles and softer pillows and new linens for the beds. She updated. She upgraded. She made a nest. She even pushed back the heavy drapes and craned up the blinds, to open wide the windows in the flat. She let the light in.

She washed Tim's clothes too. She changed his sheets. She tidied up the spare room and adorned it with tributes, photographs, his favorite books, stacked on every surface. She tucked in a cashmere throw at the end of the bed. It cost a small fortune, but what did that matter? She wanted his feet to know comfort. She got things ready because Tim was finally coming home.

Kesta read to him. She sang to him. She played old films for him on her laptop—brought into his bed where the two of them lay together—ones they had both seen many times before, quoting famous lines before the actors did because that had always made him smile, the magic of her memory.

When she bathed him, he would help her do it, holding the flannel in supple hands, soaking it in the bowl of water she held carefully at the edge of the bed. She dressed him, restored his dignity, made him a man again, not just a patient. Kesta even thought about moving him back into their bedroom.

She told him all about her plans for them. They would go down to Kent, she said, when all this was over, when he was really well again, and open up that shabby little house on the coast, the one her mother had left her. It was little more than a beach hut, really, the house that Tim once said was at the very end of the world. The house that was too remote to live in for a couple in their thirties. The one they should have gone to during the outbreak. A house that might be good enough for a future version of themselves to live in. A place where you waited it out.

Outside in the real world, far away from their little idyll, things were sliding backward into chaos because a cure remained elusive, whereas the threat of the virus returning was acute. Every day the papers and the internet posed questions to which there were no answers, so speculation and paranoia seeped into the void until it became difficult to tell the difference between the truth and a lie, between fact and wish fulfillment. London town was breaking down, and people couldn't stand it.

Kesta cared much less about this than she had done before. She worked less too, arrived late, left early every day. She only wanted to be at home with Tim. To make the most of it, whatever it was, not yet a cure, that much was obvious.

To watch him trying to laugh, to feel him touching her face, to hear him making noises that were more and more like words. Knowing he looked *at* not through her, understanding that she was the love of his life, telling him over and over that he was hers. Looking down at him lying in his bed and feeling contentment, not fear. Looking down at him looking up at her and seeing he was just below the surface. A remission.

It might have lasted a few weeks. It could have been only a handful of days.

The word *remission* means absolution. It suggests a fault for which you must be pardoned, an amnesty from your sickness, a hint of blame attached to the disease. It was *remiss* of you to get sick in the first place, it said. Your misfortune is your own, you know, so please don't be a burden to anyone else with it.

The window was open, briefly, before it began to close again. When it finally shut, Kesta forgot all about the golden light and the fresh air it had let in. She wouldn't remember ever having had the time to breathe.

CHAPTER TWENTY-TWO

There was a commotion in reception. A cluster of residents, faces she didn't recognize but who'd probably lived in the building for longer than she had, were pooling around Albert, water circling a clogged drain. They were asking questions, gesticulating at him, then bleeding off into smaller groups, transporting a low-level hum of indignation across the lobby, and it was only seven a.m. Kesta didn't notice them straightaway because she was bogged down in this mass of bodies, trying to push her way through to the exit to get to work. But they were waiting just outside.

Albert stood on tiptoes so she'd see him, more concerned with parting the waves for her than the inch-close complainants spitting in his face.

"Let the lady through, will ya," he shouted at no one in particular, waving a hand in case the bellow wasn't clear enough; sometimes people needed to be shown what to do. His glossy spectacles chain was in full swing this morning, sparkling in the overhead lights as Albert shook his head in frustration.

"They're checking the car park," Albert said directly to Kesta, "but not the flats. Might need access to the sewer system at the subbasement."

"Who?" Kesta was wedged in between two much bigger bodies, men trying to force their way past her to get to Albert. She found herself swimming against the human tide.

"The geezers out front."

Kesta shoved her way through the crowd, finally reaching the door, swiping at the lock with her key fob to release the automatic motion, the doors stuttering open with a squeak, knocking forward a woman who had been leaning against them. The woman tutted at Kesta as she walked past her into the courtyard.

There was a police van with its lights still pulsing parked in the middle of the courtyard and two armed officers guarding the gates to the warehouse. Two black dogs were sniffing their way around the cobbles, digging with urgent, feathery paws in the ornamental beds, ordered to root out something suspect from the box hedging and the cyclamen. Other residents craned out of their windows to watch. Having brought her own dog out into the courtyard, a woman in a lilac dressing gown and slippers stood huffing and patting at the poor mutt's head.

"The bleeding nerve," she said to Kesta as she tried to slip past. They'd never met before, but as with any incident in London, complete strangers were allied by a shared mistrust of the establishment and a weapons-grade desire to interfere.

Kesta squatted down on her haunches to stroke the dog.

"What's going on?"

The woman pulled her dressing gown tightly across lumpy breasts before feeling for a lighter to spark the next fag already hanging from her lips.

"The filth are here looking for one of *them*, apparently," she said, blowing a plume of smoke high into the air like a crematorium chimney. Kesta felt a tackiness in her throat that was difficult to swallow away.

"Because they found that one in the City?" she asked the dog, too nervous to look up at the woman. The dog in return flicked out a hungry tongue, and Kesta just managed to dodge it, a hand braced down for balance and luckily not in a puddle of wee.

"Yeah, they're doing all the warehouses along the river," the woman replied, flicking her ash in Kesta's general direction. "'Cause we've got underground car parks and that. Reckon that's where they'd hide, 'cause that fella was hidden in a drain, so they said." She thrust her spare hand into her dressing gown pocket, fiddling with the lighter inside. "Just want to look like they're doing something," she barked, loud enough for the officers with the sniffer dogs to hear her. "Since they missed one!" She flicked the butt end into the raised bed next to her, before folding her arms across an apron of gut.

"You're Mrs. Shelley?"

Kesta gently tugged the dog's furry bib into a twist around her fingers. She stood to meet the woman's eyes and saw that each hazel iris was rimmed with a sinister deposit, a little circle of blue-brown fat, a cholesterol-rimmed stare. Kesta should have recommended the woman have her cholesterol checked, but the burning sensation nervously searing through her own body and the fever flushing upward across her throat and her cheeks consumed her.

"Yes," Kesta said, heart *bang-bang-bang*ing in her chest.

"You lost your husband, dincha?" The woman tilted her head to one side, exposing gray submental fat to the light for the first time in years.

"Yes."

"Yeah, Albert told me."

The woman sniffed, scratching her forehead with a stained fingertip. "Nasty business, that. I almost didn't recognize you. You look, well, *changed.* From before, I mean."

Kesta thought she might faint at any minute. Sparking out on the cobbles would surely give her away. She needed to get out of there now, away from the police officers and their sniffer dogs, from this awful woman and her questions.

"Sorry," she said, flushed, stepping backward, "I'm going to be late for work."

"Yeah, you're always out early." The woman withdrew a pack of cigarettes from the dressing gown, tapping at it with the same yellow finger. "I see you. Heading off at the crack of dawn. Where do you work?"

"Up at the hospital on the Euston Road," she lied, jamming her hands down deep into the pockets of her coat, raising her shoulders up toward her ears as if she was cold. She was shaking from head to foot.

"Whatcha do?" asked the woman, igniting her third cigarette.

"Cancer care." The words quivered their way out of Kesta's mouth. The woman exhaled smoke approvingly.

"Important work." She nodded. "Funny, but—I thought you worked on the zombie thing. I thought you were Project Dawn."

Kesta could feel one of the sniffer dogs truffling around her right foot, panting heavily, a little paw scraping at the laces of her boot. Then it left her.

"Why would you think that?" was all that she could think of to say.

The woman was shaking her head, fastening the neck of the dressing gown around her squishy throat.

"Just something I heard."

"Heard from who?"

The burning sensation was running down Kesta's back and into her groin as though she had wet herself. She was shivering with the sweat. She felt numb and thickheaded, as though she were coming down with something serious.

"Oh, I don't know, Albert maybe?"

The woman was looking over Kesta's shoulder toward the police officers milling around the van. One of the dogs started to bark.

"People talk."

"Albert knows I work at the hospital."

Kesta's ears were pounding now, and a ringing was developing at the base of her skull.

"Oh well, then it can't have been him."

The woman was scuffing something off one of her slippers against the brickwork on the raised beds. "Never mind."

She smiled at Kesta as if that was all to be said on the matter.

"Me mum had cancer. God rest her soul. Pancreas. Nasty business."

She pronounced it like the train station, not the organ. Kesta was desperate to leave.

The doors to the lobby squelched open, and Albert and some of the residents poured out into the courtyard. He was looking around for someone, and when he saw Kesta talking to the woman in the dressing gown, he hurried toward them. The woman's dog jumped up, licking at Albert's hands.

"Get down, Grundy. All right?" he asked.

"How long's this gonna take?" The woman jabbed her cigarette at Albert, then in the direction of the police. Albert ignored her.

"They're not searching any of the flats"—*why is he telling me this again*, Kesta wondered—"just the underground area of the building. Where we have access to the river and the sewer system."

She could see a film of sweat had formed across the rim of Albert's glasses and was trapped in the lines of his forehead. "I've told them they'll need to come back with a court order if they want to look inside the flats."

"They're not searching *my* gaff," the woman said, cackling and stubbing out the third of her fags into the ornamental border.

Albert sighed and gestured to the metal cigarette bin fixed to the wall behind her.

"I know my rights!" She coughed, gathering her boobs and Grundy and limping toward the lobby door.

"Oh, and Mrs. Shelley?" She stopped, one hand on the doorknob. "I can't see you in there." Kesta couldn't breathe. "But I can hear you. I live in the flat below."

A hand brushed against her coat sleeve.

"You look a bit peaky, gel," said Albert, smearing away the sweat from his face with the back of his hand. Kesta looked for the woman, but she was gone.

"That woman," she stammered.

"Don't mind Cheryl."

"She asked me where I worked."

Kesta was shaking. Albert saw it.

"She said you'd told her about—" She couldn't quite bring herself to say anything. She should keep her mouth shut. But if Albert was stirring things up . . .

"I ain't told her nuffin'."

Albert was stone-faced, but Kesta could see that he was hurt. He tried again to feel for Kesta's hand or her arm through her thick black coat but ended up patting her in much the same way she had patted Grundy. "She's a nosy cow. Don't mind her. People ask me, sometimes, 'cause you don't talk to no one. And she's sensitive to noise. She's always moaning when she thinks you're being loud." He was still shifting from foot to foot, one eye on Kesta, the other on the officers being overrun by irate residents. "Sometimes she even complains she can hear noises when you're at work, and I have to tell her, Cheryl, there's no one in there."

Kesta thought she was about to throw up. She turned to dry heave into the border, tried to disguise it as a heavy cough.

"He was a good bloke, your Tim. You probably don't know how many people round here liked the fella. She just asked me how you were doing."

Kesta avoided everyone all the time. She had never stopped to think about the life Tim had had without her. When she was at work, or when he went out every Sunday morning to get coffee and the papers and bring them back to her just so that she didn't have to talk to the newsagent. Other people missed Tim, people she didn't even know, had never even met.

"Did that woman, Cheryl," she asked, "did she know Tim?"

"Don't think so, nah," Albert said, "but I told 'er what had happened. 'Cause she asked me. Told 'er what you went through. But that's it."

"That's it?"

"That's it," he said, becoming irritated with her, "but you know, she lives in the flat underneath, so, she's nosy." Albert turned to leave. "You can trust me to keep a secret."

"I don't have any."

"Yeah, you 'av. We've all got our secrets, Kesta."

———

It was 8:30 a.m. and she was now behind schedule, alternating between walking and jogging to avoid being noticeably late for work. When she thought she couldn't run any longer, she imagined that Cheryl was following her in her lilac dressing gown, and it gave her all the impetus she needed to keep going. She would have to make an effort to be quieter in the flat. She must check Tim's monitor more often to make sure he wasn't being noisy enough to disturb her. Perhaps she should go round, talk to the woman, try to win her over? Maybe she should kidnap Grundy and give her something else to focus on. Some people had too much time on their hands. They were always the ones you had to worry about.

Kesta turned left off the main road to walk through the Inns of Court, past creamy Georgian rows sequestering barristers, and lone medieval homes, now offices, symbols of London's endurance and its evolution. Steadily she walked along the cobbled street, then under an archway, past colonnades like standing sentries, through into the garden, quiet, green, empty even at this hour. A creaking sound made her look up.

A woman, four stories high, sliding open a sash window, leaning out of it to smoke. The woman waved at Kesta. Barristers don't wave, she thought, unless they're standing victoriously on the court steps having found a murderer innocent. She waved back anyway. The way things were going, she might need the number of a good lawyer.

As she reached the Embankment, she could smell the thick tang of the river. She turned left and walked right into three police vans crouched together in the middle of the road. A man in a slimy black wetsuit, with a mask on his face, a tank against his back, and two large flippers impeding his walk to the river. Another waddled out behind him. And then the thudding sound of gears crunching, the smell of motor oil, a noise so loud it became a physical pressure Kesta could feel against her chest and in her head. A tank rolled down the Embankment, past the assembled police, heading for Westminster. If there were fresh zombies on the loose, it was essential to save our most important people.

Politicians and spin doctors first.

———

Down in the belly of Project Dawn, Cooke was complaining in the break room about the raids. "Putney is all closed off around the Thames Tideway," she moaned, "and a chap I used to work with sent me a text this morning to say he was stuck in his car in Woolwich 'cause the army is crawling all over the Tidal Basin. You want a biscuit?" she said, shoving a tin of custard creams at Kesta.

"There were police searching the courtyard of my building first thing," she replied, taking two biscuits.

"Why were the police at your house?" said another woman, eavesdropping. Kesta recognized her, her lanyard said her name was M. Collins, and she hadn't realized that she was in the room when she had arrived.

"They weren't in my house," she said defensively. "They were in the courtyard."

"Same difference," said M. Collins, "close enough to scare the shit out of you, I imagine?"

"My apartment block overlooks the river," Kesta said, pretending to be Jess, mustering a haughty indignation from somewhere deep within. "There are stairs leading down into the river. So, obviously the police are checking everywhere one of the infected might have been able to hide."

"I wouldn't want to live where you are," said M. Collins, before swiping a biscuit and leaving.

"Ignore her," said Cooke, "she's in Primrose Hill. Barely had any cases up there. What with the incline."

"Listen, Cooke," said Kesta, covering herself with a fine spray of biscuit dust, which Cooke thoughtfully wiped away for her, such was their bond these days. "We've really got to figure out how Paul Mosi got infected in the first place. I think we must be missing something."

Cooke kept a watchful eye on the doorway. "You still think there's an antigenic shift, another animal in the mix somewhere, don't you? Or a separate mutation we should consider?"

Kesta shook her head.

"It just doesn't make sense yet. We need to know how the IBD became zoonotic. And typically, that involves a second species. Like, for example, a chicken or a cow that has been bitten by a sick snake, and that has then been slaughtered and introduced into the human food chain."

"We'd need an animal that is also prone to IBD, one that doesn't develop antibodies like the mice do," Cooke said. She looked up as if she were trawling through the Rolodex of her brain, searching for another species that might fit the bill. "But isn't it true that no other species have caught and gone on to develop IBD?"

"Can we find out what Paul Mosi was doing in Madagascar?"

"That's way out of our remit, don't you think?" said Cooke. "That's a government matter."

Cooke trotted off to the lab, leaving Kesta to eat her biscuits quickly and drink a hurried cup of tea that was too hot. She checked the app on her phone and saw Tim lying quite still, stretched out flat on his back, like a corpse in the morgue. She continued to sedate him when she left for work because the risk of him making a noise was too great. She followed the colored lines around and along the miles of never-ending corridor, all the while wondering what it was that had brought Paul Mosi to Madagascar in the first place.

A single man, an accountant on holiday perhaps, traveling from his home in Belgium to a far-flung, exotic island nation. Maybe he was on a blue safari, one of those trips of a lifetime that plunge visitors deep into the ocean to swim with iridescent fishes, to feed banana to turtles, to hold snakes safely as they wove themselves around your arms and squeezed you while a tour guide took your picture.

When she reached the observation room, she found Dudley and Lundeen watching Liv through the thick glass divide. The monkey was loose and waddling around on the floor as the humans analyzed her motor skills. She was talking away to herself, *ah, ah, ah.* She was delighted, it seemed, by her new-found freedom.

"You're late," said Lundeen, tapping away on his iPad. "And don't blame the raids either. If someone had had the sense to shoot down that news chopper, then we wouldn't be having to work against the fucking clock." His voice got louder toward the end of the sentence, and he let out a deep sigh, resting the tablet on the dashboard in front of him and wheeling around in his chair so that he was facing her. Kesta saw that his feet couldn't quite touch the floor.

"I'm up against it," he said, slumping forward, his head bowed, his visor resting against gloved hands. "We're all up against it. Reanimator-A is showing promise, against the odds." He lifted his head, gestured toward Liv as she darted around the room next door. "But they won't sign off on our human trials until the next financial quarter."

"We just found a zombie who'd survived," Kesta said. "I thought they'd want to escalate the trials, bring everything forward."

"They don't want any hiccups with this drug. They want us to get it right the first time, as right as can be, before they let us loose on humans. They're giving with one hand and taking with the other."

"It means we have to wait another three months before we're allowed to start testing the Reanimator-A on humans," said Dudley. "We had to cut back on the animal testing period, but they're holding us to the original clinical timeline and blaming the budget."

"Three months?" said Kesta, dumbfounded. "But look at Liv. It's clearly working." She realized too late that she had grabbed Lundeen by the elbow as she made her point emphatically. He swatted her hand away.

"Three more months," he replied. "I went to bat for us, Shelley, especially with Dave turning up as he did. We're going to give him the Reanimator-A tomorrow. Keep your fingers crossed."

"There are some side effects we've noticed," whispered Dudley. "It's why we have Liv in here today."

"Oh, those are minor, nothing to worry about." Lundeen waved his hand dismissively.

"What kind of side effects?" asked Kesta.

"Liv's hair's falling out a bit at the back, but it's nothing too noticeable," said Dudley.

"We've got a shipment of rhesus monkeys coming in over the weekend. So, we're focusing on mass-producing the isolated virus so we can get them infected with it as soon as they arrive."

Kesta trembled at the thought of the virus being mass-produced.

"And in the meantime, I'm in the process of recalibrating Reanimator-A."

"In what way?"

"Liv's blood work is still irregular—more so than I would have hoped, put it that way. I'm concerned that the effects of the Reanimator-A are wearing off. That it's a treatment, not a cure."

A treatment, not a cure. Kesta's heart sank.

"If there's anything I can do to help," she said, looking at her exhausted colleagues and finding them almost as close to the edge as she was, "please let me know. We don't have time to waste. I'll do anything, anything at all."

"Other than volunteering yourself as a human guinea pig, there's not much else you can do," said Dudley, regretting it instantly when he saw the gleam in Kesta's eyes.

"We're going to have to prepare a statement for the press," said Lundeen as he eased himself out of his chair, "which is a royal nuisance. Honestly, the temerity of the media thinking they have a right to know what we're working on here. As if they'd even understand it. But Dave has got everyone asking difficult questions."

He stopped himself at the door and turned to Kesta. "If you are approached by any members of the press, please remember that your contract with Project Dawn prohibits you from discussing its research efforts, so, simply put, talking to the media will result in your sacking or worse. Just direct any questions to the press office and let them take it from there." Lundeen disappeared into the corridor.

Kesta had a million questions of her own that she desperately wanted to ask Dudley but couldn't. She wanted to know everything she could about the symptoms Liv was experiencing, what was wrong with her blood work, whether Dudley thought that the Reanimator-A would fail completely or just recede in its efficacy as time went on. Did he think the side effects were dangerous? Was he having to administer any treatment yet to manage them?

"So, it's not working then?" she asked, trying to keep things as linear and unemotional as possible.

"I'm not sure yet," he said, "but this preclinical phase could take a while. The drug clearly needs more work before it can be given to humans." Kesta felt a clenching pain underneath her diaphragm.

"Well, how far down the alphabet are you thinking of strolling, Dudley?" she asked, trying to make light of it.

"Honestly, I can't say for sure at this stage," he said, watching Liv as she sat down on the floor to wash her face with her hand. "The recalibrated version, Reanimator-B, managed to melt through my gloves, so I've already dispensed with that. If we get to Reanimator-M, I'll be doing something fundamentally wrong."

She had given Tim the Reanimator-A almost without thinking.

"It's not just the Reanimator I'm worried about," he whispered, even though it was just the two of them in the viewing room. "It's the other research. The Gain-of-Function. Lundeen wants us to start mass-producing the more virulent strain." He gripped the dashboard in front of them and leaned into it as though without it he might collapse.

"But there are moratoria in place to stop people making such things, to stop humanity devouring its own."

"We're in an entirely new world here. London was left to fend for herself. And I think that London and maybe even Lundeen are a bit pissed off about that."

"Dudley, we need to have a plan," she said. "We need to be better prepared." The two of them sat side by side, their bottoms voluminous in their hazmat suits, squashed together against the dashboard. Kesta could feel Dudley's leg juddering against hers. "If they're going to manufacture a more virulent version of the virus and stockpile it," she said, "then it stands to reason that the need to establish an effective cure becomes all the more urgent."

"Agreed," he whispered, "and the Gain-of-Function research is actually helping in terms of trialing the Reanimator quickly. It's the irony of it all, isn't it? You have to take unpalatable risks in search of that eureka moment."

"How long do you think you need, Dudley?"

"Kesta, honestly, I don't know. We can accelerate the animal testing from next week, but I can't say for sure. We need to find a cure for this thing before we even think of blowing the whistle on the Gain-of-Function research. We have to report it to the relevant authorities, but we cannot risk doing it yet. If we blow too early, we'll lose access to everything we've been working so hard to develop, and it will leave the cure in limbo.

"But I'm going to speak to someone, someone I trust, and see what our options are. In the meantime, keep your head down, will you? The last thing we need is either one of us getting fired."

Kesta and Dudley shook on it. Turning back around to the viewing room, they saw that Liv was lying on her side on the floor. Kesta prayed she was only sleeping.

CHAPTER TWENTY-THREE

"They thought it was voodoo," said Jess, curling silken legs, one by one, underneath her, her top half arched like a witch's cat in repose. Kesta as usual sat cross-legged on the floor in Jess's living room, leaning her elbows against the walnut coffee table, pecking at the beautiful books Jess had no intention of reading.

"Who did?" Kesta asked, emptying the Pinot Grigio into Jess's glass as she flicked through a hardback about postmodern art.

"Those men in Haiti," Jess said, drinking quickly. A little cough, too much work for one woman's larynx. "Came back to life after three days, like Jesus or something." She laughed that haughty, facetious laugh of hers. "We've inherited all that we know about zombies from those cases in Haiti apparently. The sloth-like movement, the vacancy, the undeadness of them, it all came from one incident. I've been reading up on it." She coughed again, less ladylike this time, a proper hacking. Kesta proffered a glass of water, but Jess sank a mouthful of white wine instead.

"Don't talk," Kesta suggested.

"They even buried one of them," she wheezed out, her eyes tearing a little, though it could have been at the thrill of a live burial.

"Who did?"

Kesta closed the book, understanding now why Jess wouldn't bother to read it.

"The men in Haiti," Jess huffed, unknotting herself, sliding off the sofa, coughing and idling her way into the kitchen. "I read an academic paper on it and a couple of long-form reports." She was standing in front of the open refrigerator, silhouetted by its icy light. "They make a big deal of it over there. Death. Heavily bound up in their voodoo practices, honoring their ancestors, manifesting luck, good or bad. Anyway"—she removed an identical bottle of wine, bought in bulk, and began to unscrew the cork with the same force required for a lumbar puncture—"it was very interesting because it's not something anyone has looked at, as far as I'm aware?"

At this point in the evening, Jess and Kesta would usually be discussing dreams they wouldn't realize, places they wanted to travel, and people they hated at work. The last part could sustain them for hours. Kesta rested her back against the side of the sofa.

"Have you had some sort of brain wave?"

"Poison," Jess said, slithering in her stockings back into the lounge. "That fish one."

"Tetrodotoxin?"

"Yes, anyway, this Haitian gentleman had a beef with this one guy, so he had him struck with the fish poison. Puffer fish or blowfish, you know what I'm talking about. Nearly killed him. He passed so convincingly for dead that he was buried, and they had to dig him up again after."

Kesta thought about this for a moment as Jess swayed slightly in her seat on the sofa, gripping the glass, her eyes glossy with alcoholic hubris.

"I just wanted to suggest it, in case it was helpful, you know. Because the symptoms they described in the paper I was reading, they were so similar to the zombies we encountered in the outbreak. Apart from the bleeding. And the biting. But how they moved, their responses or lack thereof to stimuli like light and pain, were exactly the same."

"So, you're suggesting that this isn't a virus; it's a mass poisoning?" Kesta asked.

"Fuck's sake, Kesta, I don't know. I just read it and thought it was interesting. And I thought of you. I'm just trying to help." She drank her wine forcefully, the way a bigger fish might eat a puffer fish whole and then live to regret it. "You won't tell me anything about what you're working on, and I'm just dying to know."

"You know I'm forbidden from discussing work with you. You're not even supposed to know I work at Project Dawn. But it's not terribly helpful at this stage for you to posit your own half-cut theories."

"I just want to be supportive. I want to help."

"Jess, your job involves delousing dirty five-year-olds; telling old people that the issues they have with walking and weeing are largely down to them being old people. I don't need your help with this."

Jess was sullen, spoiling on the inside.

Kesta didn't know what to say. "I shouldn't even be here. I have . . ."

"More important things to do, right?"

Exactly, Kesta thought. She sat back on her heels to endure the silence for as long as Jess willed it to continue.

"Can you tell me anything? I know you're not allowed, but—"

Kesta sighed.

"Actually, we're making real progress but"—she paused to gather her thoughts—"but it's difficult. There's more scrutiny now, what with Dave, the guy we found. The infected one."

"The last zombie left alive," said Jess. "It's almost romantic."

"Trust me, if you met him, you wouldn't feel that way."

"Did you see about that article in the *Standard*?" Jess asked, her voice augmented by the glass as she spoke into the bowl. "The one asking for more oversight into what the Project is doing?"

"Yes, I did see that," Kesta said, gulping on the inside, "and I'm all for transparency, but the timing isn't helpful. We're at a critical stage in the research, and we don't need outside interference."

"I think people feel entitled to know what is happening with the cure after all these months." The change in Jess's voice came on suddenly, a quiet sobriety. One brow arched, her lips pursed, hands folded across her lap in a small act of defiance.

"I do need to talk to you about something, okay?" she said, and

Kesta knew she was about to be blamed for something; Jess's strange powers of obfuscation at work, a chameleon's ability to go from error to accusation in one subtle shift of color.

"You are brilliant. That's not in dispute, but are you sure you're the right person for this job?"

She looked at Kesta, a portrait of anguish.

"Because I think it's putting you under too much pressure. And you're worrying me, like, all the time."

"I'm fine."

"We both know you're not fine, but . . ."

Jess was wringing her hands in her lap.

"You've ditched me at the last minute three times lately and"—her hands were fiddling with her hair now, another of Jess's guilty tells—"to be honest, Kesta, I feel as though they, and when I say *they* I mean Dudley, pressured you into joining their team in the first place because—"

"They didn't pressure me."

"Because you only lost Tim pretty recently and you're still grieving, and I'm not sure it's the right environment for you as you're recovering from all that. Kesta, I don't think you're at all well—"

"I'm well enough to work, Jess."

"And you're drinking such a lot."

"You're drinking such a lot."

"Half the time I pretend to drink so that I can keep an eye on you while you're chugging it," she said, very soberly indeed. "And let's be honest, Dudley's always, always had a thing for you."

"Dudley's all right. He's really championed me at work, and what we're doing is so important. I feel like I'm making a real difference. It's helped me to keep going when I've wanted to die." It came out breathlessly and somewhat artificially, as if Kesta was scrambling together her defenses.

"You wanted to die?" Jess was stunned. "You could have told me that when you needed a repeat script for antidepressants. Kesta, I could get into trouble."

"Oh, heaven forfend you stick your fucking neck out and risk any-thing!" Kesta spat, and Jess cowered as if she'd been slapped.

"You're different, you know. Like a totally different person."

"I lost my husband. Half of me has been obliterated. I'm sorry, Jess, if it was his side of me you preferred."

"How dare you, Kesta? You carry on as though you're the only person in the world who ever loved and lost. People want to help you, but you won't let them. You won't let me."

"You can't help me."

"Dudley seems to help you though. Right? How you talk about him is different. I thought you didn't like him?"

"I've never said I didn't like Dudley."

Jess's lips curled into a sneer. What came next poleaxed Kesta through the heart.

"There's nothing going on between you, is there?"

Jess didn't pose it as a question. It was an accusation. Kesta felt herself swoon as though her aorta had been sliced open and all her blood was gushing out of the wound. Her face was ashen, her hands and neck clammy, her mouth gaping, a fish out of water, as she processed the shock.

"How could you ask me that?" she whimpered, though inside an inferno raged.

"I'm not judging you. It happens. People find comfort in each other—"

"We work together!"

The muscles in her arms and hands and fingers began to pulse with electricity, the administering of thousands of tiny shocks to her system. She juddered around the table to collect her coat and her bag, which had been tossed, hours earlier, by the dining table, where their finished meal was starting to stiffen and stink.

"I think I should go," she said, and began to zip up her leather jacket, when Jess delivered a fatal blow.

"You've been missing therapy."

"What?"

"I spoke to Dr. Walling."

Kesta was immobile, her legs rooted, staked into the ground, cruci-
fied. She felt the bag drop to the floor.

"She was as worried about you as I was. She actually thought you
must be dead." Jess was sobbing but dry-eyed. "She's offered to see you,
one-to-one. I think you should do it. It's for your own good."

She stood up and turned to Kesta.

"I know you'll hate me for it, really hate me," she wailed, sliding
over the parquet in twenty-denier stockinged feet, "but I've had so many
nights worrying about you shutting me out. You're just not you anymore."

Kesta had always hated Jess's melodrama. She knew her well enough
to know that there was only one way to deal with it, and that was to tell
Jess that she was right. To vindicate her, validate her, tell her, *oh, you
know me better than I know myself.*

"I am losing myself in my work," Kesta said, "because it's all I have,
and because to me, it's the most important thing in the world right
now. I'm sorry if that's pushed you out in the cold. I'm sorry that I seem
changed. Grief does that. I am grieving. I know you're here to help."

"Will you promise me you'll go back to Dr. Walling? You need to talk
to a professional, Kesta."

"I will think about it," Kesta replied, "and I will try to make time
for group." She nearly added *I promise*, but that really would have drawn
attention to its insincerity, and Jess, who was standing proudly, hands
clasped together, feeling that she'd fixed her friend in an instant by
simply listing all her faults, was beaming.

"Kesta, seriously," she cooed, "you'll always have me." She kissed
Kesta on the forehead the way Tim used to.

———

Kesta leaned against the wall outside Jess's flat and wept uncontrollably
into the collar of her jacket, Jess's words ricocheting around her brain
like a pinball machine. Then she remembered something her mother

had said to her years ago, long before she and Tim had gotten married and years before her mother had died. *People are either radiators or drains.* Jess is a drain. Tim is a radiator. Her mother certainly would have enjoyed the irony.

Everyone around her was draining the few reserves she had left. Dudley and now Jess didn't think she was handling things well, didn't think she should be allowed to work at Project Dawn.

Did they think she was a failure? Didn't they see that everything good had come out of her brilliance, her resolve, her blood and guts and sacrifice? That fucking journalist. Lundeen, Cooke even. Didn't they know how hard she was working? How much it consumed her? How dare they all question her? How dare they try to hold her to account?

She was holding everything together. If they knew, if they really knew, Kesta was sure they'd be in awe of what she'd been doing. And she had to keep going, had to keep something back, so that when the time came, she had enough in reserve to give to Tim.

As Kesta reached the curious sanctuary of their spare room, she listened out for the word that she had longed to hear for so long.

Kesta.

But the flat was silent.

"Tim?" she called out as she unbolted the door to his room.

He didn't register her presence.

"Tim," she said again as she rested her hand on his shoulder. Instead of trying to say her name, instead of reaching out to her, Tim just groaned and turned to face the wall.

The Reanimator-A wasn't working anymore.

———

The ringing of her phone dragged her out of an unusually deep sleep, one in which her endless reading into snakes of all species had come back to haunt her. She saw herself alone at the edge of a vast ocean. The sky was no longer blue, it was brown. It was moving. It was made of scales.

Kesta must fight to the death this monolithic snake, one that held its own tail in its mouth. Were the snake to release itself, it would trigger the end of the world. And so Kesta had forced her hands into the snake's mouth and been bitten by it. She thought she would die, that everything would implode, and then she saw the light of her phone shining out of the corner of her open eye.

She groped at the coffee table with her right hand, her head still smooshed against a cushion. She had fallen asleep suddenly on the sofa, angry and exhausted after her row with Jess earlier in the evening.

"Did I wake you?" asked John the American.

"Kind of," she said, "in that I actually got some sleep for once." She looked back at the phone. It was only midnight.

"I know the feeling," he chuckled, "worst thing about the kids. Listen, could you do me a favor? I was just heading home for the day when a buddy of mine called."

Kesta sat up on the sofa and opened her eyes wide, stretching her feet out in front of her and crossing them at the ankles on the table.

"Go on."

"He's just impounded a bunch of boas out by the Okefenokee Swamp."

"The what swamp?"

"Okefenokee, it's on the state border with Georgia. A lot of it is protected wilderness. I'm going out there first thing. Anyhow, this buddy of mine got a call from the wildlife refuge out there. Some kids in a boat out on the backwater had seen some big snakes out there, hiding in the weeds along the shoreline. Three of them. The snakes were all twisted up with what appears to be IBD."

"Jesus, John."

"Thing is, it's going to bring a lot of heat my way, Kesta, if IBD makes it into the news cycle out here, which it's bound to. The other thing," he almost whispered to her, "the other thing is that when they brought the snakes into the lab, they found they're a type of boa we don't even have in Florida."

"Oh?"

"Or in Georgia for that matter. It's a tree boa. Guess where they originate?"

"Madagascar?"

"Hell, how did you know that?"

"Should I tell you it's because I've learned more about snakes than I ever wished to learn and that they are the stuff of fucking nightmares?"

"Funny how you're sleeping more soundly than ever."

"So, you're going to visit the snakes tomorrow?"

"Listen," he said, ignoring the question, "I know you believe that IBD is behind your zombie virus out there, and if we have cases of it in snakes in the US, then I am morally obligated to notify the relevant authorities. I can't sit on it any longer."

"I need you to give me just a bit more time, John," she begged. "We're making progress with our preclinical trials but—"

"Kesta, we don't have time," he said bluntly. "I have non-native snakes sick with IBD, and you're telling me that the disease has made the jump to humans. If that's true, then what happened in London could easily happen over here. Right? I can't in all good conscience wait while you come to any other conclusion than that."

"Is there anything I can give you in exchange for more time?"

"You can give me the name of your Patient Zero. I've gotta know if he's on our list of smugglers."

"Smugglers?"

"Snake eggs, Kesta. Breeders who sell eggs illegally. Into China for medicine, into some parts of Africa for food, skins too, to different parts of the world. And they ship into the US, where people breed snakes and there's a demand for exotic species here. Do you have any idea how much of an issue it is in certain states, certain counties where people buy these things, and then they get too big and so they just drive them out into the swamp somewhere and let them loose?"

Paul Mosi wasn't just a tourist. He was a collector, a breeder, a man who trafficked in illegal snake eggs. It must have been why he was in

Madagascar, to buy eggs. And it looked to Kesta like he'd traveled with them into the States.

"Paul Mosi."

"What's that?"

"Patient Zero," said Kesta. "His name was Paul Mosi."

"I'll follow up with my colleagues. I think it may be safe to say that your Mr. Mosi came into direct contact with the IBD virus, even if we can't yet explain how he contracted it. It has to be the connection we're looking for. An international dealer trading in eggs and snakes, some of which must have been infected. Do you know if he'd been to the States?"

Kesta couldn't bring herself to confirm John's suspicions. Paul Mosi had traveled extensively in the months preceding his death, including to the US. If he was importing banned items, bringing snake eggs and live reptiles into the country, what if it was enough to cause an outbreak in Florida?

"I don't know anything about that, I'm afraid, John," she lied, to buy herself more time.

"Look, if you can find out where this guy lived, if he has a farm or anything, for breeding purposes, I'd be happy to have a team go out there and take a look. See if we can find anything useful. But I'm going to have to tell them here about the Madagascar connection, Kesta. I'm going to have to do it by the end of this week. I'm sorry. I just have to report my suspicions."

"I understand," she said before hanging up. If Paul Mosi had fallen ill during the yellow fever outbreak when he was traveling through Madagascar, if he'd then handled and been bitten by a snake infected with IBD, could it have been enough to set in motion the chain of events that led to the outbreak?

Kesta walked into Tim's room, where he seemed to be sleeping. She gently stroked his hair and watched as several strands came away in her fingers. Just like Liv.

One step forward, two steps back.

It was then that Kesta resolved to take a giant leap forward on her own. If Dudley was refining the Reanimator-A, she would try to find people willing to trial it. She would put the feelers out for volunteers and get the ball rolling on a human sample trial, with or without Lundeen's permission. Tomorrow night, she would go hunting.

CHAPTER TWENTY-FOUR

During what had seemed like an endless night, Tim had shed even more of his hair. Kesta had covered him with blankets because he couldn't stop shivering. It was pitiful, and she longed to restore him again the way the Reanimator-A had done so, albeit briefly. She needed to understand what was wrong with the drug.

It seemed entirely logical, practical, rigorous in fact, to the scientific part of Kesta's brain, that in order to study and fine-tune the Reanimator-A, a human trial was absolutely vital. She had thought about it a lot, in the middle of the night, waiting for the sleep-deprivation psychosis to kick in.

She'd read up on sleep-deprivation psychosis, there were lots of clinical papers and blog posts on the subject online, probably written by her fellow insomniacs at three in the morning. She was worried she might have it, but couldn't be conclusively sure. Her brain and its decision-making capabilities versus someone who didn't have to provide twenty-four-hour care for a zombie while holding down a day job—she'd need an entirely separate human trial to prove it either way.

Her knackered scientific brain told her that Tim was just too weak now for her to risk giving him anything else experimental. Someone more robust, more fortunate, needed to take the strain. Dave would likely suffer the same side effects as Tim, given his lengthy exposure to the virus before he'd been given the Reanimator-A. Without the luxury of time, a small human trial was the only logical next step for her to take.

Kesta knew that this was the morally right thing to do for her husband, if not the ethically right thing to do for the people on said future drug trial. All she really needed was twenty willing volunteers, which wasn't so much to ask for in the grand scheme of things, to help her accelerate Dudley's research. And Kesta knew exactly where to find the right demographic. Pour Decisions.

The kind of men who were young and fit and strapping enough to withstand urgent, radical drug therapies also went to bars. They were the kind of men who didn't stop to read the label on their medication, who were ignorant of the warnings attached, who drank alcohol on antibiotics, but who were also vegan and cycled everywhere.

If these men wouldn't join Kesta's medical trial for the bragging rights, or to impress their employers with their effective altruism, they would do it for the money. The financial incentive in medical trialing was always crap, but that didn't seem to stop people from signing up for shots designed to treat the effects of cholera with the unexpected bonus of an improvement in wrinkle reduction.

She hadn't worked this part out yet. She had the remnants of a bank loan left over, from when she and Tim had plans to redo their kitchen before a zombie apocalypse had put paid to his aspirations for a double oven. She might be able to scratch together enough cash to compensate ten or even fifteen twenty-somethings.

There was that otherwise empty dungeon area at Project Dawn, the one that Dudley had shown her. Kesta was confident, irrationally so, that she could have a good stab at filling up its beds.

Science is risk.

Kesta had always reassured herself of this. She always knew what she was doing. More or less. Less so nowadays but then, perhaps she should practice self-care and be kinder to herself because she had kept her husband undead for seven months in the room next door, and who else could lay claim to that?

She was ready. She had prepared. She had even worn makeup. Kesta felt anxious but not conflicted. She placed her hand against the breast pocket of her leather jacket. Inside it lay a lock of Tim's lost hair.

Walking toward her, Jess was waving. The closer she got to Kesta, the slower her pace became.

"Did you let a child draw on your face?" Jess asked her, standing back to inspect her.

"It's just lipstick," Kesta said defensively, feeling for her mouth.

"It's not meant to go quite so far up to your nose, dear," Jess said, wiping a smear from Kesta's top lip with her little finger. "Kesta, it's nice to see you making more of an effort but, babes, you look dreadful. Like a sort of Dorian Gray painting of Alice Cooper," she said, using a thumb to remove some of the charcoal from Kesta's undereye.

"Like I should be peering out at you from a drain?" Kesta said, trying to make light of it. "Well, good, that's the look I was going for."

"I'm just pleased to see you," Jess said, almost apologetically. "I was worried I'd really hurt your feelings the other night."

"Come on, I need a drink."

"Yes, but just the one, right?" Jess called after her, but Kesta was already half inside.

As she and Jess waited for the burly bouncer in the leather trench coat to administer his checks, Kesta could feel the music throbbing through her feet. She could smell that particular Pour Decisions mix of cheap aftershave and anticipation. She could imagine the odorants and olfactory receptors hanging in the air around the entrance.

The bar was unusually busy. Kesta could see an abundance of them— her targets—standing inside, clutching their drinks, laughing and talking. Young, strong, healthy-looking men, already several sheets to the wind, competing with each other for supremacy.

"Busy tonight." Jess turned to her, arms still in the air as the bleep of the thermometer signaled she was clear to enter. "Should we go somewhere else?"

"No, this is fine." Kesta was busy eyeing up a man in a tight blue polo shirt, his biceps bulging, skin gleaming in the candlelight, and she thought about where she might inject him. She threw her arms up and glared at the bouncer.

"Are you sure, babes? We can easily go elsewhere. Actually, I'm not sure I'm comfortable now, with this many people—"

"There's a space at the end of the bar. If we move quickly, we'll get it."

Kesta pushed past the bouncer without waiting for Jess, then marched her way through the inner cell mass of unsuspecting men to assume her position at the far end of the bar. *There is such early promise in this room*, she thought, staring back at every man who turned to look at her as she pressed up against their bodies, carefully moving them out of her way. For the first time in their two decades of friendship, Jess found herself bringing up the rear like a pantomime horse.

"Gosh, well done, you," she said as they commandeered the only vacant barstools. "The last time I saw this many men in one room, they were all zombies and about to be double-tapped. I might have a cocktail, you?"

Kesta was scanning the room, mentally preparing a list in order of preference dependent upon size and weight. Being this close to strangers was entirely out of her comfort zone, especially if she was to be expected to engage them in conversation.

"Actually," she said, trying and failing to get the bartender's attention, "I think I need a shot first."

"Kesta, are you sure that's a good idea?"

Of course Kesta wasn't sure it was a good idea, because it was a monstrous idea—but it was the only one she had in the moment.

Kesta stuck two fingers into her mouth and whistled like a steam train. The barman immediately stopped serving the man in the blue polo shirt and sprinted down to their end of the bar.

"Two shots of tequila," said Kesta.

"Kesta, what's gotten into you tonight?" asked Jess, slithering out of her jacket.

"I'm fine. I'm great. It is busy but that's good, I can work with that."

"Work with what?" asked Jess—and then, to the bartender, "Oh, we'll both also have red wine, thanks. Smooth and fruity, babe?"

"More full-bodied and dependable," Kesta replied, having caught the eye of the man in the polo shirt, who appeared to be making a move toward her. The barman returned with two frosted shot glasses and poured the tequila up to the rim.

"I want to start a tab," Kesta hissed as she pressed her debit card into the palm of his hand before folding his fingers tightly around it. He nodded obediently. As she watched him walk over to the register, storing her card in a long black wallet, Kesta imagined him strapped to a gurney at the lab.

"You sure you're all right, babe? You seem preoccupied," Jess said, draping her jacket across the other barstool before sitting on it rather daintily. Kesta *was* distracted, by the plethora of bare arms around them.

Such vascular men, such easy prickings.

"I'm fine. Work is just—we've reached something of an impasse. Anyway, here's mud in your eye," she toasted, downing her shot, leaving Jess to sip at hers rather gingerly.

Kesta hated tequila. But she needed that sudden, violent heat, that surging, devil-may-care spirit that only the strongest ones can evoke. And she needed it urgently.

"Anything you want to talk about?" asked Jess, gasping as she finished her shot. Kesta didn't answer.

The two of them waited in silence as the bartender returned, placing their wineglasses onto delicate paper coasters. He looked pleased with himself.

"You ladies got a big night planned?" he asked, pushing a complimentary bowl of olives across the counter toward them.

"That depends," said Kesta.

"On what?"

"On whether you leave us alone to get on with it," she said under her breath.

"Sorry, didn't quite catch that," he shouted over the music with one finger to his ear, but Jess elegantly waved him away toward the other patrons before Kesta had another opportunity to offend him.

"Oh hello," said Jess, surprised to see the man in the blue polo shirt had appeared between her and Kesta. She stabbed at one of the olives with a cocktail stick. "Who are you?"

Ordinarily, Kesta would have given him the kind of intensely repulsed death stare that would make him think she carried a switchblade and would be delighted to use it on his testicles. Tonight, she remained impassive. Discreetly neutral. As much as it pained her to talk to strangers, she would have to start somewhere.

"Hello, I'm Dan."

"Hello, Dan, I'm Jess, and this is my friend Kesta," said Jess, holding the olive and the cocktail stick in between her teeth as she shook Dan's hand. Kesta did the same when he offered it to her. She felt his grip strength would score perfectly.

"Hi, Dan," Kesta said, admiring his tanned forearms, watching them clench as he swigged from a bottle of pale ale.

"Kesta," he said, gurning idiotically, "what kind of a name is Kesta?"

"It's my name, Dan."

"Who on earth is called Kesta?"

I am, you fuck nugget, she really wanted to say, and not for the first time in her life. Instead, she steadied herself. "Are you responsible for all these men, Dan? Usually it's pretty quiet in here."

Jess shot her a look. Her friend was not herself tonight. It was as though she was possessed.

"Ha, ha, yes," said Dan, laughing at nothing. "There's fourteen of us, actually."

He gestured back at the group, some of whom smiled in return and raised their bottles and glasses, their two-fist brains trying to figure out who he was talking to.

"We're old university friends, though we haven't seen each other since, well, you know, *BTZ.*"

Kesta and Jess looked puzzled.

"Sorry, *before the zombies.*"

He laughed again. It was entirely unearned.

"We're having a reunion."

"A reunion, how lovely!" Jess shrieked, slapping her hand against the bar. "Isn't it wonderful to do something so normal again? Don't you think, Kesta?"

Kesta didn't have an opinion either way. She was trying to figure out in her head if fourteen could work as a sample trial as opposed to the standard twenty.

"You're nearly dry there, Dan," she said, gesturing toward his empty bottle. "You want another? And what about your friend over there?"

"Jacob, hello, I'm Jacob."

"Hello, Jacob."

Kesta offered her hand for him to shake and saw with great disappointment that he was avascular. She could stab away for hours and never find a vein.

"What do you gents do?" asked Jess.

"What?"

"What do you do?" she shouted again over the music and the growing din of conversation.

"I'm in finance," said Dan, "and Jacob works for a law firm just south of the river. In fact, we're mostly bankers and lawyers here, although Alfie over there, he's a structural surveyor."

Good, Kesta thought. *Lawyers and bankers.* The world could do with fewer of those. A medical trial would be a valuable opportunity for them to give something back to society rather than to keep plundering from it.

"I hope you don't mind my saying, but you both look very fit," Kesta said, somewhat lasciviously. "How would you describe your overall fitness levels?"

"Pretty bloody good, actually."

"Oh yeah, we're very active."

Kesta didn't entirely wish to know what Jacob meant by that.

"He was cross-country champion, represented our college," Dan chipped in.

"Five-minute mile, thereabouts, so, yah, pretty damn fit."

After his moment of self-congratulation, Jacob became subdued.

"Actually, Dan and I are preparing to run a marathon in the new year."

"Oh heavens," snorted Jess, "why on earth would you want to do a thing like that?"

"It's in memory of our friend. Callum. He—he died early in the outbreak."

Jess turned scarlet with embarrassment and mouthed a hopeless apology. The four of them were silent for a while, lost in loss, deafened by the artificial sounds around them. Just like that, their desire for a normal night, to laugh and drink and make new friends, seemed idle, almost selfish. To carry on after death wasn't a choice, but the manner in which you did so felt pointed.

"To Callum," Kesta said, raising her glass the way she had toasted Tim's birthday in that same bar just months before. She felt for the lock of twisted hair inside her pocket. It wasn't just to Callum that she drank, it was to what his friends might yet do for her undead husband. A circle of sacrifice she was determined to square.

"It's very admirable of you both to honor your friend," she said. "It's important that people see they have a responsibility in times of crisis. That everyone can play a part."

"I think any decent human being would want to do as much as possible to help, don't you?" said Dan.

"Absolutely," said Kesta, leaning solicitously into him and lowering her tone so that Jess couldn't quite hear her, "and what with that other zombie they found, well, it makes you wonder—"

"Wonder what?"

"About the threat of it all happening again. Because without a cure, we are all still at risk, aren't we?"

Kesta watched as the cogs in Dan's brain began to turn. Over his shoulder she saw a sofa had become available by the window. Gritting her teeth, she put her hand on that deliciously vascular forearm, imagining for a moment what Jess would do if she wanted something badly enough.

"Would you mind if I asked you something? Over there?"

She tipped her chin toward the sofa. Dan instinctively helped her off her stool. She didn't say anything, but Kesta felt Jess's eyes boring into her back as she and Dan crossed the room and squished together on the sofa. Jacob took up Kesta's seat on the stool. Jess was occupied. Kesta could get to work.

"Listen, Dan," she spoke right into his ear, trying to plant the seed as deeply as she could. "I'm looking for people to help me with something incredibly important. How would you feel if I told you that you could do something more vital than just run a marathon in Callum's name?"

"I mean, I'd say yes, obviously," he replied, sipping his beer.

Kesta looked out across the bar.

"I get the feeling that you and your friends here would like to do something more—meaningful. To really make a difference. To help others, Dan, the way you couldn't help Callum."

Dan's brow tightened at the mention of his dead friend's name. There was a sadness in his eyes as he looked down at Kesta and, she thought, a sense of shame and responsibility. Emotions she could exploit.

"What would you have done to save Callum, if you'd had the chance?" she probed.

She saw that he was confounded by his own failings, searching the room for his friends, remembering the one who was missing, internalizing a feeling that somehow it was his fault that Callum wasn't there with them. A survivor's guilt.

"I mean, I would have done anything if I'd been there," he said, convinced that he, a merchant banker, could have stopped a pack of the infected from tearing his friend apart. "I would have tried to rush the zombies. I would have fought back."

She saw his vulnerability underneath the bravado, a sense of disgrace at being left alive. "If all of us lads had been together, I think we could have given them what for, killed a bunch of them, you know, and got Cal out of there."

"He died because he was on his own and didn't have you there to protect him," said Kesta, letting her hand linger a moment too long on Dan's knee.

"That is exactly how I feel," said Dan, making the kind of emotional breakthrough Dr. Walling would be proud of. "You seem to know what I'm thinking."

"I understand how you feel, more than you could know," Kesta said, "and that's why I'd like to offer you the chance to make a real change. A meaningful sacrifice. By helping me with my work."

"Sounds important."

"It is. And I would like to start a conversation with you about how you might be able to make a difference. For Callum."

"Anything. I'll do anything."

"Excellent," Kesta said, retrieving a notebook and pen from the side pocket of her jacket. "I'm just going to make a few notes. Hope you don't mind. You're, what, twenty-seven?"

"Twenty-nine actually."

"Almost at a milestone. Don't worry, you should see thirty. Do you have any preexisting medical conditions I should be aware of, Dan?"

"Like what?"

"Oh, you know. Any allergies, heart problems, any surgeries in the last six months?"

"No, not that I'm aware of. Is that good or bad?"

"Oh, that's really good, Dan. Thank you. Any family history of blood disorders, stroke, aneurysm, clots, any family history of diabetes, childhood cancers, any recent exposure to radiation?"

Kesta began to imagine the rows of test subjects lying side by side on the hellmouth floor of Project Dawn, every man playing his part. Every man not for himself but for everybody else.

Are you on any medication, Dan?

How do you feel about snakes, Dan?

And needles, what about needles? Do you faint when you see them?

"You ask an awful lot of questions." Dan coughed nervously.

"It's because I need the answers, Dan. And this is a matter of life and death. Of national security. A chance for you to make history. A chance to trial the cure."

Even though Dan had handed over all the incriminating details of his medical history, nothing could have prepared him for this uniquely unsettling proposition. He jolted backward in his seat, as if he expected to see a syringe in Kesta's hand, as though he'd already been drugged.

"The cure? For the zombie virus?"

Kesta dug the vial out from her inside jacket pocket and held it up to the light for him to see. The Reanimator-A.

"I'd only need you for the weekend, maybe a whole week, there would be a series of injections, all done in state-of-the-art conditions, under the strictest medical supervision," she said. She slipped the vial back inside her pocket. "You'd be a pioneer, Dan. You'd be pushing the envelope of scientific endeavor."

"You must be out of your mind!"

"Think of Callum, what would he want you to do?"

"Callum would want me not to get bitten by a zombie in the first place," said Dan.

He began searching the bar for reinforcements, for a vigilant friend to signal to for an immediate extraction.

"You cannot be serious?"

Kesta felt blindsided, but rallied.

"You said you would do anything. In Callum's memory? Anything to help."

"My mate's already dead," said Dan, standing upright. "I'm not putting myself at risk for a fucking stranger. Some other time, love."

He wiped his hands on the front of his jeans. He was shaking.

"There won't be another time!" she called after him, but Dan was already blending into the crowd, becoming one with the mass of male bodies, presumably passing on the message that Kesta was not to be trusted. She would have to act quickly. She needed another shot, an extra boost to help her charm her way through the crowd when charm was the thing she truly lacked. She waded through the morass, squeezing through the spaces they deigned to leave, using their jackets, their trouser legs, anything for leverage until she hauled herself up to the bar.

After hailing the bartender, she downed another tequila and stood with her back against the countertop, feeling the heat and the light and the noise surging through her body. She was Dorothy in *The Wizard of Oz*, desperate to go home, but without anyone there to help her, marooned in an alien realm full of cowards and metal men without hearts. Kesta took a deep breath and pushed herself back out into the crowd to try again.

Something hooked her by the elbow. Before she could do anything about it, the bartender had blocked her path, smothering her like a fire-retardant blanket thrown over someone alight. The crowd of men began to disperse as though it was Kesta who was infected. Behind the bartender stood the bouncer, patiently cracking his knuckles.

"You can't conduct your business in here. This is a private establishment. You're harassing my customers."

"I'm not doing anything of the sort," Kesta blustered. She was trying her best to sound casual as she sweated bullets.

"I'm going to have to ask you to leave. Eric, will you see her out?"

"Yes, boss."

"I don't want to leave. I haven't done anything wrong."

"That's not what some of the other customers have been saying."

"What's going on here," Jess interjected, wrapping a protective arm around Kesta's shoulders, pulling her close. It was an old trick of Tim's, intended to rein her back in when she was in free fall or considering punching someone.

"Nothing. I haven't done anything."

"Your friend's been trying to talk my regulars into some kind of medical experiment," said the bartender. "People come here to relax. Not to be made responsible for other people's ailments."

Kesta was ready to rip the bartender a new orifice, but Jess took charge and pushed her toward the exit. She could hear Jess apologizing for their behavior, something about her friend having been under unimaginable stress at work. The dead-husband card was dealt. But then Kesta heard Jess deliver a sharp *fuck you all* before she flounced her way out through the velvet doorway, dragging Kesta outside and into the cold.

"Jesus, Kesta, what the hell?" said Jess, struggling back into her jacket. "What's gotten into you?"

When Kesta didn't reply, Jess grabbed hold of her, pinching the flesh by her armpit, and pulled her out into the street in the direction of Smithfield Market. When they reached the vast iron archway of the market on the other side of the road, a safe enough distance from Pour Decisions, Jess stopped, her arms folded across her chest, and tried again to reason with her friend.

"Kesta, what were you up to in there?" she said, leaning defiantly on one hip, her jaw tight, her lips bitten shut.

Kesta zipped up her jacket and tried to look nonchalant, shoving her hands deep into the pockets. She could feel against her fingers the calling cards, the notebook, and the empty prop vial of Reanimator-A all lying there guiltily.

"Kesta!"

"They've postponed my human trials," she said, as if it was somehow all her fault. "For three months. And even then, they might make us wait even longer before they will let us trial our drug *on people!*"

Kesta's frustration was palpable. She knew she looked small and angry—not fragile, Kesta was never that—but at a breaking point. Jess softened a little. She put her hands on Kesta's shoulders. Kesta was sure she was concerned, but mostly she looked confused. Her kindness made Kesta all the more despondent. Jess could never understand why Kesta was really so upset.

"What does that matter, babe," she said gently. "What's three more months if, by waiting, you get the answer you're looking for?"

"We need to move to human trials in order to make sure that the drug is safe, that it works."

"Don't you only move to human trials after the drug has been deemed safe?"

"Yes, but someone has to be the guinea pig, Jess."

"No, babe, that's what guinea pigs are for. They have to be the guinea pigs, poor little bastards."

"You're not listening to me," Kesta moaned, slumping down to the pavement, resting her back against the gates to the market. "With every new drug there is an experimental phase. If we're to make it safe for humans, we have to test it on them. Someone has to go first. Someone has to be brave."

"Yes, but Kesta, it's a really big ask, isn't it?" said Jess, crouching down next to her. "I don't think I could do it. Do you?"

Kesta let Jess hold her for a moment, their jackets squeaking together as they looked back across the road through the misted windows of Pour Decisions, where the friends of dead people, confirming their own existence by living as if everything was normal, were getting another round in. A toast for those left alive.

"Jess, I just really need for this to be over," Kesta sighed. She felt Jess reach for her hand. But before she could say anything else, the space around them flashed neon blue, a bright light circling the street and splashing across the two of them. Kesta had to shield her eyes from it as she watched two female officers jump out of a patrol car mere feet away from her. The officers headed into the bar, disappearing behind the curtain.

Someone had called the police.

———

Jess had begged Kesta to stay the night. To come home with her to her flat in Hampstead, to let her, in her own infuriatingly inept way, take care of her. Jess wanted to feed her up, she said, to run her a bath, to wrap her up in her nearly new blush cashmere robe, and to let her sleep late into a dreamy weekend. Bacon and eggs and toast and coffee and reruns of TV shows in which everyone was deliriously happy and joyfully irreverent all the fucking time and nothing went wrong and absolutely no one ever died, ever.

Jess just wanted to help, she said, but all Kesta could hear was an outline of her own failing. That she was too thin, unknowingly unkempt, unattractively tired, morose, and very, very desperate. Kesta didn't want to hear it, so she left Jess sobbing at the station, and she came home alone, dragging her duvet into the hallway, making a crude nest on the floor, where she lay down in her clothes, staring into the spare room, eventually falling asleep to the metronome beeping of her husband's heart inside the vitals monitor.

As with every morning since Tim had been bitten, Kesta had a nanosecond of bliss, of ignorance, preceding the horror of another day of this surreal unliving. Kesta pushed herself up onto her elbows, her legs knotted in the duvet, and saw him there, still clinging on, still beeping, watching her. His fingers twitched a little, and he wheezed.

Good morning, she imagined him saying.

"Morning, darling," she said, rubbing her eyes with her fingers and seeing the soot come off on her hands. "Which one of us looks worse?"

It's a dead heat, honey.

Kesta creaked as she struggled to her feet, her knees locking up, her hips crunching. She should try to take some more blood today. Maybe try to eat something. She reached for the belt of her jeans. She thought it had come loose, but it hadn't. The belt and the jeans were much too big for her now. Even on the tightest notch, everything was too loose. Kesta began to lumber toward the kitchen just as the communal doors at the end of the hall whined, just as footsteps thudded down the corridor, just as a fist knocked once, twice, and a third time on the front door to her flat.

Kesta stood still and waited. She didn't breathe. The monitor wasn't so loud that you could hear it from outside. If she hid here, silently, the person knocking would go away. She looked at Tim. She wanted to ask him what to do.

The knocking came again, louder. A hum of voices in the corridor. Two people then, not one. Kesta stayed rooted to the spot. She shut her eyes and willed the visitors to leave. Albert didn't work on weekends. Albert knew not to let anyone up without asking her first.

"Mrs. Shelley?" a woman's voice called through the fire door. Still Kesta didn't move.

"Mrs. Shelley, can you open the door please?" Then a muffled exchange, another woman's voice.

"Are we sure she's in there?"

"Yeah, the fella on reception said she came home around midnight."

Another knock, more like banging, irritated, probing, testing how secure the door was and the probability of two women being able to break it down. And then the real terror, the dread, the arrival of it on the doorstep like a vampire, but one you didn't get a choice whether or not you let come in.

"Mrs. Shelley, this is the police. Open up, Mrs. Shelley. We need to talk to you."

Kesta was trapped. There was no way out. The police were at her door. She felt her knees go weak. She needed to sit down, to collapse. She couldn't bear the weight of her own body any longer, even though it weighed so much less than it had before.

A wave of sickness began to quiver in the lining of her stomach, a pain inside the diaphragm, around her heart, spread across the ribs. Kesta wondered if this is what it felt like to have a heart attack, this dizzy, nauseated, achy feeling, coupled with an odd desire to simply let go.

"Mrs. Shelley?"

You always know what to do.

But Kesta didn't know what to do. She might be dying.

A conversation in the corridor, somewhere out there in the ether.

"Do you smell that?"

"Smell what?"

The sound of sniffing, the sense of someone's face pressed against the door, the crackle of a radio.

"Are we sure she's home? Should we call it in, do you think?"

Then a swooshing sound, a blanket being hauled across the floor, the metallic scratching of a key inside a lock, the creaking of a door opening, just a crack. A pair of black, hollowed eyes peering out from the void.

"Oh, hello there," said the officer, flinching with surprise, hand guardedly hovering over the can of mace at her hip. "Are you Mrs. Kesta Shelley?"

Kesta croaked yes, she was. She couldn't look the woman in the eye.

"Are you all right, love?" said the second officer, taller, older, kindly, maternal, like nothing could surprise her. Like she'd seen it all before. *Just not this.*

"I'm sorry," said Kesta. "I was asleep. And I don't sleep. Not normally."

"I'm a bad sleeper too," said the older officer, "makes you feel like it's the end of the world, doesn't it, when you can't sleep." Kesta nodded automatically, hugging the door to stop herself from keeling over. The younger woman stared at her suspiciously.

"We had a report of verbal harassment at a bar in Farringdon last night," she said.

Kesta lowered her head, braced it against the door.

"Can we come in, love?" said the older woman, bending down to look at Kesta. "Only you don't seem very well."

"I'm not very well," Kesta whimpered.

"Are you hungover, yeah, is that it?" snapped the young officer, folding her arms, still able to touch the mace with her fingertips.

Just be honest, Kesta. Just tell them the truth. It won't hurt.

"I lost my husband."

"Oh!"

The officers stepped away from her, leaned against the wall to give her some space, watching her sway and sob, holding herself up against the door. A feral widow, a grubby little stray, trapped between one life and the next.

"Was he bitten, love?" asked the older officer.

Kesta nodded. Just the question *was he bitten* was like being branded with an iron, and Kesta felt it in her stomach, such burning pain.

"Can't I come in and make you a cup of tea? See that you're all right?"

The officer was being nice to her. The officer wanted to help. And in that moment, a large part of Kesta, so tired, so threadbare, hardly human now, wanted to let her in to deal with what she'd done. To make that cup of tea.

"It's all such a mess," Kesta said. "I'm so ashamed."

"Ashamed of what, love?"

"Everything. You've no idea."

The two officers exchanged a look. The older woman nodded, and the younger one trundled away down the corridor, muttering into her radio. Kesta heard the rumble of the lift shaft and the bright ding of its arrival, to ferry the officer away.

"Look, love," said the officer, rummaging in a pocket of her fluorescent jacket, "it's understandable to lose your way. Grief can make you mad. I've seen it myself. But you can't go around shouting at men in bars."

Kesta shook her head, wobbling, lips crumbling, trying not to cry again. And then.

"I felt so angry with them."

"Why's that?"

"For being alive."

The officer's hand wove through the gap in the door and rested on Kesta's shoulder. It didn't rest for long, feeling the bone so close to the surface, feeling the muscle so wasted, feeling death beneath the skin.

"I get it. Fucking awful when the world has the nerve to go back to normal. Listen, love, we just came here to bring you back your bank card. You left it at the bar last night."

Oh.

"None of the men wanted to press charges. They were all just confused. Most of them were drunk, anyhow, rambling on about some drug trial or other. Saying you wanted to turn them all into zombies or something. Sounded a bit far-fetched to me."

Kesta coughed. She tried to sound rueful, convincing.

"I drink too much. It's become a problem. I promise I'll sort myself out. I'm sorry."

"You know, there are people out there who can help you with grief. It's just that people are also a bit shit. They don't always notice when you need some support. You shouldn't have to ask for it. But in your case, love, I think you should."

Kesta's body hung on until it heard the officer step into the lift and the doors close behind her. The last thing Kesta heard, before she fainted in the hallway, was the door to her flat click shut.

CHAPTER TWENTY-FIVE

Dr. Walling took her glasses off and put the temple tip end into her mouth, as she always did. Kesta had never been in trouble before. Never been given detention at school, never once been stopped or searched or questioned by police. Never driven while drunk. Never stolen.

Yes, you have, she corrected herself, thinking about the slew of medical paraphernalia and prescription drugs that she'd trafficked to her home. Never stolen and been caught.

Jess had booked the appointment. And after her behavior at Pour Decisions, Kesta knew that keeping it wasn't optional. She had no choice but to go. She had watched as the ZARG members filed out of the meeting room at the back of the hospital and into the street where she was waiting, and when Dr. Walling had seen her, beckoning her in with a finger, it felt exactly like being in trouble.

"It's been a while," said Dr. Walling.

"Only a couple of weeks," said Kesta, though she couldn't remember when she had last been to therapy.

"Four months, actually."

Kesta raised her shoulders, but it was barely a shrug. No point trying to defend the indefensible. She was distracted by a new poster in the room, nauseating in pastel blue and yellow and featuring a cheerful duckling.

DON'T WORRY, BE HAPPY!

Kesta thought about dunking that duckling in a bowl of soup and eating it alive under a napkin in the dark like the French.

Dr. Walling crossed her legs and propped her glasses on top of her head. She tilted her head in concern, and the glasses slipped a little. Kesta smiled, inside on the verge of hysteria, thinking how difficult it would be to keep a straight face if the glasses were to make a bid for freedom of their own.

"Something funny?"

"Nothing, sorry. *Duckling.*"

"So, what's the reason, then," she asked, "for you missing so many Recovery Group sessions?" Dr. Walling rarely added the Zombie Apocalypse part, didn't identify so much with that bit, just the therapeutic element.

Kesta had tried to prepare a good enough excuse. She'd thought about blaming a lab leak, claiming she'd been forced to quarantine; thought about citing a change in her shift patterns at the Project. But in the moment, faced by the good doctor, she drew a blank.

Kesta fiddled with the old tissue she'd brought with her as a prop.

"I just find it very, very difficult to—to talk, that's all. I don't like talking about it. I don't want to talk about it. Because I live with it. All the time."

"Oh, Kesta," Dr. Walling said, shaking her head, "people are making good progress here, you know? It's awful what happened—awful for everyone in group—and we've all been required to plumb new depths of grief. But people are finally starting to learn to live with their loss and to move on. Except you."

Kesta looked down at her lap, then up at the ceiling. How had she failed to notice that fan whirring silently above her? She closed her eyes and thought of it breaking loose, crashing down on top of her and smashing into her skull.

"Talking helps."

"Yes, I know, you keep saying that."

"That's because it's true. Talking helps, Kesta."

"It doesn't help me."

Dr. Walling decided to change tack. She fished a miniature bottle of vodka from the handbag splayed open at her feet.

"Does this help?" she said, thrusting her dogmatic little prop toward Kesta like a crucifix prepped for an exorcism. "Does this help more than talking?"

Kesta shrugged. A nerve under her right eye began to twitch. She rubbed it hard with her fingers.

"Personally speaking, I would say yes, yes it does."

"Well, Kesta, professionally speaking I would have to disagree and say no, no it really does not. Alcohol is never the answer."

"That depends entirely upon the question." Kesta tried to make light of the matter, but Dr. Walling's brittle countenance made it clear that the time for joking had long since passed.

"I'm sorry," said Kesta. "I'm dealing with it the best I can."

"And how's that then? By working yourself into the ground?"

"Yes."

"And what do you think you're going to achieve by working so relentlessly, Kesta? Hmm?"

Dr. Walling no longer used that soothing tone. She marched the words right out of her mouth, her manner clipped and final the way one might talk to a dog that was proving difficult to train not to keep shitting in the house.

"Working won't bring your husband back, you know?"

Kesta said nothing in reply, so Dr. Walling stood up and crouched down on the floor, resting her hands on Kesta's kneecaps.

"You have a good friend in Ms. Street," she said, "In Jess, I mean. She's very worried about you, she was in bits when she rang me. About how erratic you are. About your drinking. It's just awful. You're putting people through the wringer, Kesta. People who care about you. If you don't want to get better for yourself, at least try to get better for them." Dr. Walling squeezed down on Kesta's knee as though she was cracking a walnut. "Tim would want you to be happy."

"How the fuck do you know what my husband would want?" Kesta said, months of stored-up vitriol flung at the doctor for having the temerity to act if she'd known Tim herself.

Dr. Walling flinched, leaning back on her haunches. She glared at Kesta.

"It's like it hasn't really happened," said Dr. Walling, shaking her head, her voice devoid of any emotion. "That's what I think. You haven't accepted that he's gone, have you? And for what it's worth, I don't think they should have allowed you to work at Project Dawn, not with your history."

It was as though Dr. Walling regretted having said it out loud, like it was blasphemy or an incantation. She stumbled to her feet and returned to her chair, where she began cleaning the lenses of her glasses with the sleeve of her top. It was only when the silence started to groan between them that she confessed.

"Jess told me."

She sniffed, unable to hide her concern, not necessarily for Kesta but at the prospect that someone from the Project might come for her and bundle her into the back of a van.

"She was just so worried about you, Kesta. She didn't mean to betray your trust. She really didn't, and I won't either. You can trust me."

Kesta couldn't trust Dr. Walling. And, as she had feared, she couldn't trust Jess either. The secret had been too much for her to carry on her own. She shook her head, jutted her chin out defiantly.

"I was given all the proper clearance checks." Kesta squeezed the scrunched-up tissue like it was a rubber stress ball. "I am fine."

"Kesta, seriously, don't you think it seems irresponsible to have employed someone who's grieving so acutely for such a critical enterprise? Emotionally, I'm not surprised it's been too much for you."

She stopped rather abruptly as if calculating a particularly deft chess move and lowered her voice as she spoke.

"How did your husband die, Kesta?"

"He was bitten."

"Yes, of course he was, but—look, everyone else in the group can relive it in minute detail—"

Dr. Walling stood up, the shadow she created blacking out the lenses of her glasses, erasing those piggy little eyes and replacing them with dark squares.

"—but you can't, can you? Why is that?"

Dr. Walling was trying to get a rise out of her. To push her to the breaking point, and to what end? To give her cause to make an official complaint against her to the Project? She had to stay calm and ride out this session before she could leave. Leave without making things worse for herself.

"How did it happen?"

Walling had no right to keep her there, but if she ran screaming from the room, if she really raised the doctor's hackles, these mindless, meddlesome questions would continue unabated. Kesta was sick and tired of manipulating her grief in order to mitigate the feelings of other people, people like Dr. Walling who hadn't the faintest idea of what it was like, living in such pain.

"It's like living in an iron lung," she said, her knees quivering together, hands too.

"What is, Kesta?"

"The grief. If I stay inside it, I can breathe. I can function. I don't have to move on because I don't want to. I can't. If I try to go outside it, try to talk about what happened, it's as though everything in my body tightens up. I can't exhale. I can't take the next breath."

Dr. Walling drew her chair up close to Kesta. The two of them sat, knee to knee, the doctor still and contemplative while Kesta's legs were restless, juddering involuntarily. She tried to calm them, putting her hands on her knees, trying desperately not to cry.

God, I need to get out of here.

"Tell me how it happened."

Dr. Walling placed her hands on Kesta's thighs.

"He was bitten by an infected child when we were out shopping,"

Kesta said, "and before the virus developed, before he started to change, he ran away from me."

"So that you wouldn't become sick?"

"I suppose so, yes. So, I don't know the ending, Dr. Walling, because—because he wanted to spare me from seeing it. I only know that after he was bitten—that it was the last time I saw my husband."

"It was the ultimate act of love. He sacrificed himself to save your life."

"I wish I had been bitten too. I wish I had died too. I don't think anyone else in group wishes they were dead as emphatically as I do. But there it is. Working gives me the illusion of living. And I drink too much, but it's all I have."

"You have friends. You have Jess."

"You've seen how much grief frightens her? The hard truth of grief. We are expected to sanitize it, aren't we, Dr. Walling? To make it less extreme for other people; to make them feel that the support they offer us is adequate when it isn't."

Actually, ranting rather than talking is actually quite cathartic, she thought.

"I don't want friends, Dr. Walling. I don't want to move on. I don't want to go on holiday or find a new hobby. I just want Tim back. And if that really isn't a possibility, then there's nothing I want at all. I'm just staring into a void waiting to join him."

For the first time since she'd been forced into therapy, Kesta had succeeded in making Dr. Walling feel guilty for asking. Walling fidgeted with her glasses and then with her hair and finally the hem of her trousers, successful in making herself look as uncomfortable in her skin as she felt. Even she, a licensed counselor, able to stick a fancy title in front of her name, hadn't the faintest idea how to navigate grief when it plunged as deeply as this.

"Is there really a drug that's viable enough to trial?" she finally asked.

"I can't tell you, you know that," said Kesta. "All you need to know is that there's enormous risk involved and a shit ton of red tape."

"I can only imagine. But where's the rush, Kesta? Why start collaring unsuspecting men in a bar and asking to inject them with something you should never have removed from the lab?"

"The bottle was empty. It was just a prop," she said, sullenly, "but I need this to be over because then maybe I'll be able to move on with my life. Until then—"

"Until then, your husband died for nothing," said the doctor.

"I guess."

"Kesta, it wasn't your fault, you know."

"I know it wasn't."

"You really do have to forgive yourself at some point. Otherwise, you'll be tortured for the rest of your life. You have to let it go."

"I can't."

CHAPTER TWENTY-SIX

Fate strikes like lightning in a heat wave. When we least expect it, having relaxed into living, when we're no longer paying attention. We trip over it, unprepared, unable to brace ourselves in time. The second it's happened, it's already too late to retrace our steps and undo it. It was the same sort of thing with the little girl.

The days had once again been growing reassuringly unremarkable. Having hidden away indoors, pale Londoners who had held their breath for five weeks ventured tentatively into its wide-open spaces, blinking into the sunlight, gratefully filling their lungs with fresh air. This particular day, a Thursday in early May, brought with it the unseasonal weather that tricks you into believing that summer has arrived, balmy and benign. The Thames flowed like quicksilver in the sun, and the sky was as optimistically blue as anyone could remember. But it was simply too early to be summer.

They almost tripped over her as she lay in the road. It was so typical of Tim to go back. Kesta would have left her there and carried on; the kid was someone else's problem, and the two of them were by that point so dreadfully close to home, having gone out to the supermarket at the end of the road because the sun was out, and they had quantified the risk.

"Tim, don't touch her!"

"We can't just leave her here. She's tiny!" he said, not waiting for an answer. Down on his knees he went in the middle of Wapping Lane where the child lay, leaving Kesta with their shopping, his gentle hand on a doll's porcelain shoulder, his comforting voice asking her if she knew where she was, if she was all right.

"Tim, please, come away from her."

He brushed her russet locks away from her face to take a better look, to give the girl some air. Kesta saw him flinch, and her heart fell through her chest. The look of absolute surprise as he sharply withdrew his hand, clutching it to him, horrified, mystified, as the red-haired girl began to writhe against the cobbles. He looked up at Kesta. They both knew what had happened, what *would* happen.

Why hadn't they seen it coming? Why hadn't he listened to her? Why hadn't they stayed at home?

They ran back to the flat in silence, their carrier bags abandoned beside the twitching child. Tim was squeezing his left hand with his right. Kesta's heart and stomach were churning up a primal sickness inside her. By the time they arrived at home, Tim was sweating. Great patches of it were weeping through his shirt. He was shaking.

"It's only a scratch," Kesta said as she inspected the wound on his thumb. And it was, just a little nip, nothing like the kind of damage she knew they could do if they wanted. "Maybe the viral load is small. It might not take hold," she lied.

"I shouldn't be here," Tim said as Kesta locked the front door.

He said nothing as he watched his wife dragging the side table in the hallway in front of it to barricade them both inside. He kept quiet as she led him into the spare bedroom they used for guests who rarely visited but for whom it waited just the same, cozy and welcoming, pillows fluffed, cushions plumped. He gaped helplessly as she left him there, returning only with a blanket, which she laid down on the floor beside the radiator, and a pair of pink, fluffy handcuffs that Jess had bought them as a wedding present. Tim said nothing as she kissed him one last time because Kesta could always take his breath away. He didn't protest when she forced him down upon his knees and chained him by the infected wrist to the radiator.

Tim said nothing, did nothing, offered nothing because he was consumed by fear.

Kesta always knew what to do. She would know what to do now. He trusted her with his life. As his brain began to fog, the neurons grinding to a halt one by one, Tim could feel his heartbeat slowing, his insides throbbing deeply, profoundly, almost coming to a dead stop. A fatigue all the way down to the marrow was dragging him toward eternal sleep. *Kesta will know what to do*, he thought for the last time.

Kesta did not know what to do. She acted on instinct. She ran on adrenaline. Tim had been bitten. He would die. But then he would return. Changed. She just had to keep him safe. She would figure the rest of it out later. Nothing files the mind to a razor-sharp point like acute stress. As Tim lay in the spare room, wheezing and rasping like a rabid dog, his legs flailing against the floorboards in what she could only imagine must be agony, she could think of only one thing: How could she save him?

She felt faint. *You're in shock,* she told herself. *Don't give in to it. Buy yourself time.* She raced into the kitchen and took a bar of chocolate from the fridge and ate it in three big bites. *You need the sugar, or you'll crash.* She poured a glass of water; spilt half, guzzled it. She felt for her pulse. It was racing, her heart was punching its way out of her chest. *Bang, bang, bang!* She was shaking all over.

Pull yourself together, Kesta. Only you can do this. She took a series of deep breaths, each one slightly deeper and less ragged than the one before. She went back into the spare room and saw that Tim had vomited a thick black substance onto the floor. She would deal with that later. Tim was on his back, panting, the air scraping in and out of his throat, his mouth, that beautiful mouth with those soft lips she'd hoped to kiss for the rest of her life, hung open, his jaw slack.

Oh God, no!

She covered her own mouth with both hands to stop herself from screaming it out loud.

What do I do, what do I do?

Kesta sat down on the floor with Tim. She held his hand. She told him it would be okay. She watched him die, felt his last breath leave his body. All that she had loved in him, it vanished. She looked at the body of her dead husband. She was alone, or would be until he returned. Until he came back to her.

Alone.

The thought rattled around in her brain until it came to rest somewhere near the frontal lobe. No one else knew what had happened. No one had seen them come home. No one needed to know he was here.

Kesta edged into the hallway and moved the side table away from the front door, opened it and tiptoed out into the corridor. She crept down the communal staircase and into the foyer of her apartment block. She used her fob to open the electronic doors and walked outside into the courtyard. The sky was as blue as before, but there was a determined chill in the air now. Kesta snuck past the porter's lodge unseen, slipping through the main gates and out into Wapping. And then she ran, pushing herself forward until she was sprinting, pounding down the street faster than she'd ever run before, faster even than when she had been chased by them, right at the beginning, before she learned how to track them, to hunt them down and to hide when there were too many of them to fight back against. She ran past the coffee shop with its windows blown out, crunching across a carpet of shattered glass. She ran past the ancient pub with its makeshift barricade made of chipboard and empty beer barrels lashed together with rope. She ran past the Italian restaurant where all the workers had moved in together when the outbreak began, to take care of each other, seven of them holed up in a single room above it. She ran past the Catholic church, entombed behind padlocked gates, reinforced with pallets and dustbins to keep the infected out. She ran past the primary school, its playground still scattered with toys abandoned and games that would never be won.

Kesta ran through her disfigured neighborhood, absorbing its pain with every step she took, until she reached the underground and the two soldiers stationed out in front of it armed with assault rifles. She threw herself down on her knees in front of them and roared a scream of rage and fear and panic and grief.

Two red dots trained on Kesta's forehead.

"Please! Don't shoot me!" she cried. "It's my . . . Tim. My husband. They got my husband. My husband is dead!"

CHAPTER TWENTY-SEVEN

Tim had a bad night. His eyes began to bleed just as they had done when he was first bitten. For a few hours Kesta worried, quite hysterically, that somehow she had infected him anew, because his symptoms had returned with a vengeance.

As he lay twitching and groaning, his face pulled wide into unnatural shapes as though the bones in his face had shifted like tectonic plates, she wondered if the Gain-of-Function had already worked, and that she had transported their new iteration of the virus home on her hands, or inside the lining of her handbag, and that she had given it to Tim when she touched him. It was a kind of madness, her paranoia, the way she blamed herself for everything. She snatched an hour of ragged sleep, but she was awake by four.

The flat felt fresh as though it was filled with dew, perhaps because she had left the windows open to cool Tim's fever. She had been unable to kiss him before she left because her shame kept her from going in there. But she had seen him lift his unchained hand and lower it again, once, twice, three times, as if he was waving hello to someone. Or signaling for help. She'd left the door to his room unbolted.

Kesta wasn't thinking. And given that Kesta only ever thought at a hundred miles an hour, reasoning her decisions and revisions and dissections continually—a consequence of needing to plot your next move incessantly because you doubted everything you did, even who you were, all of it save for the two tenets of your life, love and science—she felt thick-headed, almost drunk.

Kesta trudged past the Tower of London, slower than she normally walked, her arms languishing by her sides, barely looking ahead. Were it not for the acres of clean concrete paving and the shiny office buildings, the city seemed so desolate it could have been at any time in the last millennia. She had the city to herself, so she imagined herself the only person left alive in it. It felt like what she deserved, to finish out her days cast out by the living.

They call the early morning the golden hour. Perhaps because of the luminous light of dawn. Maybe because the day lies stretched smoothly before you, untouched, ready to be molded. Or because real magic happens in the supernatural sliver of time between night and day. That morning, in spite of the amber glow shimmering across the river, the open sky warming to blue, and the pervading calm, Kesta felt nothing but an overwhelming dread. She was fearful of the day before it had dawned because there was so much that could yet go wrong with it.

It wasn't even seven before she arrived at the Strand campus. She buzzed her key fob and placed her handbag in a tray before sliding it into the curtain mouth of the X-ray machine. She caught a glimpse of the whitened image of her belongings cut in half, her keys, her wallet, a spare T-shirt balled up. She imagined herself in the CT scanner and what would be revealed of her insides if she lay down ready for inspection. Half a person sliced apart, her innermost flesh and muscle and sinew exposed, the guilt with which she was riddled on show for all to see.

Patient's betrayal metastasized. Little shadows everywhere.

"Have a good one," said the security guard, waving her through.

The building was already busy. Two men in hazmats passed her in the corridor as she walked toward the changing room. Perhaps shifts were changing over.

She realized, suddenly, what a state she must look, her dirty hair bedraggled and hanging down her back. Had she even looked at herself in the mirror since last night? She hugged tighter into the walls and picked up her pace until she reached the changing room and tossed her bag on the ground. She rooted into it, found a brush, and dragged it through her hair until it formed a ponytail, then a bun, the grease fixing it in place.

She was about to change into her work clothes, to wrap the plastic cap over her head, when she saw herself in the bank of mirrors, freshly cleaned. The skin around her eyes was inflamed, her cheeks seemed to have developed new capillaries overnight, and they zigzagged from her chin to her temples, angry against the swollen flesh. Lack of sleep, surplus booze. The white of her eyes pink. All the blood in her body seemed to have risen up to the surface as if she were ready to explode.

The doors swung open, and Cooke came in.

"Kesta, it's so early. I didn't think—" She stopped herself, wrenching off her face mask, clutching it to her chest with one hand, the other outstretched toward Kesta.

"Kesta, Liv didn't make it."

The words people use to avoid the grim reality of death. *Didn't make it.* As though living was a party you had thrown, and someone was too busy to attend.

Kesta felt an interminable sadness tugging at her arms and legs, pulling her down to the floor. She gripped the sink with both hands. She took a deep breath and turned to Cooke.

"Take me to her."

Liv was lying on her side on a metal trolley. She was already cold, but she wasn't stiff yet. Kesta slid one gloved hand underneath the monkey's stomach. The other she used to support her head, and she drew Liv to her like a baby, rocking her. Kesta began to cry. Huge, gut-deep sobs catching against her chest, tears streaming down her face behind the mask. Liv had struggled so hard, so bravely, for reasons she could never comprehend, and for what?

Had it not been for the others in the room, for Cooke, who was trying to soothe her by stroking her back, and Dudley, seated in the corner hunched over, his head in his hands, a clipboard on the floor beside his feet, the aftermath of the efforts to resuscitate the monkey scattered around them, Kesta could have carried on crying forever.

Liv was dead. And what Liv had been given, Tim had too.

"She was fine until about nine and then she went downhill," Dudley said, standing awkwardly—he was bent double, clearly shattered. Creaking himself up straight, he walked over to them. "She couldn't seem to get a breath and then—" He stopped and put a hand on Liv's back, he and Kesta both pretending, just for a moment, that she was still breathing, though it was Kesta's body, rising and falling so unhappily, that they both could feel. "We did everything we could to save her."

Kesta looked up at him through her mask. His eyes were raw.

"What will happen to her?" Kesta asked, even though she knew the answer. She needed someone else to be in charge of things, to tell her what to do, because her brain couldn't be trusted to operate independently.

"We need to see what happened." He spoke to her gently. "She'll have a postmortem, but I will do it. I will make it like it never happened afterward."

"I've already asked Lundeen if we can bury her," Cooke interjected, sniffing back her own tears. "He didn't seem to think it would be a problem, though we'll have to mark her down . . ."

As destroyed. As incinerated. Kesta knew what Cooke was thinking but unable to say. Samples, human and animal, had to be destroyed. They were diseased. They couldn't be returned to sender, couldn't be kept or memorialized in any way, either for science or as a symbol of what had been lost. Kesta remembered the little shelf of curios back at the hospital, the lung and the embryo frozen in time. She held one of Liv's hands between the fingers of her gloves, imagining the soft fur and the fragile bones she so wished to touch for real.

"Do you have any idea," she asked Dudley, "what killed her? Any idea what's wrong . . . with what we gave her, I mean?"

Dudley sank back against the trolley. "Only that we need more time to refine the Reanimator, that it needs stabilizing," he sighed.

"Reanimator-C is showing some promise. I've used the 17D attenuated strain of yellow fever vaccine together with glycoproteins, which may eventually serve as part of a vaccination against hemorrhagic fevers."

Time was the one thing Kesta did not have.

"We're monitoring Dave closely," Dudley said. "There are signs he is deteriorating too. I am thinking about giving him the modified drug, but we need to make sure he's stable enough first."

"I reckon we can probably manage without you today," said Cooke, trying to be kind. "What do you think, Dr. Caring? Can she go home? Can we do without her?"

"Yes," said a voice on Dudley's behalf. It was Lundeen. He had entered the room unseen. "We can do without Kesta, indefinitely."

Lundeen walked toward her but held back when he saw that Liv was in her arms. Kesta clutched her tighter.

"Lars, what is this?" Dudley asked, wrapping a protective arm around Kesta's shoulders. "We've all just had a terrible shock."

"You're not the only ones," Lundeen said without taking his eyes off Kesta. "Do you want to tell them or shall I, Shelley?"

"I don't know what you're talking about," Kesta stammered, and it wasn't really a lie because she didn't. She couldn't think about anything other than the image of Tim dying alone in his room.

"We've been reported to the World Health Organization by a laboratory out in Florida. I've been taking calls, trying to justify why we've sat on the information about the link to IBD. Why we failed to make other territories aware of the potential risk of a new zoonotic disease spreading to humans."

All eyes were on Kesta now. And Kesta knew what was coming.

"Your snake expert is in Florida. And he's raised the alarm. So, thanks to you, the layer of secrecy designed to protect everyone working here has been ripped off, and now our work is exposed for all the world to see and scrutinize. Now we have to share our findings. Now we lose our cutting edge. I have no choice but to cut you loose."

"Lundeen, be reasonable. You can't fire Kesta!" Dudley pleaded.

"Please, Lars. It was bound to get out eventually," said Cooke.

"You can't fire me," said Kesta, knowing she had only one card left to play, "because if you do, I'll tell the WHO what you're really up to down here. I know all about the real reason for Project Dawn's existence. We all do. Don't think I won't walk out of here and head straight to the papers about your illegal research."

"You'll do no such thing, Shelley," he spat, "because you signed a nondisclosure agreement. If you go public, the authorities will become involved. You'll be held without a need to even charge you. You'll be a risk to our national security. I won't even have to justify why I'm having you arrested."

"You can't fire me, I will beg you if I have to. I need to keep working. We all need to keep working! So that the cure—"

"—is successful? Well, Shelley, you should know as well as I do that if we do make a breakthrough with the cure, it will be precisely because we were willing to take unpalatable risks in the name of scientific discovery. I made allowances for your earlier breach when you made the IBD connection. To tolerate a second would make a mockery of everything we're working to achieve here. Now go home."

Still cradling the dead monkey, Kesta charged at Lundeen, stopping only when she forced him into a clumsy retreat. He was incensed, his back against the wall of the lab, his gloved hand groping behind him, pulling the switch on the alarm. The deafening ringing triggered wave after wave of neon lights flashing, the terrible noise soaring and plunging, like a roller coaster in free fall. Before Kesta knew what was happening, two men crashed into the lab and grabbed her, tearing Liv from her arms. She screamed as they dragged her down the corridors, up and out of Project Dawn, before throwing her out onto the street. She sat panting on the pavement in the stark morning light, wiping the dirt from her hands. Her handbag was still inside the lab, though she had her keys and her mobile in the back pocket of her jeans. She took out her phone. The screen was smashed, the picture of Tim ruptured into a thousand tiny pieces of what used to be him.

———

Kesta walked up toward Fleet Street, where she caught a bus east. She sat up on the top deck, her face pressed against the window, as the bus trundled toward St. Paul's Cathedral. She stared blindly at landmarks as they passed. Places she and Tim had been to so many times before, not always stopping because when you lived in London, you took for granted all there was to see because life gets in the way of pausing to admire the view.

"This is our manor," Tim had said as he pulled her toward him on another bus, standing room only, a real squeeze, the two of them packed in together with commuters and buggies full of wailing children, and every time the bus went round a corner, she had jolted into him and he'd caught her. "We're going to have a great life together," he had said, kissing the top of her head and holding her tightly with one arm, the other gripping the handle that descended from the ceiling of the bus, supporting the two of them so she didn't have to worry about falling over if the driver hit the brakes too hard. Tim had them both. Kesta could lean against his chest and relax. She could just let go.

She left the bus at the Tower and began the walk through the docks toward the cobbled lanes of Wapping, where her feet fell over one another and she trudged along without looking ahead, just down at her feet, thinking about how many times she'd made this walk in the eight years they'd lived in the wharf. She walked alone. She could smell the river next to her, she could hear a boat churning up the water, forcing waves toward the shore. She could sense that the tide had turned.

As Kesta stood shivering by the warehouse gates, a couple clipped past her, huddled together. The man gave her a judicious glance backward, and Kesta felt their pace quicken.

They are running away from you. She had become her greatest fear. She was a pariah; loveless, jobless, worthless. Her work had given her meaning. Tim had given her more. Without working, her chances of finding a way of curing Tim were close to zero. She could go back to stealing supplies from the hospital to try to keep him going, but she felt sure that Lundeen would find a way of barring her from her old lab too.

She looked down at her bare arms and could see only the starched ulna and the radius glaring up at her. Twenty-seven fragments of white bone in each hand. There wasn't much left of her now. Tim would barely recognize her.

———

"You're home early?" said Albert as she passed him in the porter's lodge, making tea. He waved his cup in her direction. "Don't suppose—"

"Actually, I'd love one," she said and opened up the Dutch door to the porter's lodge, pushing away the mail to the other end of the sofa and taking a seat. Albert handed her his cup, the one he'd just made for himself. It said BEST HUSBAND on the side and the rim had a chip in it.

"I'll make another," he said, disappearing to the kitchenette, which lay at the back of his office. A news channel was playing on the television. The IBD story had broken. There were images being beamed from Florida of men wading carefully through tall reeds, of tightly coiled snakes being displayed for all the world to see on a trestle table covered with a black cloth.

NOTORIOUS SNAKE VIRUS FOUND IN HUMANS? asked the chyron underneath.

"We just want answers," said a man in a sheriff's uniform on the small screen.

"Don't we all," said Albert, returning with his tea, steeping the bag with a dessert spoon, muting the sound on the television. "You all right, gel?" he asked, peering at her over the lenses, like a wise old owl.

"Not really," she said, sipping cautiously. The tea was good. It was what she needed, something warm and soothing to hold on to.

It's the amino acid L-theanine in tea that helps us, quite literally, to relax by lowering the stress hormone cortisol. That cup of tea did serve to soften Kesta, but the caffeine in it gave her a sudden sense of clarity.

"Is there anything I can help you with?" Albert asked her.

Kesta knew then exactly what she had to do.

"If anything happens," she said, "will you take care of the flat for me?"

Albert frowned. He pulled up his office chair and sat down in front of Kesta. He put his tea and the dessert spoon down on the desk behind him and drew himself closer to Kesta.

"What is all this?"

Kesta leaned toward him, the steam from her tea forming a soft mist across Albert's glasses.

"I'm just saying, because I don't have anyone else I can ask," she said, "that if anything happens to me, will you take care of my flat? Will you deal with what's inside it?"

"Nothing's going to happen to you, Kesta."

"It might. I'm not saying that it will. I'm just saying if."

"If?"

"Yes, if," she said, "if anything happens."

"Of course I'll help. Of course I'll deal with the flat for you."

"Thank you, Albert."

She brought Albert's mug upstairs with her and drank the rest of her tea while she collected a bag of her own blood sitting in the chair next to Tim. It took an hour, the blood slowly draining out of her. She felt weak, but the tea was restorative. Tim watched her, his breath wheezing in and out. She could hear a rattling sound in his chest each time he tried to speak now.

"Mmmmgggg."

"It's all right, darling. I'm here."

When the blood bag was full, she fed it straight into Tim through the cannula in his arm. She gave him fluids too, little nips of antibiotics, steroids, giving anything a try. Anything to keep him going, to buy them time while her newly formulated plan would take effect.

"We're going to have a quiet night in," she said, squeezing his hand to help the blood pump through. "But tomorrow, I might not be home till late. Or at all. I can't say because I can't guarantee that what I'm going to try will even work. But don't worry," she said, "if I fail, Albert will take care of you."

She ought to text Jess, she thought. In spite of the Dr. Walling fiasco, Jess had been a good friend to her, to them both. It wasn't Jess's fault that she didn't know what they were going through. Even if she did know, she wouldn't be able to understand it. She was on the outside looking in. Kesta shouldn't punish her for that. She texted Jess.

I'm sorry for everything I hope you can forgive me K x

Kesta ventured into the kitchen and opened up the fridge. She stood there, blinking into the stark white light. The fridge was empty apart from a bottle of wine in the door, a pick-and-mix selection of drugs on the bottom shelf, and blood samples crammed together in the salad drawer underneath. She took the one at the very back of the drawer, tucked away in the far corner. The first blood. The blood she had taken from Tim the day after he'd been infected. She held it in her palm to read the tiny label she had made and glued across it.

PATIENT: TIMOTHY JAMES SHELLEY
DOB: 12/07/84
BLOOD TYPE: O
ZOMBIE VIRUS SAMPLE 1
03/05/2023

She took the first blood and the bottle of wine and carried both into the spare room. She sat in her chair and dug out the cork, gulping it down and gasping. She saw her phone glow with a message from Jess.

Nothing to forgive. Love you x

"Can you forgive me?" she asked Tim, but he didn't move or blink or say anything to give her comfort. Just stared. She drank down another slug of the wine and then stopped herself, wiped her mouth, replaced the cork, and stood the bottle in the corner of the room.

Nil by mouth, she thought. Patient should not be given anything to eat or drink ahead of what was coming next. It would be wiser, clinically speaking. Just in case.

CHAPTER TWENTY-EIGHT

She spent the night pacing in tight little circles around the flat in the dark. Lights off, curtains and shutters drawn. Thinking, evaluating, worrying. There was so much that could go wrong, so many variables in play, the threat of human error ever present. Complications, infections, reactions, each and every possibility running maneuvers through her mind.

But she had to try it, didn't she?

Because there was no other hand to play at this late stage in this terrible game but her own. The noise of what she was about to do kept her awake. If she sat down, she began rocking, backward and forward, on the sofa in the living room, possessed by some electrical impulse to move, to run, to do something. But she had to time this just right, so she whiled away the hours creaking around the flat, stealing looks at her husband just in case they were to be her last.

At four a.m., the intercom buzzed. It was Albert starting his next shift.

"Love, Cheryl said she can't sleep for the noise coming from your flat again."

"Sorry, Albert. Can't sleep. Just walking around."

"Want to come down here and have a cuppa tea?"

Kesta did want to go downstairs. She did want to have another cup of tea, really wanted to collapse on the sofa in the porter's lodge and let someone as capable as Albert take over. But only she could do this, only she could see this through. It was her sacrifice to make for the man she loved the most.

"No, thank you, Albert. I'll try to keep it quiet up here."

Kesta dressed in her signature black, the vial hidden in her bag. She watched Tim from the doorway as she was lacing up her boots. They had reached the point of no return. He couldn't wait. Not any longer.

"I hope you know I'd risk anything for you, darling," she whispered as she kissed him goodbye.

Kesta arrived at the Project Dawn lab at six. She couldn't process the motions of normality, saying hello to the security guard, making coffee in the break room, staring down into the ocular lens of her microscope into the bright white light of the illuminator, because she couldn't get inside without her key card. The security guards had confiscated it during the scuffle. She stood out in the road to check the mobile app, to watch the live feed from Tim's bedroom. Even in its bewitching sepia, she could see that there was barely anything left of him. His skin was shedding off in great flakes that drifted down in front of the camera like snow. She would have to move quickly now.

Kesta buzzed the intercom on the wall by the entrance gates to the Strand station. She waited. Finally, a voice crackled into the ether.

"Hello?"

"I need to collect my things. They're in the changing room. My handbag. A jacket."

She waited again. Suddenly the gate began to contract, opening up to her from the inside. She slipped into the dark antechamber, the overhead lights flickering on, and she watched as the door to the security room opened too, but the guard didn't come out. She crept into the security room and saw that he was on the phone. He nodded at her to wait for him to finish. Kesta hovered by the X-ray machine, one eye on the guard and the other on the door to the lab, the one she needed a security pass to open. The guard was armed. She had no choice but to stay put, jiggling about on the spot, unable to stop her arms and legs from quivering with anticipation. In half an hour, Dudley would arrive. She looked at the guard, who was distracted by his call, covering his mouth with the receiver and his huge hands so that Kesta couldn't hear what he was saying. She could see the lanyard hanging tantalizingly around his neck. She wondered if she could rip it away from his throat and use it to open the door before he had time to draw his weapon. *What kind of damage does that kind of gun do?* she was wondering as the doors suddenly slid open again and Cooke walked in.

The two women stared at one another, each one holding her breath. Kesta thought she might die then and there, just evaporate into thin air. The sense that she was invisible, a microscopic entity lingering in the atmosphere, was compounded when Cooke said nothing to her. She smiled at the guard, still busy on his call, and let her handbag pass down the conveyor belt very slowly, before it emerged at the other side, and she picked it up. Cooke walked toward the door to the lab. She turned to Kesta, took one last merciful look, and buzzed herself inside. The door closed. But not completely. Cooke was holding it open with her fingertips. Kesta darted through it.

"Be careful," Cooke called after her as she raced down the corridor, but Kesta couldn't stop to thank her. Her stomach had contracted into a ball of acid, her arms and legs were bone, no sinew, no muscle strength, to propel her down toward the changing room. She felt brittle and wired, as though every nerve in her body was fighting its way to the surface of her skin so that it could feel everything that was happening in agonizing Technicolor. Behind her she could hear voices, shouts of distress, Cooke's was one of them, an argument already in progress. Kesta's heart was pounding erratically as she ran.

The changing room was deserted, damp with the last of the steam from the showers dissipating through the ventilation system. Kesta looked at herself in the long mirror above the sinks, itself lightly blurred with humidity, the edges of her face softened by the condensation. Eyes sunken, bleak; her hair scraped back into a ponytail. She watched the woman in the mirror untie the band holding it in place and watched her dark hair fall down around her face, like the curtain that conceals the coffin before cremation. Kesta knew what she was doing. She'd thought it all through.

Kesta stripped off her clothes until she was standing in her bra and knickers and socks. If Dudley needed to bring a crash team in, she wouldn't choose to give them more to do, having to cut her out of her jeans and T-shirt first. She folded her jeans and T-shirt politely and stowed them away under the sink, her battered combat boots tucked underneath them. She touched her fingertips to her lips and pressed a final kiss onto the broken image of Tim on her phone. A shiver ran through her body, but she wasn't cold. She hadn't felt this nervous since the morning of her wedding. She'd known exactly what she was doing then, too.

Kesta sat down on the changing room floor, her legs stretched out in front of her, her back braced against her locker. A livery of goose bumps and broken vessels spread from her hips to her ankles. Underneath the opalescence, her skin glowed brightly. She pulled out the vial of Tim's blood that she had kept in the fridge at home and the blister-packed syringe hidden in her left sock, then removed both socks—she might need traction later on, she didn't want to slip and fall when she was turning—unwrapping the parcel on her lap. The syringe broke the seal. She heard it snap and wheeze, watched as the plunger dragged backward, Tim's blood shifting from the ampule to the barrel. Kesta tucked the empty vial into the front of her knickers. When someone found her, let them find that first.

She flicked the air bubbles from the syringe and thanked her mother for her prominent veins. She speared her flesh with pure intent and pushed his blood inside her.

Kesta sat back, resting her head against the cold locker door, and thought of Tim at the moment he had been bitten. She saw his face, blanched and contorted by the cruelty of surprise, his punctured hand clutched to his chest. She remembered how violently she had felt her stomach lurching, forewarning her then that life as she knew it had ended.

Kesta felt her eyes begin to tear up at the memory of Tim's beautiful, optimistic face overtaken by the brutal revelation of his predestined death. He would have been so very afraid of what was to come.

Kesta was not afraid now. Emotion overwhelmed her, but she had accepted her fate, wholeheartedly. One way or another, she must sacrifice herself for Tim. She wiped away the tears streaming down her cheeks and saw that her hands were covered in blood.

An alien pain, hot and bright like a firework, began to boil and sparkle in her middle. She pulled her knees up, rocking back and forth, embracing the agony in an effort to control it. She breathed in through her nose, panting out through her mouth, fighting the urge to panic, buttoning her lips tightly in between to stop herself from moaning. The changing room around her had turned a night-vision, heat-sensory red from the blood in her eyes, and she struggled to wipe herself clean, to keep her vision clear. She would need a towel, some paper.

She stumbled over to the sink, dripping blood across the vinyl floor, then the countertop, as she struggled to find the strength to pull a handful of paper towels out of the dispenser, the connections between her brain and her extremities already beginning to short-circuit. She saw that she was waving one hand in the air, reaching out to nothing, then wiping idly against the glass. The steam had all but cleared now, and Kesta saw herself in the mirror once more, viscous, sweating, beaten, smeared in her own fluids as her husband's infected blood surged through her veins. The virus was taking hold of her.

Kesta pressed the towels against her eyes. The lights in the changing room were blinding, so she retreated from the sink to cower at the foot of her locker. Every inch of her was shaking, and there was nothing she could do to stop it.

Without warning, she vomited a thick tar across the vinyl. For what felt like minutes she lay there, quivering in the aftermath of it, thinking it could be over. But it had been a split second, no more, before the pain returned to her, growing and growing as she imagined contractions did, peaking higher and higher. She pressed her hands and feet into the locker, into the flooring, sliding and shifting her whole body in an effort to exorcise this demon.

But there was no end to it. This pain knew no limit, its fire branding her insides, igniting her liver, her kidneys, her lungs. Every breath she tried to take fanned the flames as the burning soared to an inferno, her arms and legs, neck and head accelerants to the raging fire. She was consumed by it.

Kesta felt Tim fighting to escape her, mauling his way out through her skin. She shared with him in death as she had in life. All of it. She felt her brain switching off and on again like a faulty lamp, the light flickering out, leaving her in the dark. She felt her body stretching against itself, her head yanked backward, stargazing.

Kesta's vision was lost to her now, a swirling mass of capricious shapes in shades of red, nothing to focus on or the ability to hold her mind still. *This is it*, she thought as she disappeared, shrinking backward, in retreat, no longer human but microscopic, redundant, obsolete. If only she could close her eyes, she might not see Death standing above her, looking down. He had come for her at last.

CHAPTER TWENTY-NINE

Kesta blinked. A hollow sound, water dripping somewhere, cavernous, cool. She couldn't see. She blinked again and heard the pumping of blood, a quiet industry. A ticking noise, tinny, automated, behind it something wet and syrupy. Somewhere down below she felt a current pulsing, a circuit rewired, the twitching of a foot, a knee twinging. Then a voice.

"She's awake."

Kesta blinked for a third time, and with this, her eyes began to sharpen, a spherical lens fluttering the images into her brain, out of focus, overexposed. White lights, white shapes, whiteness all around her, her pupils like liquid spilling from left to right.

"Kesta, Kesta, it's me."

She tried to say his name, but the word wouldn't come out because her throat was full. She could hear a sharp beeping getting faster and faster. A tube in her airways triggering panic, her blood pumping harder and harder. She tried to wrench the tube out by herself, but her right hand wouldn't join her left in the effort—something was holding it down.

"Kesta, it's okay, keep calm. Let's remove intubation now, please."

Regurgitating the plastic tube, the violation of her insides dragged up with it, snaking upward through her airways. She spat out the end, tasted blood in her mouth. She said the word again, summoning more energy.

"Tim."

She felt a pressure against her free-falling left hand and someone shifted out of the ether into focus.

"It's just me, I'm afraid," said Dudley. He took hold of her hand.

"What . . . happened?" Kesta croaked.

Dudley wiped something away from her lips.

"It worked." He smiled. "It actually worked."

Kesta blinked again and again trying to focus, to connect her eyes with her brain, willing them to understand, to remember.

This is Dudley and Dudley is crying. Why?

Because you're not dead.

She wasn't dead because the Reanimator had worked. The Reanimator-D that Dudley had given her when he'd found her collapsed on the floor of the changing room just as she knew he would when he arrived for work that morning. She had infected herself with the virus using Tim's blood, made herself sick so that Dudley would be forced to treat her with it, whether it was ready or not. She had sacrificed herself to science.

"It worked?" she said, laboring for an understanding of what these words should mean. The word *Tim* had come easily, it had been right there on her lips when she'd woken, but this was more distant. Her body throbbed, and she couldn't lift her arm. She looked at it, lying there on the bed beside her, her brain slopping around in her skull, the whoosh of vertigo as she moved. She felt sick. Sicker still when she saw the arm, her hand forced to the side, pinned back by leather restraints, a metal buckle glinting in the strip light.

She had injected herself with Tim's infected blood. And she was still alive.

She tried to sit up, but her organs lurched inside her. Her heart was too fast. Dudley tried to ease her back against the pillows, when another face emerged from the miasma. It was Lundeen.

"So, she made it then," he said with a sneer. "Not that she deserved to." He was looking at the source of the bleeping, her vitals monitor, looking for clues, shaking his head. "What the fuck were you thinking, Shelley?"

He jabbed a finger, and the vertigo that had skewered Kesta's sense of perception made her throw a hand up to protect herself from it. Lundeen glowered down at her. He seemed so tall now, and he grabbed Dudley by the elbow and the two of them left Kesta's frame of vision. She lay there, her heart and brain smashing against the walls of her body. She began to test her limits, to recalibrate, feeling about in the bed for traces of strength in her arms, her legs, willing herself to remember how to get up.

She could feel her tongue darting inside her mouth. *Am I thirsty?* she wondered, but it wasn't water she wanted, her tongue wanted something else, she just didn't understand what. Blood? No, that wasn't it either. She touched the tip of her tongue against her teeth, then slipped it between the crack of her lips. Sensation, bright, painful, strange, she couldn't process it. Taste and smell together, a new feeling. Like a snake.

Kesta could smell and sense with her tongue. She shut her mouth with the shock of it. She leaned over the restraints, heaving herself upward with her fixed arm. Dudley rushed back to her side, and with one thigh on the bed he shoved her up into a sitting position, a ventriloquist's dummy, hollow yet somehow lifelike. Dudley supported her back, tucked his arm around her waist. Lundeen eyeballed her from the end of the bed, his arms folded across his chest to keep his rage inside. Dudley saw it too and held up a hand, defiantly and protectively, to stop Lundeen from shouting at her.

"Kesta, you were very, very lucky." Dudley spoke calmly, as though it was just the two of them there. "Cooke rang me. When I found you, you were barely conscious, the virus had manifested at great speed, muscle spasms were acute, the bleeding was significant, and your temperature was 103."

He looked at her, and she saw he was tearful. "But you didn't turn." He squeezed her gently toward him. "I injected you with the Reanimator-D immediately. You've had packed cells, fluids, pain relief. You've been on oxygen. And I've just given you a second vial of Reanimator-D, just to be on the safe side. I've done a full blood profile every day. Kesta, there's no longer any sign of the active virus in your body."

"Every day?"

"It bloody worked."

"How long have I been here?" Kesta felt her stomach cramp.

"Five days," Dudley replied. He took a vial of the Reanimator-D out of his wax jacket pocket and held it in the air like the elixir of life. "It bloody worked, Kesta."

The beeping of the monitor began to escalate as the panic overwhelmed her. Tim had been alone for five days.

"I have to go home," she said, scraping at the restraints with her free hand, urging her body to comply. "I have to go home now!"

"Kesta, we need to monitor you for a bit longer," Dudley pleaded, trying hard to placate her. He leaned across her in the bed and held her down without exerting any pressure, just using his body to stop her from breaking her own wrist in an effort to escape. Dudley took her in his arms and held her, comforted her, and Kesta struggled against him, her free arm winding itself around him until it pulled him in closer, tighter, she was gripping onto him for dear life, almost sucking the life out of him. She released him abruptly when she realized what she'd done.

"I want to go home," she said, and it was then that she saw she was in that awful basement room, the only patient present in row after row of empty beds. "I want to go home now!"

Lundeen was livid, his nostrils flared as he ranted. "I told you three months of animal testing. Just three. What the hell was the rush? You've jeopardized the entire Project, do you understand that? If this gets out, we're finished!"

Kesta didn't feel much like being shouted at. She summoned what little strength remained in her muscles and used it to push herself upward and out of the bed, but her legs, like dry twigs, snapped underneath her and she fell to the ground, snagged at the wrist, a web of wires and tubing exposed, tugged out, she felt wet and helpless and as if she might faint.

The two men raced to her side, cornering her, and Kesta knew she had no choice but to submit, at least momentarily. As they raised her, stabilized her, disconnecting her from monitors and catheters, tubes and cannulas, she bore the indignity and the discomfort with her teeth clenched shut, thinking only of Tim all alone without her there to comfort him.

Her tongue darted its way through her teeth, and she could feel the end of it twitching, just a little. She was an animal snared by a trap. This is what it's like for Tim, to be devoid of agency, imprisoned by the virus, held captive by her.

A feeling flooded through her, one not defined by pain but by intense despair. So far, she had cheated death, but having been brought back to life, the worst of it appeared to have remained intact. If he had died all alone, she would never forgive herself.

She was stripped of the medical gown, washed, re-dressed in the jeans and T-shirt that no longer fit, her clavicle and ilium bones protruding like wire coat hangers under her skin. Feet stuffed into her boots, the laces left untied, she was pummeled into a wheelchair, part of the bedding wrapped around her shoulders by Dudley for added warmth, because no one seemed able to find her jacket.

Her lap would carry her handbag, and Kesta shivered in receipt of it, it felt so heavy to her, but then came the relief of finding that she still had the keys to her flat.

Lundeen forced a clipboard down on top of the keys and the bag, upon which lay a waiver of some kind. *If I die from self-infected snake disease, I will have nobody else to blame.* She signed away her name and her rights to sue the Project. She watched him recoil as she handed back the paperwork with a little of her blood having oozed out across it from the wound on her hand where the cannula had pierced. She smiled as they both saw it at the same time. She had really clenched that biro with all her might.

"Without Kesta, we wouldn't know that the Reanimator-D works," Dudley barked at Lundeen as they were leaving. She could feel him steadying himself using the handles of her wheelchair. "She did something wholly unfathomable, yes, wildly unethical, and incredibly fucking dangerous, but she has single-handedly accelerated the trial. We know we have a certain cure."

"We don't have a cure!" Lundeen raged. "None of this is ready yet. We're months away, if not years."

"You have to let me finish what I started," Kesta wheezed.

"You will never work again. You're out of your mind, Shelley."

"Dudley, help me."

"Lundeen, come on. Without Kesta—"

"Without Kesta, we wouldn't be in this mess! It is unconscionable what you did, Shelley. You put everyone's life in danger. You could have turned. You could have run rampant through the lab and killed everyone. You could have set another outbreak in motion all because you weren't prepared to wait!"

Lundeen finally paused for breath. He asked the two guards to leave. Kesta watched them walk away between the rows of empty beds. Dudley wasn't inclined to hang around either and began to wheel her away toward the exit. When the door patted shut behind the guards, when Dudley and Kesta were only halfway out of the room, Lundeen started up again.

"Where did you get the blood from, Shelley?"

Dudley brought the wheelchair to a dead stop.

"The sample. The virus we found in you. Where did you get it?"

Kesta turned around to face Lundeen. But before she had a chance to say anything she might live to regret, Dudley marched the two of them out of the ward.

They pushed through the doors of Project Dawn and out into Surrey Street. A chill rippled through her body as a rush of cold air hit her. She was shaking quite violently now, but it wasn't because she was cold. A nausea began to dredge through her insides, and her head felt disconnected from the rest of her body. So did her skin. Her skin felt stiff and rough, and she had the urge to peel it away. To shed it.

"Just put me in a taxi," she groaned. "I'll be fine."

Dudley didn't say anything. He carried on pushing her down the street toward the Embankment, a better place to hail a cab, if they could find one. She kept telling him to leave her, that she could get home on her own, that she understood why he was so angry with her. However horrendous she was feeling now would only worsen when she found out what had happened to Tim in the five days she had been away from him. As they reached the Embankment, Kesta saw that the sky was deep and black and the moon hung low over the Thames, silhouetting the grave monuments that grew up alongside the river, casting light where it wanted light to shine, and making the water pulse and sparkle as though it was lit by another moon beneath the surface. Kesta felt an uncontrollable desire to walk into the river and sink in it like a stone.

She felt Dudley put the brakes on the wheelchair. She sensed the steps he took, slow and trepidatious, until he was standing right above her. He crouched down to her level, one hand resting on her kneecap as he searched for something in his jacket pocket. His hands were shaking and red-raw, like lumps of uncooked meat. He withdrew the vial and placed it in her lap, they both saw it glinting in the light from the streetlamps, they both read Tim's name written in her handwriting on the label.

"Where is he, Kesta?"

CHAPTER THIRTY

They sat in silence on the taxi journey through London while the driver babbled away to them about the stresses of his own day as though they were unique in their significance. Something about the vehicle not being his, about a broken brake shaft, and an audacious bill from the garage. About the value of friendship, a guy he knew stepping in, offering his cab on loan, helping him out, just because. Kesta and Dudley were alone in their thoughts. It didn't matter that they didn't answer back because the driver was happy just talking.

When they reached the warehouse, Dudley threw a twenty inside the cab and they tumbled out onto the street without pausing for change. Kesta flicked her key fob at the side gate, and they entered the courtyard, the driver still bellowing thanks for their generosity as he pulled away, but it was nothing of the sort. Not generosity. They just wanted to get away. Kesta knew pain in every one of her 206 bones as Dudley shuddered the wheelchair across the courtyard cobbles, her lungs and kidneys rattling. As they reached the doors to her building, Jess emerged from the shadows.

"I called her," said Dudley, "when I thought we were going to lose you. You were in a coma for four days, Kesta, I had to tell someone."

Jess didn't speak but shot her a look of such bitter disappointment that Kesta felt across her chest for the wound. Dudley reached for Jess's hand

and Jess let him take it, but then Jess began to cry. Jess and Dudley whispered to each other, and Kesta thought how peculiar it was seeing them in league because of her. She wondered what they'd talked about while she was out cold on the ward. Had they shared stories about their weird, distant, enigmatic friend, the one who didn't return texts and wouldn't open up? The quivering of Jess's lips and the worry lines carved into Dudley's forehead told her the truth, something that wasn't open to interpretation.

They cared about her. They had been terrified she would die. They didn't want to lose her, as lost as she was.

She surrendered her key fob to Dudley, who swiped it against the receiver, which was too high for Kesta to reach from the wheelchair. The three of them passed silently into the building. They wheeled through the foyer toward the lift, and Kesta remembered the story of the hospital porter, the man who had pushed Paul Mosi's gurney down the corridor moments before he sunk his teeth into the consultant Dr. Daniels and this whole dreadful thing began.

But Dudley and Jess didn't let go. They didn't shove her away to meet fate on her own. They held on tightly to the handles of the wheelchair. Inside the lift, they huddled together, three beating hearts reverberating in a metal coffin, each one of them knowing that life would never be the same again once they entered flat number nine.

"I need you both to understand," Kesta said as she struggled for the door key, stiff hands devoid of human movement, her tongue bitten between her teeth. When they were at last inside the lock, Kesta stopped and waited, resting her forehead on the door.

Please don't be dead. Please don't be dead.

Kesta dragged herself out of the wheelchair and finally pushed it open.

———

It was the first time in over six months that Jess had been inside Kesta's flat. She looked round her, refamiliarizing herself with a place that had always felt like a second home.

High ceilings and low lights cast shadows across wide pine floorboards stretching off into the living room. A black-framed mirror over a marble-topped console table, a marquetry bowl decorated with pearlescent shapes, full of keys and loose change, a linear coatrack hung with Tim's effects. On one wall, a painting bought on an anniversary trip, a mysterious woman in a red hat looking back over her shoulder, a portrait of someone who had once meant everything to the artist.

Entering the Shelleys' flat had always been bittersweet for Jess, a tasteful, elegant spy hole into a perfect marriage—her uniformity, his mercurial eye—warm, inviting, theirs. Standing in that hallway now, Jess felt like a stranger in a different way. The flat was colder than the outside and stale smelling, a putrefaction lurking behind plug-in air-fresheners.

A life left incomplete, still to be packed up and boxed away. The picture of the woman was lopsided against the wall, hanging by a thread, the paint surface chipped behind it, marks like claws cut into the doorframes. One wall light was broken, and the mirror had cracked. Tim's coats still hung on the rack, but they had a secondhand musk. The hallway was a ruin—dusty, dank, a manifestation of Kesta left alone, not really living, inside a mausoleum meant for two. They heard a beeping noise coming from behind the wall. Jess gasped when she noticed the barricade of black dead bolts rendered to the door.

"I didn't have a choice, you have to understand that," Kesta said again, driving and yanking at the locks automatically, never taking her bug eyes off Jess and Dudley standing there, open-mouthed, their gray cells processing frenetically. Knowing, and yet not being able to imagine what would meet them on the other side of those locks, even though it was all so terribly obvious now.

Kesta shoved the door, and it yawned wide open until Jess and Dudley could see the awful truth.

He was lying on his side, chained to the radiator by an outstretched wrist, a shape more demonic than of man. A single yellow eye looked through them.

"Oh, thank God. Tim, you're still alive!"

Kesta threw herself onto her knees by the bed and wept. But for the open eye, unseeing, and the chest creaking in and out struggling for breath, Dudley and Jess would not have known that Tim was still alive. The hum of the machinery did not make him alive. The medical paraphernalia—syringes, bandages, creams, used blood bags, empty bottles—scattered across every viable surface even less so. Neither Dudley nor Jess knew what they were feeling standing there in the spare room of Kesta's flat, aside from an overwhelming sense of pity. Jess covered her mouth to conceal her shock from Kesta and to protect her face from the smell.

"I couldn't let him go. I just couldn't," Kesta said, looking down at Tim as she traced the light feathers of his hairline with her fingers. "I tried everything I could think of. Please understand. You have to understand why I did it."

"Hello, Tim," said Dudley, approaching the bed without caution and leaning over the body in it to take a better look. "Gosh, what's it been, a couple of years? You haven't aged a day."

Tim's eyes were wide and hollow, and he was sniffing softly at Dudley. He grunted, his free hand twisting toward him as though he wished to shake Dudley's hand.

"Hey, Timbo," Jess whimpered from the doorway, "love what you two have done with the place." She couldn't bring herself to move any closer, and her throat was tightening with new tears. Staccato huffs and puffs punctuated Tim's effort to prize himself upward in the bed so that he could see who was there, but he was simply too weak. He fell back against the pillow and Jess had to step out into the hallway to cry.

"It's all right, old boy. Don't tire yourself out," said Dudley. "We've got much to do tonight. Do you think you can manage a car ride? I thought a change of scenery might do you good after six months stuck in here."

Kesta swooned against the bed. She had existed for so long between two opposing worlds, this spare room a parallel realm, the real world disappearing behind her each time she closed the door and locked them both inside. Now the planets had collided; the worlds were becoming one again, and she realized she no longer held power in either dominion.

"What are you doing?" she asked.

"We have to get Tim out of here and take him up to Porton Down," he said. "They are waiting for us."

"They know about Tim?"

"They know to expect us," he said, "and we have to move quickly if this is going to work."

"What's going to work?"

Dudley put his hands on her shoulders. "Listen to me, Kesta. This is important. Cooke has reported Project Dawn to the WHO. They know about the Gain-of-Function research. She's with them now. They're going to raid the laboratory. We had to wait until we could get you out of there. It won't take long for Lundeen to realize where you got the infected blood from, and he'll try to use that against us. He'll call in the police, he'll tell them you're a threat. They're bound to send a team here to bring you both in."

"Kesta, we need to get you changed into something warmer, and I want you to eat, okay?" said Jess. She had recovered enough to start opening the wardrobes in Kesta's bedroom. "Should I pack her a change of clothes?"

"Pack enough for a few days at least," replied Dudley. "Kesta, do you have a syringe I can use?"

Dudley and Jess were working feverishly around her. This was a new reality, an unreality. Dazed, she found a sealed syringe in the bedside table and handed it to Dudley. She watched as he rummaged in the pockets of his wax jacket again. Jess appeared in the doorway, a flask of tea in one hand and a thick woolen jumper, which she passed to Kesta, who obligingly put it on.

"Do you think it will work?" Jess asked.

"Well, it worked on Kesta, so we have to try," said Dudley, injecting Tim with the Reanimator-D. "But Kesta didn't turn, whereas Tim did, and a long time ago now."

Kesta moved toward the bed, and Tim's soft sporadic moans formed one low rumble. She felt the fingers of his cuffed hand reaching out to hers like tiny tentacles, tapping, sensing the space around him. She pressed her other hand to Tim's cheek and felt him turn into it, she felt him pressing back against her. She saw tenderness in his face, she felt remembrance in his touch. Then she took the key from the bedside table, and she unlocked the handcuff that had held him there. The skin underneath the metal was almost black, indented with the cuff's foreign shape. Tim lifted the arm toward Dudley, peering at it quizzically.

"Let's get him into that wheelchair, shall we?" said Dudley.

Together the three of them maneuvered Tim out of the bed and into the wheelchair that Jess had brought into the hallway. They tucked a blanket over his legs.

"You're just going to wheel him out into the open?" Kesta heard herself asking.

"The more you try to hide, Kesta, the more people will notice that you're up to something," he said. "I mean, we could put a wig on him, dress him up, say it's your grandmother. But we don't have time to argue."

"Dudley, this is Kesta we're talking about. She'll always find time and a thousand ways to tell you why she's right and you're wrong, you know that." Jess smiled at him as she handed Kesta the thermos of tea.

"Good luck, you three." She gave Dudley a set of car keys.

"You're not coming with us?" said Kesta.

"No, I'm going to stay here and call the *Evening Standard*," she said. "Tip them off about the raid that's about to kick off over at Project Dawn. Dudley, your car's parked out on the high street. Don't let her drive, whatever you do."

"Have you met her?" He winked. "You think she's going to give me any choice in the matter? She thinks I'm frightfully slow behind the wheel."

The two of them giggled, as if to cover up their sense of dread, the responsibility they had assumed, having prized it out of Kesta's fragile hands. They parted like friends unsure if they'd ever meet again.

"Kesta," Jess called out just as the doors to the lift were about to close, "I understand it all now."

CHAPTER THIRTY-ONE

The sun was rising, silhouetted behind a bank of bloodshot cloud. Spiked hedgerows, having shed their soft autumnal colors, clawed back the fields from roads that slashed across them. These fields were sodden and pockmarked with sheep and cattle staggering through the mud, braced for winter. The roads were barren except for Dudley's little car, which groaned under the weight of their illicit cargo. Somewhere to the east of them, Sailsbury lay sleeping. Over to the west was Porton Down. Kesta was oblivious to the incandescent day breaking. She had eyes only for Tim, watching her, as yet unblinking, in the rearview mirror as she drove.

"Dudley, why isn't it working? There's no change in him."

Dudley loosened his seat belt and turned around to look at Tim crumpled in the back. He looked so ravaged by the virus, so far beyond help. His porcelain skin three layers less than it should be, all bone and breakable. Kesta was driving too fast. A sharp turn might be enough for Tim to dematerialize completely.

"You're the only person who's taken it, Kesta," Dudley said, glancing at the speedometer. There had been no change in Tim's condition since they'd given him the Reanimator-D, no change despite the silent prayers he'd watched her lips mouthing as she drove. Kesta felt Dudley pat her hand as she changed gears. "You didn't turn completely. We cannot know if the Reanimator works on the long-term infected. Tim is our only hope. Give it time. We will give him another dose when we get to Porton Down. I'll try Elizabeth again."

He bit off one of the gloves he'd retrieved, oddly enough from the glove compartment, and redialed. He whispered into the phone as if Tim were sleeping and shouldn't be disturbed. Kesta whispered too, hoping that silence might help them travel undetected. They had checked the car radio three times since they had left London, but there had been no unscheduled interruption on any channel, no breaking news of their escape. Kesta wasn't wanted, anywhere. The higher the sun rose, the greater the threat to them became. A man, a woman and an undead passenger stalking the Wiltshire B-roads, increasingly visible with every passing minute.

"It's me again, Liz. It's half past seven. We're not far off now." Dudley had been trying to reach his fabled contact at Porton Down all night, but only Dr. Ancora's answering machine knew to expect their arrival. "Hope you get this." The phone cut off. "Hello, hello?"

Either the line was dead or Ancora's mailbox was finally full.

"My battery's almost flat." Dudley shook his phone as if it might charge kinetically. "Be good to find a phone box, if they still have them out here." He fogged up the window as he peered out into unfamiliar countryside. Then he blanched. "God, what if they've been tracking us? Through my phone. Do you think they could do that?" He shut his phone in the glove compartment. "I just want her to know we're on our way."

"She'll know."

A strange frenzy, metallic and seditious, was regurgitating inside Kesta. Her skin was alive with a new sensation: of it replicating over her muscles. She imagined that if someone were to cut off one of her legs, she could withstand it, grow another. She hadn't mentioned it to Dudley, this ophidian feeling. She looked again in the rearview mirror. No change. *He may be too far gone*, Dudley had said as they were lifting him into the back seat, because he wanted Kesta to be prepared for the worst.

Kesta looked in the mirror again. She thought she saw Tim blink. Then an electric haze lit up the horizon in front of them like fireworks, the toluidine blues of her fluorescent chemistry. Malignancy perceptible to Kesta, even at a distance.

"Police."

"Lundeen must have called them."

Dudley shifted in his seat.

"I'll text Liz to let her know we'll have to find another route." Dudley spread a well-thumbed map book across the dashboard like a constellation of stars. "I'll find us another way." Kesta continued to drive toward the flashing lights.

"Take a left here," Dudley said, unconvincingly. "It should take us through a village, maybe we can lie low there for a bit, wait for Liz to send someone out to meet us." Kesta did as she was told, turning left without indicating onto a single lane packed with fallen leaves. She switched off the headlights, and they skulked down toward the village, the rising hills concealing them from view, a fog enveloping the car.

In the back seat, Tim gurgled. Then he coughed. Kesta and Dudley both turned to watch as he lifted a hand up to his mouth, patting at his lips with twisted fingers.

"It's all right, old boy," said Dudley in that same whisper voice. He reached out a shivering hand and gave Tim's knee two convivial pats before letting it rest there. "We're nearly at Porton Down. It won't be much longer. I'm confident my friend there can get you right as rain."

Kesta had to look away. This tenderness between them was devastating. She had misjudged Dudley. Perhaps he was the only person who would ever understand what she had done, because he would have done the same thing for her.

They emerged through the dawn mist into the kind of English village you might visit unintentionally on an empty weekend. A pub steeped in ivy, a jack-of-all-trades shop and post office, a church frowning down upon ancient cottages and refurbished barns competing for position by the green. They crept through at fifteen miles an hour, willing the car to be quiet, Kesta hunched over the wheel, Dudley almost hidden in the footwell, still connected to Tim, hand to knee. They were at a crossroads now, and the village signpost was of no help.

"Drive straight on, I guess." Dudley shrugged, gazing out into the thinning fog, patting at Tim's thigh absentmindedly as if they were taking their dog to be put down. Kesta rubbed her eyes with the back of her hand, dry clumps of mascara catching in the lids, making them stream with tears. She realized that she hadn't washed her face in nearly a week.

Driving one-handed, she looked at herself in the rearview mirror, smearing at the black grub defiling her lash line. She thought she saw Tim smile. She turned round to look at him, but his head was still tilted back on his spine, stargazing. She felt Dudley reach across her and redirect the steering wheel.

A relic from another era materialized half a mile or so out of the village. A red telephone box. The glass panels still intact, catching the light of the sun rising across the hills. Kesta pulled off the road onto the edge of a field.

"Let's hope it's not a community bookstall," Dudley said, grimacing as he unfastened his seat belt. He was out of the car before she had turned off the ignition, looking around them for signs of life or trouble, zipping the waxy collar of his jacket up high, almost catching his chin in it. Kesta could see Dudley's skin reddening and his eyes squint against the chill. He fought against a gust of wind to open the phone box door. She saw him rummaging inside it, waggling the receiver, pressing at buttons, listening, his face worried. Then, a radiant smile brighter than the dawn, a thumbs-up to his coconspirators back in the car.

Kesta waved in return and forced a smile. They were very nearly there. Kesta felt months of exhaustion weighing down upon her body. She couldn't stop herself from yawning.

"He won't be a minute," she whispered to Tim, resting her hand on his knee where Dudley's had been. A stream of saliva was oozing from the corner of his mouth, his lips wide open, his tongue straining against his teeth. A hissing noise escaped. Kesta wiped away the spittle with the sleeve of her coat.

"It's all right, darling," she said, looking back out of the windscreen to Dudley, now in animated conversation with someone, presumably Dr. Ancora, on the other end of the phone. "They will be able to help you at last, to get you well again." She looked back at him in the rearview mirror. "I promise you."

Kesta closed her eyes, just for a moment. The darkness gave her the feeling of a brief reprieve, though her eyes were hot and stinging.

"Let . . . go."

The voice struck her like a claw hammer and the words would stay, lodged in her brain, forever.

She had wanted to hear his voice for so long, and she had cried about how she might forget what it sounded like. This voice was flat and heavy, and it didn't sound like Tim's.

"Kes . . . ta. Let . . . . go."

The air in her lungs evaporated as she turned to face him. His stare was full of resignation.

He touched her hand as he said it. Kesta was in shock. Somewhere in the distance, she could hear Dudley talking on the phone. She heard him through her mouth, another new sensation from the snake virus, so much sound, too much truth inside that car it was deafening.

"Kes . . . ta." A foreign word mispronounced in an uninitiated mouth. "Ssss . . . stop."

Kesta felt the tears begin to prick around her eyes and nose. Tim lifted a hand to her face and began to wipe her tears away. "I'm so sorry, Tim," she sobbed. "I'm so sorry that any of this ever happened to you."

The harder Kesta cried, the more tender Tim became. He was shushing her gently to console her.

"I've missed you so much."

His lips, his jaw twitched in noiseless struggle, the muscles moving, but the product of sound was too hard. He tried, he wanted to tell her how he felt. But nothing worked the way it was supposed to. There was such frustration in his eyes, a strange knowing she hadn't seen before. An awareness that was terrible. *How must he feel? Now that he understands what he's become?*

"Tim," she cried, "look at you. What we gave you is working. You will be well again soon. We're going to get you better. I promise."

"Ssss . . . top."

"I promise you, darling. Please, can you hold on for me?"

Tim was trying to shake his head, but the effort made him choke.

"Nnnoo," he whimpered. "Nnnn."

"Tim, we're so close. We have a cure. We have to try it again. We have to try it on you again."

"Let me go . . ." he spluttered again, a bloody aspirate whistling in and out, filling the space between them.

"Tim, we have to keep fighting! Please. We have to believe that this time it will work. Or that a new version of the drug will be better. We can keep trying! Please don't say you want to leave! I can't lose you, not now."

Kesta clicked her seat belt open and climbed out of the driver's seat. She slid across the leather beside her husband and unfastened his seat belt. She cradled him in her arms like a newborn, inhaling the alien scent, caressing the unfamiliar folds of his ravaged form. He rested his head on her shoulder, mirroring her embrace, breathing in what remained of them together. As she looked into his eyes, she saw nineteen years of life distilled into a single look, one that, as always, told her everything she needed to know and do. She stroked his hair, feeling the breath in his chest catching and wheezing. Tim groaned with a pain that felt like her own. Kesta's chest tightened too, and she knew that her heart had broken.

Tim whispered something, but she couldn't understand what he was trying to say.

"But I need you. I can't live without you."

Kesta had tried courageously to fight the virus for Tim. But in the end, the simple truth was that it wasn't her fight; it was his. Only Tim could decide that it was finally over. Only he could say stop when she asked when. How she had yearned to hear his voice again, but now that same voice told her there was a limit to what it could endure—that that limit had been reached. Tim had had enough. As his consciousness improved, Kesta understood that his desire to determine his own fate, that most human instinct, had been lying just beneath the surface all along, waiting to speak up. Kesta knew then that she must listen to it, that she must return the gift of choice to her husband, in spite of herself, because she loved him. Kesta lay in her husband's arms in the back seat of Dudley's car, and together they watched as the sun rose above the trees.

"I love you so much, Tim," she said, holding his hand so tightly with her own, she feared she would break them both. In her darkest hours on the bleakest nights during the worst months of her life, when emotion overcame reason, Kesta had wondered if it wouldn't be better for her husband, the man she would give anything to keep for eternity, if he simply slipped away, softly, into that unending rest. But she had fought death with all her might for both of them. Now she saw that her husband could no longer resist.

"You've had enough?" she asked. "You want to stop?"

He squeezed her hand as tightly as he had the day they had stood together at the altar. He squeezed it then in commitment. It was part of the promise. And he needed her to honor that promise to him now.

Tim was stricken with a faraway stare. He was looking through her, past them, to the other side of nothingness. This lucidity was precious, and yet with it came the knowledge that perhaps only part of her husband remained in that car. He already had one foot in the afterlife, and she was preventing him from crossing over. There was something missing. Or rather there was something else present. Kesta couldn't be sure. She cupped his broken face with her hands.

"I will tell Dudley we can't carry on," she said, each word catching in defeat inside her throat. As she turned to open the door, Tim grabbed hold of her wrist. Kesta saw the focus in his yellow eyes had sharpened.

"Out," he wheezed, "air . . . please."

So, this was it. Tim was ready to die. Kesta had to let him go. How could she refuse his plea to sit outside the car, to breathe in life for the last time?

"Let me help you," she said, taking him by the hand and easing him out of the car, bearing his weight as he stumbled, making light of it, telling him it would be okay. Tim sniffed at the fresh air, gulping at the sky, panting, sensing the world opening up around him, tasting freedom with his tongue. He was smiling.

She felt his fingers straining against her palm, then slipping through her own as she resigned herself to losing him in increments.

She clung on. She wasn't ready yet. Dudley watched her anxiously from the phone box as he talked to Porton Down, gesturing. *What are you doing?*

All Kesta could do was shake her head at him, mouthing the words, over and over, *he can't, he can't, he can't.*

She looked at her husband, but it wasn't Tim's face she saw. It was a changeling face, an other, a thing in transition, shape-shifting, moving beneath her husband's skin. A hardening of the features, a possession of the body, a superior force working from within. Kesta was no longer looking at her husband. She had come face-to-face with the virus.

"Tim?" she cried as his fingers ripped through hers. He began to hobble away from her, his feet distorted, unfamiliar, struggling to gain ground. She called his name again, but there was no recognition, no response. Freedom to breathe had meant freedom to run. The virus had deceived her.

"Tim!" she screamed as he dragged himself away from her, never once looking back before slithering into the high grasses between them and the village down below. Toward people getting up, going out, making do with their lives.

Tim was groaning. He was sniffing at the air, lumbering forward with one leg heaved behind him. Then his half-hung head abruptly repositioned, poised on the spine, and his arms and legs became rigid and strong. Some untoward matter surging through the veins inspired him, not the cure they had forced there, but the divine inside, the virus, that which possessed his sinew and his muscle, commanding every cell, manifested deep in the marrow, a genetic instruction, a call to arms.

Kesta ran after him, cutting across the field, but Tim's pace grew urgent and hungry, as sudden as the bite had been, breaking out in long strides, his arms rampantly slashing through the grass. She could not outrun him. Tim was propelled forward with true purpose, by the fate that Kesta had stopped him from fulfilling all these months.

Transmission.

Tim swept across the open field toward the village because the virus demanded to be spread.

CHAPTER THIRTY-TWO

The glare was so strong, you had to look away. It was like staring at the sun in eclipse, the flashes of their cameras burning tiny holes into the back of his eyes, even though he tried to shield them with one hand as the other clutched the brief his solicitor had prepared, and he walked into the courtroom. A narrow path opened up before him, men and women parting like waves, standing in reverence as he walked toward his seat. Somewhere in the distance a panel was arranged, a blur of indiscriminate suits who fell silent at the sight of him. They were a somber and persistent class, although seeing him in the flesh made one quickly draw her breath.

No one in that room wanted to listen to what he had to say that day, six weeks into the inquiry, because it was all too difficult to hear. But that was precisely why it needed to be heard and why he was the person best placed to say it. To force them to listen. Our testimony is all we have. And though witnesses can be unreliable, this witness wasn't.

Dr. Dudley Caring took his seat at a single table and chair positioned in the center of the room. He laid down his papers in front of him and took a sip of water from a waiting glass. He tapped the end of the microphone and heard his own sound amplified around the room.

"Good morning," he said, and the microphone didn't screech, which was the thing he'd been worried about most, "esteemed colleagues, members of the press, and to those families who've joined us here today"—he gestured behind him to rows of grim faces, etched with recent grief—"my name is Dr. Dudley Caring, I am head of Biotechnology at Porton Down, and I was lead research scientist at the Project Dawn facility."

People gasped when he said the name. Muttering spread through the gallery, a flash exploded, and a minister asked the photographer to honor proceedings and put his camera away.

"Have some respect for the infected," said the chairman of the inquiry. "The Bourne Valley incident has left an indelible mark on all our lives. Dr. Caring, please continue."

And so Dudley opened up to them like a postmortem. They saw inside him, every bone and breath, and he let them look hard at it, the wild insides of a living human being. He hoped it would help them understand the inconceivable. He charted the events leading up to the infection of six villagers five miles outside the Porton Down biological site last November. Of how he was in the process of transporting the only zombie to have survived the viral outbreak to the facility eight months prior, where he was to receive treatment under the care of Dr. Elizabeth Ancora. He and the patient, Timothy Shelley, had been offered sanctuary by the facility in exchange for access to the pioneering drug he'd been developing, the so-called Reanimator-D. Their journey had been relatively smooth and the patient compliant and sedated throughout. And that he, Dudley Caring, had not been in the vehicle when the patient, Mr. Shelley, was somehow liberated from it. Once he had identified that Mr. Shelley was no longer contained, he had made every attempt necessary, he explained, to prevent Mr. Shelley from reaching the village at the other side of the field. He had alerted Porton Down and asked them to send support urgently before disconnecting the call and telephoning the emergency services. No, he didn't have a clear view of proceedings from his position in the phone box. Yes, he was as convinced today as he had been that morning, that no one could have foreseen Mr. Shelley's escape.

"Surely Mrs. Shelley foresaw it?" the chairman growled into the microphone.

"I cannot comment on the moments preceding Mr. Shelley exiting the vehicle," Dudley replied calmly. "The manner in which Mr. Shelley found himself to be out of the vehicle is unknown to me. I wasn't present at the time."

"Do you believe she intentionally allowed her husband to escape?" asked another drab minister, his voice like a cloth, wrung dry.

"At the risk of repeating myself," Dudley said, almost archly, "I can no more imagine another person's state of mind at a moment of acute stress than you can. We are not here to speculate but to report the facts as they are known to us. I cannot know what she was thinking at that time. I cannot even imagine it."

The ministers whispered amongst themselves, and those attending in the gallery did the same. Dudley felt his throat tighten, so he loosened the knot of his tie. He smiled. She would have found it funny that for once his tie wasn't slung over his shoulder. He hadn't seen her since she'd been in custody. He missed her.

The woman who had gasped when Dudley had entered the courtroom was trying to catch his eye, smiling apologetically on behalf of her colleagues.

"Dr. Caring, are you able to update this inquiry as to the progress of the six members of the public who were infected at Bourne Valley? Those who were rescued and subsequently treated at Porton Down under your care?"

"They are all doing remarkably well, ma'am. The zombie virus was an unprecedented and catastrophic zoonotic mutation. We anticipate their full recovery. We have reason to be hopeful with the progress of the Reanimator-D drug, the Shelley Cure as we intend to name it."

"I would like my colleagues on the panel to turn their attention to the illegal Gain-of-Function research undertaken by Project Dawn," a younger face at the far end of the panel interjected, directing her question toward her own notes rather than to Dudley. "It is important to stress at this juncture that Dr. Caring has received full immunity from prosecution in this matter as a consequence of his professional fortitude in acting as the whistleblower who exposed the nightmarish work being orchestrated at Project Dawn by its team leader, Professor Lars Lundeen."

Dudley outlined clearly and with the dispassionate tone befitting such an inquiry, the events leading up to the investigation into the activities of Professor Lundeen, his former superior at Project Dawn, and the manner in which the site itself was run.

"Were you aware, Dr. Caring, that Professor Lundeen was in fact running a covert laboratory engaged in illegal Gain-of-Function research?"

Yes, Dudley had been aware. Yes, he had worked in the shadow lab himself. And while he acknowledged the myriad ethical breaches involved in engaging in such research, such research had served to pioneer and accelerate the development of the Shelley Cure.

"Would it be your recommendation, Dr. Caring, that this government take steps to review its use of Gain-of-Function in research settings?"

Dudley sipped at the water and hoped the panel couldn't see how badly his hand was shaking.

"At times of great need, rules may need to be broken if it is of fundamental benefit to the public. I doubt there is a scientist dead or alive who hasn't felt themselves at risk of stretching their moral fiber even to breaking point to save a patient, or to move the scientific needle forward."

The minister began passing a fountain pen from one hand to the other, and he spoke without looking at Dudley. Dudley turned around in his chair. He saw the steep bank of photographers at the back of the room, all of them poised for permission. He scanned over the packed seats in the gallery. He saw Jess straining into the aisle so that he wouldn't miss her. She smiled at him, and he allowed himself to nod back at her, grimacing a little as she placed her hand over her heart and mouthed to him that he was doing all right.

"And Kesta Shelley?"

The minister looked up at him now. He'd sprung the question, to see what damage it could do.

Dudley winced. "I am of the belief that Kesta Shelley should be immune from prosecution for her actions."

"You worked with her for nearly ten years, Dr. Caring. Your opinion can best be described as entirely prejudiced."

"I don't especially care what you think of my personal opinion—and yes, it is personal," Dudley said, emboldened by the clamoring from the crowd. "Kesta did what she did for love. I don't know how. I only wish I did."

"You have the temerity to say that in light of all that has since transpired? Six people were infected because of her."

"She lost her husband."

"Six deaths could have joined his on her conscience."

"Six people were cured because Kesta took extreme risks far beyond the comfort of anyone else."

"She played God with their lives, Dr. Caring."

"It's what we do in my profession, sir. Much more than chewing pens on a government panel. We fight death to avenge the living. Kesta lost her husband to the virus. In many ways, she lost him twice. Once when he became infected. A second time when . . . well, we all know what happened."

The room fell still.

"Timothy Shelley was shot and killed by a police marksman."

Dudley could hear the blood rushing hard inside his head, the pounding of his heart in his chest, the throbbing of his pulse against the too-tight shirt collar. He had prepared his testimony carefully. He had rehearsed it over and over with his solicitor in order to do it justice, so that the truth might be recorded and preserved. But nothing could prepare him when it came to Kesta, to what had happened to the three of them. He pushed his palms into his sockets, then strained to look up at the ceiling, anything to blink away the image of Kesta cradling Tim in her lap, bracing the back of his skull with just her fingers, having so very nearly cheated death. Dudley sighed and tugged at his tie again.

"Kesta Shelley was the most loving one of any of us," he said, hearing his voice cracking over the microphone. "She didn't think that love would hurt her. She *knew* it would. True love is promises made in the dark, ones you cannot hope to keep but will die trying to, regardless. Without expectation. Without even stopping to think," said Dudley as the brilliant lights of the cameras exploded all around him.

CHAPTER THIRTY-THREE

He would have wanted her to do this. Needed her to do this, and not for him, but for herself. She understood that now, even as she sat there with her eyes closed the way she used to, legs jiggling in jeopardy, pretending it wasn't happening, still wishing they'd all go away. She felt a hand on her shoulder, and Kesta opened her eyes to see Michael holding a saucer out toward her, with a cup of strong tea. She could feel the steam rise against her cheek, the two chocolate biscuits he'd wedged against the rim beginning to ooze. Michael didn't say anything, just gave her that grim expression of wordless resignation. The international look of *oh fuck*.

Here was a man who had decapitated his own husband with an axe in the kitchen of their maisonette in Streatham. Here was a man who knew real pain, who had lost a love and taken a life, the only life that had ever mattered, the one worth two of his own.

He had counted out the blows it had taken to cleave Eddie's head into the sink. They were the first thing he thought of every morning when he woke, and they would be the last lucid image he saw through tears in the milliseconds before his own death too. Kesta hadn't appreciated it before, had perhaps refused to see it, to accept it, or even to acknowledge it. They hadn't been the same then, she and Michael. Now things were different.

Kesta reached up and took the tea, grateful for his strange blessing.

This was going to take some getting used to. She returned the smile, the shrug, and said nothing. Kesta had never felt more alone than when she was crowded by foreign bodies, so profound was her reaction to other people. Until she'd been treating Tim. And yet today, peering anxiously between the ZARG group members as they solidified, turning fluid into form, Kesta realized that she wasn't alone because Michael was there.

Michael understood her, and she him. He touched her shoulder again, cautiously, like trying to elicit a tune from an unplayed piano, then he wheezed where the words should have been, but they hadn't quite formed because, seriously, what was it exactly that you were meant to say in these moments?

I am so terribly sorry that you were detained for three months, having harbored your zombie husband in the spare room for half a year until you saw fit to set him free. Next to a village.

Michael knew what she had done. They all did. As Michael walked away, Kesta felt her shoulders sag, the teacup rattling in her hand. She was worried she'd break down completely. But then he came back, dragging a chair screaming behind him, and he sat down close to her with a sigh, a nonchalant sniff. She saw that he saw that she was shaking.

Michael took the cup and the sticky biscuits from her and placed them on the floor beside her feet. And then he took her hand and held it in his own.

Dr. Walling arrived in a flourish of angora cardigan. Bits of it were coming loose and forming expensive tumbleweed along the linoleum. Michael's hand was soft, and Kesta felt the urge to apologize for her own dry and ragged one, but then she remembered that nothing really mattered anymore. It was perfectly fine to have your bony old fingers crunched together by a widower who used hand cream liberally, and not to try to rationalize it.

"Gracious me," huffed Dr. Walling, hugging her files against her chest as she took her seat, teasing a tuft of fluff from the corner of her mouth. "Can it really be a year since the outbreak began?"

A reverential hum filled the room. Tina made the sign of the cross over her chest. Carol naturally started crying. Kesta thought of Paul Mosi and of the people who died trying to save him. Michael squeezed her hand tightly. Kesta squeezed his back. They both knew what was coming. He shifted in his seat, angling his body toward her, as if to shield her from some of it, to soften the blow. Tim would have done that, she thought, made her feel that whatever she had to face, he could be relied upon to be the armor she wore into battle. Kesta swallowed hard but she didn't flinch, didn't close her eyes and disappear inside herself, although she wanted to. Dr. Walling watched her, invisible therapist's antenna feeling through the air and the angora pile for the signal that it was safe to venture further.

"Kesta," she whispered, "Kesta, on behalf of the group, it's really good to have you back with us again."

To her surprise the others nodded and muttered in agreement. Their wide, watery eyes batted at her frenetically, soothingly, full of encouragement, sympathy—a kind of kinship, welcoming her back into their dismal fold. Michael leaned toward her. He breathed *I told you it would be okay* into her ear, even though he hadn't; he hadn't said a word, just fetched her that tea and squeezed her hand, filling the void with conciliation.

Kesta wanted to cry and to scream, but you couldn't go on crying and screaming forever, could you? The statistical analysis of her behavior over the past year had proven conclusively that to go on repeating such frenzied patterns was entirely unsustainable. The conditions had been permanently altered anyway. Living was an experiment she couldn't control and shouldn't try to. Now was the time for acceptance, or something like it.

A sudden beam of sunlight shone through the windows of the ZARG meeting room, searing over Kesta's legs, over her hand and Michael's. It burned her, the light and all that it revealed to them, the little that was left of her now, weary, depleted, grayer than before, insufficient flesh stretched taut across the bones in her shoulders.

The horror she had endured—her memories, her loss—it had scarred her. These marks were livid still, stitched up with a kind of static electricity, ready to spark and explode if someone pressed down on them too hard. It was too intense, all of it, it was just too much. And it always would be, that was the thing. The heart aches eternal.

As the group began to settle, as Michael finally released her hand, Kesta understood that they, that she, that none of them would ever heal completely from what they had experienced. You couldn't recover. But inexplicably, in defiance of the laws of science and humanity, it somehow didn't kill you. The wound was survivable. You just had to learn how to stop it from getting infected.

Dr. Walling removed her glasses, hunched forward in her chair, and asked, not without hope, "Kesta? Are you ready now to tell us about Tim?"

Kesta blinked and took the deepest breath.

ACKNOWLEDGMENTS

One *Yellow Eye* is a novel about how far we will go to keep the ones we love alive. It's inspired by my experiences with my lovely dad, Roger, during the final year of his life. He was so valiant and stoical as he battled cancer over many years, lifting the mood in every hospital ward and treatment bay he visited with his easy charm, always looking to make light of things and to make other people feel better. But it was the way in which he died, incrementally and so brutally, in 2020, that really compounded our grief.

My dad was soft-spoken, unassuming, and shy. He was a deep thinker, a constant worrier, and a first-class giggler. Everyone who met him adored him. That sounds like a cliché, but it's true. He made people feel safe. He wasn't a man to grandstand. Although he held his beliefs carefully, he never imposed them on others. He was *live and let live, life's a game and then you die.* He was a thoroughly decent human being, and there really aren't enough of those around.

I loved making him laugh. I miss hearing him laugh most of all; he could really lose it, and once you set him off, the rest of us, his family, would follow. Life is so much less interesting without him here to gently take the piss out of it. Dad loved me every day of my life, and I will spend every day I have left missing him. And being grateful. While anyone can be a father, not everyone can be a dad. And my dad was the bloody gold standard.

He would have been mortified to be memorialized in this book. Hopefully also proud, but mostly just really embarrassed. Dad, you're welcome! It's a lot less than you deserve. I know you'd rather Arsenal won the Premier League, but I'm a daughter, not a miracle worker.

My parents taught me how to love. Their love was astonishing and remains unbroken even now. Mum and Dad were always my heroes. My mum spent her career saving people's lives by looking down a microscope and making sense of chaos. Nothing I do will ever come close to the contribution she has made to this world. Mum, and my dear little brother, with whom I share this love, this history, this loss, I know you both get it like no one else does.

Onward.

Thank you to Peter Salmon, the first person who told me not to give up on writing.

To Andrew Pyper, a much-loved and exemplary writer who was generous enough to give this book its first blurb. Like all the very best we have, you've left this world too soon. I will never forget your kindness. Thank you.

Thank you to everyone at Faber Academy, students and mentors alike, for believing in this story in its infancy and for encouraging me to believe in it too.

To my superstar agent, Hayley Steed, I will have to thank you at least weekly for the rest of my life to account for how much you've already transformed it. You've given me permission to dream and to believe, things I couldn't do on my own, and will never take for granted. Thank you for everything.

Thank you to Kirby Kim and everyone at Janklow & Nestbit on both sides of the Atlantic, who've been so generous in their support of this book.

Thanks to my glorious editors, Kimberly Laws at Simon & Schuster and Sophie Robinson at Pan Macmillan. My deepest gratitude to you both for your encouragement, your friendship, and for the immeasurable ways in which you've so brilliantly brought out the story I was always trying to tell, especially through the medium of sassy AQ's. The Picpouls are on me.

Thanks to Charlie Gavshon for the pep talks. I am going to have *it's only hard because you care* tattooed across my face.

Lastly, to my exceptional husband, how very lucky I was to meet someone as special as you. Luckier still to get to split a lifetime between the two of us. I love you. Although, if there ever is a zombie apocalypse in real life, I think we both know what happens next . . .

ABOUT THE AUTHOR

LEIGH RADFORD trained as a broadcast journalist. She produced and presented arts and entertainment content and documentaries for UK commercial radio, *BBC Radio, Time Out, The Times*, and *The Sun*. A former book publicist, she is a 2023 graduate of Faber Academy. She is currently developing content for film and television through her production company, Kenosha Kickers.